Praise for *The Countrywoman*

"The sensibility is true, the passion genuine. Mr. Smith's gift for rendering speech is astonishing. . . . When every drunken Dublin writer is a genius I don't feel like committing myself to the word; but I am sorely tempted."
—Anthony Burgess, *Observer*

"No novelist among the Irish has faced our slums—slum psychology, slum insanity and slum truth—as Paul Smith faces them. He writes with fury, with mockery, with deadly accuracy; and with the most bitter and unflinching love. This wonderful book . . . a great achievement—it touches the heart, startles the conscience, and does not leave one's memory."
—Kate O'Brien

"For his ability to write of such unutterable sadness with detachment, with the riotous humor of the Irish gutter, and without self-pity, Paul Smith deserves to be saluted by all men of his profession."
—*The New York Times*

"Smith can combine black terror with riotous hilarity, rather in the way that O'Casey can do it. I realize that to put a writer's name on the same page with that of Sean O'Casey is giddily high praise. But now I think it is time for it."
—Dorothy Parker, *Esquire*

"His writing teems with subtle life. . . . A born story teller . . . A remarkable novelist"
—*The Times Literary Supplement*

"Smith has been compared to O'Casey and Joyce. . . . I'd like to add to the list by suggesting . . . Dickens and Dostoevsky."
—*The Irish Times*

"A rugged and shattering addition to English literature"
—*The Guardian*

THE COUNTRYWOMAN

Paul Smith was born and raised in Dublin. He has taught English at Uppsala in Sweden, was a costume designer at the Abbey and Gate Theatres in Dublin, and has lived in Australia, France, Italy, Canada, and the USA. He lives in Dublin.

Paul Smith

THE
COUNTRYWOMAN

PENGUIN BOOKS

PENGUIN BOOKS
Published by the Penguin Group
Viking Penguin, a division of Penguin Books USA Inc.,
40 West 23rd Street, New York, New York 10010, U.S.A.
Penguin Books Ltd, 27 Wrights Lane, London W8 5TZ, England
Penguin Books Australia Ltd, Ringwood, Victoria, Australia
Penguin Books Canada Ltd, 2801 John Street, Markham, Ontario, Canada L3R 1B4
Penguin Books (N.Z.) Ltd, 182–190 Wairau Road, Auckland 10, New Zealand

Penguin Books Ltd, Registered Offices:
Harmondsworth, Middlesex, England

First published in the United States of America by Charles Scribner's Sons 1961
Published in Penguin Books 1989

1   3   5   7   9   10   8   6   4   2

LIBRARY OF CONGRESS CATALOGING IN PUBLICATION DATA
Smith, Paul, 1925–
The countrywoman/Paul Smith.
p.   cm.
"First published in Great Britain, 1962 by William Heinemann Ltd"—T.p. verso.
ISBN 0 14 01.2146 3
I. Title.
PR6069.M525C68   1989
823′.914—dc20   89-33673

Printed in the United States of America

For
my mother
Kate O'Brien Smith
and her grandson
Paul

Down, down, down into the darkness of the grave
Gently they go, the beautiful, the tender, the kind;
Quietly they go, the intelligent, the witty, the brave.
I know. But I do not approve. And I am not resigned.

EDNA ST. VINCENT MILLAY
from *Dirge Without Music*

ONE

MRS. BAINES was a big woman, tall and lean, with a hollowed thinness pared into her white face, with a sprinkling of faded freckles across a slender but prominently boned nose. Her hair was white and washed to a shine. She wore it in a fat neat bun on the nape of her neck. She wore white blouses that smelled of fresh air and, when the pennies were plentiful, of starch and Reckitt's blue. Her coat was good, her skirt the remnant of an old biscuit-colored tweed.

After eighteen years of two rooms in Kelly's Lane, she was still as clean-looking as that evening in summer when she had first set foot in it. Her hair had been gold-brown then, her body hard and strong with life and love. She was in love with Pat Baines passionately, wholeheartedly, in a way that would cause her to flame with shame when she remembered. And she remembered often those first months when Teasey was a baby and Kitty yet to be born and the breath of country air was still on her face and in her

1

gently blued eyes. She had shown no trace then of her wanderings across the length and breadth of Ireland, following Pat from parish to parish in pursuit of the job that would last and where his wheel-making skill would be appreciated. And if he never got further than the verge of landing just such a job, there was always the hope that in the next town or county, or in the one after. . . .

She was seven months in the Lane, longer than she had been in any other place since she got married, when Kitty was born, followed a year later by Babby who, in turn, was chased by Danny, before the great innocence left her and she knew there never would be such a job and that this she had come to would always be so. The acceptance of the fact brought no change. It came and stayed unnoticed, jammed between the births of Neddo and Tucker Tommy and the constant struggle to keep body and soul together and a roof over her own and the children's heads. Around the Lane and in Rock Street, other women with husbands like Pat Baines might leave them, defying the teachings of their church and Father Rex Aurealis, their parish priest, and wonder why the countrywoman didn't do the same. But Mrs. Baines had talked to the priest, who preached patience and humility and told her to stay with her husband, and it was no use the other women telling her to go anyway because, even if she could have brought herself to go against the priest—and once she had thought she might—where was a woman with six children to go to?

But "Why?"—not why must she stay with Pat, for the answer to that she could find in her catechism let alone in Father Rex Aurealis's admonitions—but "Why?"—the question she could scarcely frame, the question neither she nor anybody else could answer, which flowed through her always like blood in her veins: "Why does he . . . ? Why is he . . . ?"

It had seemed to her that the priest would know, and she had asked, hoping that he would be able to give her an explanation she could understand, something round, defined like her immortal soul, something she could live with. But he had merely shrugged: "It is not for us to question, but accept." Other women, with such a comfort, could run to their families scattered over the Lane and the streets around it, until tempers and drunken passions subsided. They at least were sure of a place to rest their heads, but for her there was no place where she might hide from, or with, her wounds.

She had imagined once there might be. It was while she still had only Teasey, and she had written one letter then to her brother Mick in Wicklow, but received no reply, and conscience would not let her try again. And so, in time, the little farm out beyond the Seven Chapels became no more substantial than Pat's wild sometime assurances to give up the drink. Neither was to be remembered. The drinking went on, and with Mick's marriage the farm went, and with its going the vague consolation that its somewhere presence had given gradually faded from before her eyes, like the color from her hair. "It is not for us to question." She would never escape, no more than she would ever understand, the wide sweep of Pat Baines's fists, and she had long ago stopped searching for the cause. That was how it was, and how it had been always, and who cared what the Kaiser said? He wouldn't kill Pat Baines or drive him mad. Pat would, she knew, eventually return from France and the Dardanelles. And, she knew, around the Lane and behind her back women at the pipe said, "With medals and ribbons, a pension and his old thirst for Irish whisky."

For the four years he was away, Mrs. Baines was paid her allowance as regular as clockwork through the Post Office, and for the first time since she had married she knew what it was to have a week's wages from him. Debts were paid, and the arrears on the rent as well as the insurance, so that now the constant threat of a pauper's burial, if anything happened to herself or one of the children, was no longer a dread. She bought linoleum for the floor and a couple of chairs, along with wallpaper and bedding for the two rooms. The jampots were sold to Jack the Rag, the cracked ones flung into the bin at the pipe and the lot replaced by red-rose-covered cups and saucers that matched. Lace curtains replaced sacks and paper on the windows. She even paid a man to make a window box and planted it with geraniums which caused a great wonder in the Lane. She bought the children clothes and a change of shifts, and searched Dublin till she found her statue of the Virgin with the trace of a smile and dressed in blue and white robes. Then she made an altar, in a blind window over the big bed in the corner near the fireplace. She lined it with white crepe paper and put a shelf across the middle. From it she hung a piece of bleached calico that she pleated and embroidered with blue and green silk-thread flowers and leaves like those she told the children grew out in the fields and hedges of Wicklow. Behind the curtain on the sill she kept a chocolate box. It had a picture of a uniformed parlormaid on it and, inside, photographs of Teasey and Babby and a faded one of her father and mother that was yellow with brown spots. Underneath these she put her marriage lines. At the foot of the Virgin she set a red Sacred Heart lamp which burnt its steady flame night and day, casting a pink glow onto the naked toes of the Virgin and an unhealthy red one onto the tumbler at her side with its few fresh flowers. She bought a zinc bath big enough to hold the biggest of her children, which was Danny, and two iron beds because wooden ones attracted the bugs that came out of the walls in the darkness of night.

"It's like having money in the bank," she'd say when the children commented on some new luxury such as oilcloth on the table or butter on their bread or shoes on their feet.

"Sure, we don't know ourselves with all the grandeur!" she'd laugh. And true enough, compared with their poverty newly passed, they didn't.

The gradual ease from want gave Mrs. Baines time to explore the world about her, and in the second year of the war she discovered the Canal and the water fast-flowing, hemmed in between grassy banks that proudly sprouted trees. It was round the corner from the Lane and on the other side of the big row of tenements that shut out the Lane's light and left it in a green darkness such as moseyed round the trunks of trees heavy with summer. But along the Canal, the light was white, the sky high and wide, the wind unfettered as it went through the branches of the trees and spread itself down to whip the water into ripples, and splashed white spray onto the tall grass, and hurtled itself with devilment at the low-flying gulls and tore the cry from their throats with a brave jerk. Fat turf-boats lumbered low under pyramids of black and red turf between the bridges, and swans stretched bone-rubbery necks at the sight and plunged their orange beaks into the churned pink-e'en-ed mud under them. Iris, yellow and purple, bristled at the intrusion before they withdrew trembling into the protection of the wild rough reeds forever caressing them. And along the banks and under the trees, Mrs. Baines walked or sat alone or with one of the children, talking about Wicklow and the mountains while one or more of them fished for pink e'ens—and the war and Pat Baines were far away.

The spring of 1919 was early and warm and in the Lane men came home from the War, some propped on crutches, others nursing hidden wounds, and Mr. Thraill limped from his rooms to the lavatory behind the pipe on a slim walking-stick with a silver handle. Ruth and Martha Fay were suddenly widows, and so was Cocky O'Byrne. And Mrs. Thraill, when she heard, stopped going to Mass because—she said—the Devil looked after his own. The Lane, which had been whitewashed, ran wild with drink and a wave of pension books. Jew-men with dark faces and things to sell and money to lend, came down in droves, strangely easygoing in the new plenty, scattering blankets and sheets and orange-colored china dogs, and holy pictures in gilt frames, left right and center.

"I'm doing them a favor," Mrs. Kinsella said, as she made a bonfire of everything she had in her room, and replaced it all with new.

And Mr. Thraill took to wearing a carnation in his buttonhole and, on Saturdays, setting fire to his wife; Cocky O'Byrne, who never used to drink, became a drunkard; and Mary Ellen Timmons, who had been a nurse in the Army and been shell-shocked, came

down to the pipe in broad daylight in her skin and had to be
dragged back to her room screaming, and the priest had to be sent
for. Mr. Slattery, who lived in the room under Mrs. Baines, bought
a horse and black cab, and on Mondays Cocky O'Byrne and
Martha Fay hired it to go down to the Post Office to collect their
pensions, coming home again in it, roaring drunk. Mrs. McDonald,
whose husband didn't come back, threw herself into the locks and
was drowned, and her daughters went on the town. The pubs
round the Street and the one at the top of the Lane kept open till
all hours of the night, and the place rang in a moithered orgy of
fights and brawls and wild hooleys that no one dared refuse to go
to. The men came all summer, and by the winter, those who were
coming at all had done so, all except Pat Baines.

By the spring of 1920, Pat Baines still hadn't come home, nor had
Mrs. Baines heard from him except for a postcard which he sent
from England with the picture of an actress on one side and a
completely illegible scrawl on the other. She only knew he was
out of the Army because her allowance was stopped. And she only
knew he had been wounded because the Post Office man explained
that all payments to her would cease since her husband now
possessed a Disabled Pension. The loss of the money was a blow,
and Pat's disability a worry, but while there was nothing she could
do about the latter so long as he was in England, she could cope
with the former, and she set about doing so right away. Teasey
left her job for a better one in a tobacco factory, and Babby
went in as a waitress to a café in Westmoreland Street. They
were good jobs, compared to Kitty's, who stayed on in the house
in the Rathgar Road scrubbing floors and looking after three
children. Mrs. Baines herself got the odd day's work scrubbing
out one of the shops round the Street, and so between them the
rent and the insurance policy were paid regularly. Only Danny
was idle, for the city was swarming with messenger boys and the
laboring jobs went to the returned soldiers. And his two brothers

were still in school. But that was no hardship. She could manage.

On days when she wasn't working, when there was nothing left to scrub or scour in her own rooms, she took her knitting or the half-finished makings of a frock for one of the girls onto the Canal and worked there, her head bare, her back to the trunk of a tree while her thin fingers manipulated the four steel needles on a sock, and usually with either the youngest or all three of her sons spread out on the grass beside her. While her needles flashed round the heels of the scarlet sock, she remembered past days, aware at the same time of present days and of the great contentment that filled them. Still, this peace of mind could not last, she knew. One day Pat Baines would walk in, and no matter how hard she might try, or how hard she might pray, she couldn't fool herself now that he would have changed in five years.

Most of the time she tried not to think about this. The now was more than enough. Her children were good and no trouble to her or anyone else. She didn't owe a penny and could call her soul her own, and when the girls bought a bit of silk or cotton for a dress or a hat, it was because they could afford to. Her only cause for worry was the secret her husband's brother had burdened her with—and the dancing, which in itself was harmless enough, God knows. Babby, who could never have been called robust, was the worst offender. She would dance every night of the week and twice on Sundays, before and after Mass. Mrs. Baines was proud of this daughter, who won medals and anything else that was going in the way of prizes for dancing. In the Lane, where achievement was rare, it mattered that she was the best dancer and that she should be well-liked by the fellows who fell over each other in their pursuit of her. But she was well-liked by girls, too, and could—and would—twist a bit of stuff in her hands for one of them half an hour before they left for a dance hall, and end up with a new hat or a dress.

Babby was small and dark, with great eyes that slanted up and out across her face, good-natured eyes on the verge of a laugh always or desolately sad and serious if you had a headache or were worried. She had Pat's dark brows, and his hair, except that hers was as straight as a reed. She had his strong white teeth, and, smiling, they made a snowy trace. If Mrs. Baines could have put her feeling about Babby into words, she might have said that her third child was like a fleeting night mood, a blissful half-minute that's neither sleeping nor waking and vanishes even as your mind unfolds to grasp it, leaving you with a momentary pang of desolate loss until you remember how beautiful it was and turn, consoled a little by the memory.

Teasey, the love child, was different altogether in looks and manner. A solitary, surrounded in a deep private quiet. She was tall, like her mother, and blonde and blue-eyed, but, unlike Mrs. Baines, she had a touch-me-not quality and seemed forever on the brink of withdrawal. She made you think it was gross and commonplace to be other than tall, slender and blonde, and the axiom that her left hand never knew what her right one was up to seemed to have been invented especially for her. She danced as often, but not as well as Babby. Nor did she attract people to her in the same degree. Nor did she laugh as much or as often as her sister. She saved what she could, and went with a fellow nobody liked. Babby disliked Peter Tansey because it was rumored he had fathered the child of a girl who'd ended up in the Union; and Mrs. Baines because he had red hair which she distrusted, because he neither worked nor looked for work, and because she sensed, rather than knew, that he would have preferred Babby or Kitty to their sister. They were younger than he was and neither would give him a rec. A gurrier, he was, Mrs. Baines thought when she remembered that it was Teasey who paid all his expenses when they went out and kept him in cigarettes and pocket money. He was no good, and Teasey couldn't see it, and she herself held her tongue in what she hoped was wisdom, and because Teasey wouldn't have listened anyway. Her eldest daughter was determined and headstrong, with a selfishness of purpose that both her sisters lacked.

On the contrary, Kitty never calculated anything more important than the number of days to the next dance or a length of beads for a new dress, couldn't bear the time-clock existence of a job in a factory, and preferred the heavier drudgery of housework because of its variance and because she liked being alone as she scrubbed floors and did washings that caused wittles to cover her hands one after the other. Like Babby, Kitty was small, but serious, with a pointed, almost brooding face and soft brown eyes that seemed forever to be looking at things hidden from the sight of others. She shared Babby's passion for dancing, and like her would search the secondhand shops in Kevin Street for a dance frock with beads or a gay fringe round the hem or a pair of satin slippers with diamond buckles. But she was unlike Babby in her air of near sadness, and her peculiar trick of stopping in the middle of a sentence to look off and away into space.

Kitty adored Danny, who for no apparent reason took it upon himself to watch and father her, without either of them being aware of it. It was Danny who followed her to the door of the dance halls and hung around until she came out again, and waited at the corner of the Lane every evening with his eyes fixed upon the hump of the bridge until he saw her coming, when he would dart wildly between trams and carts to meet her. They exchanged no word of greeting when they met, nor was there any show of affection between them, a pause only, while Kitty turned on him a serious gaze and, after handing him a pear or a biscuit she had saved especially for him, she would say: "You shouldn't be out so late," and look past him as they crossed the street. They would walk the rest of the way in silence until they turned into the Lane, then Kitty would ask: "An' how many bags did you get today?" When she heard the answer, she would smile slow; and seeing her smile would make him laugh; and hearing their laughter on the stairs, Mrs. Baines would move to open the door, and Kitty would be home.

It was Kitty who started the cinder-picking, and after she began to work, Danny took over. Every morning sharp at six, he would take the soapbox car from the landing and go off on his rounds about the areas of the big houses of Fitzwilliam and Merrion Squares. It was important to get to the bins before the rest of the army of cinder-pickers. This way he had the best of the burnt-out coals and anything else the maids threw out. Danny was better at it than Kitty, and often came home with a loaf of bread or a hunk of cooked beef or a bowl of dripping. Unlike the rest of the pickers, who would rob all before them, he took only what was given, knowing that at certain houses a grin to a housemaid was more effective than the sleight of hand and the risk of being caught or chased and eventually cutting down his number of calls. He was quicker than Kitty had been at filling the sacks, and it was a poor morning when he didn't arrive back with them filled to the brim with good black cinders and bits of coal.

Danny was husky and tall, with broader shoulders than any of the other fellows his age around the Lane. He was on the way to looking like his father, you could tell—even as a child; but there, you could also tell, all resemblance would end.

In the room in the Lane the light from the oil lamp on the wall was richly yellow. On the line at the fire, clothes had been pushed to either side and on the hob a black-bellied kettle pouted puffs of white over the green-and-blue flames from the fire. There was a smell of fried onions and salty bacon and fried bread, and at the table Neddo, the second youngest of Mrs. Baines's children, dipped up the gravy off his plate with a piece of bread.

"Oh, for God's sake, stop licking your lips!" Teasey said impatiently. "An' it's bad manners to wipe your plate." She sat opposite Neddo, with her back to the altar. She still had on the khaki smock she wore in the factory and, even though it was clean, it reeked of tobacco, but she wouldn't take it off until she finished her tea, for fear she would mark whatever it was she had on underneath.

"Be a lot worse if he'd nothing to wipe," Babby said. She sat at the head of the table and gave Neddo a broad wink as she raised her cup to her lips.

"You shouldn't encourage him," Teasey snapped.

"You shouldn't be so anxious to pick on him then!"

"That'll do!" Mrs. Baines said, as she cut bread and piled it on a plate in the center of the table within everybody's reach.

There was a silence, until Kitty, unaware of its cause, broke it. "Esther Fitz is selling a lovely orange-colored frock."

Teasey surveyed her coldly. "I saw it. It's a rag."

"Its gorgeous!" Kitty looked at Babby. "The waist is smothered in blue and black beads, and they're good ones, you can tell by the shine."

Teasey laughed. "Catch Click-Clack selling anything good. When did you see it?"

"In Willmore's. On Saturday night."

"It wasn't dresses catching your fancy Saturday night," Babby said teasingly, her smile quick and white in the faint dimness. Kitty looked studiously at the rim of her cup, and Babby laughed at her. "An awful-lookin' ibex, that Gibblers is! Don't know how you stand the sight of him."

"Is that so?" Kitty retorted. "Well, your Nick is nothing to write home about. Mr. Sensible wouldn't see his heart on a white plate."

"Maybe," Babby nodded, "but you can tell which way he's going. Still," she said with high seriousness, "it's nothing to mock at, God forbid an' all harm!"

Danny laughed, and so did his two younger brothers.

"Ah, no!" Babby pretended to scold them, sitting up straight in her chair, looking down at them with her eyes crossed. "Ah, no! Fair is fair," she mimicked Kitty's fella, and Mrs. Baines tried not to laugh. "Will ya habe a dice creab or a boddle a Bimto, Kiddy?' Babby went on, hers eyes still crossed and her top lip forced down over her upper teeth.

Teasey giggled, her blonde head shimmering with the movement. "How does he get round the floor in the Cigarette Dance?" she asked wonderingly.

"He feels!" Babby said.

"He's terrible. He's a sight!" Teasey held out her cup for more tea.

"Is that so?" Kitty suddenly flared out at her. "You're just jealous."

Teasey roared. "Of that? Why, I wouldn't piss on him if he was on fire!"

"Mind your tongue, my girl!" Mrs. Baines said swiftly.

"You better not let *your* beauty hear you talk like that," Babby warned. "He doesn't think butter would melt in your mouth."

"She needn't worry," Kitty quipped. "He won't be able to keep her in *want*, let alone butter. So he'll never know."

Teasey half-turned to the attack again, but just then Babby shrieked. "Onions! Oh, Mother!" Her hands flew to her mouth, while she stared wide-eyed at her mother.

"Sen-Sen," Teasey and Kitty said together.

" 'Clare to God, but you put the heart across me!" Mrs. Baines gasped.

Babby jumped to her feet, muffling with the scrape of her chair the timid knock on the door. When it opened, on the knock, Esther Fitzgerald came in. She stared from Babby to Mrs. Baines and, quickly sensing the mood of the room, asked, "What's up?" And without waiting for a reply, she added, "An' youse are not ready." The question and comment followed by a request. "Would y'ever have a go at me hur? Just cast your lovely wans at it, will ya?"

"I ate onions," Babby said.

"Sen-Sen." Esther opened the black-beaded bag in her hands. She took out a white packet decorated with violets and poured a few square specks of black into Babby's open hand and watched as she threw the lot into her mouth and chewed desperately.

"A mouthwash would be better," Mrs. Baines said.

"Me mother says them things is unhealthy." Esther's glance rose from the table to Mrs. Baines, who gestured to Neddo and Tucker Tommy, who drew closer to Danny. Without a word, their mother took a clean cup from the dresser and poured tea into it.

"What've ya on?" Kitty asked.

Esther, two years older than Teasey and the same height as Kitty, was dressed to death.

"Everything," Babby answered for her, and Esther giggled. Then, with everyone's attention on her, she opened her wrap-over pink coat to show a yellow dress underneath. It came to her knees and had a heavily fringed matching overskirt. Where the fringe began at the hips, green beads took over and ran riotously up over a slightly protuberant stomach to a flat chest and a cluster of artificial Parma violets on a narrow shoulder strap. Her stockings were salmon-colored silk, her shoes black-pointed satin, to which she had attached bows of black silk. Her mousey hair was sparse and cut to a bang on her forehead. Two side pieces were brought high across her cheekbones to stab each side of her nose with wispy points. Her make-up was heavy, her eyes kohl-smeared, emphasized by a white nose and chin that cupped a tiny crimson cupid's bow.

Kitty, overcome, gasped her admiration.

Esther tossed her head. "Wait!" she cried, whipping off her coat to expose her arms, on which, like welts of flesh, she had put multicolored bracelets. "Aren't they gorgeous? Aren't they the absolute!" She held her arms high above her head while she danced a saraband to the hope they held.

Mrs. Baines tushed her lips in wonder, but it was Babby's approbation that Esther wanted, and she came to a halt before her.

"You're lovely," Babby said gently, though her eyes were suddenly clouded, as if saddened by the sight, knowing as she did that the effort was wasted as far as Esther was concerned, because no man wanted to marry a woman generous to all men—not even the Black and Tan fellow Esther was going with now. Esther was a soft thing. To rid herself of the momentary, but accountable, mood, Babby laughed. "We won't get a rec with you tonight," she said, and turning to her sisters, "Come on. We better hurry."

"Is Nick calling for you?" Mrs. Baines asked.

Babby shook her head. "No, I told him I'd meet him there."

Mrs. Baines moved to sit with her sons at the far end of the table away from the fire and the looking-glass over the mantelpiece. Babby took the kettle from the hob, Teasey lit the candle, and the curtain to the little room closed after them.

Esther Fitz never asked for anything outright. She simply said, "I've only got threepence and I need another penny." Her look caught Danny's, then his mother's. "I'll give it back tomorrow."

Mrs. Baines got to her feet and took her purse from behind a jug on the dresser. She handed Esther a threepenny bit.

"I'll give it back to you tomorrow."

"There's no hurry." Mrs. Baines sat down. "It'll do when you have it." Trouble is, you never do have it, God help you! The thought came swift, but remained unspoken. "Did you get your tea?" she asked.

Esther nodded, taking another slice of bread and buttering it before she masticated it daintily in the front of her mouth.

Kitty came out of the little room, holding a towel up to her chin to hide her breasts. "Is it true," she asked, "about Nancy O'Byrne?"

Esther looked at Danny and his brothers and hesitated. Then she said, "Yes, an' isn't it terrible? Course, I'm not surprised. What with her father an' all. An' Cocky on the drink. Besides, she threw herself at him, so what could you expect? End up in a Home or the Union, me mother says."

"I hope not," Mrs. Baines said.

And Teasey, listening in the little room, turned to Babby. "Wouldn't that hoor's melt make you sick? An' her going round with a Tan?"

"She'll hear you." Babby peeled a black stocking off her leg.

"So what?" Teasey asked.

And Kitty came back into the room.

"Maybe I should a got a lend of Rosie's necklace to go with the dress," Esther spoke to herself in the glass.

Behind her, Mrs. Baines sat listening to the splash of water coming from the little room. She didn't answer Esther because she didn't hear her. She sat with her elbows on the table, her every sense alert to the scene going on behind the dropped curtain. Babby was laughing at something Kitty had said, a light airy laugh, as clear and as pure as a bell. She could hear Teasey lifting the lid of the little brown tin trunk and she held her breath. The girls' best slips and knickers were in the trunk, and Teasey would hardly go rummaging beneath them, or beneath the spare sheets and pillow cases, and find what was on the bottom. Still, she did not breathe again until the pause was ended and Kitty had begun to talk again and Mattie Baines's guns and ammunition remained undiscovered. They had been there a whole week now, and would stay there until Pat's brother came to take them away, or the Tans, in which case she and her children would be taken with them, the way Mrs. Anthony and her two sons in Rock Street had been, in the dead of night and bayoneted to death on the Canal.

A laugh interrupted her train of thought, and she knew Babby was taking the cover from off her dress hanging on the back of the door. Her mind's eye hurried from the one imagined sight to this other. She could see the very expressions on the faces of her daughters as they hurried about the room. Babby's eyes would sparkle like delph in the candlelight, and her face newly washed would be white as snow where the light caught it, matching her rounded shoulders and her firm tilted breasts. And the shadows between her breasts and in the curves of her face would not last, because she would never stay still long enough. There would be a flash of raised arms against the red-raddled walls as she pulled her dress over her black head, and a dancing shadow as she eased her body into it. Beside her, Kitty would be standing at the table with the basin on it, scrubbing her teeth with a little brush dipped into a tumbler, spitting into the zinc bucket on the floor. Are they white?: she would ask presently, before she put on her clothes, and Babby would say, as she always did: Spotless. Kitty hardly cast a shadow, but Teasey would from the end of the room, a tall shadow cut in halves at the shoulders where the wall gave way to the low sloping ceiling, and her corner of the room would be neat and tidy, with everything in its proper place. She would rub swansdown cream from a round silver box over her pink and white face and into her hands, with their faint lingering smell of tobacco, before she sat down on the edge of the bed to smoke the cigarette that Mrs. Baines pretended not to know about. And Babby would rush to open the window to let the smoke out. They knew she didn't approve of women smoking, and though their liberty had grown with their age, they preferred to keep her in what they thought was ignorance about this. But she knew. The giveaway was the slightly raised voices of Babby and Kitty before the sudden swift opening of the window, which was pushed down as far as it would go, whatever the weather.

Esther Fitz, bored with Danny's pointed talk about "the plunder and the murder being done the length and breadth of Ireland" by the Black and Tans and beginning to feel, by her association with one of them, in some way responsible, moved away from him over to the curtain. "God! An' are youse never going to be ready?" And she drew aside the curtain and went in.

There were giggles and whispers, and Mrs. Baines knew that she, too, was having a drag from Teasey's cigarette.

Danny stood up. "I'm going out." He waited, and Mrs. Baines nodded.

"Me, too," Neddo said doubtfully.

"No further than the corner, mind you." But Tucker Tommy, edging with him to the door, was called back. "It's too late for you," Mrs. Baines told him, and she brought him with her to the fire to wait for the girls to emerge, like butterflies, from the chrysalis of the little room. She would clear the table presently, and wash the delph, and tidy up the little room when they'd gone, but right now she sat with her youngest child, savoring to the full the delight and deep contentment that it pleased God to give her. For, what should have been a familiar routine mood for her this moment when she had her children about her was, she considered, in actual fact, a mercy granted to her by the goodness of God and His Holy Mother, and in a great feeling of thanks and peace she turned her eyes to the little altar.

"God is good!" she was fond of saying, and she said so now.

"And His Mother's not too bad, either," Tucker Tommy added, as one or another of them always did.

She smiled at the familiar joke and watched him take up the doll's cradle that had come down to him from Teasey, and through all the others. But God *was* good, she affirmed to herself. He had given her five whole years of release from fear and let her and her children go unhindered and unchastised all that time. She wasn't a religious woman, and didn't go to Mass every day like Mrs. Chance in the room in the hall below, or like Nellie Ennis who took fits and rolled in the gutter if a day passed without her going to the chapel. Mrs. Baines never went to Confession and only to Mass on Sundays, but she believed that God was aware of her personally, and that He knew she did her best and tried to live and bring up her children in a way that was right. This she believed, and only her neighbors discounted it. Father Tithe, the parish priest who for some forgotten reason was called Father Rex Aurealis, on one of his visits to the Lane had tried saying that more, much more, was needed from her before she could claim to have God on her side, but, confronted with her simple reasoning, had had to admit without actually saying so that there was more than a modicum of truth in what she said, and had taken his shilling for the Chapel Building Fund, imparted his blessing and gone his way.

A cinder, red and square, fell onto the hearth, and the girls came out of the little room, all radiantly excited and strangely beautiful in their eagerness for her approval. They twirled in front of her, white faces and arms mingling with the reds and blacks and yellows of their dresses, devouring the lamplight and robbing of their gleam the dresser of shining delph and the bed with its spread of polar white down to the stiffened valance. All hurry, they clustered round the mirror, each trying to edge the other for a better position, and nobody succeeding.

"How do I look, Mother?" Babby asked. And Teasey pushed a hair-tongs into the red heart of the fire.

"You're lovely, pet," Mrs. Baines answered, and, beside her, Tucker Tommy saw her eyes caress tenderly the dark beauty of her favorite child, lingering on the black-lashed eyes that mirrored all her dreams in their wide, luminous depths. She swallowed the unaccountable near hurt that rose in a tight knot into her throat, and dragged her gaze away to Kitty, who waited softly, excitedly, smiling. The fringe on her forehead tonight was new, and shone from brushing. She was looking so young, so vulnerable, that before her mother could speak she had to think what year it was that Kitty was born, and to remember that she was indeed old enough to be going to dances with her sisters. "Musha, but you're a treat for sore eyes," she said.

Kitty laughed into the exclamations and into the sudden smell of burning, as Teasey deepened with the tongs the natural wave in her hair.

"She'll scalp herself," Esther Fitz said, opening the door to rub her powder puff on the red-raddled wall of the landing and, afterwards, proceeding to rub her cheeks with it methodically.

Teasey did not ask how she looked, but was told nevertheless. "There won't be a soul nor sinner to hold a candle to any of you," Mrs. Baines said, and was gratified by the near-smile that touched Teasey's pinkly pouting mouth.

"Oh, we're something!" Babby laughed as she put on her coat.

And, eager to be off, Esther was saying, "If youse don't come, there won't be a fellow left to dance with."

There was a chorus of assurances, and the next minute they were off, and Mrs. Baines was looking out the window after them, until they turned the corner of the Lane and were gone on a last laugh from her sight.

TWO

Mrs. BAINES had finished cleaning up the little
room and washing the delph when Neddo came back with a
rush, taking the stairs two at a time. She swallowed the panic
that had made her heart beat quicker, her mind came back from
the tin trunk to his grinning face and she spoke her relief out
hotly.

"I don't know what class of feet you have at all. You take them
stairs the way you would a mountain," she told him, as he settled
himself with his lesson books at the table. She handed him the
pen and bottle of ink from the dresser and took her chair on the
other side of the fire opposite Tucker Tommy. She would sit by
the fire now until the girls and Danny came home. It was no use
Babby telling her she should have gone to bed, because she
couldn't have closed her eyes until they were home, and in the
meantime she could be doing something useful. She would do the
mending, and help Neddo with his spelling. He was a bad speller.

yet he could correct the mistakes in the newspapers, which was something she couldn't understand. And because he was full of energy, he had to be talking or doing something every minute. She saw now that because he needed a haircut, his face looked thin. The room was quiet, except for the quick scratch of his pen, and warm. But outside, night fog from the Canal lay sodden and trapped in the well of the Lane, stuffing the yawms of the open doorways and the black stairs with a swirling swell of vapor, and leaving the naked laths of ceilings and the red-raddled walls wringing wet.

Here and there, a light in a window glowed drearily behind drawn lace curtains. Behind them bent or twisted silhouettes crawled with the pace of the slow night across the smoky flame of an oil lamp or the guttering spire of a candle. In the middle of the Lane, the pipe, squat and crowned, dripped a slow rhythmic drop into the shore beneath, and behind it the high whitewashed wall of the lavatory cowered under the higher menacing green-slimed wall of the railway. In the lowering darkness, the watery flame from the gas lamp outside the Slatterys' room gave a puny light, and a song, like a sudden burst of pain, shot through the uncurtained window of Cocky O'Byrnes's room. Granny Quinn, on her way down the stairs to the pipe, paused to listen, and at the fire Tucker Tommy joined in the just heard refrain. So did Mrs. Slattery in her room below, and for a moment Mrs. Baines beat time out with her foot.

"Kruger kept them marching . . ." Tucker Tommy sang.

And his mother added, "And he blew them out of sight."

And together:

> "Sound the bugle, sound the drum!
> Give three cheers for Kruger.
> Death to the Queen, an' her oul' tambourine,
> And hoorah for Billy Kruger!"

"I can't think," Neddo said, important, from the table; and over on her own stairs, Granny Quinn shook her bugles, her cameo, her glittering bonnet, and made the sign of the cross as she passed Cocky's door.

Annie the Man's room was silent and dark, and Granny Quinn wondered where she could have got to at this hour of the night, but from the Thraills' she could hear the sound of someone crying. The Mullens were playing their new gramophone, and in the room beneath them Mrs. Carney, whose son had been gelded by the Tans and died of it, put her head out the window to shriek obscenities because the gramophone had wakened her baby. Her daughter appeared behind her and tried to drag her from the window. Failing, she joined her mother screaming futile protests as the gramophone went on and on. A train on the railway overhead burst to devour the darkness and puked down soot and cinders onto the clotheslines and Mrs. Baines's window box and drowned for one screamed moment the Lane's sounds, which rose more strident in the new quiet.

In the Slatterys' room underneath her, Mrs. Baines heard the children clawing and tearing each other for more room in the crowded bed.

"Youse bastards!" Mrs. Slattery screamed lazily from her bed in the big room. "If I have to get up an' go into youse, I'll swing for the whole shaggin' lot."

The threat reduced the kids' cries to a whimper that would continue fitfully for the rest of the night.

Granny Quinn, carrying her half-bucket of water, moved reluctantly from the pipe and dragged herself back up the stairs to her own room again. She would come down to the pipe twice more tonight before she went to her bed.

In Rock Street, at the top of the Lane, the pubs were making fitful pretense at closing and when Neddo spoke, Mrs. Baines stirred on her stool by the fire. "Aye," she said, "but it's time you were both in bed."

Neddo pretended he hadn't heard. She spoke again, and he raised his head. "In a minute," he begged, "but tell us first."

Neddo could mind mice at a crossroads, she thought. And for

a second she wondered where she would begin to teach him, as far as she could, about the times he was living in. "I don't rightly know where all this strife started," she said. "All I know is, we seem to have been in the midst of it since '16, an' now we've got two governments, an English one and an Irish one, with nothing to choose between either. However, the I.R.A. want the English to clear out, but the English'll never be driven. So they've poured all these lousers into the country to rob and murder and plunder all before them."

"The master told us the Black and Tans went into a pub in Richmond Street last night," Neddo interrupted, "and fired shots up through the ceiling. Then they drank for the rest of the night." He paused. "Whisky. And do you know what they paid the man?"

Mrs. Baines shook her head.

"A shilling." Neddo eyed her gravely.

"What's the Black and Tans?" Tucker Tommy asked.

"Well, without making you an impudent answer, son, the scum a the earth! The scrapings of every jail in England. Though, God forgive me but! I'm sure most of them are some poor mother's hard rearings."

"What's them?"

Neddo hushed his brother. "Is our Uncle Mattie an I.R.A. man?" he asked.

He smelt of salt, thought Mrs. Baines, as she began to run her fingers through his hair. "I think I'll put you into a bath before you go to bed."

He shook his head free. "Is he?" he persisted.

"Now how could he be?" she asked. "Isn't your Uncle Mattie a jockey?"

Neddo nodded. "But couldn't he be an I.R.A. man as well?"

He could be and was; and so was his English wife. "No," Mrs. Baines said, "he couldn't." But Neddo's look told her he didn't understand why not.

"Was our father a jockey?" Tucker Tommy asked.

Pat didn't know one end of a horse from another. "No," she said. "Your father's a wheelwright."

"Not a farmer? Like our grandfather?"

"No! Your father's a town man, and so was his father before him. An' I've told you all this a hundred times."

And she had, but her children never tired of hearing about their mother's life in the country or about the farm and her brother Mick and her father, and about how she had first come to the Lane when Teasey was a baby. Well, she would tell it again and let them set her straight when she diverged, as she sometimes did when, in the telling, her mind became a dragnet for memories . . . and questions.

Why had she married Pat Baines? Looking back over the twenty years of their married life, she could remember the time when she had loved him as she had dreamed of love, wandering through her father's meadows and staring up at the blue mountains of Wicklow. Her father hadn't liked the tall handsome wheelwright. Landless, her father said, a man of the towns and, though not a drunkard, fond of drink; but perhaps . . . He listened to her assurances, her father, that big soft gentle man dignified in gray homespuns, treated with deference even by Pat. So she had married, and been happy with her child and her husband. He could leave off drink any time, he told her. The next town was to be the new start, he told her. And went on telling her even after she had stopped listening, told her in the dark of night smelling of resin, and sent her wild with love, with what she imagined was his need for help, and then with passion as she took him to her, losing her doubts against the want in his mouth and in her body . . .

"But, c'm'ere?" Neddo recalled her.

She began slowly to see his puzzled serious face.

"Florry Connors says we're country," Neddo said inquiringly, and thought his mother was looking at him as if she hadn't seen him every day of his seven years of life.

"You were all born in the Lane," she said. "Only Teasey was born in the country."

"And you?"

She nodded. "And me."

"And our father?"

"In Cork."

"And Uncle Mattie's wife?"

"In London."

"So she couldn't be an I.R.A. woman, could she?"

She grinned at the trap he had set for her. "Lots of English women are." And she thought, And well you know it. "But your Aunt Zena isn't!" she said flatly.

"She's a doctor," Tucker Tommy said.

"No, she isn't," Neddo contradicted him. "She was going to be a doctor, but Uncle Mattie stopped her. Didn't he?"

Mrs. Baines smiled. "That, and other things." She glanced up at the clock on the mantelpiece. In a little while, her three daughters would leave the dance hall for home, and Danny, the pitch-and-toss school in Fallon's Lane.

Neddo, noticing her glance, anticipated her. "In a minute," he begged.

She shook her head. "You'll never get up for school in the morning."

"He hasn't finished his exercise yet," Tucker Tommy made his own effort to draw the night out.

"I have. I wrote a composition on the Black and Tans." Neddo watched his mother take the zinc bath from behind the bucket on the tea chest and fill it with hot water from the kettle and cold from the bucket. He began to strip himself reluctantly. "Mr. Ben," he said, "took Florry Connors in his car today. But he wouldn't take us." Mr. Ben was the insurance agent. "He doesn't like boys, only girls."

He stood still in the bath, as she lathered his sturdy legs, and giggled and tried to put his arms round her, as she drew his initials in soap on his belly.

"Queenie Mullen's mother hid the gramophone in the lavatory when Bedell came today," he said. "She even took the pictures down off the wall and hid them up on Granny Quinn's landing."

Mrs. Baines nodded. "Aye, I heard."

"Why?" Tucker Tommy peered at them through the bars of the doll's cradle in his hands.

Neddo looked back over his shoulder at him. "Because if she didn't, she wouldn't get the seven-and-six relief money, would she, Mother?"

"Why?"

"Because if she had pictures an' all, he'd think she didn't need it, wouldn't he, Mother?"

"This," she said, "is something you can fight out among yourselves. I'm not interfering." She wrapped a towel around Neddo and, with a heave, lifted him out of the bath onto her lap.

"Why don't we get the relief money?" Neddo asked.

"Because there's others that need it worse. And besides, I couldn't stand the constant threat of that get sweeping down on top of us at all hours of the day or night, throwing fits if he saw a cup of tea on the table or a spark in the grate, that's why."

"If you must know," Tucker Tommy added.

"But doesn't the government have to give you relief?"

"No, only if it suits them, an' it mostly depends on whether or not Bedell thinks you need it. If he doesn't think you do, you don't. An' a short answer or a cross-eyed look is enough to decide him."

"Aunt Zena wouldn't be able to bring her flute when she came, if we got relief, would she?"

"No," Mrs. Baines replied. "Nor that bed couldn't boast that white quilt, nor the table the oilcloth. Now," she said, as she took Neddo's flannel nightshirt from the line and held it out to him.

She took Tucker Tommy's things from him as he undressed, and after she had washed him, she cleaned up and made them a cup of cocoa which they drank in their shirts sitting by the fire.

When they had finished, they both made to jump into bed. And when she had reminded them, they both knelt in silence by the side of the bed that they shared with her, their eyes on the altar over it. She took the cradle from Tucker Tommy, who reluctantly relinquished it, then watched them bless themselves before they tumbled into their place at the foot of the bed.

"Will you waken us if Kitty or Babby has chocolates or paper hats?" Neddo asked, turning his face out to her.

"Aye, surely," she smiled. "Now go to sleep, son."

He turned his face to Tucker Tommy's back and the altar with its red glow of the Sacred Heart lamp. "I'm going to be a doctor when I grow up like Danny. What are you going to be?" he asked, but his younger brother was already asleep.

Mrs. Baines stoked up the fire and threw on a shovelful of cinders, then poured more water from the bucket into the kettle steaming on the hob. She glanced at the clock, took up the trousers that she had been patching, and listened to Mrs. Slattery call out to the "living Christ to witness the burthens of a mother who's borne fifteen children." She thought of Zena with none, and Mrs. Slattery with her roomful. She thought, for no reason, of Nick, Babby's fellow, and wondered if she would bring him home with her as she sometimes did after a dance. Her glance skimmed the room. She liked Nick, and hoped that her daughter would marry him. She raised a needle to the light to rethread it, and her gesture froze in mid-air.

In the Lane, now that Mrs. Slattery's lazy laments had died away, she heard short uncertain footsteps. She heard a laugh—a woman's laugh—and thought it was Annie the Man, but didn't get up to look from the window. The footsteps were short and uneven and heavy. She waited for them to pass, knowing they would not. She did not move, not even when they sounded on the flag floor of the hall, and she could hear the unsteady searching for the first step of the stairs. Her hands fell back into her lap. Annie the Man's laugh, if it was she, continued to rise from the Lane, and the footsteps, more sure now, slowly drew nearer until suddenly, yet quietly, the door was flung open, and larger than its frame stood Pat Baines.

He was grinning, he was drunk, and as he stepped into the room, he said, "I'm back."

She thought of the girls, on the way home that moment from their dance, of Danny, of Nick, of Pat's wound and a young girl and a young man in a Wicklow meadow, and even as she spoke, she dropped the trousers from her lap and went swiftly to greet him.

He pushed past her. "And I'm thirsty."

He didn't look round, as you might expect a man to do who hadn't set foot past his own threshold in almost six years. He looked neither at her, standing now with her back to the door, nor at Neddo, raised up on an elbow, staring up at what to him was a complete stranger, though she could tell that the son had recognized the father. And yet he did what you might expect Pat Baines to do, removed a pint bottle of whisky from the pocket of his overcoat and threw the coat and his hat onto a chair.

"I ask for nothing," he said with drunken gravity, "right now, except a glass."

It was the answer to her question, all the answers to all her questions. She moved to get him a glass, and shaped her face to smile. It hid nothing. You could hear it in her voice as she watched him fill the glass and pretended gladness that he was home and saw him drag cigarettes from one pocket and four medals on a striped ribbon from another and, with no awareness of what she was doing, sat down at the table opposite him.

Neddo crept to the end of the bed to see the medals, and Pat looked round to stare at him. Neddo stared back, and when his father put his huge hands up to his hair he saw that they were bruised and scratched. His black hair fell onto his forehead and joined his wing-shaped brows. He looked away from Neddo to his wife, and on a new mood he grinned.

He leaned towards her. "I bollixed the whole Kaiser's army," he said confidentially. He swayed on his chair. "That was a war," he said, "to end wars!"

"You were wounded?" she began tentatively. "Bad?"

His head swung to and fro, as she had seen her father's bull do. "I've got maybe a year left. Maybe a month. Ah, that was a war!" His head reared up, like a bull as it bellows. He gestured. "What's happening here?" He shrugged with contempt, then looked at her, clean, still, with the fire casting shadows on the smooth planes of her face.

She drew back, without seeming to, from the reach of his hand, and began to smooth the oilcloth with the tips of her fingers. "Where were you at all?" she asked casually.

He continued to stare at her, sullenly, with his big scarred hand on the table between them. "In England." He lifted his glass and drank in a great thirsty gulp.

"And when did you get back?" she asked, her voice mildly chiding, and she knew he had noticed her withdrawal.

He shook his head. He could not remember leaving England, but certain things that happened later were hazily grasped. He had been in a fight. He had picked up a woman in the first pub he had gone into. He had been in some room with her and afterwards she had slept. She had slept and woke and, when awake, she drank, and in her sleep, she had nightmares. He had her hoarse, but it was like flogging dead mutton, and he had left her in disgust, in that room with the blind drawn to shut out the daylight, but he could not remember when.

"Maybe today," he said. "Maybe yesterday."

And Mrs. Baines wondered if he was answering her question.

"You know," he said, "there isn't another man in the length and brea'th of this country that's seen what I've seen. With these very eyes. And I've good eyes."

"None better," Mrs. Baines laughed lightly. "But tell us, what kept you in England?"

He would not be sidetracked. "Sweet Jesus, that was a war! To put everything that's gone before in the ha'penny place. Do you understand?" But he didn't wait to hear. He began to talk of trenches and guns, of Big Bertha and Hindenburg, of strange place names and "devastations" and "slaughters" and incidents from which he emerged with monotonous regularity the hero, and to prove it all, he was home again, with medals and a pension.

When she asked him again if he'd been hit bad and where, he shouted that he had the pension, didn't he, and what more proof was needed? None, she assured him, and Neddo watched from the curved iron of the bed. He wanted to get up and go over to where the medals lay, but he didn't. He sensed something uncommon in the boasting blurred voice, something sharp and querulous—undertones in the Irishman's petulant whinge that held him still and—it was suddenly important—unnoticed. He heard his father dismiss contemptuously what was happening in Ireland now, and held his breath when he thundered:

"Why, even their priests are against them!"

"Aye," Mrs. Baines said, as if this wasn't anything new. "So Mattie says."

"Mattie?" The name was exclaimed through Pat's confusion.

"Aye, he's here. Living in Dublin and married to an English girl who was at Trinity College. But I'm afraid she's given that up, and is now devoting herself entirely to setting Ireland free."

"And Mattie?" Pat asked.

"Both."

"The ridiculous bastard!" Pat spoke through her. "Them an' their molly-coddlin' fight for freedom!" He turned his face away to regard the mind's sight with unfocused eyes, and then got up to move with uncertain steps around the room. "By Christ, I come from a war that was a war!" All the time, he talked in streeled dislocated sentences.

Mrs. Baines watched him, wary, her every sense alert. And Neddo remembered his Uncle Mattie, who gave him lessons in history whenever he came to the Lane, told him how the priests and bishops of Ireland had always been against the people, given him dates and a saga of events his mind could not grasp, so that the excommunication threat of the Bishops in 1172 against any Irishman who refused to acknowledge Henry of England as his king became confused with the Rebels' excommunication in '98; and the Famine of '48, when the people, already dying of hunger in the ditches with grass and weed juice running from their mouths, were told to hand up their crops, sometimes came before, sometimes after, the prayers of thanksgiving that the Bishops offered up for the capture of Robert Emmet. And the song about Robert Emmet, that Mattie sang and Mrs. Slattery when she had a drink taken, ran through his mind and came to a halt when he saw that his father had tired of belittling his brother and his wife and was heading off on a new track. "Earl Haig," he said, "and me." And his father began again about the war, but pausing to stretch out a dark-cloth arm every now and then and squeeze his mother's shoulder and her breasts. Neddo watched the huge hands, scratched and bruised, strong, impatient. His mother sat quite still under them, and his father drew them away and scowled. But his mother exclaimed admiringly with her lips at what he was saying, and he saw her smile in her efforts to coax him out of one mood to another. But his father muttered with a sound of anger, and touched her, and Neddo watched her face tighten, her eyes steal desperate furtive looks at the clock. He watched her hurry to do his father's bidding, preparing a meal his father didn't touch but pushed aside to grab hold of a glass of whisky, and then get up to pace the room while he interrupted what he was saying about Earl Haig and sang a bit of a song that ended abruptly as he began another story.

Pat Baines was a big man, and the floor trembled and groaned its unheard protest at his great weight. But on the dresser the cups swung and tipped each other as if in a game, as he went round the room. He was a town man, but with none of the town man's slightness of frame or quickness of movement in his body, which filled out to a smoothness his dark serge suit. His thighs almost burst his trouser seams down to the calves of his legs, which jutted into a hard stand. All the flabbiness he once had was gone.

He was now all muscle, and moved slowly, like a boxer taking the measure of an unknown untried opponent. Neddo and Mrs. Baines held their breath each time he went near the lamp, for his approach sent the flame rushing up in a gust of air, blacking the rim of the thin globe of glass and threatening to explode it to smithereens. Pat's gestures grew even slower and broader, as the whisky in the bottle grew less and less, and when he turned over a chair and fell down between the table and the bed, Neddo gave a startled cry. It was lost in the clatter of things falling, for as Pat went down he made a clumsy catch at the table and dragged the cloth and everything on it to the floor. Mrs. Baines rushed to help him, but he pushed her aside and staggered, unaided, to his feet.

And then, as if for the first time, he saw his sons. He towered over them and tried to focus his eyes on Neddo, kneeling up in bed, staring wide-eyed at him, afraid. But, as yet, his fear was unnecessary, and the meeting without acknowledgment, for after pointing vaguely in his direction, Pat muttered incoherently and turned away.

"You better sit still, till I clean up this." Mrs. Baines swept the broken delph and food with a floor cloth onto a shovel.

"Aye." He grinned, and reached out suddenly and pulled her standing.

Slowly she straightened up under his hands and tried to twist away, but the effort was useless. He laughed thickly, pulled her close to him, and, mumbling, backed her up to the table. She turned swiftly, unsmiling, and was suddenly free. When he made another grab at her, she said, "The child."

Pat gazed at her stupidly, all trace of his good humor evaporating. "Well, what the hell are you waiting for? Get the bastard out of here!"

Neddo was lying with the bedclothes dragged up close to his face. His mother bent over, whispered to him, and took Tucker Tommy up in her arms. He got up quickly and, keeping close to her, went into the little room. His brother had slept through the change, but even with him beside him, Babby's bed was big and cold and the blackness very black except for the sliver of light coming through the parting of the curtains from the big room. He heard his father talking, his mother's voice answering him. He heard her stoking the fire, and two heavy sounds as something fell to the floor. Sitting up quickly, he peered through the curtain slit and his father stepped into his vision: barefoot, stripped to the waist, his head back drinking straight from the bottle, and one hand closed over the bulge in his trousers. The next sound was the bottle dropping empty to the floor, then his father breathing harshly and moving with a grin out of Neddo's vision, a laugh and the rip of cloth, his mother's exclamation and his father's curse and the bed creaking beneath a great sudden weight, and after a time the beginning of a persistent hard rhythm as the laths were worked back and forth.

Through the curtain, the light began to flicker and die. He was asleep before the ultimate darkness came and the sound, half-cry. But he dreamt a man's voice laughed and the man's voice said, "Wrap yourself around this."

It was late when Mrs. Baines heard her son's and daughters' footsteps on the stairs, cautious, hesitant, like the steps of the blind. They halted together for a second outside the door, before the handle turned easily, and Babby, in her stocking feet and her shoes in her hand, crept in followed by the others. Behind them, Danny closed the door softly, then they grouped together to stare unbelief towards the bed.

Over the broad rise of Pat's naked chest, Mrs. Baines murmured, "Is that you?"

Babby's whispered reply was inaudible.

Mrs. Baines turned her head then, as much for her own sake as for theirs. "He's home. He's come back."

They made her no answer.

"Wet a cup of tea for yourselves," she added quietly.

In the faint glow from the altar lamp they could see Pat's dark
head, a dead weight on the pillow, and the long line of his body
under the quilt. They stared, shocked but not really surprised at
their father's sudden appearance, for hadn't they always known
that one day he would come back? But somehow as the weeks,
then months, then even years went past without him, they had,
unbeknownst even to themselves, assumed that he was gone for
good. Confronted with him now, like this, in the early hours of the
morning, they, who only a short while ago were grown-up adults,
assured as they went gliding round the dance hall in the arms of
their fellows, were suddenly reduced to fear and, even, trembling.

Danny sensed this, as he herded them into the little room.
"We're not hungry," he said, because they couldn't.

"Go to bed so, with the help of God," Mrs. Baines murmured.
"You'll never get up in the morning."

They went, and, long after they were gone, she was still awake,
staring wide-eyed up at the ceiling. In the Lane everyone slept,
and in the house, in all the world; and, Mrs. Baines thought, in
heaven God and His angels slept, but she prayed nevertheless,
moving her raw lips soundlessly. And beside her, her husband
snored long snores that ended in a pettish gurgle up in the darkness,
then came to a stop altogether and, awake, he raised himself again
to take her.

THREE

"TELL that to your dirty mother and your friends in America!" Mrs. Kinsella screamed.

Mr. Bedell, the Relief Man, paused in his rush down the stairs to glare back up at her and, behind her, the greater heaved bulk of Mrs. Slattery.

"Ya hoor master!" Mrs. Kinsella cried.

"Is that so?" Mr. Bedell's fleshless ferrety face twisted with anger. And as he sought for words, Mrs. Slattery laughed. "Go—wan," he cried, "you pair of misbegotten bitches with your begging pusses and false pretenses!" He shook his fist at the two women on the landing. "I could have youse up for this."

Mrs. Kinsella roared and darted forward, Mrs. Slattery making no effort to restrain her, and in one jump Mr. Bedell had cleared the stairs and was shouting his feeble abuse up from the well of the hall.

"Gowan, you filthy Locke Hospital leavin's!" Mrs. Kinsella shrieked. "Go an' stick your lousy seven-an'-six up your la-la!"

"*And* your hungry Monda'!" Mrs. Slattery interrupted, and laughed. Cautiously distributing her weight, she went to peer over the bannisters with Mrs. Kinsella to make sure Bedell was gone.

He was.

"Mind." Mrs. Kinsella, after listening, eased the other's weight off the bannisters and grinned. "Well, we made short work of that pox bottle!"

Mrs. Slattery laughed back.

"But, Jasus, what'll I use for money now?"

"It was the shaggin' cot," Mrs. Slattery said. "If only we'd 'membered to take that below."

Mrs. Kinsella exclaimed. "Ah, but wouldn't you think that dyin' lookin' puke'd have some nature in him? Sure, I had to get that cot if I didn't want the oul' mattress to walk out the door with the weight a them kids' piss. Wasn't it to save the bed I got it?"

Mrs. Slattery nodded and sighed. She had expended all the effort she was capable of in a single day, and she would have liked now to go back down to her own room and lie with a wet cold cloth on her head till it was time to get up and go out to the afternoon two-penny rush at the Palace or the Mary-o. But, ahead of her first was the job of lugging back up from her room the contents of Mrs. Kinsella's.

"It was the cot," she said. "Just the same. Did you not see his oul' galdy eyes rivet themselves onto it the minute he set foot past the door?"

"Ahhh!" Mrs. Kinsella screamed now, for no reason. "Bollix him and the cot!"

"We shoulda hid it," Mrs. Slattery repeated calmly, marveling at Mrs. Kinsella's energy.

"What?" Mrs. Kinsella asked incredulously. "And have that youngwan knocking the nails from the boards with the strength of her t'rottle? No shaggin' fear."

"Well, it was that what did it," Mrs. Slattery said.

Alice Slattery could be terrible one-track-minded, Mrs. Kinsella thought.

"Didn't you hear him say you seemed to have full and plenty, thanks be to God? An' run his hand along the bars of the oul' cot?"

Mrs. Kinsella nodded. "Maybe now I should keep the kids in a shaggin' cage?"

"If only we could!" Mrs. Slattery sighed. With effort she folded her massive arms, bare to the elbows, across the wide sweep of her chest, and impatiently eased her big breasts into a more comfortable position. "Who told him Phillo was working, I wonder?"

And Mrs. Kinsella thought, nothing could contain Alice Slattery, she rose and overflowed all bounds. "Th'oul' bollix's fancy woman, who else? I told Leather-Lips to take them overalls off on the job, an' not wear them in an' out a here. But d'you think he'd listen? The men in this kip lose the run of themselves when they have a day's work. An' what matter, if I was any the better of it? Nothing to be ashamed of, he said, when I told him—not that I ever said there was. Him an' his shaggin' badge a courage! I'll put a match to them overalls when he walks in here tonight."

"More power to your elbow!" Mrs. Slattery said, then beckoned her to silence by a look, and both women nodded by way of greeting to Pat Baines, who had come into the hall and onto the stairs without either of them hearing him.

Oul' creeping Jesus, Mrs. Kinsella thought, and on her face there was no answering smile until she remembered suddenly that, what with one thing and another, Mrs. Baines might not have heard him come into the hall, and so, she said, "It's Mr. Baines!" She hoped her loud warning wouldn't go for nothing. Too shaggin' bad if it did, she thought, as Pat said: "An' I hope it's fit an' well I find the pair of you this lovely day." They saw his quick glance dart past them into the bare room before he grinned knowingly, and Mrs. Kinsella nodded.

"Come and gone," she said bitterly.

Pat gestured his understanding. "He's a powerful assessor, that man," he said.

"Oh, a genius!" Mrs. Slattery replied, and both women hoped that what they felt for Pat Baines in his good dark suit and black overcoat wasn't showing on their faces.

"Of course, you can make another application," Pat said.

"I can and will." Mrs. Kinsella stepped aside to let Pat by.

"If I can help you," he said, "you've only to ask."

"Aye." It was not quite a question, and neither woman said another word until the door of the Baineses' room had closed behind him.

"Would you think that was hard enough to break eggshells?" Mrs. Kinsella asked.

"Whisht!" Mrs. Slattery put her hand to her mouth and, without moving, inclined her head towards the Baineses' door, but no sounds reached them. "How long is he back now?" Mrs. Slattery rocked upright again.

"A year. Twelve long months. I know to my cost," Mrs. Kinsella said, " 'cause I don't know what it is to sleep the night through since the oul' bastard came back. I as much as told him so the other morning, but all he said was that that was the trouble in these rooms, no privacy. And a person could be heard scratching their back."

"If that was all!" Mrs. Slattery said. "But you'd wonder he stays in the Lane. Him an' his grandeur. You'd think with all the balls he sprouts about what it was he came from, he'd have a country house to retire to."

"Aye, the bragging he goes on with over that family of his is enough to make you sick, especially when you know, as we do, the two representatives of it—him an' that Republican brother."

"That's another poor unfortunate," Mrs. Slattery sighed. "That English wife of his."

" 'Course he had to marry her," Mrs. Kinsella said.

"Go 'way!" Mrs. Slattery stirred closer.

"Ah, I don't mean that! I mean the Rebels made him marry

her because they needed a doctor they could trust, someone to look after their wounded."

"I wonder if that's true?"

"Well, it's one reason. Though what an educated woman like that was doing to get herself entangled up with him and his lot for, I'll never know. The daughter of an English surgeon, Mrs. Baines said."

"An' barren!" Mrs. Slattery mushed her lips together.

Mrs. Kinsella laughed. "Well, Mattie Baines is making up for it. In the past year, there's been at least four girls down here with bastards in their arms for him. And ya knew that young fella living round the Canal with Mad Mary is one a his."

Mrs. Slattery nodded. "I know." She jerked her head towards the Baineses' room. "I was in with herself when the last one arrived looking for Mattie. A fine big country girl, she was, with a fine healthy baby in her arms. She wanted her to take it, an' her stretched out after that miscarriage. An', you know, I think she would've, if Pat hadn't been lying on the broad of his back up in the Union and likely to walk in the door any minute."

"That was the miscarriage after he sold his pension book?"

Mrs. Slattery nodded. "Sure, wasn't that the hand of God, and wasn't she saved the expense of going to Mrs. Ennis to get rid of it."

"She never would've," Mrs. Kinsella frowned. "She'd never have an abortion, the poor fool!"

Mrs. Slattery's eyes were brooding. "He must a got a lot for that pension book. A whole lot."

"Why?" Mrs. Kinsella asked suspiciously.

"Well, he was away three months on the money."

"And when he'd pissed every penny of it down the drain, he went into the Union."

"Lying up in the Union's getting a habit now," Mrs. Slattery said. "After every bout of badness. Do you think it's his conscience? Do you think, maybe, it's because he can't stay to face the depredation he's done?"

Mrs. Kinsella laughed. "Conscience? You know what they say about a standing prick!"

"God forgive the low tongue in your head." Mrs. Slattery felt she ought to make the sign of the Cross, and hoped God would accept the thought for the deed.

Mrs. Kinsella went on easily. "Now, don't you know he goes up to the Union after a bout for the same reason he goes when the dealers come looking for the money they've lent him? Because there's nothing left he can beg borrow or steal. And it gives that poor creature in there a chance to gather herself and the childer and a few things round her again, just long enough for them to begin to think he's gone for good. An' the very minute they do, back he comes with all his badness."

"You'd think the war would've changed him," Mrs. Slattery said sadly.

"The war? You heard it was him an' Earl Haig won the war, I suppose? Only mostly him. Which gives him an excuse for the greater thirst he came back with, and puts him in the way of getting the money to quench it from the British Legion and all the other patriotic bodies in the city."

"Them shaggin' places should be closed down," Mrs. Slattery said, " 'cause all they do is encourage every pisspot in the city a Dublin to imagine himself a hero."

Mrs. Kinsella shook her head thoughtfully. "Pat Baines, drunk or sober, would still be the scourge he is. You should see him now, lying there in bed from morning to night, being waited on hand and foot."

"She must be out the door trying to keep him in luxuries," Mrs. Slattery interrupted.

"If that was all!" Mrs. Kinsella looked skyward. "Listen, last night I was looking for a bit a salt, so I went over. He was singing, like he does—usually, 'The Dublin Fusiliers'—but I knocked anyway and went in, and there he had them all standing to attention round the table. And only then I recognized the song was 'God Save the King'!"

Mrs. Slattery giggled. "Go 'way!"

"No, honest!" Mrs. Kinsella drew her hand across her mouth. "Come on," she said, and both women descended the stairs to Mrs. Slattery's room.

"What'll we bring up first?" Mrs. Slattery asked, not listening, wondering if Mrs. Kinsella couldn't manage the lot by herself and sighing internally. Overhead she could hear the heavy step of Pat Baines, as he walked about the big room. "Maybe I'll wet a cup a tea," she suggested, spreading her hands across the pit of her belly.

Mrs. Kinsella caught the gesture, and Mrs. Slattery nodded.

"It's the good feeding I'm giving Tom," she laughed, "but this time I'll hansel Sadie Ennis's couch whatever happens." She shook her head. "I'll have to."

"I never said you shouldn't," Mrs. Kinsella replied.

"I know, but you had the look in your eye Molly Baines gets when she knows a person's about to go against nature, although, God knows, if I were her, saddled with a man who cares nothing for his children except to give them a hiding when he fancies they've discommoded him, by a laugh during the Rosary or a unsuitable expression during one of his war stories, I'd never be away from Sadie Ennis." Mrs. Slattery sat down, breathing heavily.

"Well, your Tom won't disappear till it's all over, anyway. And then turn up afterwards to carry on about whose bastard fattened you. At least Tom admits they're his, which is more than that hoor's melt does."

A woman came into the hall and paused at the open door. Mrs. Kinsella's nod was brief, but Mrs. Slattery said, "Come on in, Mrs. Chance. You're just in time for a cup."

"I've just seen Aggie off," Mrs. Chance said quietly. She was hatted and coated and, unlike the other women her age in the Lane, she carried a handbag.

"Ah," Mrs. Slattery could bring herself to say no more, because she had heaved herself up again to make the tea, but she was thinking, Thanks be to Jasus! For with Aggie Chance out of the way, her daughters' fellows were safe again, although this last time, Aggie had seemed to be concentrating her energies on Danny Baines. And a lot of good it did her, because, unlike his father, Danny didn't seem to know why the good Lord had given it to him.

"I have a feeling," Mrs. Chance said and paused, and both women turned to look at her, "that this time the call in Aggie was very strong. Stronger, I'd say, than it ever was."

Mrs. Chance gazed piously over to the picture of the Sacred Heart above Mrs. Slattery's bed, then to Mrs. Kinsella, who was trying to remember when Aggie's mother hadn't thought the call was strong in Aggie. Aggie Chance had been going in and out of the convent in Ranelagh ever since she could remember, and she was as near to being the nun her mother wanted her to be now as she ever was.

"What she needs is a little patience," Mrs. Slattery said, " 'cause its a hard life she's chosen."

What she needs is a buck nigger! Mrs. Kinsella thought. She looked at Mrs. Slattery, who giggled as if she had read her mind, and said to both women, "Sit over," handing them each a cup of tea.

"Course, it would make a great difference if my Aggie had a little money," Mrs. Chance said, and was sorry she had because it admitted a need of something more than the Call that came three or four times a year.

"Or Father Tithe on her side," Mrs. Kinsella said.

"How do you mean?" Mrs. Chance always cautiously skirted the possibility that anything outside Heavenly Intercession could affect her daughter's future with the nuns.

"What I say," Mrs. Kinsella went on. "She needs Father Tithe on her side to put a word in for her with the head nun. That would do it. A word let fall from his thin lips into the ear of the Reverend Mother'd be enough to make Aggie a fully fledged nun in a week."

"How?"

"How what?"

"How could he do that?" Mrs. Chance asked.

"How can he do half the things he does?" Mrs. Kinsella retorted. "How can he persecute the life outa poor oul' Cocky and her daughter Nancy? How can he tell that woman upstairs to put up with that man? How? Because there's no one to stop him, that's how. And if he wanted to get a girl made into a nun in the morning, he could do that, too."

Mrs. Chance smiled wisely, the tolerant smile of the converted, Mrs. Kinsella thought, though the former was a natural-born Roman Catholic.

"God, an' you're holding the priest responsible for an awful lot!" Mrs. Chance lightly scoffed.

"Well, he must shoulder the responsibility for what's happening up there!" Mrs. Kinsella gestured with her head to the ceiling, and all three women listened expectantly, but there was silence. "I heard him when that woman first come to the Lane, with my own shaggin' ears—tellin' her it wasn't her place to question the ways of God or His Church or His workings through a man like her husband, when all she asked him was to give her some reason why Pat Baines should be the way he was."

"Ah," Mrs. Slattery joined in. "I remember that. A lovely creature she was in those days. With the clean cut of her and the great blue wanderin' eyes and gold hair."

"But do you think One-Ball'd tell her?" Mrs. Kinsella interrupted.

"Ah, well, after all, Pat Baines isn't an ordinary man," said Mrs. Chance. "I mean he's not like anyone I've ever come across. What would you have him say? Father Tithe, I mean."

"It was the priest's business to say something, to explain somehow so that woman'd understand, instead of tellin' her her place was with her husband and that was all she needed to know."

"But what about the Sacrament of Marriage?" Mrs. Chance asked gravely.

Mrs. Kinsella laughed. "Sacrament, my arse!" she cried. "What's sacred about two people wantin' to go to bed with each other?"

"That's not what marriage is!" Mrs. Chance said.

"Not in all cases, I'll grant you. Some don't even have that, but it *is* in ninety-nine cases out of a hundred. And it's about time we cut out this balls about the Sacrament of Marriage. It's nothing of the sort."

"What is it then?" Mrs. Chance tried to sound sarcastic, but failed. She was terrified of Kinsella, Mrs. Slattery thought, and hadn't the stomach to go the whole hog.

Mrs. Kinsella sat back and ran her hands up and down her spread thighs. "It's what happens when we like the way the other fiddles, or when we see in them, or they in us, the shape of the thing we want. F'rinstance . . . ."

Mrs. Slattery screamed. "No, stop it!" she cried reluctantly. "For Jasus' sake!"

"I was only going to say," Mrs. Kinsella said, "that Phillo said it was . . ."

"Stop!" Mrs. Slattery held up her hand.

"But, c'm'ere," Mrs. Chance repeated, "if it isn't a Sacrament, what is it?"

"Well, it's got hundreds of names," Mrs. Kinsella replied, "but I don't think anyone in their senses would call it a Sacrament." She grinned. "It's just not so good on a windy hill on a wet night. Any fella'll tell you that. Their feet can't get a grip on the grass, so they rush us to a priest or parson and have them say a few words over us, then head for bed."

Mrs. Slattery laughed and wondered what was keeping Mrs. Chance from getting up and going out the door as she always did when Kinsella started on the facts of life, not, indeed, that with six unmarried daughters and a molly of a husband called Alexander, she didn't already know them! But then, every tinker had his own way of dancing, and if Madge Chance wanted, at her age, to pretend that that sex-mad daughter of hers had the makings of a nun and believed a woman's every pregnancy was the direct result of the mysterious ways of Christ, then let her get on with it. "Have more tea," she said.

Mrs. Kinsella shook her head, and Mrs. Chance said, "He kept me from my sleep last night."

"Who, Alexander?" Mrs. Kinsella's eyes widened in surprise.

Mrs. Slattery giggled, and Mrs. Chance put down her cup and drew her coat a little tighter to her. "No," she said emphatically.

Mrs. Kinsella grinned. "Well, I was going to say!"

"Does he never get tired listening to his own voice?" Mrs. Chance asked. "And his language!" Her eyes lifted towards the ceiling. "Alexander wanted to go up to him, but I was afraid of what might happen if he did."

"So would I be if Alexander was my husband. Sure, he'd a et, bet an' threw up Alexander as quick as look at him!"

"I don't know so much about that," Mrs. Chance demurred. "My husband, God bless him, 's a great temper when he's riz."

"Whisht!" Mrs. Slattery gestured them to silence. Both women looked at her, then upwards. "He's at it," Mrs. Slattery said.

The sounds continued until, across the floor of the Baineses' room, someone ran. Mrs. Kinsella jumped to her feet, and Mrs. Slattery followed her more slowly. On the landing above they heard a door open, and when Danny Baines got to the foot of the stairs they were waiting. His look bid them to silence. Then, suddenly, from above them there came a half-scream and a thud. Mrs. Kinsella reached out and grabbed Danny by the arm.

"Don't!" she cried.

Danny shook himself free and cleared the stairs in two jumps onto the landing, with his hand stretching for the handle of the door. They heard the door slam open and shut, then a muttered confusion of men's shouts that died under the hammer-weights of blows. Mrs. Slattery stifled a scream, but Mrs. Kinsella shrieked Allelujah and clapped her hands hard above her head.

"He's knocking the bejesus out of him! Allelujah!"

Mrs. Chance sidled round and past them, her face set in distaste, and disappeared into her own room behind the open hall door.

Overhead, there was a shouted obscenity, and a woman's scream.

The door was flung open again and, unmarked and unharmed, Danny backed out onto the landing with his mother pushing herself against him, urging him away. But Danny held his ground, and against his anger her strength was useless. Conscious that she might be heard, Mrs. Baines was whispering, her face still gripped by recent pain. Pleading with him to go, she must have been, they realized, for they could distinguish Danny's troubled "No!" Then, finally, they heard: "It'll be worse. It'll only be worse, if you stay." Her head was shaking, and she was looking at him, as he tore himself from her.

The women drew quickly aside as he rushed down and out the hall past them. They stared after him, then slowly looked back and up for Mrs. Baines, but she was gone, and the landing was empty.

"Help us," Mrs. Slattery said after a while, and with a laugh Mrs. Kinsella moved to do so.

Mrs. Kinsella took an egg cup from the top shelf of the dresser, and from it gave Neddo Baines one of her last two shillings. "Maybe you'd come in after, son, and give's a hand up with me things from below?"

Neddo nodded. "Are you getting the relief?" he asked with grave interest.

"I am," Mrs. Kinsella replied. "An' isn't it time?" She grinned at Mrs. Slattery sitting at the fire. "Bedell hasn't deigned to pay us a visit since Mrs. Slattery and myself threw him down the stairs six months ago. Until today, that is."

"That's a cross-born get," Mrs. Slattery said contentedly. "Don't forget," she said, moving on to more important things, "to go down to the Room-Keepers' about the Christmas coal."

Mrs. Kinsella laughed. "Never fear. He won't do me outa that."

"Me mother says she'll give you this back tomorrow." Neddo eyed the damp cold cloth tied round Mrs. Slattery's head. "Does that stop your pain?" he spoke directly to Mrs. Slattery.

She gazed at him, puzzled.

"Your head," he gestured.

"That an' Tom Slattery!" Mrs. Kinsella grinned and shooed him ahead of her towards the door. "Go wan, your mother's probably waiting."

Mrs. Slattery waited until the door had closed behind him. "That youngfella would buy an' sell the lot of us."

"Wouldn't he want to? With the ram of a father he has. Still," she added thoughtfully, "he hasn't half the nous of some kids round the place, or like his sister Teasey."

Mrs. Slattery nodded gently. "Ah, that was the fly wan! Getting married with not a word to a soul an' going off the way she did."

Mrs. Kinsella dipped her spoon into a tin of condensed milk on the table and sucked it before she put it into the cup of tea in her hand.

"Of course, he hated the ground that creature walked on."

"Who?" asked Mrs. Kinsella. "Neddo?"

An expression of pain ran across Mrs. Slattery's features. "No, Pat." She paused. "That," she said, indicating the condensed milk, "is going to fill you with worms."

"So Phillo says." Mrs. Kinsella laughed. "Well, it's either him or them. But sure, Nature never intended me to go empty."

Her glance met Mrs. Slattery's, and to the question in the latter's eyes, she nodded. Mrs. Slattery looked to heaven, and Mrs. Kinsella smiled.

"The trouble is, I like babies."

"An' that's not all."

"Have another sup of tea," Mrs. Kinsella laughed. "It'll take your mind off your sins."

Mrs. Slattery looked thoughtfully at the stream that stretched and contracted, as Mrs. Kinsella raised and lowered the pot. "It's funny," she said, "but I've never heard that man throw a kind word to one of them childer. It's as if he hated them all." She took the spoon from Mrs. Kinsella, who was nodding agreement.

"Hatred or indifference," the latter agreed. "I'm not sure which.

All I know is, I've never known a man to be so unaware of his own, or of any responsibility to them, in the whole of me natural."

"He's not human," Mrs. Slattery said.

"He's not shagging well anyt'ing. Except an Antichrist!"

"And yet," Mrs. Slattery said ponderously, "he's a learned man."

"He's a learned . . . !" Mrs. Kinsella broke off. "That man doesn't know his arse from his elbow, no more than he knew them three daughters of his were grown-up women, or that Teasey was planning to marry Peter Tansey until she did. An' th'oul' get hasn't got over that yet. An' sure, look at Danny! It took that hiding he gave him that time to make him realize he had a man on his hands."

"Jasus, that was a day!" Mrs. Slattery laughed lazily. "What with us cleaning Bedell, and Danny Baines knocking the scutter out of Pat!" Her face creased her satisfaction.

"Herself," said Mrs. Kinsella, "told me afterwards that he lay on the floor pretending to be kilt, until she got Danny out of the room and it was safe for him to get to his feet again."

"The dirty slieveen!"

"It was the first an' only time that man's brutality has ever been checked in that room."

"And the last," Mrs. Slattery added her amen. "Though, mind you, it doesn't seem as bad up there as it did when he first come home."

"He restrains himself, God save the mark, so long as Danny's in the neighbourhood, for he knows that, for all Danny's easygoing ways, he could, if the humor was on him, sweep the Lane with him, and the only reason he doesn't is his fear that Pat'll take it out on them or the mother after. He's still sleeping under the stairs, y'know?"

"I know. Maybe he's getting a decent night's rest, now his sisters have stopped using the place as a Conference Hall. Kitty wasn't so bad, but Teasey and her fella kept me awake for months adding up shillin's and pence to make the pounds that'd take them to Birmingham. Teasey's marriage can't have surprised Danny."

"Nor the mother," Mrs. Kinsella added. "And Pat didn't even know she was gone from the house till three weeks after."

"A fortnight."

"No, three weeks," Mrs. Kinsella said emphatically, and although Mrs. Slattery waved a hand weakly in capitulation, she went on: "No, I remember the morning Kitty told Danny. As you know, she smuggled out the jug of tea and the bit of bread to him every morning. Well, she told him on the morning Teasey was married, and that was the day Phillo got laid off. Then three weeks later, Phillo got a week's work on the Custom House, and that was the day Pat Baines found out his eldest daughter had taken the step and gone to live in a room near her factory. An' by the livin' sweet Jesus! will I ever forget the ructions that followed that bit of enlightenment? Aye, it was no wonder that at the end of it Kitty was after her. And, although the bit she was bringing in was a loss to her mother, you could hardly blame her for wanting out."

Mrs. Slattery agreed, and decided against warning Mrs. Kinsella to lay off the condensed milk.

"He was beside himself over Teasey's marriage," Mrs. Kinsella sounded pleased. "Into a black knot, the bastard wound hisself. And blamed herself for colloguin' with Teasey. And tried to beat her whereabouts outa Neddo, who was running messages from herself. And," she concluded with a roar, "stayed home an' sober for one whole month!"

Mrs. Slattery sighed. "I remember," she said. "Issuing his orders from the bed in the middle of the night, and . . ."

"And," Mrs. Kinsella interrupted, "in the day, lying on his back sleeping or reading. But at night! I was comin' back late from Fawan Barton's that time, and wasn't he chasing those poor girls down the stairs? He refused to let either of them set foot outside the door, y'know. And there he was, in his striped shirt an' nothin' else, like an avenging angel, with the big hairy legs on him. When he saw me, he went up faster than he came down, but he was kicking Kitty an' Babby before him."

"That was the time he burnt the dance dresses! Oh, there's no end to the badness of Pat Baines," Mrs. Slattery murmured.

"Fed the fire with them, he did, and anything else he could lay his hands on!"

"Well, there isn't a lot for him to burn now!" Mrs. Slattery turned in her chair, and faced Mrs. Kinsella fully. "I was in yesterday morning for a lend of her iron, and the room's empty."

"Did she have the iron?" Mrs. Kinsella asked, and Mrs. Slattery shook her head, "I thought not. Sure, she's had to pawn anything she could, to keep him in drink an' tobacco an' the meat dinners he won't go without. Bejasus! I know the meat dinners I'd give him!"

"How long is Teasey gone now?" Mrs. Slattery asked.

"Five months, and Kitty half that. God help her!" said Mrs. Kinsella. "Poor Kitty! Only to Dartmouth Square she was going, to do indoor work. After all, she told her mother, it was only over the bridge, it wouldn't be like Teasey getting married and going to England, she'd be able to come home on her days off and give up something out of her wages every week. Oh, aye, and now she's in America with her Gibblers."

"Schenectady," Mrs. Slattery liked the sound of the word. "Schenectady."

"She'd like Babby to get married," Mrs. Kinsella said, "but Babby won't. Won't leave her, and neither will Danny. Because, although it's difficult to get to England from here now, it's not impossible, but he won't go."

"He's a good fellow," Mrs. Slattery said, "and if Babby doesn't take him, Aggie Chance will."

Mrs. Kinsella looked at her. "Who're you talking about?"

"Babby's fella. Nick Ryan," Mrs. Slattery said, confused at having to account for the order of her thoughts. "She's home again, you know."

And Mrs. Kinsella knew now who she was talking about.

"She came outa the convent yesterday evening," Mrs. Slattery said, "and what that girl's got to give she's offering with two hands. Serving it up on a platter, she is, to any fella fool enough to take it." She leaned forward and said in a whisper, "I heard her in the hall last night on her way in from the lavo, talking to Danny Baines, an' if he's as hot in his britches as his father is, it isn't a nun she'll become." Mrs. Slattery laughed. "Wouldn't it be the height of that wan if she was fattened up with some fellow's bastard? Jasus, that would take some explaining! Her mother would hardly be able to claim that as the hand of God."

Mrs. Kinsella rocked herself back and forth. "It would," she said. "But Danny Baines won't spread that girl's legs apart. He's got enough on his hands with Queenie Mullen."

"I never heard!" Mrs. Slattery turned from the fire with more than her ordinary energy.

"Take it gently," Mrs. Kinsella replied. "There wasn't nothing to hear except Phillo saw the pair of them sitting on the grass on the Canal the other evening, an' he said that, to all intents an' purposes, Queenie Mullen's body was acting independently of her brain."

"I never heard," Mrs. Slattery said again, her great face forlorn, then went on, "Well, she better mind herself, if she doesn't want Father Tithe to get cracking on her!"

"He'll leave Queenie alone," Mrs. Kinsella sneered. "After all, he has a father and mother to account to there, not like poor Nancy O'Byrne, who's a half-orphan and, with the way Cocky's going ever since the death of Peewee, almost a whole one. Which reminds me—Mr. Pughe came down the Lane last night to ask her to marry him."

Mrs. Slattery nodded and looked pleased. "I got every living word of it from Granny Quinn? She saw it all through the door."

"Go 'way!"

"He came with flowers, an' his hat on an' his best yeller boots. And Cocky let him in and sat him down and sat opposite him with Peewee's coat t'rown round her shoulders and Mr. Pughe's flowers in her lap."

"But how did Granny Quinn see it all?"

"Cocky left the door open, on purpose, so the granny could see what was taking place. She said Cocky sat very respectable, and didn't shout or sing, and she'd done up the room and her hair for the visit. She'd put a white cloth on the table and it was set for tea, but between the cups she had set Peewee's phota, because, Granny Quinn said, she didn't want Peewee to feel he was being left out. However, Mr. Pughe didn't want the phota between them, and asked Cocky if she'd put it on the mantelpiece out of harm's way, and Cocky did. Then Granny Quinn said, she sat back down and looked at Pughe, serious, and said, 'Did you know my Peewee, Mr. Pughe?' Your man shook his head and said he'd never had the pleasure. An' Cocky laughed, threw back her head an' laughed as if he'd said something funny, which he hadn't. You know how solemn Pughe is, God help him! 'That's a laugh,' Cocky said, 'that is. Pleasure! Oh, Jesus, pleasure! Listen,' she said, and she leant towards him. 'He was a beauty, my Peewee. A living beauty! No man had the right to be as beautiful as my Peewee. He was the most gorgeous thing Christ ever created. I used to lie beside him, when he was asleep, just watching him. Just watching him, mind you. I used to kiss his feet. I used to kiss him all over, but I used to kiss his feet like the Japanese do.' And Mr. Pughe asked her who told her the Japs did dirty things like that, and she said Peewee did. On the soles of his feet she said she kissed him, and in the arches of each foot. An' then she did something awful. She threw Peewee's coat off her shoulders and stood up and began to take off her clothes. And when Pughe saw what she was doing, he nearly died. Granny Quinn said she could see the blood rushing up the back of his neck to his head. And Cocky was saying she wanted him to see the marks that came when she just *thought* of Peewee." Mrs. Slattery paused. "No, it's true," she said, "the granny told me that when

Cocky took off her blouse you could see on her arms and on her breasts the kind of new-dinge marks a man's fingers'd make."

"Like a stigmata," Mrs. Kinsella said.

Mrs. Slattery nodded. "Exactly."

"And what happened?" Mrs. Kinsella asked.

"Well, Cocky showed Pughe these, and said, 'Pleasure! Oh, Jasus, pleasure! You little undersized runt! You talk about pleasure! You whip up enough courage to come out from behind your counter to come down here to ask me to marry you and . . .' An' then Mr. Pughe got to his feet and said something, but the granny didn't hear what, because Cocky began to roar at poor Pughe, and swaying. You know. The way she does in drink, only she wasn't drunk. That's for sure, Granny Quinn said she'd been in cleaning herself and the room the whole evening for Pughe's visit, and she hadn't a drop on her. But it was as if suddenly something he said, or something she thought, set her off. An' then she began to tell him how Peewee made love to her an' how he . . . well, you know, an' all. And how often. And about the way she an' Peewee had stayed in bed for a whole two weeks, an' what they did. The granny says it was disgusting."

"She would, the bitter bitch! Go on!"

"Anyway, she then whipped round the table to Pughe," Mrs. Slattery said, and then broke off suddenly. "For two whole weeks!" She looked blankly at Mrs. Kinsella. "Doing what?"

Mrs. Kinsella laughed. "Go wan with the story, you dirty-minded oul' faggot!"

"Oh, God!" Mrs. Slattery giggled. "Anyway . . ."

There was a knock on the door and the handle was turned and Neddo Baines stood looking from one to the other.

"I'll help you bring up the furniture now, Mrs. Kinsella."

Mrs. Slattery was vexed at the interruption. And so was Mrs. Kinsella, but if she was to get her things back up before Phillo came in, she would have to accept Neddo's offer now, or do the whole thing herself. "All right, Neddo," she said, and as they rose to their feet, she said, "Well, what happened after?"

"Oh, I'll tell you again," Mrs. Slattery said. "But it ended up with Pughe going out quicker than he went in, and Cocky screaming out the window after him."

"She threw his flowers out at him," Neddo said. "Tucker Tommy and me saw it from our window. And they all lay dead on the ground. But Florry Connors took them up in the morning and brought them up to the teacher in school." When Neddo saw that Mrs. Kinsella was interested, he added, "The teacher put them on the altar."

Mrs. Kinsella laughed, but she noticed that Neddo did not, as she nudged him before her out onto the landing. "Is he home?" she whispered.

Neddo nodded quickly, and ran before her down the stairs.

FOUR

"Holy Saint Ann, send's a man!" Babby Baines
laughed, and despite the irreverence, her mother laughed with
her as she put a plate of coddle before Danny, who was shaking
his head.

"God help the fellow gaum enough to saddle himself with
you!" He bent into the steam rising from the mixture of sausage,
onions and potatoes, swimming in a milky water.

"Is that so?" Babby, with mock impertinence, leaned towards
him. "And what, may I ask, is wrong with me?"

Danny chewed gravely a moment before he answered. "An'
well you might."

Tucker Tommy turned solemn eyes from one to the other and
reached out to take another cut of bread. "All's wrong with Babby
is she's flighty."

"An' who made you so wise and your ma such a fool?" Babby
twisted in her chair to regard laughingly the baby of the family.

54

"Granny Quinn told Mrs. Chance at the pipe." Tucker Tommy was all importance.

"It's a pity now that oul' bugle-bonneted reprobate wouldn't have something better to do with herself, instead of scandalizing me and the likes of me round the pipe all day!" Babby cried in near anger. "It's in she should be with her Rosary beads getting herself ready for her next life!"

"I thought you didn't care what the neighbors had to say about you." Danny grinned at his sister's temper.

"I don't," she snapped. "But, if it's something to occupy her mind with she wants, let her look over her own shoulder."

"What else did you hear?" Mrs. Baines asked, her voice matter-of-fact as she refilled Babby's cup with tea.

"Nothing," Tucker Tommy answered swiftly.

"What do you mean, 'nothing'?" Mrs. Baines was familiar with his ways of hearing, and telling, the gossip he overheard in the Lane, and round the pipe in particular. She repeated her question.

Tucker Tommy counted the cuts of bread left on the plate. He flattened a lock of hair back from his forehead and chose that moment when all eyes were on him to grab two, knowing the gesture would go unnoticed, and afraid that if he didn't grab while the grabbing was good, there'd be nothing left in another minute but the empty plate. He kept the bread under his outstretched palms, and Mrs. Baines spoke again.

"Well?"

"Granny Quinn said Esther Fitz ought to be ashamed of herself going round with a Free Stater, and that men must be hard to get when girls went to such extremes. She said Nancy O'Byrne is living with Kevin Hely, and that Father Tithe is out to get her. And . . ." He took a bite of bread and looked down.

"An' what else?"

Tucker Tommy looked at his mother. "Granny Quinn said you were a gun-runner, 'an you'll have us all murdered in our beds if you're not careful." He bit into the bread again, and over his head Mrs. Baines caught Babby and Danny's swift stares.

"An' what else?" she asked inexorably.

"Granny Quinn said she saw a soldier giving the bins a gate-a-going last night when she came down for water, and she asked him what he was looking for, and he said, 'Without making you an impudent answer, ma'am, me health.' And then he saluted her and went up the Lane."

Tucker Tommy bit his bread more openly now and chewed noisily, but Mrs. Baines hardly noticed. She sipped the tea, growing lukewarm in her cup, before she spoke again. "An' what else?"

"Granny Quinn said we're Rebels an' should be drummed out of the Lane before death an' destruction done in the lot of them."

"Was there anybody else there when this was going on?" Babby asked.

Tucker Tommy gazed at her. "Only Mrs. Chance. And Mrs. Kinsella. And Annie the Man. Aggie Chance's frock an' coat is hung out on the line, and her mother says Aggie's got the call again. And Mrs. Kinsella laughed and said Aggie was always the bridesmaid, but never the bride, of Christ."

There was a silence. Slowly, carefully, he edged himself off the chair, and made for the door. He looked back at the three who were deep in their own thoughts. "Let's out?"

Mrs. Baines turned to him. "No. But go out and tell Neddo to come up, an' when I leave my hands on him, I'll take his life."

They waited until the door closed behind him.

"Are we, Mother?" Babby asked quietly.

"What?"

"Gun-running?"

Mrs. Baines gave a tired nod. "Mattie and Zena left them here the other night."

Babby jumped to her feet.

"Well, what was I to do?" Mrs. Baines's glance shifted from Babby to Danny. "He couldn't take them with him, and them gougers losing the run of themselves around the place in their new suits."

"But, Mother!"

"But, Mother, nothing! Show some sense, child." She saw Babby's eyes dart to the unlikeliest hiding-places in the room. "They're in the trunk," Mrs. Baines said, wearied into the further revelation by the repeated weight of Mattie Baines's secrets.

Babby stared at the curtain of the little room. "Oh, sweet God, if it isn't one thing. . . . Only a year ago their bloody treaty was signed!"

Danny snorted. "Treaty!"

Mrs. Baines exclaimed. "I know nothing of treaties. He said if he could get in tonight to take them, he would." She stood up.

"He might? He might do anything." Babby spoke in the fret of anger. "They all might. They might give people a chance to live, instead of keeping the whole country in an uproar with shooting and killing. If they must kill, why not each other? Why do people like us have to be dragged into it?"

"Have you finished?" Danny asked.

"No, I haven't. If Mattie and his cronies think they're man enough to shoulder guns, why the hell don't they? What did he want to leave them here for, that's what I want to know? He won't free the country by keeping guns in a brown tin trunk."

"He might," Danny said. "Anyway, that's where they are. Isn't that enough for you?" He was irritated by the sight and sound of his sister's fear. When she wheeled round at him, he went on in a softer more reasoning tone. "As me mother says, the place was crawling with soldiers, and there was nothing Mattie could do but what he did. He was hard set as it was to get away without carrying ammunition with him. That would've been asking for trouble."

"Trouble?" The word was saturated with irony. "Have we ever known anything else with Mattie? Or his brother?" Babby continued contemptuously. "Him an' his Irish poems an' his spoutin' about a free Ireland an' a free people. He wants to set us free, but at whose expense. As long as I can remember, it's been at ours. He's used this place as an ammunition dump for years!"

"That'll do," Danny said quietly.

"It won't." Babby's voice, too, was pitched low, but Mrs. Baines recognized the near scream. "*Your* heart may be with the Republicans an' their tuppenny-ha'penny 'free nation,' but mine isn't. And neither will yours when the soft knock comes on the door in the middle of the night and we're taken out the way Tom Carney was."

"It'll never come to that." Mrs. Baines made a gentle motion with her hands.

"No, Mother!" With her whole stance, Babby rejected her mother's making light. "I'm sick hearing about reprisals and betrayals and innocent people being hanged, drawn and quartered, first by the Black and Tans, now the Free Staters and the Republicans. I'm fed up a Mattie an' all the other Matties in Dublin, play-acting with guns and speeches about things that don't or shouldn't concern them. The ignorant lot of gombeens! It'd suit them better to get out and earn their living instead of cadging the drop to drink and the bit to eat, from us an' the likes of us, hedge-and-hall hopping with a pack of half-cracked oul' bitches who should be on their knees telling their beads and asking God to forgive them and the other mongrels for the allegations and bloodshed they're responsible for!" Babby paused.

And out of a fitful memory evoked by her daughter's blazing eyes, Mrs. Baines spoke into the silence, quietly. "I agree with most of what you've said. Now let's hear no more about it."

"I haven't said half the things I could!" Babby protested.

"We all could, child." Mrs. Baines sighed. "We all could."

In the Lane, Cocky O'Byrne broke the hush sharp and quick. They listened to her scream lance the air and didn't hear Mattie and Zena Baines come into the hall and up the stairs, until their knock came at the door, the door was open and Babby was staring at them both as if hypnotized.

"Well," she cried, "there's nothing like a real live Republican for putting the heart across you!"

The scene held for a moment, with Babby staring her amazement into the man's wide Burberry-covered shoulders, while

Danny noticed that, without appearing to move at all, Mattie's sharp quick glance flicked over every inch of the room. He went forward smiling his welcome, into the mild confusion that was buffeting the greetings, and behind him Mrs. Baines began to whip the dirty delph from the table, and rushed to make the room look respectable.

"We never heard you coming," she said in answer to Mattie's greeting and the grinned smile that exposed the same white teeth of his brother Pat, for whom now his gaze went in search. "He's not here." Mrs. Baines took clothes off the line over the fire and pushed them into a bundle into the press at the bottom of the dresser. "He's above in the Union," she added lightly, not so much in apology as thanksgiving, Mattie thought, as she looked beyond him to Zena standing with her flute in its case behind him.

Mattie shook his head as if he should have known, as indeed he ought to have, Babby thought, watching his glance linger on her mother.

"And how are you all?" he asked in his heavy Irish brogue.

"Grand," Mrs. Baines replied. "We're all grand, thank God!"

Babby shook her head free from his hands cupping it. "And we'll be a lot grander after seeing you!" She began to spread clean paper across the table with angry slaps.

"That'll do," Danny whispered.

"That'll do, the pair of you!" Mrs. Baines snapped. "Go and help your Aunt Zena with her coat."

Babby did so with a smile to Zena who, after handing her flute to Danny, glanced in quick doubt at her husband.

"How's that?" Mattie asked.

"How do you think it is?" Babby replied. "I mean, it's a lot better we'll be when you get that arsenal out of here. That's how."

Mattie Baines laughed. His smooth tanned face turned back and up in the lamplight. "Ah," he said in mock understanding, "the scapulars!"

"Around here, guns are guns."

Babby's reply wiped the grin from her uncle's face. His glance, wary, skimmed from one to the other. "They haven't been taken?"

Mrs. Baines laughed easy. "Not at all," she said; but in the same breath Babby cried scornfully, "Hah! *that's* all you're worried about!"

In the embarrassed hush that followed, and while they stared at each other, Mattie turned to Babby. "I'm sorry."

Impulsively she reached out and touched him on the arm. "I am, too. It's only . . ."

"I should never have left them here," Mattie interrupted. "I never will again!" He gestured. "It's only . . . when you find someone you can really trust, you go on trusting them," he said dramatically, his lips stretched in a mournful grin. He looked at Babby from under lashes as dark as her own. "I was out of me mind."

His wife shrugged. "So that's new?" she said, but there was no criticism in her voice, only a terse comment.

Mrs. Baines, anxious to get beyond a mood which might, with Mattie, become contrary, said, "Ah, it couldn't be helped." Then, to Danny, "Raise the wick, son," and to the visitors, "Sit over to the fire."

Babby, at her mother's gesture, took her coat from the back of the door and flung it round her shoulders before she took some money from a handleless cup on the dresser. As she hurried out the door, Mattie looked after her. He turned to Mrs. Baines.

"Now, don't go to trouble."

"It's none," she assured him. "And you must be famished."

"Where are you coming from?" Danny aimed his question at Mattie, but it was Zena who answered.

"The Featherbed." She stretched long thin hands to the fire.

"In this weather?" Mrs. Baines could not see Zena's eyes, deep, dark in the bones of her bent face. But even if she could, she knew they would not tell much, no more than the words she spoke.

"It's the only safe place remaining to us."

Zena's way of speaking was tidy, English, to the point, and Mrs. Baines heard her in silence.

"Babby seemed upset," Mattie said abruptly. "You haven't had trouble?"

"Not a bit," Mrs. Baines said lightly.

"I gather from what Babby had said something happened."

"Oh, something did!" Danny laughed. "Tucker Tommy heard some of the oul' wans round the pipe call us gun-runners."

"Don't let that worry you," Mrs. Baines said.

"We'll take the arms tonight." Zena seemed to be answering an unspoken question.

"You're never going to traipse them mountains again tonight?" Mrs. Baines looked from Zena, who had not turned her head from the fire, to Mattie. "You can't."

"We are," Zena said quietly. "We have to."

Mattie glanced over at his wife's bent shoulders. "It can't be helped." A hardness crept into his voice, and made the muscles of his lean face flex as he continued. "We must clear that stuff out of this house tonight. Tommorrow might be too late."

"Tomorrow she might be dead." Mrs. Baines glanced at Zena's carelessly drawn-back hair and the too-white bony cheeks in the fire's light.

"Molly, if one knows, twenty do. Tomorrow you might all be dead." Mattie pulled up a chair and sat down, facing the fire opposite Zena.

"They say the Staters are like ants between here and Rathfarnham."

Mattie nodded at Danny's remark. "So they are," he said tiredly.

"Then how will you manage?"

"There's a family group. . ." Mattie rolled his r's, and his grin was quick and sly. "Going out from the city at twelve tonight to a wake, and the funeral tomorrow."

"Oh, dear God! where is all this to end?" Mrs. Baines asked. "All this strife and murders be going on now since 1916. Six years! Aye, and more. And still no end to it!"

Molly Baines was too simple by mind and nature, Mattie thought, to follow the tangles and arguments of the times she was living through. But then, craftier eyes than hers had had the wool pulled over them by the so-called "Free" State of Ireland with its Treaty and its shopkeeper, landholder government. He shrugged.

"It won't end," Zena said, looking up now into Mrs. Baine's troubled face, "until the Irish realise freedom won't come from yellow-bellied chicaneries in Westminster, which is the Free State's way, nor from organized murder, which is ours." To a gesture from her husband she said sharply, "Yes, it is. Murder. Arson. Pillage. All of those. It will come—freedom will—from open war." She turned wearily back to the fire. "Geneva Convention," she ended disconnectedly.

"What have you got against the Peace Treaty, Uncle Mattie?" Danny asked.

"It's illegal, son."

Which meant, Danny thought, that he didn't object so much to the conditions laid down by England as he feared the darkening of the warm fire of Republicanism. The Republic must come now, his uncle and hundreds like him felt, or it would never come, it would die, the young men would lose the image of freedom, turn away from the phoenix; a free Catholic workingman's republic, Utopia, would be lost in the industrial undertakings that peace promised.

"So, instead of accepting it, the country's plunged into civil war. With Irish eating Irish?" Nobody answered Mrs. Baines. "Arragh, we always have! I'll wet the tea." She banged four cups unnecessarily on the table.

"May I wash first?" Zena said.

And Danny continued to Mattie, "I believe the Republicans are grabbing the houses and lands of Protestants and the Free Staters are handing them back?"

"Ah, now don't believe everything you read in the newspapers, Danny," Mattie began.

"We'll go inside." Mrs. Baines guided Zena by the elbow and, turning from the table, lifted the heavy black steaming kettle off the fire. Zena smiled her thanks for the candle Danny lit and handed to her. To her husband's question: "Isn't that right, love?" she answered: "Yes, Mattie," though she hadn't a notion what he'd been talking about, and followed Mrs. Baines into the little room.

"What about your things, pet?" Mrs. Baines poured water into the basin.

Zena laughed. "I'm dosed with flea powder," she said, beginning to unbutton her blouse, shaking back her thick heavy hair, stiff and coarse as a horse's mane. Mrs. Baines watched her strip, then opened the trunk and took out the knickers and the undervest that were hiding the arms at the bottom. Quickly she let the lid fall, and began to warm the underclothes in the palms of her large, thin, worn hands.

"Hot water!" Zena sighed. She held her head on one side. "I dream of hot water, gallons of it, and white baths." Her hands plunged and glistened and plunged.

Mrs. Baines lowered herself onto the edge of Babby's bed.

"Hot water and white baths and big clean beds," Zena said. Her eyes, caved, reflected the candlelight. "And you, Molly?"

"Of haggarts filled with good golden hay," she said, and felt, as she often did, that Zena, the Englishwoman, a stranger in this strange place, needed to be loved, mothered even, away from the sight of her husband. "And the Wicklow hills. In all seasons. And sometimes of my father." It was what she told the children when they persisted, what she was telling Zena now while she waited to have the disturbed heart sensed in the woman this evening explained. There was a difference tonight: not the known difference of class and country. Something else. A thing that mattered.

"And what else?" Zena asked.

"Of the table set for Sunday dinner at home," Mrs. Baines said. The Sunday dinner used to fill the room, unlike the other days of the week. "Of whole hams with the bone, pink and bare and rounded, and flitches of bacon hanging from the ceiling. Of cambric." She gazed at Zena. "And the smell of thyme. Of Mrs. Farrell, who, after the death of my mother, took over the running of the house. With the flour running up her arms, mostly I see her. And the earth. I suppose this most of all. The black spine of it." She spoke into the candlelight. "You could feel that under the soles of your feet, and you spread them, like a duck, so's you'd not miss any of it. You couldn't have, of course."

Yes, you could, Zena thought, but you never did. She rolled her hands into a tight soap ball.

"And you, pet?" Mrs. Baines took Zena's skirt and moved closer to the flame of the candle. She raised the seams. They were furrowed with traces of fleapowder that looked like old snow tussocked with the near-stunned crawl of red-brown vermin. They died between her thumbnails, made a sound in the room, and marked her thumbs with blood. She wiped each carcass onto the top of an old silk stocking on the floor beside her, but the blood on her thumbs dried quickly into congealed splashes and spread across the nails to a point on the flesh of her fingers.

"I've crushed them between my front teeth at night when I couldn't see to kill them otherwise," Zena said. "And afterwards dreamed of flowers. I dream a great deal about flowers. Arranging them. And writing letters. I used to write scads of letters to girls I was at school with. They were always getting married. And for a time they wrote back, then, gradually, they would stop and, except for an occasional announcement of a child, I never heard."

Mrs. Baines looked up.

"Oh," Zena smiled. "I was dark. And thin. And awkward. So I was left. But I was at home and didn't mind. I did, but I wasn't supposed to. I was clever. There were 'other things,' my mother said. When she talked to me at all."

And she had worn hats and gloves, Mrs. Baines thought, and learned—not cooking and cleaning and mending and washing, because nobody who had the rearing of her would have envisaged the necessity. And it might never have arisen if some folly had not led her to Ireland.

"How can you know?" Zena asked. "When you're young?"

"No," said Mrs. Baines, "that's a time when all's astray."

But something would happen, Zena had thought. But when? She could not wait. This was something they had not taught her to do. Her mother had been middle-aged when she was born, Zena, her first child, a gay middle-aged forty with her second husband, concerned, amused until the novelty had worn thin and her baby handed with care into the care of strange women who kept her in closed rooms and pushed her through parks and listened and waited with her for a voice to call, for someone to walk in and coax the long wait to life. —You must be good, her mother said abstractedly. You must behave, brush your teeth and your hair. You must study and do what Miss . . . She would stare then, blankly, and touch her own red hair, filling in the time until the stranger's name was brought to her, until the friend called or the carriage was brought round, her head bright and as hard as her eyes in the dim room's light, and impatient. —Not looks, darling. You could hear the despair. But brains. It was the next best thing, the only thing. I do believe Zena's clever. And sometimes Father saw and nodded his eyes, and Miss, to be heard, to be known, to be smiled at, would say: Zena will be a doctor. Later, others said it. She would be like her father, they said. In this she might resemble him, but in nothing else, she knew. She was thin and dark, and her father was handsome. Mattie was like her father in his big handsomeness. And in this, she knew, he might resemble her father, but in nothing else. Mattie was mad. He laughed. He was warm. He made her warm. Afterwards she knew he had married her because she was useful. To the Cause. To *his* Cause. And yet she loved him.

She drew a comb with force through her dark hair, and fastened her eyes on Mrs. Baines's face, and asked a question.

The reply was slow in coming, and short. "He's gone a week now," said Mrs. Baines. She bent her head back to her task, and in the room only the long hiss of the hair being combed and the sharp snap of death broke the silence. Zena would not persist, and she was grateful, for somehow before Zena she felt shame and embarrassment when they discussed Pat. And she hoped that Mattie's wife knew as little about her life with Pat as she knew about theirs. And she knew very little about Zena, she supposed. She knew she wrote books about Ireland and addressed meetings in the streets after dark and that she was great with the Countess Markievicz. That she had met Mattie at an I.R.A. gathering, and married him after a short acquaintance: this she knew, and the things Mrs. Kinsella knew, heard, like her, from the mouths of the stray women who came looking for Mattie in the Lane. But there had never been time for herself and Zena to get to know more about each other, ever since that first night when Mattie had turned up with her and said: Meet my wife. They had done little more than shake hands, then or since. Now, when he and Zena came, it was hurried, unexpected, between journeys to or from meetings that they talked about, or from one ammunition dump or another which they didn't. It was surprising perhaps that, being so different, herself and Zena should like each other. And yet they had, from the first: Mrs. Baines, because she liked the tall colt-grave gentleness and the still discernible angular awkward girl in the woman of thirty, the English speech and the really beautiful manners, the quiet good taste and the eyes that saw even those things you wished them not to see. They were alike in this, herself and Zena. They saw many things, but in the end they would both react differently. Would what Zena had seen, was seeing now, in Ireland, break her, or would she survive? Would either of them? Zena would not have her reasons, though. Zena was childless. And too good for Mattie, Mrs. Baines believed. Fond as she was of her brother-in-law with his quick laugh and sober ways, there was still that about him which made you know he'd be forever answering the come-away call of the gentry in the meadow of a summer's eve. This incapacity to roost for longer in one place than you'd be looking at him, he shared with his brother Pat. Mattie was training to be a jockey when politics claimed him and took him from his job in Kildare to the city. Then, like the Dummies, who were Protestants for as long as

anyone could remember, suddenly turning Catholics, he turned
to speech-making, and his subject was the Salvation of His Country. He developed a hatred of everything English, even the language, and changed his name to Kavanagh because he couldn't
prove the one he had was Irish. He liked Mrs. Baines and her
children, and was good to Zena, but he took other women and was
constantly being pursued by one pregnant girl after another. What
matter if they were camp-followers and the Cumann na Ban
rossies, it was still, Mrs. Baines told him, disgraceful! What Zena
thought of it all, you had to guess. She never said. But it was her,
Mrs. Baines knew, who had to dig into her purse every time a girl
turned up. All Mattie did was throw his hands in the air and say:
Another little bastard for the Cause! while a grin spread from
his mouth to his eyes and the episode turned into a sour laugh.
The man had children all over the place, and there was poor
Zena with nare a one. Better so, if it must be reared on the run;
but there was no consolation in that thought, because she knew a
child was the one thing Zena wanted.

Mrs. Baines ran her hands quickly along the seams of the skirt,
pressing the raised cloth back into place, and looked up. She surprised Zena's quietly musing gaze, and, because she didn't speak,
Mrs. Baines said, "They were big enough to carry you off, pet."
She held out the skirt.

"We don't spare your sensibilities," Zena said, following the
statement with a solemn smile. "What would I do without you,
Molly? What would any of us do without you? But me? You've
given me so much."

"Musha, hush!" Mrs. Baines watched Zena fix the buckle on
the belt of her skirt. Then she bent and gathered up the discarded
underclothing which she would wash out tomorrow.

"No, it's true," Zena said, but with no trace of a smile now.

"Will ya whisht!" Gratitude was embarrassing.

"What happens is turned over, put away, and left," Zena said.
"You feed, clothe, wash and delouse us."

Mrs. Baines had looked away, as Zena wandered back from the

new path she had pursued for a moment; listening, she began to sense that it would be said now, something momentous. With the clothes in her arms, she half turned and stared in sudden wonder at Zena, who was crouching, gripping with one hand the head of the bed while the other spread clawlike along the side of her face. Mrs. Baines was shocked.

"Zena," Mrs. Baines whispered, unaware that she did. In one movement, she was beside her, taking the ridged hands tightly in her own.

"I saw a man die," Zena said. "I held him in my lap, but he died. We had nothing. He could not be brought to a hospital, and so he died."

"But you have seen other men die." Mrs. Baines did not understand. There was this on one side: the life of men killing men in the dark of night, on country roads and in city lanes; and on the other: herself and the children and the people they lived amongst, as remote as dreams from that other except when, as now, it was brought to your door. "I always imagined it wouldn't be so hard for you?"

"Sometimes it's worse than other times." Zena bit her lips. "It's as if one was quite mad. Or as negative as air." Her breath dominated the silence. "I can't get used to seeing men die."

Mrs. Baines felt the tension rush from her. In the violent shiver that followed, she drew her down onto the side of the bed. I shall wait, she thought, I shall love her and wait. Her arms encircled the bony shoulders.

"I'm sorry, Molly. I'm sorry." Zena spoke after a while.

"What ails you child? What is it?"

Zena shook her head. "Nothing. It's tiredness. I'm tired. We haven't slept a whole night through since God only knows." She raised her face. In the candlelight her eyes shone hard and hurting, like brilliants under water. She could not express in words what as yet had no shape, only the unalterable fact. Leaning back, breaking the halter of arms, she said, "Also I've had a miscarriage."

"Oh, my God!" Mrs. Baines's exclamation shot into being, hovered and was shattered by Zena's aimed: "Yes, another."

"Oh, child! That man dragging . . . He must be out of his mind!"

"He didn't even know I was pregnant." Zena's voice wavered and grew bitter.

"You never told him?" Mrs. Baines was incredulous. "But how did you manage?"

"Like Mary—in the manger."

"When?"

"That last night he came in alone."

"But he just said you were not well that night and I was so worried about Babby or Danny finding out I'd taken them things there from him again, that I hardly asked." She stared from the trunk to Zena. "Dear God and His Blessed Mother!"

Zena forced a smile.

"You can't go back with him tonight," Mrs. Baines said. "You stay here with me now, and let me look after you for a bit."

Zena shook her head. "No, we've eight cases of flu out there, and it may spread. Something else I've got to get while I'm down here is medicines." She smiled. "The weapons of life, Molly, not only the weapons of death. Besides, he'll need me.

"If only to see that no harm comes to him!" Mrs. Baines was silent for a moment. "Well, then stay this one night."

"We can't," Zena said and shrugged deeply.

The curtain was pushed aside, and Babby said, "Mother, I'm back."

They stared at the interruption, then Zena bent to kiss Mrs. Baines on the side of the face. Her skin was soft and smelled of soap. They looked at each other before Mrs. Baines said, "We'll go so."

Tucker Tommy was waiting now with Danny and Mattie, listening with his eyes never still, watching his mother wet the tea, following Babby's motions as she fried rashers, glancing up solemnly at Zena as she drew her chair close to Babby at the fire.

"And where's your Nick?" Mattie asked. "We haven't seen him round here for a long time."

"Working," Babby replied and shook the pan emphatically.

"He never stops," Mrs. Baines said. "He's getting as much money as he can to make a home for them."

"And when, if ever, is she going to marry that poor chap and put him out of his misery?"

Babby, sensing from her mother's and Zena's attitudes that everything was not as it should be, felt sure her uncle was in some way responsible. "I'm in no hurry to tie myself to any man!"

"Watch out now for those rashers, girl!" her mother cried.

Mattie grinned. "You're like your father," he said. "More like your father used to be."

"I wouldn't know how my father used to be," Babby replied. "I only know how he is now, an' it's nothing to brag about."

Mattie shook his big head portentously. "The war made a great change in Pat."

"The war!" Babby said. "The war had nothing to do with it. He was like this before the war, and so were the rest of the insane ex-servicemen roaming the streets. The war is simply an excuse now to legalize their blackguardism."

"If you don't want your Aunt Zena to go hungry, pay more attention to what you're doing," Mrs. Baines said.

"We-ell?" Babby questioned, giving the word the two cheeky notes that never failed to amuse Zena.

She spoke now across to Mattie. "I thought Danny was the one who most resembled your brother."

Mattie shook his head. "In appearance, yes. But it's Babby who has his temperament. I often remember when we were chiselers, Pat and I, and how it was. He was quick-tempered then, an' nothing could hold him once he was started. He once set fire to the O'Hegarty property because a pike he had caught in their stream bit him and got away. He blamed the O'Hegartys for it, and went away and came back with a gallon tin of paraffin, and dumped it into the river. To poison it, he said. He swore he would empty that river of fish. And the fire caught onto the bank and burnt up a barley field."

"And you think I'm capable of being so spiteful?" Babby asked.

Mattie shook a firm denial. "No," he said, "but you'd be a great help to the cause, and you'd be a wonder on the platform."

"What cause?" Babby asked.

"The only one," Mattie replied, serious before her scorn.

"And people like us have time for causes?"

"But you're exactly the people who should!" Mattie exclaimed.

"You mean you are," Babby replied. "We've got our hands full trying to deal with the men left over from the real war."

"And what do you think this is?" Danny asked.

Babby grinned. "You need to be told?"

"You've been listening to Pat," Mattie said.

Babby laughed, "We haven't discovered a way not to."

" 'Ey, did he empty the river?" Tucker Tommy interrupted. "Our father?"

Mattie grinned. "Yes. Yes, son, he did!"

Mrs. Baines swept round on Tucker Tommy. "An' where's Neddo?"

"I didn't see him." He sidled round to stand between his uncle's knees.

"Would you see him if he was tripping you up?" Danny asked.

"I'm not an ijut," he answered, taking his uncle in, and the newly set table with a quarter pound of sliced cheese on a plate in the middle of it.

"You will be, from the clatter I'll give you if you make another answer like that, me bucko!" Mrs. Baines told him.

Tucker Tommy looked quickly at Zena. "Are youse not going to play the flute?" he asked.

"We are indeed," Zena smiled. "And tonight I'll give you a lesson."

"When then?"

"As soon as we've had a bit to eat." Mattie drew his chair up to the table. "But right now, my belly's stuck to my back."

"That's the last of the bread," Tucker Tommy said seriously. He looked at his mother. "And tomorrow there mightn't be a bit to be had in the shops."

Danny moved and spoke because his mother couldn't. "Come away out of that!" He dragged his young brother to him.

"Pay no attention to him." Babby's face, like her mother's, was crimson. "We've galores in the press."

A look passed between her and her mother, as the latter found her voice. "Oh, wait," she cried threateningly. "I'll give you 'the last a the bread'!" She reached across Danny and made a swipe at Tucker Tommy, but he ducked, and her hand tilted the bird-cage on the wall, that held the polish brushes, the spinning tops and bits of string.

"You're quite sure?" Mattie asked.

Mrs. Baines breathed heavily, glowering at Tucker Tommy, then smiling at the others. "Of course," she said. "Eat."

They did, and the meal of rashers and cheese was soon got through, though it was noticed that Zena hardly broke fast, and that Mattie had finished her plate as well as his own, and that while he talked, she barely said more than two words. Her silence was not disconcerting. She was never, at the best of times, a talker, preferring to sit and listen while her husband took the floor. His laugh and Babby's back-chat, modified and tempered by remarks from Mrs. Baines and Danny, sped the evening. Afterwards the table was cleared and pushed aside, the chairs drawn closer to the fire, and then began what was becoming a ritual when Mattie and Zena visited them and Pat was out of the house—what Neddo and Tucker Tommy referred to as the Music.

Part of the ritual was the getting-ready. The flute in its case was taken from the bed and handed by Danny to Zena, and the empty case taken from her by Tucker Tommy, who carefully set it back on the bed. Mrs. Baines would check him and his brother, or nudge Babby to remove something from sight, such as the slop bucket, or she would slip twopence to Danny for a packet of Woodbines, knowing that what she did went unnoticed while

Zena was preparing herself for the playing. The preparations never
varied. She would look for specks of dust, flick the keys with a
handkerchief and rub the mouthpiece carefully, as her lips, long
before she began to play, would shape themselves. Then, leisurely,
almost tentatively, Zena raised the instrument to her mouth and
a tune was started that at first was only a dark troubled hush
over the sounds in the room and those coming from the other
rooms in the house. Then, gradually, it grew in constant strength
to fill out the room and all the sounds, until finally they died
themselves and nothing then could be heard but the music, which
went on and on until the room took on a lilt and the pictures on
the wall were pushed into the paper and in your eyes and in your
head there was nothing but the music that did away with even
the rush of the trains. For her parents, Zena had not been able to
do it. Her music, they said, did not have its beginnings outside
herself, it was like the instrument she chose, new, unknown, un-
ladylike, and her music was born of the dark, angular like herself,
the thwarted passionate self she would thrust upon them, while
she stood listening, immune, they thought, to criticism, sullen,
unconcerned. But for the Baineses, Zena knew, her music existed,
and neither they nor the room could hold it. It welled over, like
Molly Baines's compassion, and they rocked to its deep strange
rhythm or clapped their hands as if to ward off its threat to over-
power their innocence, for in Zena's music there was always the
recognizable, the felt indication of distress and desolation from
which they backed away as from a scalpel and remained, she
knew, untouched by her own laceration, and in another key she
made the touching simple shapes that made them laugh.

The tunes she played them were familiar ones: "The Last
Rose of Summer" for Babby and Mrs. Baines, who liked to cry
over it; "The Flower of May" for Danny, who kept its images
and his emotions to himself; "My Dark Rosaleen" for the Kin-
sellas and Mrs. Slattery who could be heard starting to sing in the
room beneath just as Zena came to the last bars, causing her and
the others to laugh. The laugh was the call for a livelier tune, and

Mrs. Baines, catching hold of Tucker Tommy, was up to dance round the room. The floor shook and trembled and the cups joined in on the dresser but nobody took any notice, and Mattie beat time while Babby and Danny clapped their hands and shouted approval and encouragement until the tune came to an end, and Mrs. Baines, with her hair loosened and falling across her brow, sank with her son in her lap into the nearest chair.

"More luck to youse!" Mrs. Slattery screamed up.

"An' more power to your elbow, Molly," said Mattie.

And into the laughter, Neddo came.

Neddo was born lucky, his mother said. And she was right tonight. He escaped a hiding now for staying out, because of Zena and Mattie's presence; and escaped most of the chastisement owed him for his wildness, by the grace of God Who intervened, Mrs. Baines believed, on his behalf at all hours of the day and night. He was taller than Tucker Tommy, and fatter. His belly pushed at the cheap wool of his blue gansey, and gave it a rounded smoothness at the back as well as in front. He had his mother's blond hair stuck up like a pennant over his forehead, and her blue eyes without the gravity, and was considered in the Lane a marvelous knocker-outer because of his knack of finding the best bins with the biggest cinders in the mornings, and because of his genius for never coming home empty-handed. Even now, as he stood unsure of his reception, balancing himself from one foot to the other, his hands clutched a newspaper full of fish and chips, which he held towards Mrs. Baines. From his expression, he might have been holding a peace-offering or a bribe. His face had lost its nervous look and the natural wariness fled from his eyes, as he took in the scene before him, for he knew he was saved, whatever his mother might say now about dealing with him afterwards.

"Where were you?" she asked at once.

"Nowhere," he answered. As she took the paper of fish and chips, he turned his quick smile onto Zena.

"An' where's that? An' why weren't you to be found when I was looking for you?"

Mattie pulled Neddo to him. "Tell the truth now, you scholar, and shame the devil!"

"Down the street with Florry Connors," he said.

"An' where did you get these from?" Mrs. Baines held up the greasy package in her hands.

"We bought them," Neddo stared back at her, and edged away from Mattie to stand at the far end of the table.

"An' where did you get the money?" Mrs. Baines asked, but without waiting to hear the answer, she began to share them out. "Sit down there," she said to him, "and don't let me see you make another move till I tell you." As she gave him his share on a saucer, she added, "I'll deal with you later for staying out all day without a by-your-leave, and for not doing what I tell you."

Anxious to divert attention from himself, Neddo looked at his Uncle Mattie. "Florry an' me got the money from the Staters," he said. "There's whole lorry-loads of them in Rock Street going from house to house. They're stopping everyone. They sent us up to knock on doors, and came and hid behind us on the landing till they'd seen who opened up."

Mattie shot to his feet, and Zena rose, more slowly, beside him. Mrs. Baines looked from one to the other over hands that had flown to her mouth in the instant's panic, and she took a quick uncertain step towards the little room.

"What'll we do?" she cried.

Without answering, Mattie grabbed his Burberry from the back of the door and emptied the pockets of cigarettes and a manuscript belonging to Zena. While he struggled out of his jacket, he barked orders to her. "Split them up. Half each, and the same with the feed. We'll go separately."

She couldn't have heard him, Babby thought, because he had to tell her again, roughly. "What are you waiting for?"

Zena sprang then to do as he bid, while he turned back to Neddo. "This side?"

"Yes." Neddo mashed a cold chip in his fingers.

"How many?" When Neddo looked blank, Mattie cried angrily, "You didn't count them?"

"I didn't know youse were here. But I will." Eager to help, he got to his feet.

"No!" His mother and sister spoke at the same time. "There might be sniping."

"I could just look." Neddo's eyes shone with an excitement only he could imagine. He reached out his hands to his mother, and with a sudden burst of fear, she slapped them from her.

"No!" she screamed. "Get into bed, or I'll brain you!"

With his hands to his mouth, Neddo slunk back to the corner of the fire beside Tucker Tommy who was regarding the scene in silence.

Mattie stared his uncertainty, then hurried with Mrs. Baines into the little room, where Zena knelt beside the trunk. Six revolvers and three rounds of ammunition lay on the floor beside her. Mrs. Baines drew back, but Mattie went down on one knee and with speed began to divide them between himself and Zena who, with a calmness that Mrs. Baines would afterwards marvel at, began to secrete them inside the waistband of elastic and the top of her knickers. Mattie filled his trousers and coat pockets and left the rounds of ammunition to the last. These he dumped into Zena's handbag, then slung the strap over his shoulders so that it rested under his armpit next to his shirt, Mrs. Baines helped him on with his jacket, then his Burberry. Listening, Danny's brothers and sister didn't see him slip out or come back, until he was in the room again and at the door of the little room.

"You'll never get out the Lane, Uncle Mattie," he said. "There must be a hundred Free Staters round the street and the bridge, and they've shut the pub. Both sides of the Lane," he concluded, anticipating Mattie's question.

"The curse a God on every hoor's ghost among them!" Mattie said. "We'll have to go over the yards so, an' make for the Adelaide Road." He sounded apologetic as he said to Zena, "We've no alternative."

"We never have," she replied.

"True for you," Mattie said, his words and manner impatient, "but it's certain we can't stay here."

Mrs. Baines caught him at the door. "No, but you could leave them things behind. If you're caught with them, you won't have a chance."

"What chance would *you* have, Molly, if they found them here? Talk sense, woman," he concluded roughly.

"He's right." Zena said softly. "Don't worry." With a rare coarseness, she patted her belly. "Mrs. Large will go over those walls like a two-year-old." She laughed, as she fastened the collar of her coat under her chin.

That chin too pointed, too sharp, Mrs. Baines thought. She wondered that Mattie would not see, and realized it was not his nature to do so, and even if he did, his sense of duty to his country would absolve him from duty to his wife. "You must take care of yourself," she said to Zena.

Zena nodded. "Soon now, there'll be peace."

"Peace," Mrs. Baines murmured, studying its implications. Then Danny could go to England, perhaps the jobs would be better in Dublin, and Zena could have the house and home with Mattie that she'd never had. She might even have the children she craved for.

"I made sandwiches," Babby said, appearing among them. "And there's tea in the bottle."

"Musha, but you're the right of it!" Mattie took her face in his hands as he had done in the first of the evening, and as if to answer the questions he had raised, "You're your mother's daughter, alanna," he said.

"And here!" Tucker Tommy held the flute out, in its case again.

Mrs. Baines knew it was useless to ask Zena to leave it behind, and tried not to feel angered at her for giving herself this added encumbrance. She went to the window and cautiously drew aside the dark green blind and peered into the darkness of the Lane. There was neither a soul nor a sinner stirring. Nor did any strange sounds catch her ear, only the known which came from the lighted rooms and, further away, the strident brawled muted sounds from Rock Street. Mattie spoke and she came from behind the blind.

"Aye," she said. They stared at each other, anxiety and fear between them, until Mattie moved.

"We'll go so, with the help of God! An' let yourself and the childer hit the hay." He opened the door and peered through the slit at the dark of the stairs. There was no sound in the house, nor in any of the rooms. He turned and flashed a grin at the children behind Mrs. Baines, and said to Zena, "Now!"

Swiftly, Zena kissed Mrs. Baines and Babby, then without a word she disappeared into the darkness after him. They listened to the protest of the stairs, and Mrs. Baines held the door open for its pale light until she heard them reach the hall. When she closed it, she turned the key in the lock, hurried back to the window and cautiously lifted the blind again. She was just in time to see Mattie, and Zena a little behind him, turn the corner of the Lane that led to the Nolans' pigsties and to the backyards of houses that would eventually take them to Adelaide Road and, with the help of God, safety.

"Have they gone?" Babby spoke behind her.

Mrs. Baines nodded and, about to draw back, stopped to stare in instant wild disbelief at the woman standing across the Lane gaping up at her. She squinted to distinguish the silent black bulk, unable, in the pale green light from the sputtering gas lamps, even to be sure that it was a woman. She leaned out the window further and strained shortsightedly to see. But the black bulk remained unmoving and unrecognized as it stared back up at her. The only movement in the Lane was the rise and fall of the gaslight. It was the banshee, she thought, and made the sign of the cross at once, but even as she raised her hand, the bulk stirred and shuffled forward and sideways until it was directly under the window. Only then did it raise its face into the light.

"Glory be to the hand of God!" Mrs. Baines spoke the prayer as she looked down onto the round noseless face with the cancerous hole in the middle.

"Ah! I sawn you!" Annie the Man sniggered up at her. "Sawn you nicely." She groped for the cotton skirt that streeled over a bundle of indescribable underskirts onto the ground, lifted the sides of it and twirled about in a drunken dance. "Annie the Man sawn the Countrywoman lettin' go the Rebels!" With me two poor galdy wans, I sawn you!" She stopped and shuffled forward as though to get closer to the woman in the window. "But it's between us, Molly darlin'. It's between us." She tittered over a clot of phlegm in her throat, blew into the heel of her hand and flung the snot and her defiance upwards.

Mrs. Baines shivered. She drew herself in, away from the window.

"Who was that, Mother?" Babby asked. "I thought I heard somebody."

Mrs. Baines tried to sound matter-of-fact. "You did. Annie the Man. She saw Mattie and Zena going." She stared back into her children's stares. "I'll wet a fresh drop of tea."

Danny put down his book. "Did she say?"

"Twice. And in no uncertain terms."

"She'll tell," Babby stared. "She'll tell the Staters, or Jesus knows who! She told on the Carneys and wasn't Tom taken out in the middle of the night and . . ." Babby could not utter the thing that had been done to Tom Carney.

"True for you," Mrs. Baines said slowly, "but they set fire to her for that."

"Annie the Man could make trouble for them, serious trouble." The thought worried Mrs. Baines. Ah, but she wouldn't, she must by now have learnt her lesson. And if she hadn't? Mrs. Baines shook her head, the physical exertion crystallizing the memory she had been trying to draw back from, until it streeled itself before her like a stream of matter.

It was in March, late in the evening. She had just finished putting out a few things on the line when Annie the Man turned the corner of the Lane on her way to her room. —I want none of your talk, Mrs. Baines had said in answer to a sniggered remark,

and Annie the Man had stopped to laugh. —Youse haven't a
civil word for me since young Carney, the Rebel, was taken out. But
sure, I had nothing to do with it, nothing whatever, she said
airily. A wonder came over Mrs. Baines at the brazen effrontery
of the woman. —Ah, g'long with you, and ask God and His Holy
Mother to forgive you, she said, the words hardly out of her
mouth when Tom Carney's mother and two sisters appeared as
if from nowhere, with a can of paraffin and a burning twisted
coil of newspaper. Hurtling abuse at Mrs. Baines, Annie the
Man didn't see them, and by the time she did Josie and Mary
Carney had drenched her with the oil and Mrs. Carney was
shoving the lighted paper at her skirts and into her face. Mrs.
Baines could still hear Annie's screams as though it were only
yesterday, and over them the unmerciful screamed vengeance of
the Carneys as they kicked the writhing mass on the ground.
She could hear too Mrs. Carney's "Traitor!", screamed at herself as she tried to knock out of her hands the bucket of water
she was pouring over Annie the Man. The sight and the woman's screams would be with her till the day she died. It was
after, that Mr. Carney, Tom's father, drowned himself in the
Canal, and when Annie the Man came from the Union she was
as bald as a baby and wearing the hat she had never been able
to take off since. No, she didn't think Annie would run to the
Staters the way she had to the Tans.

"We'll wait and see," she said. "I'll find out before long what
she intends to do." Her smile to ease their minds was fleeting.
"You'd better go into your bed," she said to Babby, who slept
with her when Pat was away.

"Yes." Babby spoke slowly and tiredly. As Danny turned into
the little room, she began to undress before the dying fire, her
hands moving like languorous moths in pursuit of a resting place
over her slim body. "Ah, Mother!" she shook her head with distaste.

Mrs. Baines had taken down a small bottle of camphorated
oil from the mantel and, having poured a few drops onto a sheet

of brown paper, was beginning to warm it at the fire. "Your cough was bad last night." She reached for a strip of red flannel hanging on the line and pinned it to the paper. "Now," she said.

With good-humored reluctance, Babby dropped her rough shift down to her waist while across her breasts and under her arms, Mrs. Baines spread what she believed was the cure for her daughter's cough. Babby giggled. "It makes me smell like the Lane."

"It needn't then. If you wash well enough in the morning. And you do."

"You're a great one for the washing and the water!" Babby said between a laugh and a yawn. And Annie the Man was for the moment forgotten.

"Go asleep, like a good child," Mrs. Baines said into the soft darkness, and went into the little room. She disturbed nothing in the dark on her way to the bed where Neddo and Tucker Tommy slept, and after tucking round them the coats flung over the worn blanket, she bent over Danny.

"Are you afraid, Mother?"

"I thought you were asleep." His voice had surprised her, quiet, husky in the darkness, nearly a man's. "No," she said. She brushed his head with the palm of her hand. Sleep, son."

Back in the big room, she crossed over to the window and looked out, unable to go to bed until she had done this, custom overcoming fear. The Lane was empty, and quiet except for the drip from the pipe. Above the irregular line of roofs to the houses opposite, the sky was dark and heavy with threatening rain. From Rock Street, sounds came, easy, slow, except for an occasional gunburst that might be coming from as far away as Rathmines. A raw shout following the heavy rumbling of a lorry probably full of Free Staters was followed by the shrill laugh of a prostitute, strongly clear, back-chatting with the enemy.

She liked this ending to her day, when her children were safe in their beds behind her, and before her the wide softness of night stretched its benediction over the world. It was the one waking hour of her day that was her own, a time when she could think, pray, or just stand and look without knowing or wanting to, why the night with its great fall of darkness was a constant cause of wonder to her. She didn't hear Danny get up and look for the white christening shawl that she usually placed round her shoulders when she went to the window. But when he slipped it under the blind and pressed it round her, she smiled and tush-tushed, pleased at his gesture but twinged by uneasiness that she had been the cause of his leaving his warm bed. She stood, alone in her cultivated vision of distance, but with Teasey, with Kitty so lately married it seemed, though it was more than a year now, and away in America; and with Mattie and Zena out there somewhere in the dark. She murmured her request to God to watch over all of them. And as the rain began to fall, she remembered Annie the Man and slowly withdrew from the window, from the summertime into which her mind fled for one brief second where the whole world drowsed and the white stone house at the foot of the Wicklow hills was slashed with light.

Babby was asleep when she lowered herself onto the bed beside her. In the little room, Tucker Tommy cried out in a dream. She waited for the cry to repeat itself; when it didn't, she lowered her lids and slept.

FIVE

IN THE morning, in the sun, Mrs. Baines started home from the bakery on the north side of the city. She carried a loaf of bread in a clean pillow slip and kept to the side streets because of the Republican funerals, the sniping and occasional plundering going on in the main ones. She had gone first to Wexford Street, which was nearer the Lane, but today, all that was left of the bakery that was there the day before was a charred smoldering gap, like a tooth torn from a gum. Nothing was left of the great glass front with the gold letters, or of the brass-plated counter. Instead, what met her eyes was the back of an envelope pinned against a beam, and on it a scribbled obscenity, and below that in some joker's hand, "Up the Rebels!" She read it before she turned away, half in anger, but mostly worried. Tucker Tommy had been right, with his bit of news last night, sifted down from the Councils of Rebels or Staters, to a shopkeeper here or there, to some of the women of the city, to the pipe in the Lane, to him. Bread was, indeed, hard to get, and a bit of flour impossible. This morning, Neddo and Tucker Tommy had had the last of the bread from yesterday and now there wasn't as much as a crust left. Even as it was, what she had given them after Babby and Danny got their share wasn't enough. She was about to turn off Wexford Street, not sure where to, when a woman had nudged her elbow.

"It's that Spanish-American bastard, de Valera, who's responsible for this!" She gestured with her face towards the burnt ruins of the bakery. "It's him and his rebels doing all the depredation an' robberies all over the country because he can't pay them." She shook her head vigorously. "There isn't a man, woman or child in this country who isn't against them. Even the priests is on the side of the Staters!"

"They would be," Mrs. Baines said, remembering Mattie and Zena. The priests were always on the winning side. She stared at the woman's fat face, creased with dirt, and puckered now into an expression meant to combine sympathy with worry, and had to restrain herself from saying, "Up the Rebels!" She glanced back at the ruin of the bakery.

"Terrible, isn't it," the woman said, "the way them lousers are allowed to torment the lives outa decent people? Burning an' thieving everything they lay their filthy hands on. I tell you, there's no knowing where to turn to keep heart an' soul together these days. Am I right?" She waited, and Mrs. Baines nodded. "I suppose your husband's out?"

Mrs. Baines understood that the note of concern in the woman's voice was due to the fact that after her remark about the priests, the latter didn't know where she stood and considered it safer to know more before she went too far. Mrs. Baines shook her head. "No," she said, unthinking, "he's above in the Union."

"An ex-serviceman? Disabled?"

Maybe, Mrs. Baines thought, but she wasn't sure. Pat said a bullet in his thigh had affected his kidneys, and he hadn't long to live. But she couldn't see where, or how. All she knew was what he said, and you didn't question what Pat said. She nodded to the woman, who sighed.

"A man in our house turned into a savage," she said, "when he came back from France." She came closer. "His wife woke up one night and found him devouring the baby. He had one of the poor thing's arms right off and half the face before she caught him. It was funny. For a few nights previously, she found chunks out of the child's legs an' she t'ought it was rats. An' even at the hospital they said it was rats. An' it wasn't them at all, but him. An' she'd never a known if she hadn't caught him down on his hands an' knees at it, like some class of animal. What do you think a that?"

Mrs. Baines had drawn back step by step. Now she felt that her tongue had swelled in her mouth. "I've never heard anything like it in my life," she said finally.

The woman gestured, "Ah, sure that's not the half of it!" she cried carelessly. "You'd want to be living where I am to know the things them dregs a men are gettin themselves up to."

"And all in the name of War!" Mrs. Baines said.

The woman tittered. "Oh, now." She nudged Mrs. Baines, looked left and right and, on a different track, said, "Sure amn't I sick sayin' it: but where's the use in all this slaughter? Where's it going to get us? I ask you, ma'am, where? But lookit!" she said in the same breath, "I'll share with you, ma'am, an' what could be fairer nor that?"

She edged closer, and from under her arm she took the black oil-cloth bag she carried and, opening it just wide enough, she said, "Look!" She had four loaves of bread. "An' two of them, ma'am, you can have outa the God-given generosity of me ever big an' open heart. An' it won't cost you a red penny over what I give for them, meself, an' that's as true as the ground under me." She paused and surveyed Mrs. Baines through narrowed eyes. "Ah, but sure, ma'am, an' I needn't tell you, for you've on'y got to cast your God-given wans on me to see the class of a soft oul' gaum I am."

"How much?" Mrs. Baines fretted her question.

The woman smirked. "Go wan!" she said. "Take advantage of me."

"I don't want to," Mrs. Baines replied.

"Well, you're the first honest person I've met on the streets a Dublin since I caught the eye of Laughing Boy, hisself."

Mrs. Baines readied herself to meet another story about Michael Collins, but saw the woman's shifty eyes weighing up the profit to be gained by some farfetched anecdote of some unlikely encounter on Grafton Street and deciding against it, as she had decided against continuing to vilify the Rebels.

"How much?" Mrs. Baines said quickly into the calculating mood.

"Well, we won't split hairs about it," the woman replied. "Sure, I'm a glutton for punishment." She laughed and nudged Mrs. Baines and said rapidly, "Five bob an' I'm robbin' the daylights outa meself."

Mrs. Baine's heart sank. "Five shillings," it was whispered. That was twice what she had to get her through the day. She shook her head and made as though to move away. "It's too dear," she said.

The fat woman grinned. "Ah, now, c'm'ere, ma'am! They're not growing on trees, ya know."

"An' well I know it," Mrs. Baines answered. "But at that price, the teeth ought to be supplied to eat them with."

The woman laughed and pulled at her sleeve, and it was then the little woman with the coat flung round her shoulders, known vaguely to Mrs. Baines by appearance, darted panting and shouting round the corner and across the road towards them.

"Don't cut, shuffle nor deal with that wan, Missus!" the newcomer cried, before she turned to attack the woman with the bread. "Gowan," she screamed sneeringly, "big fat hearty Julia-darlin', with the bread you took outa the childer's mouths! An' a shaggin' lot a good it'll do youse!"

The fat woman drew herself back and up. "Is that so, Tessa Doyle?" she cried vehemently. "Ya fugitive from the Locke Hospital! It'd suit you better to go an' give yourself the belt of a bar of soap, instead of molesting clean decent people like me. You begrudger!"

"Gowan, you brasser, an' have a Mass said for yourself!" Tessa cried. "Ya lavatory scourings! Oul' ride, you an' your mother before you!"

"Is that so, little farthin' cunt! Dirty yellow-bellied Tessa, who had to bate the molly of a husband to the altar with the point of a gun!" She swung the black bag with the bread inside it at Tessa, who jumped to avoid it and landed on the other side of Mrs. Baines.

"Go wan, ya poxy bitch! An' peddle yourself an' your bread somewheres else!" Tessa Doyle leaped in anger now, to scream in abuse, and didn't notice Mrs. Baines disentangle herself from the crowd that was gathering, and walk away, until quite suddenly Tessa paused and looked round and saw her at the corner of Cuffe Street. "Missus!" she yelled, and ran after her.

But Mrs. Baines had had enough. All she wanted was to get her hands on a loaf of bread and get back home. Rows sickened her. The swift-erupting passionate violence of the city women was something she couldn't understand. She never had, though to survive amongst them she had, like her cultivated vision of distance, schooled in herself the manner to meet and match the sprawl of their vengeance, and on their own terms. Nevertheless, it was with familiar apprehension that she turned now and waited for Tessa Doyle to catch up with her, her hands tensed on the empty pillow slip pressed to her stomach.

"Sweet dilapidated Jesus!" Tessa exclaimed. "But isn't that thing the right animal!" She drew her coat to with one hand and reared her head up defiantly, remembering things she might have said and hadn't, and wished now she had. "But it'll rot in the hoor's gullet, an' that it may." She blinked small gray eyes up at Mrs. Baines. "C'm'ere, ma'am, don't I know you?" she said. "Aren't you out of the Lane?"

Mrs. Baines nodded.

"Mind you, I thought you were. You'll know Nancy O'Byrne then?" She gazed at her earnestly.

"Aye, I do." Mrs. Baines's admission was cautious.

As if, thought Tessa, she was being asked to give something away. "Well," she said suddenly, "Father Tithe practically read her name and address out from the altar on Sunday, did you hear?"

Mrs. Baines had not been to Mass, but she had heard, and she nodded now.

"Made a livin' show of her, he did," Tessa said excitedly. "The dirty bad-minded oul' thing! Said we were to hunt out the fallen among us. Make an example of them, was what he said. Otherwise we were lettin' ourselves in for contamination and committing sins ourselves because we condoned theirs. As if people had any say in the matter! He started the sermon with the Scarlet Hoor a Babylon an' went from that poor creature to Nancy. Oh, he didn't say her name outright. Just said about this girl who we were all familiar with." Tessa broke off. "How he compares Nancy O'Byrne with that wan in Babylon, I don't know, since she was an out-an'-outer, and Nancy, God help her, has never, to anybody's knowledge, looked at another man except Kevin Hely." She shifted her position, and an old pain in her back made her remember something the dispensary doctor had told her, but over the hump of this she fled towards the faces of her children, and the terror of the bed in the Union or in the Hospice for the Dying receded in the comforting presence of Mrs. Baines. "Can you make that man out?" she asked. "I mean, Father Tithe. Classing a woman who's gone to hell for one man alongside wans with twenty?"

"No," Mrs. Baines said, "I can't." She was hesitant to criticize a man of God, but she wondered, as often she did, at the unaccountability of human nature. Because, surely it was up to the priest to help Nancy, and if he couldn't help her, then leave her alone to work out her own salvation. But leave the girl out among the known and loved and familiar, and not behind the high gates of some home.

"Neither can I," Tessa Doyle said, "and I said so a Sunday. An' me only regret is that I wasn't able to say it to his face." She laughed. "God, I'd a loved to! She's living with him, isn't she— Kevin Hely?"

"I don't know," Mrs. Baines said lightly. "It's not often I see the girl, except when she runs down to swap or borrow something from my daughter Babby."

"A lovely girl, Babby," Tessa said. "I remembered, even while I was looking at you, who you were. I used to dance," she said, "an' so I knew Babby an' Teasey an' Kitty. She's in America now."

"Kitty is," Mrs. Baines said.

"That's what I meant," Tessa said. She made small sucking smacks with her lips. "But c'm'ere. What I wanted to tell you was that Williams' in Parnell Street have bread. Machine bread. An' if you hurry, you'll get a loaf."

"Parnell Street?"

"Yuss. Williams'." She laughed wryly, caught up on an earlier mood. "God! But I could a gutted that wan."

"You could," Mrs. Baines smiled agreement. She wanted to get away now, to hurry to Parnell Street, but Tessa Doyle still had things to say.

Her face crumbled into a sly smile. "C'm'ere," she said, "but did you see the look on that hoor's plattered puss when she saw me coming? She didn't know whether she was plum or currant by the time I was finished with her." She lowered her voice. "But I shouldn't get meself worked up over the likes of that wan, an' me expecting." Her gaze was quizzical, and she caught Mrs. Baines's glance sweeping down and over her. "I hardly ever show." She laughed coarsely, good-humoredly. "Himself says he never knows where all his hard work goes, for I never look anything the better of it. Seven, I have, an' another on the way."

Tessa's look plainly said that this was more than any woman ought to be asked to bear. But Mrs. Baines understood. The attitude was part of this woman and the women in the Lane, who complained bitterly about being, as they said, "in the way," and about Paddy or Jamesie not keeping to their side of the bed and letting them get a night's rest in peace; for, apart from their enjoyment of sex, there was also pride in being able to brag about a husband's virility as well as one's own. And there was a continual race amongst themselves as to which of them could be pregnant in the shortest time and the most often. They had great pity and compassion for the rare and barren among them, and were quick with cures and charms, such as three licks of the Blessed Salt before and immediately after the love act. But their pity and compassion went as deep as water on a duck's back, compared to the depth of scorn and ridicule with which they regarded the Empty Fork and his wife's empty arms.

"It's a drag, isn't it?" Tessa said, and grimaced as though weighed down with sorrow, while all the time she wondered how a woman like Mrs. Baines, with a houseful herself and a husband who spent one half his life on his back up in the Union and the other half in every pub in Dublin, could be out in the streets before nine o'clock in the morning, spruced and polished and as shiny as a new tanner. She stared for a moment, frankly unbelieving, until she remembered all she knew about Mrs. Baines and that, indeed, she did have childer, because hadn't she known them? And as she watched Mrs. Baines walk away, she muttered aloud the Dubliner's irritation when faced with country wans, because they were a queer clean lot, God help us!

Mrs. Baines had found Williams' open and with bread for sale, and consoled by the weight of it, she turned finally into the straight narrow cobbled stretch of Rock Street again and the twin row of Georgian tenements that leaned palsied towards each other, ague-ridden and tormented by the little hucksters' shops jammed between them. The strong air of the Canal at the top of the street got trapped between the lanes and alleys and open doors and was bet helpless against the powerful smells rising up and over the horse-dunged cobbles. Dealers, black-shawled and white-bibbed, sank high black-button boots into the staring eyes of herring and whiting, smashing the heads to a mash under rotten fruit and vegetables. The refuse from the square community "bens," emptied once a week by the Corporation, overflowed and spilled down the

sagging steps and across the pavement to add to the heap made
by the dealers.

The dirt and confusion went almost unnoticed by Mrs. Baines
as she made her way up the street towards the Lane and Miss
Fogarty's huckster's shop at the bridge. She didn't distinguish the
rasp of a gramophone shrieking from an open window over the
clang of the trams that couldn't quite drown the foul abuse of a
dealer swinging a skinned rabbit after the bald head of a young-
feller who looked something like Neddo, nor did she hear his
startled cry as the rabbit landed squarely on his head. Familiarity
had robbed the scene of any wonder, for the street had been her
first introduction to Dublin and, in the way of the poor, had held
nothing back, but given itself over fully, in all its brazen vitality,
exposing its great streel of a self at their very first meeting.

A jeer of laughter and high mocking screams halted Mrs. Baines.
And a woman beside her roared and said, "Will ya look?"

She did—at Cocky O'Byrne, big and buxom, doing a wild lament
of a dance in the middle of the road. Cocky's clothes were held
up at the back, stripping bare her buttocks and thighs for all the
world to gaze upon. And her legs, covered up to just under her
darkness in brown silk stockings, sprawled like a baby learning to
walk. Her face with its triangular spread bones was hidden under
a loose mane of hair. She made no sound as the dealers began to
clap their hands in unison and sing the song they always sang
when they saw her coming. Nor did she stop her grotesque gyrations when a couple of kids with a black wet-skinned mongrel
dog pushed each other around and against her.

The street was alive with shouts. A tram had to stop because
Cocky was dancing in the tracks, and the driver, a pale runt of a
man, made pale dirty remarks that made the dealers shake with
laughter. Having gained an inch, he took a mile and, hopping onto
the street, grabbed a handful of damaged tomatoes and began
aiming them at Cocky. They splattered onto the ground like
clots of blood around the door of a pub on a Sunday morning.

Suddenly Mrs. Baines pushed her way through, fury blinding her normal reticence as she flung herself against him. "You mean cur!" she screamed, before she was aware that she did.

At the rage on her face, he lowered his arm. "No need to get yourself riz," he said, stepping back. "Just having a bit a gas, that's all," he said, cautiously edging back onto the metal platform on the front of his tram.

"You're lost now for a bit of gas!" Mrs. Baines stared up at him. "Maybe it's a bit of gas you want, at your age!" Trembling, she pushed her way through the people around her.

The driver, his courage restored at the sight of her back, shouted, "Get her outa the road!"

Mrs. Baines couldn't imagine what had made her interfere, but when she saw Cocky, still turning in her brooding aloof dance, she was glad she had. Cocky looked like a horse, worrying the heels of her feet against the cobbles as if by so doing she could still a hurt. As Mrs. Baines moved towards her, Cocky fell down, a soft boneless length, onto the filth and the egg-smooth cobbles.

The diversion was over with a shriek and a smattering of hand-claps, drowned by the insolent clang of the tram going past and the general busyness as people turned back to what they were doing before Cocky drew them away. Mrs. Baines tried to lift her and stared distressed, until Mr. Pughe came suddenly, his wig gleaming like a seal's head, from the doorway of his shop. He ignored the cheers that greeted him, and, catching Cocky under her arms, dragged her over to his door. Inside, he propped her against the base of the counter and, as he fussed about her in his small rounded plump way, straightening her clothes and drawing her spread legs together, Mrs. Baines looked in the door.

Mr. Pughe drew his black-suited self erect and turned eyes like wet onyxes in saucers of watered milk on her. He murmured in-audibly, moving lips that were dry, pink, and beautifully curved, that seemed to have been placed temporarily by someone with no sense of proportion on his porcelain-fine fat white face. "It's dread-ful," he said, and the neatness of his black wig and starched wing-collar with its virgin-white points—like a coif on the wrong end of his face—made the dreadfulness all the more so. "What's to become of her?" His chubby, beautifully kept hands flew together, for guidance or protection, against his smooth black serge chest. He gazed at Mrs. Baines.

But all she could do was shake her head. Then, sensing Mr. Pughe's despair, for his face remained smooth except for a twitch of his mouth, she hurried on to comforting words. "Ah, but it won't last. One of these days she'll be as right as rain again."

Neither of them believed what she said, and Mrs. Baines wondered that, knowing this, Mr. Pughe would still marry her. Everyone knew that he had asked her a year ago and Cocky had laughed him out of the place. He had never set foot in the Lane again, but waited in his little overcrowded shop behind the polished brown-veined counter for Cocky to come to him. She came, but not for marriage and not until the last of her pension money was gone and she was unable to get her hands on a penny elsewhere. Then she turned up, disguising her purpose with quick short grins that preceded her demands. She never tried to tell Mr. Pughe a lie about what she wanted the money for. In fact, she didn't say anything much more than naming the amount, knowing that whatever she asked he would hand over only half. And no matter how often she asked, he never refused. But he never asked her to marry him again, and he cut her requests for money to halves because that way he was sure of seeing her other than in her present state. He was aware she used him and kept him the laughingstock of the street, but as long as his passion for her persisted, he would go on being a butt for the gougers and corner-boys around the place.

Mrs Baines saw him look down now at the figure sprawled against the counter that he wouldn't even let the children touch, and knew that there was no sign of what she called his "fondness" for Cocky abating.

Cocky was just married when Mr. Pughe first came to the Street and was the first person to set foot past his door on the day he opened his shop. Upright she was, and bold the way she held up the bundle of sticks that he had wanted to charge a penny for, and her laugh and cry of "Bester!" had drawn a crowd round his door for a look at someone more brazen even than themselves. —Aye, a penny! Cocky had cried her amusement to the crowd as she held up the sticks for everyone to see. —Gowan, you dirty oul' robber! Sure, you'd get a whole orange box for a wing, a girl younger than Cocky screamed in at him. And in the small silence between laughs and shouts, Cocky slammed the sticks down on the counter and leaned across to him and said: You have your glue, mister. But she was smiling, not sullen like the others, and when he took his eyes away from her face he saw her yellow coat with its thin dark fur collar, and when he looked again into her eyes, he forgot to be timid and respectable and Protestant. But when he heard himself saying: Well, you can have them for a ha'penny, and when she laughed back at him on her way out, he remembered to be all three. After that, he remembered every time she came into his shop, and when he no longer remembered it was because it no longer mattered. The thing was, she came—and laughed and made him laugh and in some strange way made him feel as though he had taken on a new lease of life. He had always been a neat well-dressed man, buying a suit as he needed it from the best second-hand shops in the city, but in less than a week after he met Cocky he went and bought himself the first brand-new one he had ever owned. He bought a hat too, and a white silk scarf for around his neck, and new shoes, not sensible square-toed black ones, the kind that could be expected to last a man his age and habits a life-time, but narrow and brown with shiny pointed toes that made the wearing of them an agony to be borne only under the admiring glance of Cocky and on Sundays to the lonely Protestant church on Adelaide Road. Because he felt and was aware of no mental anguish at being "fond" of a married woman—the word "love" being studiously avoided as wicked and somehow lewd—he welcomed the discomfort of the shoes as a private pennance for doing something he secretly felt guilty about and—to himself—referred to as his State. This State suited him perfectly. Had it been otherwise he would have run a mile. As it was, he stayed and wore tight shoes and was happy over the years until Cocky's husband died and she stopped coming into his shop. And when he at last found the courage to admit that he missed her, he asked her to marry him. And Cocky had laughed him round the room and out of it. Yet he had felt no anger, only a loss, as he went back up the Lane, while behind him he could still hear her laughing. He was in love with her. The word and the admission came to him as he let himself back into his shop, while the kids that had followed him from the Lane hammered on the door that he locked and double-bolted behind him. Cocky had come next day and asked him for the lend of a few shillings, and almost every day after that—and he stopped wearing the brown pointed shoes.

As Mrs. Baines made the signs of departure, Mr. Pughe nervously shifted his weight. "You'd never stay? Until she comes round?"

"I couldn't, Mr. Pughe. Sure, it'll be ages before she moves again."

"But I can't leave her here all day."

"Well, maybe we could carry her into your room beyant?" Mrs. Baines suggested helpfully.

Mr. Pughe shook with surprise. "Whatever would people say?"

Mrs. Baines put her loaf in its pillow slip onto the counter. "They'll say it anyway." She looked him full in the face, then bent to gather Cocky's feet together. "You take her shoulders," she said, as he stood hesitantly.

"Very well, then, but they're so bad-minded around here, and you know . . ."

"It's no good worrying about that now." Mrs. Baines cut him short, and together they half-carried, half-dragged Cocky into the little room at the end of the shop.

Mrs. Baines had never seen the room before. Unlike the rest of the shopkeepers, who left their doors open to show off what they had behind them, Mr. Pughe always closed his. It was a nice room, and a grand double bed, Mrs. Baines thought as they heaved

Cocky onto the colored quilt. The room was small and square, with a window looking into a small yard. The curtains had been pushed aside to let in what light penetrated the yard. Under them was a rough deal table with a mat in the middle, on which Mr. Pughe had placed two pink and two red paper roses in a glass vase. Behind the roses on the sill stood a jug which Mrs. Baines surmised was filled with milk, and a saucer covered by another saucer which she knew was butter, kept there for coolness. There was no fireplace, only a paraffin stove, and on the wall over the bed, colored pictures of mountains covered in snow. There were no photographs and no altar. She remembered that Mr. Pughe was a Protestant and felt sorry for him, and because she did, she said, "You're a good man, Mr. Pughe."

He finished covering Cocky before he turned to her. "Am I?"

His question confused her, and to hide it, she said, "Your room is lovely."

"I make the best of it." He looked round, and his hands flew together.

Mrs. Baines moved to go, and Mr. Pughe moved with her. "I'll sit outside," he said, and took a furrum, like a child's, from beside the oil stove and put it in the open doorway. Everyone would be able to see him here, he thought, as he sat down neatly with his soft black boots together and his white hands folded over each other in his black lap. Behind him on his bed, Cocky slept. And across the street in another room, her daughter Nancy was forcing herself to drink a tumblerful of senna tea, while Mrs. Ennis, with man-size hands, pressed down on her belly.

From Mr. Pughe's doorway, Mrs. Baines started across the street, but changed directions to avoid the glance or greeting of Father Tithe, who stood looming like a dark and bony mountain crag over purse-lipped Mrs. Chance gesticulating up at him with a look that despaired of ever reaching the summit.

Mrs. Baines crossed Rock Street beyond them, to Miss Fogarty's shop beside the bridge, to get potherbs for the soup for the children's dinner.

Miss Fogarty kept her best fruit and vegetables on flat wooden trays outside the shop for her Lady Trade, and potherbs, damaged fruit and commonplace cabbages and turnips inside for the women of the Lane and the Street. Measle-red in the face and in her late forties, she was called Juicy-Eyes because her eyes were ringed with red raw flesh behind her thick glasses. She blamed indigestion for the flush and a bad back molar for the rawness, and dosed herself with Seidlitz powders and Sunday trips to Mount Argus at four o'clock for the relic. In the Lane they said she was a "fella in skirts," with her man's voice and gestures.

Mrs. Baines watched her wrap the potherbs deftly into a bit of newspaper, and in answer to her question said, "Yes, I got a loaf."

"Thank God!"

Miss Fogarty liked Mrs. Baines and her way of looking right at you when she asked you how you were, as though it mattered, also the proud tilt of her head and the wide sweep of forehead, the sharp well-defined temples, the strange cool thin face that seemed to have nothing to do with the blue eyes which lived a life unbeknownst to its other features. She made her feel sad—though Miss Fogarty thought "unrestful."

"Them kids have the heart scalded outa me!"

"What kids?" Mrs. Baines paused, about to go out the door. "Don't tell me it's Neddo?"

Miss Fogarty would minimize Neddo's part. "Not him alone but," she said, "it's Florry Connors and Theresa Slattery."

Mrs. Baines waited.

"Theresa came in on the way to school and asked for a ha'penn'-ort of damaged. Well, I hadn't my back turned when Florry and Neddo lifted half me peas and disappeared over the locks and away with them." She peered at Mrs. Baines. "Now no need to go an' worry yourself. I wouldn't have mentioned it except that they're demons, them young wans, and'll get him into serious trouble if he's not careful."

"If I've told him once, I've told him a thousand times about it," Mrs. Baines said. "Wait now till I get my hands on him."

She felt ashamed that Neddo, who was neither hungry nor dry, should join in the petty thieving that went on against the shops around the Street and against Miss Fogarty's in particular because of its position near the bridge, and therefore on the way to school. It was no use Miss Fogarty making light of it by telling her they all did it and always had and always would, and for her not to think any more about it. You tried to show children right from wrong, to rear them as best you knew how; and all you asked in return was that they should grow up right and decent and without making a show of themselves and you. Unlike Miss Fogarty, who was saying that the Lane was to blame and how could children be expected to know better when all around they saw grown men and women behave like savages and getting away with it, she neither accepted nor admitted that as enough reason for blinding oneself to the ethics of right and wrong. And especially not when you had someone there to explain the diffcrence. She opened her purse, trying not to think further than the present moment.

"How much do you think they took?"

Miss Fogarty tossed her question aside and tried to brush away the look in Mrs. Baines's eye as well. "You'll do no such thing. I wouldn't've uttered if I'd known you'd take it like this. Sure it was not more than a handful." She smiled.

"No, I'd rather." Mrs. Baines held out her last shilling piece, her voice and manner preventing any further objections Miss Fogarty might have considered making.

Reluctantly she said, "Sixpence," then, as she took the proffered coin, "You're a terrible woman!", easing the transaction as she fiddled in the tin box that she used as a till.

To smooth the awkwardness of the moment and of her going, Mrs. Baines smiled. "There's good drying out today. Give me a chance to get a few things rinsed out before they're in on top of me."

Miss Fogarty walked to the door and looked out and up at the sky. The light was on her thick glasses. "If it lasts," she said, "I might get a bit done meself."

The street was quieter now, Mrs. Baines saw, emptier. Father Tithe and Mrs. Chance had disappeared. She crossed the road and turned into the narrow sunless mouth of the Lane between two shops. The shops of Rock Street were backed by houses that gave way to the Lane proper and were high enough to keep the sun from ever penetrating further than the first-floor windows. They kept the ground stories in perpetual mourning gray and the cobbles black and wet. At the bottom on the left was the circle of houses where, in Number Four, the Baineses lived, towering over them the railway wall, gray, streaked with green slime that had dried into veins of hard green plush from which ferns grew. Beside them, waste, mottled with gray-white like the belly of a snake, oozed from the railway into the drain beneath the mushroom-shaped pipe. Trains belched clouds of elongated black soot, peppered with hard cinders that scorched the wash hung on lines across the yard and filled the rooms with a fine black cloud that smothered everything.

The window box with its geraniums showing just above its top thrived in spite of the soot under Mrs. Baines's care, displaying the only flowers that ever graced the Lane from one year's end to the other. Her eyes on her window box as she turned into the circle of houses, she missed seeing Annie the Man, who scurried ahead of her into the hall and sat grotesquely grimacing at the foot of the stairs, who muttered viciously at Mrs. Baines's exclamation that the heart was put across her and said:

"My, but you're easy frightened! It's your guilty conscience, Dotey, that's what it is." She raised her face up to Mrs. Baines. "Ah, but sure what would a fine woman like yourself have on her conscience?" She heaved her arms over her flaccid breasts and edged forward in a low laugh.

Mrs. Baines drew aside and back. "I haven't time to stand here with you," she said as she made to pass.

But Annie the Man was too quick, and with surprising agility she sprang to her feet, blocking Mrs. Baines's attempt to go by. "We're all in a hurry," she said; then in a whinging voice, "An'

plenty to rush to an' poor paupers like me with shag all." She
stopped. When she spoke again the nark had gone from her voice.
"But I'm the last to begrudge, God help me! Oul' ijut that I am,
live an' let live is what I say."

"What are you getting at?" Mrs. Baines eyed her impatiently,
sensing a threat in the woman's slow spinning of a rigmarole.

"What *would* I be getting at?" Annie the Man asked.

"If it's to borrow, you've come to the wrong shop," Mrs. Baines
snapped.

"Borrow, is it? Me?" Annie the Man laughed. "An' what," she
sneered, "Dotey, would I be borrowin' from you? Your grand
pianner?"

"Then what are you looking for?" Mrs. Baines stared angrily
into the noseless face with its lashless red eyes, each squeezing
out thread-wide silvery snail tracks that moseyed down from the
corners to prong the sides of her mouth before they spread V-
shaped onto her tufted chin. Her anger gave way to revulsion
and a prayer to God to bless the mark, and in the busyness of
her reaction, Annie the Man shot forward and grabbed the pillow
case with the loaf of bread. She tore the bread out and threw the
case back into Mrs. Baines's face as the latter darted forward in
an effort to grab back the loaf.

With a twist, Annie the Man was past her, crouching forward as
she readied herself for the expected attack. None came. "It's more
than a lousy loaf of bread I'd get from some quarters if I was to tell
the thing I sawn going on last night," she said. "If I was the kind
that couldn't hold me tongue . . ." Here eyes narrowed to slits
while she waited for Mrs. Baines to make a move, and the tenseness of her crouched body alerted to restless articulation the mass
of skirts and coats that covered it, making them stand apart in a
stiff aware bigness.

She sniggered suddenly. "Well, what are you waiting for? Is
it windy you are, I'll tell the Free Staters about your lousy Englishwoman an' her rebel husband?" She lurched forward. "And it's
right you are to be afraid," she said, pushing her face close. "And

if you know what's good for you and the rest a them lousy bastards, you'll stay afraid!" She threw back her head and slapped the loaf with the palm of her hand. "And there'll be more where that came from!" Her laugh rose to a roar that smashed into the gray dimness of the hall and brought Mrs. Slattery from her bed to open the door beside them.

Mrs. Slattery's fat arms were bare to the elbow and she held them up to the wet cloth round her head. Her glance fled from Mrs. Baines to Annie the Man who was crouching in the doorway with her back to the light. "Ah, I mighta known," she cried, "that you were around, ya scourge!"

There was no softening of the face when Annie the Man smiled, just a widening grimace that puckered the flatness flatter and shot the black hole where her nose should have been into a startling focal point. The absence of a nose robbed her of any definite change of expression, so her moods could only be gauged by the variant tones in her voice as it rumbled raucous from the bulk of clothes rather than from her body. She was malevolently good-humored now as she jeered back at Mrs. Baines.

"We brung poor Alice Slattery from her bed," she laughed.

"Go now, you wicked oul' thing, an' ask God to forgive you." Mrs. Baines trembled with impotence.

"Is it go? An' us after taking big fat Alice off her back?" Annie the Man laughed towards Mrs. Slattery. "It's tired you are," she began, the tone of inquiry growing with her words. "Maybe you had Tom up an' doin' all night long, or did he let you down because you had the rag up there as well as round your head? Tell us, Alice, am I right?"

Her amusement at herself brought her forward defiantly, and at that moment Mrs. Slattery screamed and raised a powerful arm to down her. But Annie the Man, experienced in the art of avoiding sudden blows, ducked out the door. She didn't go far, no further than out of arm's reach. From there she laughed, before she spat suddenly at the two women staring at her and with a contemptuous swish of her skirts streeled across to her own room.

Mrs. Slattery made as though to rush after her, but her size, weight and disposition made sudden hurried movement impracticable. All she could do was scream after Annie the Man who, by now, had disappeared into her hall leaving Mrs. Slattery to hurl her abuse in impotence, and because she knew it and because she felt powerless to do other than scream, she began to cry.

"Th'oul faggot! The dirty oul' faggot! I'll swing for her! As true as God is me judge, I'll swing for her!"

Mrs. Baines took her arm and led her back into her room. "Don't upset yourself," she said. "She's not worth it." She eased Mrs. Slattery back onto the wide bed that touched the floor in the middle.

"What did she want?" Mrs. Slattery asked.

"To borrow," Mrs. Baines said quickly.

"From you?" Mrs. Slattery was puzzled, despite Mrs. Baines's quick assurance. "That oul' cow'll rot in hell!" she cried, and her arms, ringed with old water marks, lifted her hands to her head again.

The red-and-blue-striped flock mattress on which her eleven children had been born and on which four of them still slept along with her and her husband was half-covered with a bit of sheet, and across herself she drew the faded pink quilt that was worn to ribbons and a conglomeration of discarded worn coats, and she settled among them into the sag of the bed, like a child sinking a finger into a mud pie.

From where she stood amongst the debris in the room and on the floor, Mrs. Baines surveyed her. "I'll get you a cup of tea."

But Mrs. Slattery didn't want tea. All she wanted was to lie quiet and not have to move until Tom or one of the kids came in and gave her something to eat. By the time she had eaten it and drunk her six cups of tea, it would be time for her to get up and put on her hat and coat and, with her tuppence in her hand, go where she went every afternoon, wet or fine—to the Palace, where she sat until it was six o'clock and time to make her slow unhurried progress home again. After tea she would stand at the hall door and gossip while Sadie or Bridie or one of the others possed over the floor or rinsed out a few things for morning. She didn't like upsets in her routine and would discuss this morning's doings tonight after tea with Mrs. Baines or Mrs. Kinsella, but right now she wanted to sleep.

Mrs. Baines watched her eyes close before she quietly let herself out of the room. She felt guilty about Mrs. Slattery. She thought the whole thing was her fault, as she let herself into her own room; and in the despair at losing the loaf, she turned angry with herself for letting Annie the Man get away with it. She should have torn her limb from limb before she let herself be bested like that, and she grew tense with a loathing for herself because she had. The reason why eluded her in the worry over the loss of the bread. Then, when she remembered Annie the Man's threat, she realized that the loaf, precious as it was, was a small enough price to pay for what might mean their lives. But what about the times there wouldn't be loaves of bread to hand over? What would Annie the Man demand then? The thought jumped to life before her eyes and found no answer except that, used as she was to facing decisions when they cropped up, she would face that one also.

SIX

"IT'S Protestant bread." Neddo dumped the half-loaf onto the table. "I told the woman me father was in hospital, an' she told me to come back Saturday an' she'd have old clothes for me."

Mrs. Baines stared at her son. "You mean you begged off some woman?" Her voice was incredulous.

Neddo gestured swift denial. Then, as if she would not understand until he had explained it again to her, he began to tell the ins and outs of the half-loaf of bread, explaining as if he were telling it to someone his own age.

He was careful not to say that he and Florry Connors had taken off their runners and hidden them in the bushes growing inside the gates of the house on Northbrook Road, so that they arrived at the door barefooted, relying on this bit of strategy to soften the heart of whoever should come in answer to their pulls on the brass bell. Nor that a kindly servant new to Dublin had brought them inside to wait while she went to get them a glass of water, because that was all they asked for at first; but once inside, they asked for bread followed by a whispered request from Neddo for any old clothes, accompanied by a shamed: "Oh, my God, you're an awful beggar, Neddo Baines!" from Florry, grinning nevertheless up at the bewildered country maid who listened and nodded in perplexity to accents she couldn't make head nor tail of.

To the white-haired lady in a blue crepe dress who, on her way down the curved broad stairs, commanded a clear uninterrupted view of the trio in the hall, the girl appeared mesmerized. Without hesitation she bore down upon them and smiled at Neddo and Florry before she dismissed her maid, so that the latter might hurry away to tell the cook about the two little foreigners talking with Madam.

Of course, Miss Warr had no difficulty understanding what was required of her, however much she might doubt the necessity. But one never knew, and in her wisdom, garnered from a life spent in easing the trials and tribulations of hundreds of orphans, she preferred and was happiest when she could prove herself wrong. Her seemingly vague gray gaze disguised an aptitude for the assimilation of minute details that was accurate to the point of being photographic, and it pleased this thrifty brewer's daughter to note the beautifully neat darns in the little boy's navy-blue gansey and the threadbare well-patched breeches that were obviously home-made but done with much care and attention. His replies to her gentle questioning, she would not set too much store by, she thought, when he told her his father was up in the Union and that there was barely enough money coming into the house to pay the rent man, let alone buy enough food to feed them all, and as for clothes . . . He stopped to draw her attention to his bare feet. Miss Warr smiled at his earnestness and surmised that while his shoes might not be good, they kept his feet remarkably clean.

Then she turned her gaze full upon Florry, who, Neddo noted with dismay, looked worse off then he did. Florry, aware that attention had at last shifted from him, gazed in solemn silence,

letting her cotton pinny with its rips and stains speak for itself.
Her hair, drawn taut and parted in the middle, was twisted into
pigtails tied with twine and lay limply on her bony shoulders. She
varied her Miss and her Ma'am, but never the preface of her
answers, which was "No" to all Miss Warr's questions, except when
she asked if she had any brothers or sisters at home. Then the
number and names sprung in a litany from her lips and made
Neddo step back in an attempt to dissociate himself from her,
for he thought she was overdoing it and would spoil it for him.
But Florry, with her love for what she thought was "getting
the better" of someone but which was in fact play-acting, was
blessed with a knack of knowing when to over- or underplay
and, egged on by the deep interest on Miss Warr's face and the
concealed becks that Neddo was making behind her back, poured
forth a saga of hardship and want that would have moved a stone.
Who did Neddo Baines think he was, Florry asked herself as,
without seeming ever to take her opaque gaze from Miss Warr's,
she saw him hop from foot to foot as if he wanted to go to the
lavo. She'd show him! And did, until at last, heady with suc-
cess, she stopped, and drooped a little, flickering to silence like a
candle under a harsh breath. And Miss Warr, after telling them
to wait, hurried away to disappear at the end of the long polished
hall. They heard a door close behind her before either of them
moved; then, with a shake of her narrow head, Florry laughed.

"We-ell?" she said.

When she tossed her head and said, "We-ell?" like that, Neddo
forgot how near he thought she had gone to risking their being
sent away empty-handed. There was a world of gay defiance on
the pink lips that robbed her face of its dawniness and made
their escapades deliriously joyous while they lasted and the consequences somehow easier, when you remembered what had
gone before and the promise of what was still to come. All Neddo
thought was that she was a laugh, and she was and so he giggled
with her, and while they waited for Miss Warr to come back
their eyes swept the hall in case there should be something lying

about worth lifting. But there was nothing except a couple of oul' umbrellas and a walking-stick in a big jar on the floor beside a table that had nothing on it but a brass dish and a gong. A door near them was closed, and Florry whispered daring him to open it. He hesitated, then went towards it with caution, only to stop suddenly when it was flung open and a girl came out. Her blue calico dress ended below her knees over long black stockings. She peered at Neddo and Florry from the seclusion of a wide-brimmed straw hat with a black ribbon circling its high crown. The three children stared their distrust at each other, then the girl turned and sped swiftly up the stairs. Neddo and Florry looked after her.

"God! isn't she old-fashioned!" Florry said, "Did you see her stockings? Like she was in a Home or something, and her a lady's child." Her voice was heavy with wonder. "God! fancy that! Me mother says I'm too young for long stockings, but I can tell you one thing: when I am old enough to wear them, they won't be black."

"What color?" Neddo asked.

Florry pulled at the elastic band in the leg of her knickers until it snapped. She grinned with satisfaction. "Salmon," she said. "Like Esther Fitz. Salmon color is gorgeous. Have another try." She nodded towards the closed door again. "Gowan." She grabbed his arm and pushed him.

Neddo shook free. "She might come back."

"She won't," Florry whispered fiercely. "Have a decco."

Neddo shook his head.

Florry looked disgusted. "God! you're no good. I'll look meself then."

At that moment, Miss Warr came back, followed by the maid carrying a small bundle of clothes in one hand and a brown paper parcel in the other.

"It's all I can find," Miss Warr smiled. She took the clothes from the maid and handed them to Florry along with a half-crown. To Neddo she gave the brown paper parcel that contained two half-loaves. "You divide the bread," she said, "and if you

come back Saturday morning I may have some clothes for you."
She looked at Neddo.

"Thank you, Miss," he said, one hand closing round his parcel,
the other cupping the half-crown he had also been given.

Florry, clutching the bundle to her breast, bent her knee and
bobbed and thought she wouldn't get outside quick enough to
root through her bundle and examine her half-crown.

Miss Warr stood looking after them as they went down the
wide scrubbed steps. She would see more of that boy, she thought,
as she closed the door behind them. They heard the soft click
before they darted running to the gate and the bushes where they
had hidden their shoes.

"Don't forget half-o on the bread, Neddo Baines!" Florry
slipped her feet into runners. "The woman said you were to half
with us."

Across from Miss Warr's house, Lucky Lane began its crooked
way up to the Canal, so it was here that Florry and Neddo made
for to open their bundles. The back gardens of the big houses in
Northbrook Road ended in the lane and were hidden from sight
by high walls spiked with blue and green glass to keep intruders
out, a futile deterrent to the kids from the streets like Florry and
Neddo who, in the autumn and late summer, Boxed-the-Fox to
their hearts' content.

In Lucky Lane, prostitutes, less successful than their sisters who
hustled the four sides of the Stephen's Green, stood: huddled
raddled women with stark white faces frozen into meaningless
silent smirks that crumbled like chainies when they emitted a snarl
in the way of a greeting to the furtive men who hovered around
them. The kids called the lane Lucky, because they sometimes
found a halfpenny or a penny or a few sweets screwed up in
the corner of a brown paper bag or Pigs' Balloons which they
put between their lips and tried to blow out. And it was here
Florry and Neddo went to open their bundles, and in their excitement did not see the man who had come after them, until he stood
beside where they were kneeling on the ground.

"What did she give youse?" he asked hoarsely, though he had seen. The end of his soiled ragged coat brushed against Neddo's suddenly raised face.

They jumped to their feet and shed their sudden first terror when they saw that it wasn't a policeman.

"What d'ya think?" Florry said; and Neddo said, "Nothing." His eyes fastened to the dark red face and the short bristling hair, silver-tipped around the chin and mouth before it dulled to gray on his cheeks under the shadow of a peaked cap.

"That oul' hoor is a Protestant," the man said, moving in on them as they edged away from the shadow of the wall into the center of the lane ready to run for it. "She's damned," he muttered. His words clung in the sound he made. "And she's a sinner," he went on, moving always towards them as they backed away, though he didn't seem to move at all. "And youse know what happens if youse touch anyt'ing out a her hands, don't youse?"

"She's a good woman," Neddo said.

"She's a black Protestant!" the man cried.

Neddo knew all about Protestants. On the one hand there were the songs he and the other kids sang:

> Proddy-Woddy on the wall,
> A half a loaf'll do youse all.
> A farthin' candle to give youse light
> To read your Bible all the night;

on the other hand, there was his Uncle Mattie, who claimed it was the Prods who wrote all the books and fought harder than anybody to free the country. Neddo entertained both opinions judiciously. He did not answer now; and neither he nor Florry moved their gaze from the fanatic eyes topping the bulk that came closer and closer, blocking out the sky above and behind him with the intensity of his stare, loaded as it was with threat.

"Youse'll rot in hell!" he said and reared to spring.

Florry screamed and Neddo ducked under the outstretched grabbing hand that smothered him with a burst of smell before he twisted jerkingly, like a dismembered puppet, and was free. They ran blindly, wildly up the lane until, with a look behind, Neddo saw they were not being followed. Panting for breath, they stopped and looked back. The man was still where they had left him.

With distance safely between, Florry screamed, "Ahr, ya dirty oul' bla'guard! King a the kids! Itchy back! Yellow belly!" The names poured in a torrent of abandon from her open mouth, interspersed with panted yells from Neddo, who danced round her.

They saw him make mock runs towards them, and were goaded to greater taunts at his inability to come more than a few steps at a time, and their jeers grew in volume until the echos rebounded around the long narrow lane like the tormented yells of caved demons. They waited, thrilled with shivers of fear that palsied their limbs with readiness for flight, and leaped in real terror when a prostitute, annoyed, flung a badly aimed empty wine bottle that smashed itself into green pieces at their feet.

"You better mind yourself," Florry cried belligerently, before turning her attention back to the advancing man.

"Belly a pups! Put a foot in it," Neddo shouted. "Get a move on, will ya?"

"I hope you're not left that way," Florry laughed, as the man, now only a few yards away, beckoned to them.

"What d'ya think we are—ijuts?" Neddo called, and suddenly fell silent.

They both stared, shocked, at the man who had now flung open his overcoat and stood exposed while he pantomimed obscenely around the gaping fork of his trousers. Florry and Neddo turned and fled silent up the lane.

Near the bridge under a tree on the Canal, they shared the bread, and Florry surveyed doubtfully the striped uniformlike dress, the blue coat and the strange boots that buttoned up each side.

"I wouldn't get out in them." Florry was disgusted, holding up the boots for Neddo's inspection. "A nice sight I'd be!"

"But there's not a brack on them," Neddo pointed out this important fact.

Florry wiped her nose on the hem of her skirt. "You wear them then, but I wouldn't be seen dead in them."

Neddo grabbed the boots, but Florry wasn't interested.

"Ah, sweet Jesus!" she cried. "Will you have a decco at the frock?" She held the white-and-blue-striped dress against her wiry body and began to strut importantly, before she flung it to the ground and picked up the navy blue coat. This she put on, and it was much too big for her; but it had possibilities, to judge by her rapt expression as she turned back the cuffs and bent up the end of it. But this, too, was discarded when Neddo laughed. She bundled them back up again and, as they started away for home, she wondered what her mother would get in the pawn on them.

"A lot." Neddo hugged his bread and half-crown and now a pair of boots. "Three shillings maybe, if Mick was in a good humor."

Florry held out her half-crown. "C'm'on. Will we go into Pughe's?"

But Neddo wanted to get home. His mother had murdered him when he had come home from school, for robbing the peas from outside Juicy-Eyes' shop that morning, and when he was coming out, she warned him not to leave the Lane, but he had and was afraid she might have missed him and perhaps there would be another hiding waiting for him when he got in. There might have been, except that in the delight of getting bread and a half-crown Mrs. Baines forgot that he had left the Lane. She only remembered later that evening when it was too late, she thought, to do anything about it. Neddo never mentioned the man in Lucky Lane, and when he was finished with the story of how he had come by the bread and the money and the boots, Mrs. Baines had in her mind the picture of a benevolent old lady who had almost forced Neddo by tears and entreaties to accept her great munificence. Neddo was born lucky, she thought; and with wonder, she decided that whoever she might be, Miss Warr was indeed very good.

The boots fit nobody but Tucker Tommy, not even after Mrs. Baines got Miss Keogh the bootmaker to stretch them on the last, hoping to make them big enough for Neddo who needed them worse than his brother. The boots, however, remained too small and narrow for Neddo, and were finally given to Tucker Tommy after the toes had been stuffed with paper since they were too long for him.

On Saturday morning, after coming home with two sackfuls of cinders, Neddo went alone to see Miss Warr. Florry declined to go with him, because the morning before he had grabbed a bin in the area of a house she had always considered her property. Therefore he had transgressed, and on Saturday when he called for her she decided to punish him by showing absolute unconcern about himself and Miss Warr. Nothing he could say would change her attitude, so he was forced to go alone to the house in Northbrook Road. He came home not only with a bundle of old clothes but with a job for Mrs. Baines. After questioning him for some time about his mother, Miss Warr had withdrawn and returned with an envelope which she explained he must give to his mother to take to the lady whose name and address were written on it: Miss Plum, Prince's Terrace.

SEVEN

THREE things contrived to go wrong with Pat Baines that Saturday. The first was when the ward sister came up to where he lay on the broad of his back in the corner bed in St. Jude's ward and told him in her concise voice that it was time he got up and out as they needed his bed. The second was that the minute the news of his departure spread from bed to bed and even across the landing into the next ward, men came running with demands for payment for tobacco and newspapers that he owed them. And this led up to the third, because by the time he met their demands, which were small but many, he had exactly one penny left out of the seven-and-six relief money that Mrs. Baines had collected the day before and sent up to him by Neddo. The result of his having no money meant that he had to walk all the way from what was called Number One James's Street past endless pubs in Thomas and Francis streets through the Coomb, lined with more pubs, even past those in Kevin and Camden streets where on other days he had lorded it grandly while he downed whisky faster than the barman could pour it. But today he was forced to walk by them without as much as a drink of water passing his lips, although at a couple of pubs where he considered he was well known enough to be able to run up the price of a couple of drinks until another day, the barmen had politely refused, pointing out in case it had escaped his notice the cardboard propped against a row of bottles: "Do not Ask for Credit, as a Refusal Often Offends." Pat Baines was offended and said so, but was unable to do anything other than mutter a cursed advice as to what they might do with the drink they refused him.

As usual he considered that his wife and children were responsible for the torture of his walk from the Union and for his agony of longing for even one drink. Filled with resentment, he kaleidoscopically attributed the rest of his bad luck to them also, starting from the moment the nun asked him to leave the hospital up to the last barman's rebuff. It never dawned on him that his wife and children were more unaware of Sister Eustace and her existence than she was of theirs, or that even if they were not, they were still as powerless about getting him asked to leave as her decision that he should do so was unquestionably final in its authority. It would have suited him to lie up another week in his bed in the corner with nothing to do all day but sleep, eat and read and be waited on hand and foot by the remnants of men who for one reason or another found existence within the prisonlike walls surrounding Number One easier than trying to live outside. Nor had he relied on their feeble ministrations only.

Nurse Foley, a tall gaunt woman with a gibbous chin and a lower lip, who had spent her life in one Mary Magdalene Asylum after another before she ended up as a nurse in the Union, also waited upon Pat Baines with the air of one who is at last in the presence of her god and is fully aware of being found nondeserving. She forgot to be frightened when he smiled his white-and-black grin at her and was unaware that anyone but herself saw his hands reach up to cup her breasts under the starched sail of her apron, that anyone but him noticed her man-size hand linger caressingly, unnecessarily long on the lower rise of his body underneath the tightly tucked-in sheet. She was unaware that because of Pat's whispered rough threats, loaded with insinuations as to what he wanted to do with her and delivered with the expert knowledge he had of their effect upon her and women like her, and because she imagined herself loving and loved, she would grow careless and brazen, thinking she saw in the distance a place fashioned by the outcome of his desire for her, a place free from the restrictions of her semicloistered existence and the rigid discipline of the nuns. But Sister Eustace, whose gray eyes missed nothing and whose ears could hear the grass growing, saw which way the wind was blowing and determined to stop it.

She could not discharge Pat without consulting the doctor whose charge he was. Unfortunately, Dr. Barry, who had been appointed to the Union for the sole purpose of attending on British ex-servicemen, made only irregular visits, so that she was forced to wait a week before she could put into effect her decision that Pat must leave. He had, she knew, some minor kidney ailment of so slight a nature that his application to any other doctor or hospital would have gained him no more than the advice to switch from strong liquor to barley water; they most certainly wouldn't have dreamed of giving him a bed, and neither would she, if she had any say in the matter, but she had none, yet. In the meantime there was something she could do, and because she departed from her customary thought-out caution, she made a mistake. She could, she knew, dismiss Nurse Foley. But nurses were difficult to get and, if they knew their jobs, impossible to keep in an institution that was more workhouse than hospital. Not that Nurse Foley knew her job, but, brought up to the exacting rigors of religious houses, the habit of hard work came as easy as the habit of making the sign of the cross. Both were mechanical, as natural as eating and sleeping, something you and all around you did. You didn't question either, no more than Nurse Foley questioned the nuns' right to put her suddenly onto the night shift while there was still two weeks of her day duty left to her. Sister Eustace had not expected any trouble from this move, and got none, though she searched the querulous face hoping to catch some show of rebellion that would justify her desire to teach the woman a lesson. But Nurse Foley accepted the change without a murmur, and Sister Eustace had to content herself with the promise that a time would come for a more thorough lesson and the fact that a more immediate danger to herself had been averted; for she would not have to witness the goings-on between Pat and the nurse, and she would not now be tormented by thoughts that drove her to excessive self-imposed penances. She would turn her mind now to the end of the week when he would go, and she tried, as she wrote her letter to Dr. Barry asking him to discharge the patient on his next visit, not to remember the hard dark voluptuousness which turned her mind from God and her hoped-for near promotion to the post of the Union's next Reverend Mother.

Sister Eustace had her way. On Friday Dr. Barry told her she could send Pat Baines out the following morning. She did so, never suspecting that for the past week, after lying in his own bed by day he had lain by night in the cubicle on the landing used by the nurse on duty, and that her desire to teach the woman a lesson would come to fruition sooner than she hoped, because Nurse Foley was well on her way to being pregnant as Pat Baines walked out through the gates of the Union Saturday noon.

He left without a thought for the woman whose lover he had been, except to muse momentarily that it was too bad he had waited so long before finding out about her. The time wasted caused him to shrug before he grinned and thought, what the hell! There was plenty more where that came from. And there were, for him. There always had been—when he was younger, and even now that he was thickening out in middle age and rapidly approaching what should have been the evening of his day. True, the white smile did not flash quite so quickly as it had when he was courting his wife, nor was he any longer in possession of the laughing gay forthrightness which his youth and dark Spanish looks embellished and which had made the young girl he was to marry advance without doubts into the life his charm and open-handedness promised. The women who took him now took him for what he was, the man foreseen by brother and friends when they tried to convince the young Molly not to marry him. But she, with the simple trust in the innate goodness of people that was to be characteristic of her always, went against advice and warnings, counseled only by her implicit belief in Pat, and he upheld that belief until he grew bored with it and resorted to tricks to test his power over her, telling himself that he could stop, whenever he liked, the craving for drink and the tumbling into bed with any woman that happened to catch his fancy. But it was the game that mastered him, not he the game, and as its ascendancy grew, his lusts came to bend him to their will like a straw. He made no attempt to arrest their quickening power. That would have entailed effort, a denial of the things he had come to consider rightfully his. It was not a question of responsibility. Pat Baines was not a man to dread responsibility or consciously shirk it. He simply could never imagine he had any. He was devoid of imagination, but possessed the peasant's cunning for foraging out the necessities of his life and would beg, borrow and beat, but not steal, to get them. And he'd have them now, he was thinking, if his wife and children weren't such a worthless pack as to shame a man like himself. They were responsible for his long thirsty walk from the Union, and the bad luck that dogged his days. The thought—because he had thought it—became part of the bedrock of his existence. And in this mood he turned into Rock Street and between the shops into the Lane.

"I'll see you Monday then, please God," Mrs. Baines was saying, but the words died on her lips as the door swung to with a click in her face. Bewildered, she climbed the area steps onto Prince's Terrace and looked up at the fat fluted columns each side of Miss Plum's front door. Her window was above, and the room where she had talked with Mrs. Baines. God help her, the latter thought now, all alone in that big old house with a gorgon of a cook-house-keeper as her only companion! She crossed the road into another crescent of gray-fronted houses that led onto the Canal, suddenly oppressed at the thought of going into that house and facing those two again on Monday. She would, she thought, give anything to stay away, but she had no alternative. She had to be there at nine o'clock on Monday, and her mind fled her oppression before she could admit it, for to accept it would have given life to her stupid fears. And six shillings a week and your food was not to be found on the streets, her thoughts coming staccato, as she planned what it would do. It would pay the rent. She could leave something off shoes for the kids in one of the shops every week. Neddo and Danny were in their bare feet. And in the Daisy Market suits of every description hung, all reasonably priced, so, with a little stretching, she could give a shilling or eightpence off one every week for Danny, who hadn't a stitch to his name. Babby was all right, and managed by cutting and turning to hold her own, but there were the little luxuries that she would have liked to be able to give her, such as the odd bottle of Bovril or a good cough-bottle or a flannel shift which would keep the life in her instead of the ones she wore now made out of flour sacks. These, no matter how much she bleached and washed, remained rough on the skin and, what was worse (for Babby), kept their blue ink letters. It was all right to have the name and address of a firm of mil-lers on the bed sheets, and many was the Sunday morning she had lain with first Teasey and then Babby, so down to Tucker Tommy, tracing with their fingers the blue letters spread over them. It was from the sheets that she taught them their alpha-bet. It took four flour bags to make one sheet, and when they wore out, what was left she made into shifts and shirts. Neddo and Tucker Tommy liked wearing shirts you could read, but Babby had always hated them and was bitter in her complaints even as a child against the roughness. Now Mrs. Baines thought with the extra money she would be able to afford a little better for Babby and the rest of them. She would get Babby the flannel shift first, whatever happened! And in anticipation, her uneasiness about the strangeness of her new job left her, until finally forgotten and receding altogether in the rising murmur of the new shift that spread itself white and woolly warm before her eyes and then sprung giant-proportioned and heavy with the goodnesses her mind endowed it with.

A constant yet wholly unconscious dread had nagged and gnawed at Mrs. Baines from the first moment she had laid eyes on her third eldest daughter. There had been a not-for-here-long look about Babby from the day she was born, and not once during the years when she was growing up, nor even now that she was a grown-up young woman, had she lost it. Her birthdays as they came surprised Mrs. Baines without her being aware they did. And her sigh and relief at another hurdle surmounted were only sensed. All she knew was that for some reason she was more than grateful that another year had been lived through. When she hurried to the chapel to spend whatever few pence she had on lighting candles, she never knew what it was she feared more than anything else in the world, and she was constantly blissfully ignorant of the reason promoting her thanks. She was consumed with a desire to reach out protectively towards her child, to hold her forever in an impregnable armor against the butts and roughages of the life she had bred and borne her into, in which only the strong survived, strengthened on the heaped abuses of the multitude.

Not at ease with herself about Babby, she worried and fretted if she saw her with a sign of a cold or if she looked more tired than usual, either after being on her feet at work from eight in the morning to six in the evening or after being at a dance the night before. She wished Babby wouldn't go to the dance halls as often as she did but was loath to deprive her of a pleasure, the one immoderation in an otherwise very moderate young wan. The expression: "You'll be long dead," which came naturally to her lips when one of the women about the place, or one of the kids, was doubtful about indulging some extravagance, was never said to Babby.

Her roseate thoughts about the fine shift she would buy her were disturbed by the memory of Babby's coughing the night before, and she frowned suddenly, as though she were listening again to the soft regular hack of the cough that passed into her limbs and crowded her breasts every time her daughter's head moved on the pillow beside her. —It'll go as soon as the fine weather comes in, Babby had said when her mother got up and filled a cup with water from the zinc bucket beside the window. —Wait'll you see. And she had smiled up at her in the lamp's glimmer.

With the help of God, Mrs. Baines thought now and cast back in her mind for the earlier mood of happiness. Yes, she would buy Babby the new flannel shift. The trace of a smile touched the corners of her mouth and turned the worry in her blue eyes to softness. She would have liked to laugh openly, for her thoughts and the day that was in it, and she would have except that people seeing her would surely think her mad. She had to content herself with the near smile, while unknown to her the shift took on the semblance of a relic endowed with miraculous benefits.

And unknown to her, as she turned out of the sunlight on the Street into the shadow of the houses in the Lane, was the fact that she would not be able to buy the flannel shift, that her husband was out of the Union again and was sitting staring moodily into the fire waiting for her.

This time, Pat Baines's absence had been shorter than usual, though it was, as always, long enough for his wife and family to begin, if not to forget their dread at his return, at least to hope with that perpetual wonderment of the human heart that when he did return he might be different, but he was not. He was, as Mrs. Baines, after her first shock of seeing him sitting at the fire, saw instinctively from his crouched position and from the way he said: "Where were you?", the same.

Wryly in the first wave of despair, mocking herself, she thought that he was still the same old twopence-ha'penny. Then she was overwhelmed with a fatigue she strove to push aside when she remembered her near hope and the things she must now remember to do. He watched her hang her coat behind the door and the fawn felt hat over it, and repeated his question.

"I went down after a bit of work," she said, and moved towards him while she tied the sack apron around her.

"Yes, and did you get it?"

She nodded, and he listened to her descriptions of the frail gentle spinster and the bad-tempered cook, his expression sullen, making no effort to push aside his chair as she tried to poke the fire into a flame and put the fat-bellied kettle on it.

"You look grand," she said finally, as she straightened up and surveyed him.

"I don't feel it. I shouldn't be on me feet at all," he complained. "An' I wouldn't a been if it wasn't for that oul' bitch of a nun up there. But I'll not forget or forgive," he said with threat.

Mrs. Baines waited, knowing better than to question him or show what he might consider too great an interest in his affairs. He was sober, querulously so, and the least thing would be enough to start him off. She glanced quickly around the room and saw that the bundle of clothes Neddo had brought in that morning had gone. She had left them on the bed with the intention of going through them when she came back. Maybe Neddo had shoved them into the trunk out of the way, she thought, and cautiously she began to spread two clean sheets of newspaper onto the table. She started back when Pat turned suddenly, his chair creaking as though it would break under the sudden twisted weight of him.

"Shouldn't be on me feet at all," he said. "But where am I going to lie up, tell me that?" He leaned forward on the back of the chair to glare at her. "Other men have sons and daughters to keep them if they never did a day's work for the rest of their lives. All

I have is a crowd of bastards that are no good to themselves or anyone else. I haven't one to give me as much as a drink of water if I was dying."

"Has anyone?" Mrs. Baines asked tiredly.

"That's not the point. I had to clear outa that kip this morning because they wanted the bed I lay on. And on top a that indignity, I didn't even have the tuppence for me tramfare out of it. Me! A man who went through the war to end wars, an' in my state a healt'! Not to be able to rattle tuppence on a tombstone!"

"But you had seven-and-sixpence yesterday?" Mrs. Baines spoke her surprise.

He sprang to his feet, and she reached her hands behind her to grip the table.

"So I did," he said, and pushed his face close to hers before he drew it back slowly. "And whose was it?"

Your family's, it should've been, she thought; but answered, "It doesn't matter. You had it."

"Yes," he said slowly. "I did. Relief money, that's what it was. An' you have the bloody nerve to mention it and ask me what I done with it. *This* is what I've come down to: relief money! And you ask . . ."

"I didn't ask," Mrs. Baines said.

"An' why didn't you? What's stopping you? I've been questioned by your betters." He waited for her to make some reply. When she didn't, he moved back towards the fire. "There's me, depending on a pauper's handout. A man who went through four years a hell at Earl Haig's side! And what thanks do I get?" He pushed his chair out of his way and began to move about the room.

Mrs. Baines set the few cups and plates on the table, watching him without seeming to. She had heard all he said many times before, knew it off by heart, and had developed the habit after so many years, not of deafening her ear to him, but of listening to the sounds his voice made without hearing what he said. She could gauge instantly the extent of his wrath and, when he was sober, whether or not to expect violence, by the near shading of the rise or fall of a sound that alerted her and put her on her guard. Today she guessed that there would be no violence, at least not yet; but to avoid the possibility, she had to do something.

Pat's voice went on and on, and into the middle of it came Neddo with Tucker Tommy behind him, and Neddo was handing his father a pawn ticket and money. After counting the money, he threw the ticket onto the mantlepiece. There was no need for Neddo to sidle around to where she stood spreading a bit of dripping onto the pan over the fire and to whisper: "The clothes." She knew. She had known when she saw that the bundle from Miss Warr was no longer on the bed. Nor was it any surprise to see Pat keep the money and throw her the ticket without comment. That too had happened before. But she must pacify him at least until she tested his mood about Danny. It would be a risk, but one she had to take, and now, before she could think about it.

"It's a bit of mutton," she said by way of a preface to the more serious topic to come. "Is that all right?"

Pat just looked at the bit of meat she held up and nodded his massive head as she laid it onto a plate and began cutting it into three sections. She cut the biggest piece for him and left the two smaller pieces aside for Babby and Danny. For herself and the boys, she had a couple of sausages.

"Danny'll be in," she said into the silence. Her voice seemed to shout over the screeching sizzle of the meat on the pan.

Pat turned from where he stood at the window, his movements sucking in the ordinary sounds like the swally-hole in the Canal devouring the bits of sticks the kids threw into it. "In where?"

The question in the silence was a blast from big guns.

She drove herself to pretend ordinary surprise. "Why, to his bit of dinner. What else?" she said. She was aware that Neddo and Tucker Tommy had edged around to stand near her and knew that if she looked, she would see the fear in her mind reflected on their faces, the fear that mutely begged her not to cross him, knowing in their young yet old wisdom the outcome. It was this silent pleading, this grave reminder of themselves, that so often forced her to acquiesce to Pat's demands and so gain a temporary peace. Like Danny, she herself had little fear of his violence and now, as in the beginning of her life with him, would gladly have gone to her grave rather than let him get away with his assumption to claim a wrong was right. Only because of the sufferings her stands against him caused her children and because she could not bear to inflict heavier burdens upon them by her efforts to stem a tide that she knew would eventually crash in any case, did she give way to him. She knew well her powerlessness against him, there were so many channels by which he could attack her, and in the beginning, like cold air searching out the decayed holes in teeth, he found those ways and used the knowledge with the force of cannons. But in order that her children might live at all, she was forced to make them unhappy and hope that by doing so they would eventually reap the rewards of what must seem to them senseless actions. Because it was for them she must fight, she pretended now not to see Neddo edging closer and closer or to feel Tucker Tommy's fingers tug fitfully at the side of her skirt in his effort to quiet her, while he stared with wide blue eyes across at his father.

She continued chopping the onion into the large pieces he liked until he came within an inch of her, then she looked up.

"I told you you weren't to let that thing across the door, didn't I?" he said, and wiped the table bare with one sweeping gesture of his arm.

Neddo and Tucker Tommy made small sounds, but neither moved from where they stood on each side of her, though each followed with his eyes the flight of food and plates.

Mrs. Baines stepped back from the sudden burst of anger that darkened his face. She stared at his black eyes narrowed to slits under his coarse lids, while he calculated how far he should go.

"You can't throw a young chap like that into the streets," she protested. "There's no knowing what might become of him."

He did not answer her for what seemed a long time. Then he leaned his hands on the table and bent towards her. "There won't be any streets for him to be thrown into if I leave me hands on him. I'm telling you an' I told you before, how many times do I have to tell you—to keep him outa my sight?" His voice had risen now to a shout, but still he made no move towards her. "Maybe you don't think I mean what I say? Maybe I don't tell you often enough, is that it?"

She shook her head. It was, she saw, no use to go easy now. Whatever happened, she would have her say. "It's not right nor natural," she cried, "to shut the door on your own son. It's a shame an' a sin in the eyes of God."

"It'll be a worse sin if I lay me hands on him." Pat brought his fist down with a crash and a shout onto the table. "And if you mention him or go against me in this . . . !"

He kicked upright the chair that he had knocked over, and sat down. Mrs. Baines watched him until Tucker Tommy's whimper penetrated into the noisy anger seething inside her. She looked down to her son and automatically raised the hem of her apron to wipe his eyes, and suddenly the fight seemed to go out of her. She bent down to pick the things off the floor, her motions slow and done only with great effort. Neddo bent down to help, followed immediately by Tucker Tommy, afraid of being left alone up above the table with his father. She looked up in terror as the door opened, and Babby came in. She had thought it might be Danny, and in her relief that it was not, barely noticed the flight of the smile from her daughter's face or heard her indrawn breath as she surveyed the man with his back to her and her mother holding a bent silent communion with Neddo, who slid past her out the door.

Pat Baines turned and stared at his daughter, neither pleased nor displeased at what he saw. He did not like Babby any more than the rest of his family. If anything, he hated her dark almost laughing aloofness and the element of contempt which she communicated in her dark eyes whenever she looked at him, and whether he saw her or not. It was a barely definable look which made him loathe her because he did not understand it and because she refused to hide it. She was more daring than her sisters had ever been, and would answer him back however hard or persistent his blows might be, and she never cried, only uttered dry piercing screams. Between blows the contempt she felt for him never left her eyes and wavered only in sudden more vicious pain or when she ducked. She dared to answer his lewd accusations against her morals, and even went so far as to tell him he should be locked up, braving him head high, while behind the outward show of defiance her belly churned with fright.

Babby hated Pat Baines. Even as a child she had disliked the feel of his big hands round her body in his rare moments of playfulness, when for some unaccountable reason he took notice of her or Kitty or Teasey. His sudden movements plunged her into darkness as he swooped and swept her up in his arms to the light that made her head spin and robbed her eyes of sight after the impenetrable blackness. His laugh at her shock, which he kept up while he prolonged the outrage; the way he said something you couldn't hear, because the words seemed not to leave him but to stay close to his mouth; and, when you went near to hear what was said, the clout on the side of the head—and you knew then he had tricked you: Babby had seen him do these same things to Teasey and Kitty and Danny, and the sight stunned her into a consciousness of all his other mean tricks of violence. But she was probably not fully aware of the man and his deeds until she one day saw her mother raise her hand to her face over the glow of a burning welt that showed in stripes between her fingers. This sight tore at Babby and froze her into a hard narrow core of hatred, but it terrified her too into a dread which she was never to lose; though as she grew older, while her hatred never lessened, it became tempered with a contempt that in turn gave ridicule to her fear, until now she could face him with a certain equanimity that successfully hid her fear and exposed only her contempt.

He sneered now. "Are you still here?"

Babby hung her coat up over her mother's, and came into the room slowly. "Where else would I be?"

Their glances clashed until Babby withdrew hers to meet her mother's, which bid her hold her tongue. She knew she had come in on a scene but could not guess its cause until Tucker Tommy followed her into the little room and told her in whispers. She knew then that Neddo had gone out to tell Danny not to come home. She stood listening to the sounds her mother was making, getting the meal ready, and thought enviously of people who could come and go and live lives not constantly threatened by ructions for which there was neither rhyme nor reason, and of the past few weeks, filled with peace and the semblance of comfort that somehow, though God only knew how, Mrs. Baines managed to surround them with. She thought of Teasey in England and Kitty in Schenectady, both far from Pat, out of his reach, and knew they couldn't be blamed for getting out as soon as they were able. She thought now that she should have gone, too. She had as many reasons, and *more* opportunities. But maybe that was the trouble, maybe she'd had too many opportunities. Maybe if a fellow wanting to marry you was the cause for wonder to *her* that it was for other girls around the place: maybe then she *would* have gone. Her trouble was perhaps that she couldn't feel as those others did that Anything was better than Nothing—like Teasey, for instance. But when she remembered Nick, the logic in her reasoning went awry. Nick loved her, and Nick worked hard. And at the back of her mind, she knew she loved him and there was no reason why they could not get married. He asked her often enough. He was, she knew, in a position to keep her—and in the way to which she was not accustomed. And what was important, he had her mother behind him. Her mother hadn't liked either of her sister's husbands, and had tried to persuade Teasey and Kitty to wait before they rushed into marriage. About Nick, she felt differently, pointing out—in case Babby should overlook them—the advantages of a husband who clearly worshiped the ground under her and earned good money "at electricity." Furthermore, her mother often ended her cataloguing of Nick's qualities by voicing an inner, small as yet, worry of her own that she would like to see Babby settled.

Why, loving Nick, she did not marry him; or why, when she thought of doing so, the idea of the time spent in preparation and of the actual separation from her mother should fill her with apprehension and panic: she had never reasoned.

She recalled this now in the little room, and last night, and Willmore's Dance Hall in darkness except for a red light over the bandstand, and the glow of cigarettes that the management passed out for the Cigarette Dance, and Nick's arms around her. They were strong arms and he seemed to fold her up in them like wings. . . . —Without end, he said when she told him. If we were married, he added rapidly. We must get married. It's the logical and expected conclusion, according to me *and* your mother. Then, softly gliding them both past the rough of desire, he asked, When? When? Even in her need for him, she turned her mouth from his. She would not hold Nick to her with promises, and when he touched her face with his hands, she drew back. —I don't know, she said. I don't know. Sometime. Maybe. Maybe never, Nick. He was stiff with expectation. —Is that true? His voice lumbered, and carried them, bound together like the music, their eyes staring intently into each other's, Nick unable, and unwilling, even to attempt to navigate the treacherous waters. He bent forward, out of the heights, and now she felt released from her own body and imprisoned in his. —Why do we wait? he asked. She was close to his breathing, close to his fire, entering with him into a state that she knew he was beyond questioning, engulfing her in an emotion that was like darkness pressing down. She let what she felt, like the music, take her and fling her into its dictatorial stream the way Zena's music sometimes did, her body bent to the thing and the music and what was happening was strange and dark, like Zena, and along the wall the sad girls nudged because they didn't understand —Sometime, she said suddenly. Sometime. —But definitely? He stared at her out of the music of the passion they had entered and over which, for one stretched moment, lost control; but, although there was still music, she would resist its current. She remembered, and touched his arm, and said again,

—Maybe, and they danced; his face fierce and tight in the shadows, hers smiling because he was holding her as if she were some small precious object. The moment was all deception. She laughed, but at Esther Fitz who swept against them floundering in her own sea of excitement. Esther loved a waltz. —I want to die waltzing, she said in passing, as the music swooped and caught up the colors and the bodies that rose and fell on its wave, spraying all with laughter, but also, for Babby, with premonitions that she shook from her as unnatural. . . .

"Did you get the jam?" Tucker Tommy was touching her on the arm.

Babby heard him out of the turmoil of what had been her own body. She smiled quickly and bent to open the cardboard attaché case in which she carried her black dress and white-frilled cap and apron which she wore in the cafe, and took out the two small sample-size jars of jam which the proprietress gave to the girls every Saturday and which she gave to her brothers. She gave Tucker Tommy his and then sat down beside him on Danny's bed, making sure to turn back the white quilt and not crease it. She watched him prize the lid off and swing his bare legs back and forth as he dipped his finger into the jam and sucked it. Absorbed, he did not hear her sighs, or see the look of deep pity suddenly in her eyes as her arm went round him.

Nick would not wait forever, nor could he live all his life in dance halls. He could provide for her . . . and life was endless. He wanted to be married now. He wanted sons. Less constrained, Esther Fitz said he needed a woman and, once in a mood without charity, she had said that if Babby didn't want him then she should not lead him on so, because there might be others who did . . . with or without a wedding ring . . . in bed or up against the wall of a hall. —It isn't quite fair, even Mrs. Baines had said. If you don't intend to marry Nick, you should say so. You mustn't let this continue, just because it's begun. —You want to get me off your hands! —No, darling! No. But you must decide. —Maybe I'm not the kind of girl who gets married. Probably I'll never marry.

—An' go through life barren and lonely? You weren't meant for that. What was she meant for? She didn't know. But marriage . . . ? It was as though she could not afford that in-between state which was like being caught in the middle of the road with the path you had left, behind, and, ahead, the one you had yet to reach; only now you belonged to neither, and even as you went forward, time desperately precious was in flight. It was this sense of time and dread of wasting it that kept her from Nick and made her savor like a delicacy on her palate the weeks when Pat Baines was away, when the rooms were a restful place and her mother seemed bemused with peace, and she longed for the nights to fade so that another new day of being unafraid would begin, when before her stretched hours of minutes and seconds that could be grasped and lived as though each might be her last. But Pat's return pushed her forward into an abyss of longing that drew the skin of her face tautly back while her nose and lips reached out, urgent for the days to pass until he would go away again. And the time spent in waiting filled her with a desolate sense of waste.

She turned from thought and filled her eyes with Tucker Tommy. "Come on. We'll get our dinner," she whispered with a grin to take the mystery out of the mysteriousness of having to whisper.

He grinned back at her, but when they lifted the curtain to go back to where Pat Baines sat, there was no trace of emotion on their faces except the passivity of a mask in which only the eyes in watchfulness moved.

Neddo came in while Babby and her father were eating in silence at the table. Behind Pat's back at the fire, Mrs. Baines dished onions and a sausage onto three small plates for herself and the children. Because he would not allow the children to sit at the table with him, she had long ago fallen into the custom of eating with them. This had its advantages. As well as keeping Neddo and Tucker Tommy from doing anything that might discommode and cause a row, it enabled her to keep a warning or encouraging eye upon whoever was sitting at the table with him. Reassuringly she nodded at Babby now over his head, before she sat down with her plate on her lap.

Babby knew that Neddo had been successful in intercepting Danny. She knew also that when her mother thought she wasn't looking she would hand over her own portion of food to the two boys. They ate in silence, interrupted only when one of the children began to say something that was quickly stifled to a whisper and, at a movement from Pat, died away altogether.

Mrs. Baines was aware that Babby watched her as she divided the food on her plate, but she couldn't let good food go to waste, and she couldn't eat it. She had tried, but every mouthful threatened to choke, and it was only with effort that she had been able to get the first bit past her lips. Now, with the pretense over, she began to speculate on how she might have overcome Pat's decision about Danny. Her stand against him seemed inadequate, until she remembered the look in his eyes as he slammed his fist onto the table. But even so . . . her brain reeled at what she knew were useless suppositions: if she had said or done this or that? Other than she had? But useless, all her suppositions! Pat Baines was implacable. And you could not ask him to explain, nor reason with his whims and orders. It was useless trying to reason, useless trying to understand a man unlike any other you, or anyone else, had ever heard about. Why? Useless, too, to ask. He was like something from hell sent to scourge the life and soul out of them, an implacable demon that God Himself must be unaware of, otherwise why was he allowed to go on day after day, year after year? There was no answer to that question, either, as always; and in a wave of bitterness she stirred herself to find a way of getting out a bit to eat for Danny. She had hidden away in the bottom of the press the piece of meat she had meant for him, but would have to wait until she could cook it unbeknownst to Pat.

The opportunity to do so did not come until four o'clock in the afternoon when Pat disappeared into the little room to sleep: after he had taken half Babby's wages from Mrs. Baines, and prior to his visit to the pub at the corner of the Lane where he would spend it. Knowing Pat's routine, Babby had carefully gone over the little room before he entered it, hiding anything she thought might cause his comment. Now while he slept, she scrubbed the bare boards of the floor in the big room in case he should be only half asleep and hear the meat her mother was frying on the fire.

From time to time Mrs. Baines would half her preparations of the meal and Babby would stop the whisk of the scrubbing brush to listen uneasily while they stared silently at each other, resuming their labor only when they were sure it was safe to continue. When at last Mrs. Baines covered the steaming food between two plates and wrapped a cloth around them, Neddo stopped rubbing his foot along his shin long enough to take it from her. Nervously he waited for his mother to fill the jug with tea and put the saucer on top for Tucker Tommy to carry, along with the slices of bread and butter which she had wrapped in a bit of newspaper. His expression matched his mother's solemnity. Strangely adult he looked beside the grinning Tucker Tommy, who was aware that this was a serious moment but, despite that, couldn't help feeling it was also an excitement.

"Stop your laughing!" Neddo whispered fiercely, as Mrs. Baines stood hesitating in case she had forgotten something, before she let them out the door.

"I amn't laughing," Tucker Tommy, who was, answered.

Then they cautiously crept out and down the stairs on their way to the Canal, to the tree where they knew Danny would be waiting.

EIGHT

ON THE Canal, the night was black and in the sky the moon had ripened. It was big, white and veined with Queenie Mullen's dark hair. Queenie was like the moon, Danny thought. She swelled inside clothes that could not contain her, her breasts threatening to overflow the confines of her blouse. She was seventeen, and big, and shy, and the blood stayed close and shaded her skin in daylight. In the dark she laughed down at Danny, who had turned over on his back on the grass.

"An' isn't there the great hurry on you this evening for a change?" he said. And she saw his dark face laughing up at her. She listened to him stretch his length on the grass.

"Well, look who's talkin' about bein' in a hurry!" She shook her hair that hung each side of her face. "I like that!" She looked behind her to the trees and the water. "It'll surely rain," she said. But Danny thought it unlikely.

There were insects in the air, and in the trees birds tittered, shrill through the leaves. She brought her head back, and the moon took on a drunken look.

"I like talking to you," Danny said.

"You do in your hat!" But her voice lacked certainty. "Sure I only see you when you're out on gur."

Danny drew himself up on his elbow. "I do, honest."

"Why?" Queenie groped, conscious that she had brought their conversation back to personal issues instead of him trying to explain the present political state in Ireland and then about books, which was what he had got on to when she threatened to leave him.

"Because you're honest," Danny said, "And because when I'm talking to you, things somehow take on a shape in my mind that they didn't have before."

"Believe that, an' you'll tell me more! I'm sure you say that to others."

"That's not true," Danny protested.

"How do I know?" Queenie asked. "Sure you might easily have a girl an' none of us would know about it."

"As if that were possible! Can you imagine having a secret in the Lane?"

"Some could." Queenie shrugged.

"You think I'm a fly bucko, don't you?"

"I don't know, but you're a bit strange."

"Because I haven't got a girl?"

His directness confused Queenie and was one of the things that made her understand him less. Another fellow would not have been so blunt, but would have gone skirting the issue for ages, giving hints that would have prolonged the intimacy of what had started as a game, until she had teased out of him what she wanted to hear. But then, other fellows wouldn't sit you down in the seclusion of the Canal without chancing their arm on you the way Danny Baines did. He was a bit innocent, Queenie thought, Danny was.

"Oh, you're awful," she said out of her confusion and irritation at her inability to turn her doubts into an explicitness she could

understand, to twist the moment into what she called "normal."
She saw that he was not looking at her but at her hands, which
every winter became blistered with wittles and in early June burst
and lay deflated in scaly circles all summer, hardening again with
the first cold snap of autumn. Quickly she drew them behind her,
ashamed that he should see. She recognized his concern and
laughed. "Me Ma says it's the height of me. Going into housework
where me hands are in water all day, instead of into a factory or
a restaurant like your Babby."

Danny's grin matched hers, and hid the compassion he felt as
he reached and drew her hands back onto her lap. "You should use
a poultice," he said, "instead of lettin' them with a needle or open
on their tod. Would you have liked that?" He looked up at her
as he turned her hands in his, and she forgot her shame of a
moment ago in her awareness of the closeness of his face and the
easy pressure of his shoulder against hers under the thinness of
her coat.

"What?" she asked.

"To have gone into a restaurant, like our Babby?"

Queenie shrugged. "Nobody ever asked. Nobody ever asked me
what I wanted," she said. "I just had to get a job. It didn't matter
at what. At first, though, me ma said I needn't stay if I didn't
like it, but by then it was too late. She'd got used to my few
shillings every week, and couldn't do without them." Queenie
drew her hands away from his, and smoothed her thick hair.
"That's the way," she said slowly. "That's always the way." She
shook her head. "An' you, Danny," she asked. "What would you
have liked instead of the sandbank?"

Danny grinned. "I was never asked, either. But I can tell you
shovelling sand wasn't it."

"What was it then?"

"A doctor." Danny laughed. "I was ambitious, wasn't I?"

"In a hospital?" Queenie asked.

"Aye. When I was a kid I wanted to be a doctor in a hospital."

"Would you still like to?"

"Yes, I'd still like to."

"Is that what you think about when you're here alone?"

Danny shook his head. "Sometimes. But now that I know I never will be, I don't think about it as often as I used to."

"What do you think about now?" Queenie asked.

"Other things."

She persisted. "What kind of things?"

"Just things. About getting away from here."

"From the Canal?"

"From the country. I'd like to go to another country."

"Which country?"

"Australia, maybe. Or Canada. Or America."

"Kitty's in America, isn't she?" Queenie asked. "New York."

"Schenectady, New York," Danny said, looking off.

She remembered Danny and Kitty, and the way he used to hang around her and wait at the top of the Lane for her in the evenings, and the way people, seeing him trotting up the Lane, were able to tell the time just by seeing him. "Is that all you think about?" And she added quickly, "An' I suppose if you went to America, you'd live with Kitty?"

He shook his head. "No," he said, answering both her questions. For that wasn't all he thought about. Sometimes he thought about the girls who, now that the weather was warm, came and watched him swimming in the Canal, and when he came out, threw themselves down on the grass beside him and waited. Clumsy girls, but free and easy in their talk and gestures, who hissed like geese when a kid or another fellow strayed too close, who traced with quickened hands the hair on his chest and the thin dark line of hair that ran down his flat belly and disappeared into the top of his swimming trunks. Unshy girls who could not stare enough at his near nakedness and whose talk came in bits and, thick with desire, quivered in half-sounds through their open mouths. You could hear it. See it. And because you felt only pity, you let them touch at last the mound of their want. Demurring only at suggestions, at a mouth lowered in the darkness, the touch of teeth, a hand closed and gathering roughly to guide blindly, and you tossed them off you, and they sometimes cried then or laughed bitterly, belting like a boot the palpitating thing that had not and would not take place. —Are you afraid? The question drew down the corners of their mouths. But you would not answer, except to promise another time, another night, and could not tell them you didn't know how. And they thought that only girls were virgins. —No, he would say, and after they had gone, would reflect, No, I wasn't afraid.

Danny's glance slid over Queenie. "I think about other things."

"What then?" she asked.

"About what keeps me here," he began, but he would not explain that to Queenie. "About some of the things I'd like to do in this place before I left."

"What kind of things?"

"Well, I'd like to arrange things so every Irishman could get work and a living wage. But that'd be easy, beside what I'd like to do most. What *somebody* ought to do!"

"What, f'rinstance?"

"*Some*body ought to be able to abolish the power of the priests over the minds of the people."

Queenie drew back, more puzzled than surprised. "Why? What's wrong with the priests?"

"Everything," Danny replied, "but mostly the way they teach people to accept."

"Accept?"

"Yes. Rule from England. Poverty as a way of life. The way things always have been instead of the way they might be." He paused, and, since she seemed to be considering deeply what he had already said, he went on. "Brutality," he said. "To accept and endure brutality in the name of God. That's the worst of all."

"But how do they do that?" Queenie asked.

"By refusing to face reality, by refusing to deal with the reality of *our* lives—their sheep, by refusing to answer questions. By telling us not to question at all, but to submit. Submit like animals.

For reasons that have never been proved. These are the things I think about."

"God!" Queenie was all awe. "I never think like *that!*"

He smiled. "What kind of things do you think about?"

She laughed. "Don't know. Clothes, maybe. Going to dances. Fellows," she admitted shyly.

"What kind of fellows?" Danny asked.

"*Some* fellows."

"Fellows you know?"

"Course," Queenie replied, remembering one she didn't, but whom she had met every morning for a week on her way to work, and about whom she used to think all day. Even now she remembered his tweed sports jacket and flannel trousers. She guessed he worked in an office, because he was always clean. "And about Bank holidays and bikes. I'd love a bike. Me mother says she doesn't care if she never sees the sea or goes to Liverpool, and that happiness is all that matters, but I'd like to. I'd like to go on the sea to Liverpool in a boat like the one your Kitty went on to America."

It was a picture post card, Queenie was remembering. Kitty had sent it to his mother, and she had shown it to everyone in the Lane. Some people had even borrowed it. Mrs. Kinsella did, and kept the card on her mantelpiece for two days, and his mother had to ask for it back because Babby wanted to show it to the girls in work.

"You'd like that, would you?" Danny asked.

Queenie nodded, and he stirred uneasily in the grass, and again the moon was veined with Queenie's hair.

"I would," she answered, forcing her voice over the sudden hurt dryness in her mouth, her breath—under the swell of her breasts —labored because he was looking at her, and because she was waiting.

"And what would you do when you got there?" Danny asked, taking her hands back into his, and feeling sorry because they were hers, and sore, and scarred, and because . . . He let go her hands and lay back, and because he must put his own hands somewhere, he put them behind his head, and after a while he saw her slide from where she was sitting, to lie beside him. The long grass showered up between her feet as her legs settled into it, and her head came to rest on a level with his. His eyes, under their lids, traced the soft voluptuous rise in her limbs under her cotton dress before it dipped and rose again over the hard swell of her breasts, stretched to burst into rounded points that reached for the sky.

"You're awfully pretty, Queenie," he said, and clumsily, but with an urgent hurry, cupped her breasts with his open hands.

"Am I?" But there was no uncertainty in the long pointed smile she gave, but it fled as he changed his position and leaned hard against her.

"Are you afraid?" he whispered.

She drew his face down to hers. Motion beat swaths of grass flat, and in the sky the moon pressed close on the sound of a turf boat, freed from the narrow mouth of the lock at Rock Street, riding out onto the swollen water of the Canal on its journey from one bridge to the next. In the trees, the moon hushed the birds to silence and then all one could hear was the thud of the horses' feet, beating out a metallic rhythm on the hard earth like a drum in the distance. Sounds scattered and dropped and gathered . . . and listened to the horse approach. Now it was close. You could hear the drag of its rope, the sudden single slap as it hit the water and rose taut and tight between it and the boat. There was a shout, and on the boat a clang of metal. The horse heaved forward and past, protesting through the smell of its own sweat, and when it was gone its presence still trembled in the air.

At the next bridge, the lock-keeper swung the gates open, and in the grass Danny lit a cigarette, dragged deep long gasps and handed it to Queenie who smoked in silence while she went through the gestures of tidying herself.

"I must go," she said after a while.

They got to their feet, and she held out the cigarette to him.

"I'll walk a bit with you," he said.

"You can't go home?" Queenie asked, as they neared the railway arch, because he had slowed down.

He shook his head. Her eyes, he thought, were wider in the light, large and staring, as if she was frightened.

"You're not sorry?" Her look was shy suddenly, as she reached out, as if she must touch him or hold him.

"No. Are you?"

She shook her head. "I only wondered. They say fellows think nothing of you if you let them." She paused, and they looked through the gas light into the depths of each other's eyes.

"It's not true," Danny said. He touched the side of her face. Now there was nothing left for either of them to say, and still they lingered.

"Could you not go home when your father's asleep?" Queenie's sudden desire to protect him was mingled with her fear that there should now be a moment when she would not know where he was.

"Maybe later," he said, though he knew it would not be possible.

"I better go so. Me ma will kill me for being out so late." But still she made no move to leave him. "Will I see you tomorrow?" She questioned against her will, against the intuition that told her she should have left to silence, her desire.

"Yes." His reply was grinned and swift. "I'm glad," he said. "Are you?"

She nodded and turned away, slowly quickening her pace only when she knew he was no longer looking after her as she headed for the Lane.

Danny went back the way they had come, to the hollow where they had lain together. It was where he would sleep tonight, tomorrow night, and until Pat Baines went away again or until rain or the police drove him to the halls and stairs of the Lane for shelter. He lay, forcing himself to think of Queenie, her velvety breasts and the soft cradling of her thighs, thus to forget the tight fright in Neddo's face when he had threatened that afternoon to go home and face his father. Neddo's fear had reminded him of his mother's. At seventeen, Danny feared nobody, facing men twice his age and size who lost their tempers when they lost their pennies in the pitch-and-toss school and who thought, because he was quiet, he was an easy mark. The softness men suspected in him was there, but reserved for his mother, for his sister and two young brothers. There were, he knew, better jobs to be had in England, but he also knew that his complete departure would leave his mother alone to the mercy of Pat, removing, as he thought, the only obstacle to a total and final malignity. It was because he would not desert her that he sometimes wished she might die. The Church would not release her from Pat; she would not, sinning, release herself; only death would free her, and him too—from this burden love forced him to bear.

He turned over and stared up into the dark blue sky that was spattered now with gusty clouds. How long, he wondered, would Pat stay this time? He closed his eyes, shutting out the cold, the sky, all except Queenie's voice asking him if he was sorry; and under the sound of the lie of his own reply, he was suddenly asleep.

From the window in the little room, Babby saw Queenie Mullen come round the bend in the Lane, keeping close to the lighted windows as she made her way to her own hall. Babby looked beyond her to the Fitzgerald's windows, wishing Esther would hurry.

In the front room, Pat Baines lay in his bed with a *Black Mask Magazine*, while Mrs. Baines sat mending shirts and expecting the call from the hall any minute. It was part of the plan, but she was nonetheless startled when she heard Esther's voice.

"Babby!"

Mrs. Baines got up in time to see Babby drop her coat, wrapped around a pair of shoes and a dress, out the window to where Esther Fitz and Nick were waiting to catch them.

"Esther Fitz is calling you," she said, loud so that Pat would hear.

Babby came and stood looking down at her father. "Can I go out for a minute?"

He waved her away with the magazine. "Don't have me to go looking for you."

Mrs. Baines listened to Esther Fitz's laugh coming up from the hall and the husky tones of Nick's voice, before a sudden flare-up in the Slatterys' room below drowned both with sharp shrieks over which Mrs. Slattery screamed sad blasphemous complaints as she flung whatever she could lay hands on at the children. Lifting a turned collar to the light, Mrs. Baines glanced at the statue of the Virgin and the lowered indifferent face hovering eternally in chalk-eyed blindness over the bed below. Timidly her mind approached the face of the statue, reluctant even in her need to burden someone carrying the imagined weight of the world on her shoulders. Perhaps, she thought, she might get her requests in sideways as it were, just whisper her wants so that they might be recollected in passing and without causing the least tremor of exertion to the One Who heard.

Her fingers moved silently.

NINE

THE rain that Babby escaped, that lulled Mrs. Baines into a tired dreamless sleep, woke Danny and sent him hurrying to the shelter of the trees. The downpour was steady and minutes old before it penetrated his consciousness, having soaked through his jacket and worn flannels. He stood close to the black trunk of a tree and made quick futile efforts to dry his face and head with a bit of rag that he finally threw angrily away. Overhead the branches sank beneath the weight of the rain and each leaf poured its stream onto him, and made pools around his feet. In front of him the Canal throbbed under the rain's onslaught and rose in noisy answer to devour the night's thunder into its heaving swell; and across it the black wind tore, whipping the water to a frenzy of impotence until it looked like a sliver of the Atlantic imprisoned between grassy banks.

He waited for the rain to abate, until it became clear that it would not, then made a dash for the Lane, running from tree to

tree as a rat skims under cover of the reeds at the water's edge
in a perpetual search. At the railway arch where he had left Queenie,
the protection of the trees behind him, he walked, afraid to be
seen running by a policeman or a Stater patrol who might arrest
him just for diversion. Around the corner, Rock Street was silent
and empty, and the Lane as well, but he remained cautious and
kept to the middle, giving the open hall doors a wide berth until
he reached his own. And even that he approached with caution,
before he ventured into its black yawn. Quietly he tested the dark
recesses of the hall and the small alley that ran alongside the stairs,
a hiding-place for him when he was a kid, the quiet place where
Kitty swore she had seen a little green boy disappear into the wall.
It was blocked up now because children had been raped there.

Softly he crept up the stairs to the first landing and back down
to the hall again, satisfied that there was nobody but himself in
the passage. He sat down and took off his shoes, which he wrung
out with a twist as though they were cloth. He did the same with
his socks, and took off his jacket as well, but put it on again because of the cold. Huddling into a corner of the stairs, he listened
alert as any animal to the noises of the house. A rat crept from
under the stairs on its way out to the bins at the pipe, the scrape
of its feet hidden under the whimper of Mrs. Kinsella's last baby,
who keened ignored in its misery. Overhead a board in the floor
creaked suddenly, sharply protesting, and he leaped to his feet,
waited for the sound to repeat itself and, when it didn't, settled
down once more, drifting almost at once into a doze, from which
a gasp that was almost a scream woke him and sent him running
out into the Lane and into the lavatory, leaving behind him in the
arms of her fellow, Mrs. Chance's eldest daughter Nan, who recovered quickly from her fright at suddenly stumbling over a man's
outstretched legs as she came into the hall, for it was nothing beside her surprise that her fellow had not only taken her home from
the dance but had actually come down the Lane with her as well.

The lavatory was clean, thanks to the vigilance of Granny Quinn
whose mission it was to wait outside the door ready to inspect it

immediately after use, to the annoyance of them she accused of not knowing the difference and for the benefit of those like herself who did. But not all Granny Quinn's lavish use of Jeyes Fluid could kill or even diminish the smell that assailed the nostrils. He did his best to ignore it and searched round on the floor for a position in which he could find the most comfort. Here he would at least be dry, he thought, as he drew the bolt across the door and sat down with his back to it, his legs stretched out between the basin and the wall. He knew enough about the habits of the Lane to be confident that what was left to him of the night would not be disturbed. He stuffed the ends of his tie up his nostrils, suffering this discomfort in preference to the other, and stared wide-eyed into the darkness that hid the finger-stained walls and the illiterate scribbles . . .

. . . and slept until someone pounded on the door and streaks of daylight made a gray edge around it.

Danny waited until the knocking stopped and he heard someone walking away, before he got to his feet. His first feeling was one of anger that the hour was so late. In the Lane and around the pipe he heard women shouting and children crying and calling, and he cursed himself for sleeping so heavily that he had let himself be trapped like this. Someone else came and tried to push the door open and went away shouting that whoever was in there better hurry up; but still he hesitated, afraid to face the laughter of the women around the pipe and the mockery of the kids. His legs were stiff and his back ached as though it had taken lashes across it while he slept.

Against the door now, fists began to pound impatiently, then angrily as the crowd swelled. Danny ran his fingers through his hair and knotted his tie neatly. He drew his hands over the black stubble of his beard and tried to see his crumpled clothes, and because he knew the sight he must present, he lingered still, while outside he could hear them ask each other who the shagging hell was in there. The pounding on the door grew more insistent as the kids, in a new diversion, joined in. He knew he must get out

or be dragged out, and suddenly bewildered by the raucous sounds
he flung the door wide open and, blinded by the sudden light,
lunged past them, heedless of the laughter of the women and the
jeers, as he ran from the Lane to the Canal, to the place where
so lately he had lain with Queenie Mullen and thought himself
a man.

From her window Mrs. Baines watched him go.

"What's that?" Pat flung the question from the bed.

Mrs. Baines stared as though she hadn't heard him. With a decision reached and passed, she twisted her shoulders into a kind
of shrug. "Nothing," she said bitterly. "The gougers, that's all,
having a laugh for themselves."

Sunday dragged itself out, wounded and gray, out of sight on its
belly under cover of pigs' cheeks and cabbage smells and weeping-
Jesus soft rain and shouts of fights and laughs that rose above the
tinny screech of gramophones and the tambourined and brass-
horned frenzy of the Salvation Army—the Sabbath: ignored by
Mrs. Timmons and Mrs. Thraill and the other women who con-
tinuously passed each other at regular twenty-minute intervals,
small begrimed tugs in the lea of a busy port, on their journeyings
to and from the pub with jugs of porter held in the crook of an
arm under a coat or a shawl. Occasionally they recognized each
other's passage by a silent nod, depending upon whether or not
they were on speaking terms or upon the amount of porter they had
consumed or the strength of a thirst, or whether, like Mrs. Thraill,
your husband was sitting at home counting up to ten on his
fingers, in which case you couldn't spare the time it took even
to nod for fear of being overdue whereupon your husband would
upend the table and pour water over you, or whether, like Mrs.
Timmons, your husband might strip himself naked and stand in the
window for all to see if by any unfortunate chance you went over
the allotted time for your trip to the pub and back.

In the halls and on the stairways, kids sat and played, and

youngfellas at cards, flirting with girls their own age who knew why their fathers or mothers had sent them out into the Lane and turned the key in the locks behind them. There was no mystery left to them and they pretended none, except to the young ones, Neddo's and Tucker Tommy's age, who never questioned, but spent the time going from door to door with buckets to collect food, leavings from those lucky enough to have any, which they sold to the pig-yard in the Lane for a penny a bucket.

The used-up afternoon gave way to evening and night came on the strength of chapel bells from Haddington Street and Rathmines, mournful, disturbing the dark chill of the Lane into which Granny Quinn and Mrs. Chance, old maids like Nelly Murphy and elderly bachelors like Tom Flanagan, stepped resolute, detached, suited and hatted and smelling of jam, clutching heavy worn prayer books—lifebuoys—on their way to the only devotions they knew: the envied, whose only concern was the state of their souls.

Apart from the half hour that Babby and Neddo, with Tucker Tommy between them, spent at Mass in the morning, the Baineses had not moved outside their door. Mrs. Baines, instead of going to Mass, had gone looking for Danny to give him the bread and butter she had smuggled out unbeknownst to Pat and the shilling borrowed from Mrs. Kinsella, enough to get him a meal or a night's lodging in the Salvation Army in Richmond Street. Pat never set foot outside the door except once when he went down to the lavatory. For the rest of the day he sat or lay in bed reading, maintaining the silence that was customary when he was home. He was still in bed on Monday morning as first Babby, then Mrs. Baines, set out for work, and was gone when Mrs. Baines came home in the evening.

Relief at his absence overcame her tiredness as she saw the empty bed still showing the sag from the impress of his body, and on the mantelpiece his razor edged with hardened soap and hairs beside a mug filled with dirty water, out of which stuck a shaving brush. She emptied the dirty basin of water that he had left after him on the table and hung over the line by the fire the towel he had flung onto the chair. Mechanically, from long habit, her glance swept the rooms to see what was missing, and the curtain which hung from the altar shelf and behind which she kept her own few possessions caught her eye. In mounting dismay she rushed to search behind it. She had only to glance, for he had made no effort to conceal. The chocolate box, in which she had kept Babby's three silver dancing medals, lay open and empty on top of scattered birth certificates, the few letters from Teasey and Kitty and the neatly tied bundle of photographs. But it was after the medals her mind groped, as she tried to think what he would do with them.

He'll pawn them, she thought hopefully, or sell them. But from this possibility her mind fled, unable to imagine the loss of the precious and only visible proof of her beloved daughter's accomplishment.

"He'll pawn them." She spoke the thought aloud as though by giving it voice she could will the destiny of the missing medals. She ran her fingers over the empty box, repressing the anger and the sense of loss. Many was the time when, needing the few shillings they would fetch in the pawn, she had resisted the temptation, preferring to go without rather than let them go from her hands into the hands of strangers who might lose them. They often lost articles in the pawn. And they certainly wouldn't take anything like the proud loving care that she took of Babby's medals, polishing them till they shone, and wrapping them against the damp's tarnish in the softest and finest tissue paper she could find. Now they were gone from her hands and her care, and the loss, even though temporary—for he would, she thought, eventually come back and give her the pawn ticket for them—wearied her so that the sudden remembrance of the four shillings' rent which she had left in the jug on the dresser and which, running now to see, she found was also gone, added nothing to her feeling of deprivation. The money's absence merely leavened her despair in the way of the known and familiar, as she put the empty chocolate box back behind the curtain, and went to the window to call Neddo in from the Lane.

Immediate needs drove the medals into the back of her mind as she began to stretch like elastic the shillings in her hand that she had earned for her day's work. Now it must not only feed, but bed them as well. There was no knowing how long Pat would stay home. While he was here Danny must stay out, therefore she must provide, if not some place where he could sleep, at least something that he could sleep on. Straw was cheap. For fourpence she could stuff a couple of sacks with it and leave them out on the landing where he could get them at night. She tried to console herself with the thought that even two sacks full of straw in a corner on the landing would be better than where Danny had slept on Saturday night.

She gave Neddo a half-crown, sent him off and set about cleaning up the rooms. But the memory of the misery she had felt on Sunday morning when she had watched Danny being driven out of the lavatory tore across her mind and smote her to a stillness where her tasks were forgotten in the blazing shock of its compulsion, shriveling her in a whirl of noises, her own—voiceless because they would have been useless—protests.

TEN

BETWEEN them Neddo and Florry Connors carried the straw out of the yard at the South Circular Road and up the Street. Their progress was slow, interrupted by the Street's distractions, and when Florry spotted an elaborate black crepe done up in a large butterfly bow and pinned onto a hall door, they stopped altogether. Neither of them could resist a wake. A death in the Lane or in Rock Street drew them irresistibly.

Florry let go of the bundle of straw first, to stare at the hall door, which, out of respect to the dead beyond it, was closed over without being latched. "Neddo," she said.

Fighting a losing battle with himself, Neddo pretended not to hear. His mother had warned him to hurry home with the straw, but even if she hadn't, he knew it was essential that the sacks be filled and in their place on the landing before his father came home.

But, "Just for a minute," Florry begged.

150

And a minute seemed so little a time to waste, excitement beckoned so tantalizingly through the slit of the door, and Florry was so near the door already.

"Ah, Neddo!"

He dragged the straw up the steps and into the hall, and together they crept up the stairs towards the room and the low murmur of voices. As they neared the room, they arranged their faces into expressions of piety, knowing that this was the way, assured by experience that they would not only be admitted but allowed to stand at the bed, for the grownups would step back to let them near the corpse, believing the prayers of children did the soul of the departed more good than theirs could. The door was open, and inside, people stood or sat and talked between sips of stout or bites of corn-beef between cuts of bread. The only light came from candles each side of the bed, throwing the mouths and chins of the men and women into yellow moving relief and casting the shadows of brimmed hats, owned or borrowed for occasions like this, over bright beady eyes. Some of the mourners were cronies of the dead woman and saddened themselves by recalling past events, a mixture of truth and fable, claiming an importance in her life that they never had so that her sons and daughters, fattened with moneys from insurance companies, might be relied upon to keep them supplied with drink for the two days that the wake and money lasted. A few, like Neddo and Florry, came for the diversion other people's troubles offered, lessening their own in the need for commiseration and giving them a chance to set foot across a door that had never been open to them while the woman on the bed was alive, an opportunity not to be missed of assessing what the living standards of the dead had been.

Wakes were remembered, not for the amount of lamenting that was done but for the quantity of liquor and the quality of food. And often when the insurance money was enough to buy a coffin and open a grave but no more, the surviving members of a family ran into debts they never recovered from in order that the drink might flow and the food be plentiful. The amount of brass on the coffin was also important, as were all the trimmings with which death was surrounded, receiving attention and care that was never given to the business of living. But then, death was wide open and exposed them to the mercilessness of themselves, permitting them to hide from the uncharitable gaze nothing but the wall at the head of the bed, covered with a borrowed sheet on which a black crucifix hung, the bed itself, spread with another borrowed sheet on which the corpse lay, and the mirror that faced it over the mantelpiece, hidden with newspaper for fear the face of the dead might be reflected or their own grief shown shadowed maybe with guilt.

Florry and Neddo shoved themselves through the mourners standing round the table spread with food and bottles of stout and port on a cloth that still showed the knife ridges where it had been folded. They scanned its wide surface for the cake, reserved mostly for the young and the teetotal, along with the always inadequate supply of lemonade. If there was not a big slab of fruitcake bought especially from the Home and Colonial Stores in Camden Street— and they had gone to wakes where there was none—then neither of them would stay, let alone kneel down, but would depart shouting their scorn on the stairs for the poverty of people too poor to buy a bit of cake for a wake.

But today that wouldn't be necessary. Cake—currant-black— was in evidence, and Neddo's whispered assurance was unnecessary too. Florry had seen it before he had.

"Come in, daughter, come softly in."

A woman heaved herself up from her knees at the side of the bed to make room for Florry. Her great mouth opened with the effort of her exertion. Florry, her eyes raised in wide innocence, waited, because things shouldn't always be easy for grownups.

And the woman, between gasps, got to her feet alone. "Say a prayer for her, dotey. You have His ear, the Almighty Most Merciful ear. Like a good little girl, say a prayer for her poor soul into it. Say the things a fearful sinner like meself hasn't the neck to say.

Speak it, daughter, an' He'll hear ya. Like a good little girl, say a prayer for her poor soul."

The woman shook her head wisely at the people near her, as if giving utterance to some special knowledge of her own, and there was a general murmur of agreement as room was made for both Florry and Neddo who, without raising their eyes to look at the woman on the bed, knelt down beside it.

Neddo looked first, timidly up the stretch of valance that hid the bundle of bedclothes which had covered the bed while the woman lived but had been flung under it out of sight by her married daughter, who sat now breast-feeding her baby in her lap. The stretch of white ended at the long straight line of the brown habit, sharp and smooth and flat as though there was nothing beneath its small mean folds except near the top under the white letters which he knew meant, "I Have Suffered." Over the breasts the hands rose, chained together with rosary beads wound through the long stiff fingers, the look of martyrdom giving the lie to the happy release they claimed death to be. Around the neck of the habit was a thin white pleated band cupping the dark chin of the worn old face, shadowed with the sharp rise of the cheekbones and nose, stretching the skin taut in its sparsity. The eyes of the dead woman were caves of dark under the bony temples which reached up from the pillow as though to escape the fleas crawling around the tide of her hair, marauding unnoticed and unseen in the dim candlelight—except by Neddo, who stared through the cold gray-white silence near his face and around and over the body on the bed, mesmerized into wonder rather than shock at the strange sight.

He nudged Florry, and she, thinking he meant to go, blessed herself and stood up, backing away from the light and the bed to the table. Neddo followed, and together they stood where they couldn't be missed—beside the table and right in front of Mrs. Sly's daughter with the baby on her lap. Unconscious of their presence, the woman regulated the flow of the milk from her nipple between two fingers into the mouth of her baby, who sucked un-

concerned at her distraction as she listened to Granny Quinn
volubly issuing platitudes and pious sentiments about her loss.

"She's better off," Granny Quinn was saying. "Sure what is
this life for anyone but trouble. Trouble an' worry. The poor
craytur, when I think . . . !"

Florry and Neddo glared impatiently at her, and Mrs. Sly's
daughter quietly took her breast out of the baby's face and tucked
it back into the opening of her dress.

"Maybe you'd like a bottle of stout?" she asked.

"Well, now."

"Or a sup of tea?"

As Mrs. Sly's daughter got to her feet, Granny Quinn, with careful consideration, said, "Well, maybe a drop of stout'd give me
heart again—because since your mother went I haven't the will to
set one foot before another."

As she took the bottle of stout she was handed, Florry and
Neddo drew attention to themselves by coughing, whereupon Mrs.
Sly's daughter asked them if they would like a piece of cake even
as she cut two chunks from the brown-black slab. They grabbed
the cake and waited, hoping she would also offer them a bottle of
lemonade. When she didn't, they departed, finishing the cake
between Florry's whispered words of abuse about the meanness
of some people. At the bottom of the stairs they sat to lick their
fingers, and with a toss of her head, Florry said, "Some people
wouldn't see their heart on a white plate."

Neddo tried to console her by reminding her of past wakes where
they had got more than they could eat, but this only added to her
chagrin. "You're too easily satisfied, Neddo Baines," she cried,
suddenly resenting his attitude of satisfaction. "God! Easy to see
you're not used to much!"

Neddo would rather laugh than squabble, and he did now, and
gave her a push on her bare arm.

"You're always wanting to fight," Florry shrieked as she flung
out her arm and hit him across the face.

They jumped to their feet and glared at each other.

"You're a proper slieveen, Florry Connors!" he said, his eyes smarting with the blow.

"Am I?" she made a grab for him.

But this time he was too quick for her. He ducked under her outstretched arms and came up with a push that sent her reeling across the passage against the red-raddled wall. She made as though she were going to charge him but thought the better of it, and as suddenly as it had begun the fight was over. She flattened the hair back from her face and began to examine her arms for black-and-blue marks. But there were none, and she had to content herself by finding imaginary new rips among a multitude of old ones in her blue cotton frock.

Neddo watched her warily, then sat down beside her. He giggled as he wiped his eyes with the end of his gansey, and Florry forgot the rips in her dress.

"Some people," she muttered, "wouldn't give you the daylight if they could keep it from you. An' Kathleen Sly is a mean oul' bitch!"

Neddo looked from Florry to the straw he had left behind the door and jumped up. "I'm going. Me mother will murder me."

"God! Can't you wait?"

He dragged the straw out of the corner and flung the hall door open. The crepe bow fluttered and caught Florry's eye.

"Give us a hoosh, Neddo," she said, staring up at it.

"Are you going to feck it?" he asked, awed at the idea of touching a thing belonging to death and therefore in some way holy.

"Ah, fa God's sake! What d'ya think I am? Course I'm not. I on'y want a look."

"What for?"

"To see how old she is, if you must know." Florry was already in position for him to lift her.

He bent down and grabbed her legs and pushed. The huge black bow came away from its pins easily, and when he let her down she was holding it in her hands He gasped and ran, leaving Florry alone undoing the bow.

"You'll go to limbo, Florry Connors," he called from the bottom of the steps.

Florry's laugh was brazen. "That's what ya think; but little do ya know! When I grow up I'm going to commit every sin in the calendar!" Under the skimpy dress, she contorted vigorously as she draped the black length of stuff around her head and across her shoulders. She laughed and began to strut, imitating the gyrations of grown women. "Ah, Neddo, I'm on the stage. Like the wans we sawn in the Panto, 'member?" And she began to sing in a thin nasal voice.

On the far side of the street, people stopped dead in their tracks, unable to believe their eyes and ears. Neddo warned her, but Florry was past caring.

"Let them," she screamed. "They'll know me the next time." She tossed her head back and began to kick and sing louder her disregard for the onlookers.

"She'll not have an hour's luck, the brazen rossie!" an old woman shouted over at her.

"It's a shaggin' hidin' she wants," a younger woman cried, and blessed herself.

But nobody made any attempt to cross the street. And Florry, like someone possessed, cavorted and pranced unconcernedly at the shouted abuse and warnings, waving the crepe in her own frenzy.

"Look out," Neddo shrieked as the hall door behind her was flung open and against it for one breathless moment she was poised, paralyzed in shock.

"I'll strangle you!" Mrs. Sly's daughter made a grab at her.

But Florry sprang the steps in one jump, landing beside Neddo on the path, just in time to escape the sudden rush of the people across the street.

"Plattered face!" Florry laughed up at the woman on the steps, before she grabbed hold of the straw with Neddo.

Together they fled across the road and up the street to the Lane. Neither lingered in case someone should have followed them, and when Florry came to her own hall door she darted with a laugh into its darkness, trailing behind her the crumpled symbol of death like a pennant triumphant after battle.

Neddo was saved from the consequences of his disobedience by the presence of the Rent Man, who was in the hall on his arrival pounding on the locked door of the Slatterys' room. Behind it Mrs. Slattery stood, silent, waiting, and with no intention of doing otherwise until she heard him mutter threats about evictions and dispossessions as he went away and it was safe to resume being home again: unlike Mrs. Baines, who worried when she had to face him empty-handed and who now gazed in distraction at Neddo and from him to what was left of the wages from Miss Plum. There was no need for him to tell her the rent man was in the house. She could hear the heavy ex-policeman's steps upon the stairs and dreaded meeting the fat red face, the muttered abusive threats when she told him that she couldn't pay him this week, and his way of looking you up and down as he said: "If it's not drunks I have to deal with, it's paupers!", in a voice that the Lane could hear. "If you haven't got two weeks' rent for me next week, out ye'll go," he would say. No matter how often she heard this, it never failed to instill in her the fear he intended.

"I can't face him," she said, turning the two shillings and eightpence in the palm of her hand, as though a miracle might turn them into pounds. The shock of losing Babby's medals had overshadowed the loss of the rent and put it from her mind. Even so it was too late for her to lay hands on any money now. The pawns were long since closed, though even as she thought this she knew she'd nothing that would have brought four pennies, let alone four shillings. "God blast him!" she said suddenly.

And Neddo knew she meant his father. "I'll tell him you're not in from work yet," he whispered into the noise of the knock on the door.

"No, that I'll give it to him next week." She hurried into the little room.

"Jasus, Mary and Joseph, but youse are the right lot!" The rent man's loud ejaculation, tinged with ever constant surprise, roared over the near silence his presence caused in the house and the Lane. "It isn't shagging well good enough," he shouted down at Neddo who gazed, unperturbed, up into the taut swell of a soiled waistcoat from which several buttons were missing between the tracks of dried runny stains. "Where's your mother?" he asked suspiciously as he heaved his bulk against the door to widen the careful slit that was all Neddo had made.

"She's out," he said as the rent man pushed him aside and looked around the room.

"She's out, all right," he said, his eyes on the curtain of the door to the little room. "Moryah!" He drew back out onto the landing and, with his foot carefully placed to prevent Neddo from shutting the door, he knocked on Mrs. Kinsella's.

Mrs. Kinsella had her rent ready and an extra ninepence off the arrears. She winked at Neddo and waited with a look of satisfaction for some sign of approval from the rent man, but all he said was, "I hope you're not breaking yourself," as he turned the money over in his hand.

You ill-manned pig, Mrs. Kinsella thought, her satisfaction quenched under the contempt in his face. "I am," she said, "but I wouldn't want you to lose your appetite over it." She looked across him at Neddo and past him into the empty room, as the rent man laboriously marked her rent book. "Thanks be to Jasus, this isn't going to last the rest of our lives!" She said serenely.

"What isn't?" the rent man eyed her suspiciously.

"Paying rent." She looked him in the face. "When the Republicans take the country over, the country'll belong to the people, and we'll pay no more rent, rates or taxes." She looked triumphantly at Neddo, who was her authority on current events. "Amn't I right, Neddo?"

He nodded, thinking, Well, I never told her *that!*

The rent man sneered. "That'll be the day. It's a shagging Ethiopia youse are wanting!"

"An' that's what we're going to get, isn't it?" Mrs. Kinsella

laughed. Neddo nodded, and when she cried, "Up the Republic!",
he giggled.

"And when is that woman in?" the rent man asked with a jerk
of his head.

Mrs. Kinsella looked him up and down. "Will I tell you now,
or will you wait for it?"

He gave a grunt of disgust, and she sniggered.

"Away in her country house, takin' the air for the summer,"
she said over to Neddo conversationally, "or has she gone to
London to see the Queen? Or maybe it's just out of her mind,
she's gone. Ya can have your pick."

"None of your oul' lip, an' go easy on that talk about the Queen.
I on'y asked a civil question, that's all."

"An' you're getting a shaggin' simple answer," she snapped
back. "Diggin' ya snout into other people's business as though they
owed you something!"

"They do an' all," he told her, handing back the signed rent
book.

"An' you'd let them . . ." She scrutinized carefully the place
where he had marked her payment.

"You want to clear up them arrears," he said importantly, fingering the money in his trousers pocket while his eyes darted search-
ingly from her to the room behind Neddo.

"An' that's not all I want to clear up," she answered, irritated
by his manner and by her two youngest children who had begun
to pluck at her legs in their efforts to escape onto the landing.

"It's a good thing for you and the likes of you that you have a
generous man like Benny Spirer for your landlord."

Mrs. Kinsella threw back her head and laughed. "Oh, terrible
generous he is. A heart a gold, that big fat Jew has. He'd give his
piss to the dogs any day. Like yourself!"

He looked at her threateningly. "You're anti-Semitic!"

"I am an' all," she laughed, "an' on Saturday nights, I'm Auntie
Flo!"

"Youse are all too ready with your tongues around here," he said, taking a final look past Neddo.

Her laugh was derisive. "We'd want to be."

"Suit you better to pay your way."

"Look a that now!" she called after him as he made his way down the stairs. "Suit you an' oul' Benny One-Ball Spirer better to clean the bugs an' filt' outa the lousy kips that youse are charging through the nose for."

"Ahr!" he shouted back up at her. "Put a sock in it!"

She flung herself against the bannister and screamed irrelevant abuse. "Gowan, y'oul' dirty blackguard! You an' your fancy woman below in the Locke! D'you think we're as thick as you are, ya dirty trollop!"

"Any more a that an' I'll take a summons out against ya!"

Mrs. Kinsella laughed. "You will in your la-la! Them days is over, Mickser, we're a free country now. Did your ma not inform you? The clouds over our heads are green, white and yeller now, me beauty," she shrieked; and then, as to herself more quietly, "An' a whole shaggin' lot a good it's doing us!"

She stopped suddenly and listened, but no sound reached her from the well of the hall. With a laugh she turned to Neddo, and looked past him into the room where her two children had wandered, staring in the strangeness of a new place.

"Settled that oul' bastard, I did," she said, as she swooped down on the children who screamed to escape. "He's gone, Mrs. Baines," she called.

Mrs. Baines pushed aside the curtain. "Thank God!" she smiled her relief, and the smile widened as she went on, "You're a holy terror when you start!"

Mrs. Kinsella tossed her head. "Well, who does that oul' bollix think he is?"

"He knows now!" Mr. Kinsella spoke from the landing. "You could hear your t'rottle a mile away," he told her good-humoredly. Sweeping the cap, white with the dust of bricks, from his head, he turned into his own room.

Babby, who had been behind him in the Lane, stood in the doorway. Her anxiety gave way before the ordinariness of the scene confronting her.

"You shoulda been here, Babby," Mrs. Kinsella laughed. "You shoulda seen that oul' moffadite take them stairs when I let me tongue loose on him."

"Oh, it was as good as a banquet," Mrs. Baines agreed, searching her daughter's face over Mrs. Kinsella's head.

Babby grinned, and Mr. Kinsella, without his coat and cap, came out to bring in his wife.

"Lookit," he said, "are you not going to give us a bit to eat?"

"Ah, hold on to yourself, can't you?" With a child under each arm, his wife followed him.

Babby's look was rueful as she hung up her coat and hat on the nail in the back of the door.

"You look jaded." Mrs. Baines's concern shadowed her eyes as she followed her daughter's movements and saw her sink onto the chair at the fire. "Sit still then, till I get the tea."

She hurried to prepare the meal and told Neddo to get out the two sacks from under the mattress in the little room and divide the straw into them, and told Babby not to budge out of the chair when she made as though to help him. Babby did as she was bid, unable to shake off the languor that kept her slumped in her chair, luxuriating for the moment in the ache of her limbs and in the small of her back. She only half heard her mother recount the events of the day, and shut them out altogether but furtively when Mrs. Baines turned her back, by closing her eyes. She was startled when she felt a hand on her forehead and opened her eyes to see her mother gazing anxiously at her.

"Is anything wrong?"

Babby shook her head, got up and moved swiftly to her place at the table in an effort to reassure the troubled eyes. "Honest, Mother, it's nothing. I'm only a bit tired." She would keep to herself about the cough that showed pink on the handkerchief she held to her mouth that morning. Her mother would cause a commotion, and stop her from going with Nick to the first dance in a new dance hall on Saturday night. The dance she considered too important to miss, just because of something which, according to Gyppo Clancy who had come into the washroom while she was coughing, might have been brought on by a crust of bread. Certainly it wasn't anything to get excited about, she thought, as she braced herself to seem like her usual self, hiding the effort under a barrage of questions about her mother's new job, Miss Plum and Mrs. Ross, her bad-tempered housekeeper.

They talked in between interruptions from Neddo, who kept repeating what Mrs. Kinsella had said about not having to pay rent once Ireland was a republic, and from Tucker Tommy, who as usual had come in late ready with a word-for-word account of what he had seen and heard around the Lane all day. Nobody mentioned Pat, though their consciousness of him showed every time an odd sound penetrated the chatter in the room or whenever a foot was set on the bottom step of the stairs, when in a sudden pause they arranged themselves to meet him. In this way they flew from topic to topic, like fingers skimming the strings of an instrument without actually touching it. Mrs. Baines, quick to sense the moods and strengths of her children, knew that Babby was not well, and coaxed her in vain throughout the evening to go to bed. She offered only a small resistance to Babby's plea when Esther Fitz called from the hall. But when Babby came back up to the room and began unpicking the seams of a dress that she wanted to turn and remake for the dance on Saturday night, she lost her temper.

"Why don't you rest?" she said roughly, sensing a new thinness in her daughter's face and a gleam in the eyes raised to her in surprise, a hard brittle gleam feverishly bright in the dull amber glow of the lamp on the wall.

"But sure, this isn't work, Mother," she answered. "Look." She ripped a seam in one stretch of her hands, the stitches giving way easily with a dry crackle.

Mrs. Baines looked away, confused, unable to understand her

uneasiness or what it was that kept her from drawing Babby to her breast. She emptied into the slop bucket the basin of water that she had washed out two ganseys in, and hung them over the line at the fire, placing them at the very edge of it so as not to keep the heat from Babby. Then she took the slop bucket and the bucket for fresh water off the oilcloth-covered tea chest by the window and went down into the Lane to empty one and fill the other. She did not linger at the pipe with Mrs. Kinsella and Mrs. Slattery, not even to talk to Granny Quinn who said she would be getting a few rabbits at the market on Friday and would she keep her one? She told her yes, and hurried back to the room. Babby was still working on the dress. After raking through the cinders and adding a fresh shovelful to them, she took a half-finished sock from the drawer of the dresser and sat down opposite her.

Babby watched her fingers dart and dance around the wool and the four steel needles that clicked with the rapidity of a tommy-gun. And because she knew that she must have seemed headstrong and overbearing, she said, "Mother, are you annoyed with me?"

Mrs. Baines looked up. "No, pet," she began, her voice gentle, her eyes absorbing, "but you don't look well, and a long sleep would do you the world of good."

Babby, with her hands in her lap now, was silent for a long minute. "I don't like to leave you alone with him when he comes in."

Mrs. Baines resumed her knitting. "Musha, you needn't worry. He won't get drunk on what he had today." She added up the four shillings' rent he had taken and what he would have got in the pawn on the medals.

Pat could always borrow from the dealers in Camden Street; but on Mondays they collected what was owed them and seldom if ever lent. Still, he had got loans before on a Monday. Her contradiction of Babby's fear was, she knew, neither right nor sensible, but done because she suspected Babby was pretending to be feeling better than she was, and because Pat might come home drunk. Babby, in fact, could not believe he wouldn't, and was determined to sit with her mother until she saw for herself. She longed for bed, and had to force her eyes away from her mother's bed time and again, denying herself the sleep she needed for fear her mother would need her more.

"I'll stay up just for a bit?" She looked at her mother to confirm her decision, disguised as a request.

"All right so," Mrs. Baines sighed. Blessed she was, she thought, as she considered her children's concern for her; and when Babby asked suddenly what she was thinking, all she did was smile.

They sat sewing and knitting in silence, broken only when Babby asked advice on a seam or how to disguise a tuck, or when Mrs. Baines remembered something else about Miss Plum and her big house with a surprise in her voice and face that seemed strangely young and caused Babby to smile. They never noticed the Lane's sounds change or the footsteps on the stairs until the woman was halfway up them calling out in the darkness. She reached the door almost as Mrs. Baines did.

The lamplight fell onto a strong weatherbeaten face that was manly in the strength of its bones and in the large rough shape of the head that shook backwards and forwards as she spoke with lips, red and wet, parted over a torrent of words drenched in spit.

Mrs. Baines stared confused under the woman's attack, understanding nothing from the repetitive phrases except the anger. This she shouted down suddenly, and the stranger grew quiet under the unexpected counterblast and began to tell her story, no less excitedly but more coherently.

"They shouldn't a done it," she began. "They shouldn't be running the streets doin' depredation left, right an' center, interferin' with people they've no right to meddle with." She stared balefully past Mrs. Baines to Babby, who had come up behind her and recognized Mrs. Sly's daughter, Kathleen.

"Who done what?" Mrs. Baines asked.

The question exasperated. "Whipped the crêpe off me mother's door, an' her above in the room laid out!"

"Who did?" Babby asked.

"Florry Connors and your Neddo." Her voice screamed Neddo's name.

"Dear God!"

Mrs. Baines's exclamation of shock startled Kathleen Sly into satisfied silence, quelling any necessity she might have felt for extra exertion. Being denied the privilege of a good scream, however, irritated her so that she turned resentfully to Pat Baines who had come up the stairs without their hearing him and stared from his wife to his daughter to Kathleen Sly before he asked, "What's up now?"

Quick to grasp her moment, Kathleen Sly hurried to tell him, afraid she might be done out of her chance by the women beside her, who were making deprecatory gestures in, as she thought, their attempt to minimize.

But God Himself wouldn't have stopped her, Mrs. Baines thought bitterly as she heard the woman elaborate her story and Neddo's part in it, and saw Pat drunkenly steady himself as he bent solicitously to calm her with muttered threats of chastisement for his son. She saw the deathly pallor and knew it was the result of a feed of whisky, and goaded by her foreknowledge of the outcome of his spite roused by the drink and the woman's tirade, she flared out in anger at her.

"You've little to do," she cried, "but to go round rising murder at this hour of the night!" Then, more reasonably: "Why didn't you come to me when it all happened?"

"It's a bloody pity about you now!" Kathleen Sly sneered and broke into a self-pitying sniffle that ended almost as it began, when Pat lurched past her to send his fist crashing against the half-opened mouth of Mrs. Baines.

Babby screamed, drowning the sound of flesh on teeth as her mother gaped chokingly over a gurgle of blood that spurted from her mouth onto her chin. She jerked herself upright after Pat, who had staggered past her into the room towards the bed where Neddo lay.

"I'm here."

Neddo's voice, a whisper in the little room, guided his father to where he knelt in bed with Tucker Tommy, bare thigh to thigh. To save his brother, Neddo reached forward to the fists and screamed his pain as he came into contact with them, blinded in the swirl of light that split the dark. Pat's drunken savaging flailed the room, crowding it with pain as he smashed his strength against his children and his wife who tried to save them: pain from his blows and from the iron of the bed and the tin trunk that seemed to hurtle themselves against her, impeding the way, until finally, satiated, he stumbled out into the troubled light of the outer room. In the darkness behind him nothing stirred except the bugs in holes that pockmarked the red-raddled walls, their heavy musk smell pervading and weighing down the stifled sobs like an ether bag across a vaguely protesting pain-riddled mouth. And Kathleen Sly had gone from the open door, careless in her frightened guilt of the faces showing through the narrow slits of other doors and the muttered comments that followed threateningly as she hurried out of the hall and up the Lane.

Pat Baines kicked the door shut and removed his coat, not noticing the blood-spattered stains on it or the black strands of Babby's hair that clung damply between his fingers until he wiped them off against the legs of his black serge trousers. He paced the room restlessly, kicking aside anything that hampered his progress, while his vast shadow swung like a pendulum back and forth in front of the lamp, sending its flame flaring up the glass globe in desperate gusts that blackened the rim before it shrank back captive to its withered glow. Suddenly he halted his pacing and with a roar called his wife and his children out from the sanctuary of darkness.

Mrs. Baines came first, dragging herself upright from the crouched position which had afforded her a little ease from the one pain which dominated the others numbing her body. With one hand she held a cloth to her mouth. Her other arm spread protectingly across the heads of Neddo and Tucker Tommy, who clung white-shifted to her. Beside them, Babby was tall and dark, her frailty hidden beneath her outrage, standing as though she must defy destruction, although across her white face livid welts ran wide and clearly marked and her eyes burned in feverish pain. Her blouse, like her mother's, hung in tatters, exposing her bruised shoulders from which angry scrobs grew to her slender throat. They stood like statues barely whispered into life in order that they might bleed.

Neddo raised his battered face from his mother's hip, no longer able to hold back the pain which the flow of blood brought to his eye. A sob crept out of him as his father grabbed the black rosary beads down from where they hung on a nail at the side of the altar, and said in a deeply solemn voice:

"The Joyful Mysteries. Oh, my God," he began, "I offer you this rosary. The Joyful Mysteries!" he shouted, and they knelt.

Mrs. Baines could see Neddo's eye. He whimpered as he met her gaze, frightened by the shock he saw there and the moan that twisted her face as she snarled a curse over at Pat. Without flinching from the kick he aimed at her, she let the cloth fall and drew her hand with tenderness across Neddo's face, careful not to press upon the eye which, even as she looked, was closing like some exotic bud in the center of pear-shaped petals.

"Hail, Holy Queen! Mother of Mercy, hail our life, our sweetness and our hope . . ."

The gesture of her hand across Neddo's face was a last and final effort, and to Pat's intoning she made no response, but directed a prayer that was like a cry to Her to Whom she had always looked in her hours of need and thankfulness and to Whom she cried now in bewilderment. In her eyes, looking over to the Virgin on the altar, there was no acceptance, only a mute appeal that twitched into gradual disbelief before she lowered her head in a nod of bitter resignation. She should have known better than to expect help from that source: the thought never came. She was aware only of a terrible loss, of trust given in error. And for her children and her beliefs she moaned aloud suddenly, "Ah, wurristhru! Ah, wurristhru!" intoning over and over to Mary the great pity that had been denied her.

Neddo tugged at her elbow, and when Pat interrupted himself to tell her to shut up she did.

". . . mourning and weeping in this valley of tears; turn then, most gracious advocate . . ."

Mrs. Baines began to pray, the words issuing in gasps through a new gap where teeth had been. Her lips, swollen to twice their size and black from dried blood, stayed still, motionless. Unable to kneel, she squatted as though she had fallen untidily out of her standing, with her face bent to her hands which lay loosely touching the floor at her knees. Against her, shivering with chill from shock and pain, Neddo and Tucker Tommy pressed themselves, their weight unfelt as they dug their bodies closer and closer into the lean jut of her hips, pinning her arms against the shreds of her blouse and the cage of ribs, sharp under her flesh.

". . . how our Lord Jesus Christ, being come to the place of . . ."

Babby, isolated, knelt upright, the back of her head touching the birdcage, her gaze on the cross-rungs of the table against which Pat sat, his prayers and her responses punctuated by the drag of the crucifix as the beads rose and fell in his hands. The monotonous rumble of his voice glided deliberately slow over the recital and would continue until he had had enough or reached some point in the litany such as the Presentation of the Crucifixion, when he might stop to liken his own travail to Christ's, or fling the rosary beads into their faces and scream at them to get out of his sight. She let her eyes rise cautiously to the bent head and handsome drunken face, in which, never without astonishment, she recognized her own likeness. He might, she knew, force them to stay up hearing his war stories again or listening to him sing. Whatever he intended, you never knew or could predict what his moods were going to be, not even her mother who was still caught unawares against the lightning changes of his tempers. And yet there was a pattern, as predictable as the Mass, to life with Pat Baines: the period of comparative peace, with him either at the Union or in the country; then his return, and a period of knocks and squalidness, culminating in some brutality, such as had driven Teasey, then Kitty, then Danny, from home; and finally his departure into the Union or the country again. One of those times, she prayed, let him not return, let me be here then by my mother's side! As she watched him, Pat's thick fingers slackened on the beads. Unnoticed, she nudged Neddo to alertness.

"You shame me!"

His shout rocked the hush, and he crashed his fists down onto the table, staggering to his feet and sending his chair crashing against the side of the bed. In his new frenzy he rose to tear the pictures from the walls and scatter anything his hands chanced upon, roaring abuse and obscenities over the noise of crashing delph and the new frightened cries of Neddo and Tucker Tommy who rose with their mother as Babby half-lifted, half-dragged her to her feet. The movement distracted him and he swept round on her with arms held aloft like the heavy stumps of trees.

"Take yourself and your bastards out of my sight!"

He did not wait to watch them back away, but turned through the debris and the slosh of water from a bucket he had overthrown and was asleep almost as he flung himself fully clothed onto the bed.

In the darkness of the little room Mrs. Baines and her children huddled together on the edge of Babby's bed, unmindful of their wounds as they hid waiting in the darkness until it was safe for them to look for sleep. They could see the lamplight gradually fade through the thin cotton curtain on the doorway, filtered through faded traces of climbing flowers that vanished altogether as they neared the string the curtain hung from. They waited and grew anxious when they felt Mrs. Baines relax her hold on them. But she knew now that it was safe for them to lay themselves down. She could hear the beginning of snores, the unlabored breathing of one who might have been sleeping the sleep of the just.

Cautiously she loosened herself from her sons' grips, settling them for sleep with easy gentle hands, whispering sounds that calmed and assured them it was all over and things would be better tomorrow, they'd see. She took off her shoes and lay down on the bed beside Babby.

"Your mouth. Is it hurting you?" Babby put her arm across her mother's breasts, drawing herself close to the angular body that tentatively touched the mattress at shoulders and hips, making a hollow rise under the arched back.

"A bit." The reply was drawn on a sigh through the split upper lip, swollen out over the gap and dragged gaumishly open with pain.

"Go down to the hospital in the morning." Babby's whisper hardly reached her mother.

Scooped clean in the darkness, Babby's arm across her was the only hold she had with the night, pinioning her back against the anguish of her hacked body, from which her mind sought escape.

"Mother?" The urgent whisper drew her back, worried her into consciousness of the treachery of the night into which she stared blindly, listening for any sound, any warning that might elude her.

She turned with awkward tenderness to embrace and comfort. "Whisht, pet." The words came parched, dry like paper caught in the spasms of a dawn wind dragging itself across the cobbles of the Lane. With her free hand she rubbed the tension out of Babby and gradually felt the slim body under the hated roughness of its flour-bag shift sag softly into her to find its resting place.

From the bed in the corner, Neddo or Tucker Tommy sobbed a short bitter childish sob, arresting the soothing motion of her hand on Babby's back while she waited for the cry to be repeated. But the exclamation of pain dreamt or remembered passed into the approach of the dreary gray light, against which she shut her eyes. But on it crept, in streels through the bits of lace curtains on the windows, over and up the side and top of the brown tin trunk, a cadaverous cowardly specter following with wary sniffs the track of the hunter, devouring with sly spite the leavings of the night.

ELEVEN

THE Outpatients' Dispensary in St. Connla's was square with low white-tiled walls and a red stone floor lined with brown chapel benches set in rows of six in the center. Opposite, white doors with doctors' names in black letters faced the patients. At the far end of the hall an altar of gray-veined marble occupied the entire width of the wall. From its flower- and linen-decked top, a statue of a tomato-colored Christ with opulent eyes narrowed to slits looked down with a musing banality onto the benches of people sitting with their faces towards Him. They waited silently, patiently, afraid to appear restless or uneasy lest they be rebuked openly by one of the nuns who flitted about with importance and thoroughness. Caught for a moment by a glance or a word from some favored doctor, the nuns would halt their busy flight to comment on something that would amuse or interest them, or both. They paid scant attention to the rows of patients, except when a remembered face or complaint caught their eyes

171

and they stopped to admonish for the continued attendance which, from the sanctity of their cotton-wool existence that knew neither ills nor privations, they felt indicated a lack of determination and effort. They ran the dispensary with prisonlike rigidity to rules born in the abundancy of leisure, forgetting—if they ever knew—that children must be fed and washed and someone found to leave the baby with since they objected if the dispensary's white hush was broken by cries and they were made uncomfortable at the sight of a feeding breast.

Overstaffed with nuns and understaffed with doctors, the hospital passed its patients from one religious to another like snuff at a wake. Only if the need was desperate did you by any chance see a doctor. Neither Mrs. Baines's split lip nor Neddo's black eye was considered urgent, and so after hours spent in sitting on benches in their chase from one nun to another, they were at last confronted by Sister Mary Joseph.

"What's the matter with you?"

The question was as gracious as the nun's abrupt halt and stance as she stood scrutinizing Neddo who had dropped his card and was bending down to retrieve it. As he rose, he tossed his carefully combed hair, and his mother tried to flatten it down again to keep him looking tidy.

"Never mind that. What's he here for?"

Mrs. Baines got to her feet, and in her confusion remembered irrelevantly that she had forgotten to genuflect, as was the custom of the poor in the presence of nuns and priests.

"It's his eye, Sister." She glanced from the nun to the flesh-colored patch on Neddo's eye, for which she had paid threepence in the chemist's.

"Well, what's the matter with it?" The nun's impatience harried Mrs. Baines and made Neddo nervous.

"He was hit," Mrs. Baines said.

"You don't say?"

The sarcasm was not lost on Mrs. Baines nor was the quiet titter from the benches of those who wished to ingratiate themselves with the nun. Ignoring their smirks and Mrs. Baines's embarrassment, she stretched her large hand from where it rested, fingering the belt underneath her long white loose scapular, and whipped the eyepatch from Neddo's face.

"What are you jumping for?" she asked as his hands flew to cover the eye. "What happened to him?"

"He got a bang in it." Mrs. Baines answered quietly, trying to isolate herself and the nun from the open-mouthed curiosity of the people beside her. The effort was useless. Sister Mary Joseph's loud questions rose above her soft replies and fell hammer-heavy onto the heads and raised faces of her listeners.

"Who gave it to him?"

Mrs. Baines crushed the pink card in her hands. Her reply was inaudible.

"I suppose somebody gave *you* a bang also?" The mockery in the voice brought forth a titter. On the end of it, the nun turned. "Well, come on then. Let's have a look at the damage."

Humiliated, Mrs. Baines was unaware of the whispers that attended her stumbling progress out of the pew, from people who were complaining that they had been here before her. She was bitterly sorry she had allowed Babby and Mrs. Kinsella to persuade her to come and wished for the courage that would allow her to tell the nun what she thought of her—and her hospital.

"That will need a stitch," the nun announced, her face close to Mrs. Baines's, examining the lip and swabbing the wound with some colorless liquid that caused the latter to flinch. "Lie down there," she said and dragged a trolley over to the head of a couch.

Her hands were large and remarkably gentle as she worked, swiftly and efficiently, on Mrs. Baines's mouth, drawing the sundered flesh together with deft practiced fingers. Not once did she hesitate until, the operation completed, she straightened up and spoke with the same satisfaction she might have shown if she had just turned the hem on one of her habits.

"There now." She surveyed her handiwork, contemplating the

neatness of the patch of gauze over the yellow stain, before she turned to put away her instruments. Over her shoulder she said, "You can get down now."

Mrs. Baines felt dazed and her face enormous, her mouth dead in the lingering pain, confused into a shape over which she had no control. Slowly she drew herself up into the darkness made by her eyes, open only to slits.

When the nun said, "You feeling all right," she shook herself to nod her yes. "Sit down there until I have a look at this fellow." Sister Mary Joseph led her to the chair that Neddo vacated.

Mrs. Baines watched Neddo, staring helpless apprehension at her, as the nun drew him over to the couch. Her eyes, strangely void as though she were witnessing a scene that couldn't concern her, followed him with a detached watchful gaze but without recognition and with no trace of comfort or care in their lost blueness, unmoved, except for the gradual return of life, pulsing in a slow hot throb back into her mouth, until Neddo with the first cold douche on his eye screamed: "Mother!" and shocked her from her chair to his side, all bewilderment gone as she moved to console him.

"There, there, son." She spoke with effort, and grasped the hand he reached out to her. Her eyes met Sister Mary Joseph's over his head, the nun's speculative under the shadow of the stiff side falls of her faintly transparent veil.

Without preamble, she said, "Your husband?"

Mrs. Baines felt compelled to answer, quietly and with half a nod. "Yes."

"Why?"

"I don't know why," Mrs. Baines replied. "I never have known."

"But there must be a reason," the nun probed.

"Must there? Well, I've never found it. Neither has anybody else." But maybe the nun could. Mrs. Baines eyed her, and waited.

"I suppose he was drunk." The nun turned away to search along a shelf of brown bottles.

Mrs. Baines looked at her broad impassive back. "He's done it sober," she said.

"It's a curse, the same drink." The voice was matter of fact and went on to Neddo, "Open that eye wide. Of course, a man isn't responsible for his actions in drink. We have to remember that," she said, echoing word for word Father Rex Aurealis. "How many children have you?" she asked unexpectedly. Mrs. Baines told her, and she mused in silence on the number. "How old is this boyo?"

"Nine."

"Is he the youngest?"

Mrs. Baines shook her head. Speech was difficult, but the nun disliked evasion, even when she was ferreting into circumstances that were none of her concern, and before she had replaced Neddo's eyepatch over a thin wet bit of gauze, she knew what she wanted to know.

"I suppose you can't pay for the treatment?" She took the card from Mrs. Baines, and looked briskly from her to Neddo. "No, I didn't think you could. And where did you get that?" She gestured towards the eyepatch.

"I bought it," Mrs. Baines said, looking at her squarely.

Sister Mary Joseph restrained herself, no easy thing for a woman who was used to saying what she thought without having to fear the consequences.

Mrs. Baines cut through the stern look, knowing full well the cause. "I'm sorry I'm not able to give you anything, Sister." Her apology was murmured, and barely intelligible through her bandage of gauze. "That took the last few coppers I had, an' he couldn't go round with an eye like that before people." She looked for some sign of understanding and, finding none, looked away.

Neddo stared at his mother who, masked and strange, stood with her hands twisted together on the front of her worn brown coat. The silver ring that Danny had made for her out of a two-shilling piece was worn to a smooth gleam from work and wear, thin under the hump of a rough white knuckle. Her coat was loose around her shoulders which today were bent in a way that was new. It dragged heavy. Her hat was low, covering all her hair except around the sides near the collar of the coat where it showed white and thick, shielding her eyes and completing the masklike effect of the bandage on her mouth. He had a sudden remembrance of his face pressed into her back last night, and the stuff of her blouse against his mouth as he cowered behind her out of his father's reach, and the great open way she had said: "Ah!" when it was all over, just before she reared her face against him in the twists of her pain. He had not seen her face, but he knew it was stretched long, as if the bones were growing and growing behind the white skin, leaving the eyes in shadows behind the red sounds that came from within her, hiding the middle of her face in an even straight line from her mouth up to the delicate blue of her temples. He was reaching for the memory of her face brushing his and her twist out of his grasp as he stretched out to her and felt her mouth soft and wet beneath his fingers, when the nun spoke.

With impatience at the terrible pride of the poor and worse still their vanity, Sister Mary Joseph said, "Well, perhaps, when you come back to have the stitches removed." Her smile made the implication obvious.

"I'll try, Sister," Mrs. Baines moved towards the door.

"We must forgive those who hurt us." The nun's pious addition arrested them. "You must forgive your husband and ask God to help him overcome his craving for an invention that could only come from the devil. There is a chapel around the corner. Go in now on your way out of here and say a prayer."

Mrs. Baines gazed dumbly at her.

"You do go to Mass?" It was the nuns and priests of Ireland's remedy for every ill.

Mrs. Baines nodded.

The nun seemed relieved. "And the children?"

"They all go."

Satisfied, Sister Mary Joseph opened the door. "Go in now to the chapel like I told you." Her loud command ushered them out. "Come back Saturday week and we will take those stitches out."

"Thank you, sister," Mrs. Baines said, but the nun was already moving away.

Again Mrs. Baines remembered when it was too late that she had let the nun go without genuflecting to her.

During the days that followed, she shrank from the eyes of the Lane, but she couldn't pretend that they were not aware of her bandaged mouth and of Neddo's black eye, nor that because she stayed close to her room, only leaving it to go to her work or to the pipe late at night or very early in the morning, the Lane did not know what was happening. It did. And men as drunk as Pat, but milder, in the houses opposite, threatened to force their way out and over to fight him and were restrained by their families' assurances that their threats would be more effective in the morning. But in the morning their drunken bravado was forgotten.

Neddo went twice in two days to Miss Warr's. The bundle of clothes she gave him the first time fetched only half a crown in the pawn. The second day he came away empty-handed. By the week's end the room had been stripped to the barest essentials, iron beds crisscrossed with laths lashed into place with wire having no value in the pawn, no more than the dresser, rat-gnawed and patched with old lids of biscuit tins. The cinders Neddo gathered in the mornings were sold to anyone who would buy them. On Saturday week, unable to face Sister Mary Joseph empty-handed, she borrowed two shillings from Mrs. Kinsella and paid it back the minute Babby came in from work.

Sunday morning was interrupted by the ponderous knock of the man who went from room to room and door to door collecting coppers for the chapel. Brazen in his demands and bad-tempered today with the paltry few coppers he had received, he knocked a second time before he slyly turned the handle of the door. It swung open upon his breathless ejaculation at the scene within.

The sound froze Pat. He dropped his upraised arm and leaped with a curse back into the bed. In an instant, Babby grabbed her mother by the elbow and with one push was out the door past the Chapel Man and Mrs. Kinsella, who muttered to them to hurry. They were halfway up the Lane before Pat realized what had happened. Neddo and Tucker Tommy in panic gazed from their father, who was shouting at them to close the door, to Mrs. Kinsella, who was making frantic signs to them from the landing to come out. With a gasp Neddo darted forward, dragging his brother after him. Mrs. Kinsella swept them into the room behind her before she drew the door of the Baineses' room to. She shook her head at the Chapel Man and disappeared before he could get his mouth open to ask her for her contribution.

He was knocking on Mrs. Chance's door in the hall when Neddo and Tucker Tommy, carrying two old coats in their arms, crept down the stairs and out the hall past him. At the top of the Lane, Babby and her mother waited for them, forcing onto their faces smiles that did nothing to assuage their anxiety. From the shadows of the Lane into the Street and around the corner onto the Canal, they hastened to Mass. They knew even as Neddo said it that they would have to come back.

The devastation that met them on their return, aweing in its ruin and loss, was not so important as the fact that, at least, he was out. Clutching at that relief, they crept behind Mrs. Baines into the room, stumbling in the darkness over the mattresses flung across the floor or kicked against delph strewn in smithereens. The fire was black in the grate, as was the altar lamp, and the mantelpiece had been swept clean, Mrs. Baines knew as her hand searched along it for a match with which to light the lamp. Babby knocked on Mrs. Kinsella's door for a lighted paper, and in the new sudden flare as the flame touched the broad striped wick, they saw the havoc they had felt.

"Ah, he's the right oul' bastard," Mrs. Kinsella, who had followed Babby in, spoke her mind. "I heard him raging round the place like a lion after youse went and I knew he was up to no good.

But would you believe that anyone in their senses would go and do a thing like this?" Her eyes swept the room. "Oh, sweet dilapidated Jesus! will ya have a look?" Her voice rose as she pointed to the mattress which had been ripped open and the straw dragged out and scattered the length and breadth of the room. "Why, I ask ya? Why?" She turned to Mrs. Baines and was astonished to see a dreamy smile on the woman's face.

Why? It was the question she had asked the priest, the question she nor nobody could answer. It flowed through her always like blood in her veins. And she laughed bitterly within herself at the absurdity of giving it utterance. She shook her head at Mrs. Kinsella, and stood silent, only beginning to comprehend the extent of the destruction. There was not a cup or a saucer left on the dresser nor a picture on the wall. The curtains, hanging in shreds from the window, led a trail to cinders dumped over the contents of the mantelpiece which had been swept onto the hearthstone. The white and orange china dogs that had stood each side of the alarm clock lay powderlike under the flung poker and between them the clock face downwards and still ticking. Babby picked it up and shook the crumbled glass away before she put it back in its place.

"He missed nothing," Mrs. Baines said. Her eyes sorted out from the debris the little box which Danny had made for Kitty to hold her bracelets in, and which now served Tucker Tommy for his pencils. She found foot room and gathered up the pieces, worn smooth by children's hands.

When Tucker Tommy unnecessarily asked, "Is it broke?", she nodded and hesitated before she put the small bundle of sticks under the shelf of the altar.

"I'll wet you a cup of tea," Mrs. Kinsella said.

When she came back with the cups in her hand, Mrs. Baines had begun to make some order out of chaos.

"Mother!" Babby's shriek from the candlelit little room brought them rushing to see a new outrage, to stare from her bewilderment to the mutilated disorder of the thin brown trunk beside which she knelt. "He's cut up every stitch I have." Her voice rose to a near scream as she showed them the remnants of the few clothes she possessed. "Look." She held up the pair of shoes she had just bought through the weekly installments of a club. Pat had slashed them to ribbons with his razor. Hastily she flung them from her and rummaged through the trunk for anything that might have escaped the razor, but nothing had. Hats and dresses had been ripped to streamers by his hands or cleanly cut with his blade. And in a flood of anger Babby began to cry.

"The curse of God on him!" The cry burst passionately from Mrs. Baines, out from the rising throb of her heart, from the pounding pulses under the hand she held up to her bare throat. "The curse of Almighty God on him!" Her voice rose. Her face turned up to the ceiling. "The curse of Almighty God on the mother who bore him!" She screamed with a power that stretched her taut and pulled her up to stand almost upon her toes in a forward surge, emitting fierce screams filled with the echo of animal howls, the remembered recent pains of her mouth and of the minutes, the hours, the days past.

Deaf to the frightened cries of Babby and Mrs. Kinsella, she swayed in an abandon of misery, her screams giving way to pitiful singsong moans, a heartbroken lament as low as the music for a threnody rising from the stirred uppermost layers of black moist earth. Powerless, they clutched her bare arms held stiff to her sides like a frightened child's, until her moans became words and she spoke aloud again. Pat's new and old abuses she catalogued, shaking herself violently free from the hands that held her in a remembrance that she shrieked to the flickering candle in a final blaze of anguish, a last torrent of words. Presently her voice stumbled into a tired dazed silence, and alone unaided she staggered towards Babby's bed.

Babby flung herself on her knees beside her, and stroked her face with long-drawn-out motions beseeching with whispers a return from the depths of despair to which her mother had gone. She was terrified by the deathlike inertia which surrounded Mrs.

Baines and blamed herself bitterly for mentioning the clothes, begging God's and her mother's forgiveness for doing so.

"You couldn't help it, love." Mrs. Kinsella leaned down to her. "Sure you couldn't help it." She touched Babby on the shoulder awkwardly, marveling to herself at the beauty of the white face, the wide slant of the soot-black eyes turned back and up to her, beauty that made her uneasy until her husband, followed by three of her children close to the legs of his trousers, put his head inside the door and, with his worried face on one side under the wispy hair, asked if he could do anything.

Mrs. Baines stirred in Babby's arms, and Mrs. Kinsella said, "Whisht, will ya!"

Mrs. Baines's eyes flew open and she made a move to get up, but Babby still sat with her arms around her and she leaned back upon her elbow seeming to search the dim-lit room until she found her daughter's face.

"I'm all right. I'm all right." She forced a smile.

"What would you say to a cup of tea?" Mr. Kinsella's voice startled them, and in their silence, his wife replied, "Not a word, Phillo," sending him hurrying out until she called him back to take the children with him.

"I better start to tidy up," Mrs. Baines said, sensing her sons' need for reassurance. "An' you can help me."

Neddo, eager to begin, led the way, but Tucker Tommy sidled over to her, solemn, watchful as though he must still be cautious in the sudden transition from the crowded torment to the present that began to move in the slow warm motion of reality. He felt the familiar trace of her fingers move through his hair and instead of pulling away as he always did, he waited with pleasurable patience, guessing without understanding the effort it took for her to face again the ruins of the room. More sensitive even than Babby he was to his mother's needs and moods and sometimes saw in her sighs and distant looks her desire to escape not from the room or to the Canal, or even to the mysterious place she called the Country, from which she had come, but to some place where she might only go alone and without them, but especially without him; and then, as now, her withdrawal terrified him and he coaxed her away from the dreaded journey which would take her from him, by the only way he knew. Urgently he pressed his head against her, turned his face into the band of her skirt at her waist, circled her hips with his arms in a tightened hug that relaxed only when he felt her drag away in a flash of addled impatience. Then she looked down at him, after a breathless second like those before he plucked the top off a scab on his knee; and he saw her remember him. Her sigh of resignation escaped him, passing unrecognized under the burst of peace into which the gentle pressure of her fingers again searching through his hair returned him. The others had begun to tidy the other room.

"We better go so," she spoke the intention suddenly; and like conspirators they looked at each other as she took up the candle in its jar and blew it out. His instant giggle rose to a laugh the way it did when he had won at marbles.

Mr. Kinsella came back with the tea, his wife and Babby had restored the room more or less to a semblance of its usual tidiness, Neddo had managed to stuff most of the straw back into the mattress and the floor had been swept, broken delph mingling with ashes in a heap under the grate. The window gaped cold and black without curtains, and the dresser looked bare. They gulped the hot tea and set the remaining things to right, and at midnight Mrs. Kinsella departed, laughing and embarrassed as she brushed aside their thanks, belittling her help under the pretense that she was in no hurry to stretch herself down beside Phillo. The allusion caused her husband to titter before he ordered her out to her bed, to which she went with a laugh.

In the hush that followed, Mrs. Baines and Babby settled down for the long useless wait for Pat's homecoming. She had put Neddo and Tucker Tommy to bed long before. Now, afraid that Mrs. Kinsella's laugh might have roused them, she crept into the little room. Neither had stirred, except that Neddo in his sleep had stretched out an arm across his brother's shoulders. She saw the gesture for what it was, the sight stirring in her a new wakefulness, a new demand on her strength to protect them both. Her mind shied from their hurt, unwilling in the passion of her love to admit her helplessness. Her prayer was silent as she drew the thin blanket up over Neddo's arm. The white bar of the shift on his thin shoulder seemed to strap him into place and thwarted her efforts to loosen it without waking him. She stared down at his face which was turned into Tucker Tommy's back. Then with soft steps she went out into the lamplight of the other room.

"He's not coming back." Babby spoke into the hour striking from the clock on the steeple of the town hall in Rathmines. And when, long afterwards, it struck another hour and there was still no sound of Pat's steps in the Lane or on the stairs, she got up from where she was sitting over the dying fire and said, "We'll go to bed."

Mrs. Baines stopped in her walk between the table and the door. "It's early," she said. "He might still come." She drew the back of her hand across her eyes.

"Let him." Babby's tiredness showed in the clipped retort, explosive and aired with defiance.

"Yes. Let him." Mrs. Baines spoke parrot-fashion.

Babby turned the wick in the lamp to a glimmer. Without protesting, her mother allowed herself to be led into the little room to Babby's bed. With the help of God, her father wouldn't come back tonight! Babby's wish was fervent as she watched her mother undress. Though she remembered the dance she was to have gone to tonight and the clothes reduced to rags, she shrugged off that oppression and characteristically turned her mind to wonder that Pat had missed her and her mother's coats on the back of the door and the black dress with its white collar and cuffs underneath them that she wore to work. Idly she tried to imagine at what point in the room Pat had started on his bent of destruction. At the same time the sight of her mother with her head out the window—for despite her fatigue and her need of sleep Mrs. Baines had resumed her unbreakable habit of looking out into the night's darkness—

caused a smile to touch Babby's lips. As she drew her mother away from the window, and heard her whispered: "Yes, pet, I'm going," and saw her lower herself onto the bed over the snarled protest of the straw in the mattress, she mused on this strange custom of her mother's. She had never understood it, or what her mother sought from the night. She had never asked. Her question, she thought, would have been in some way an intrusion.

She felt her mother's arm reach out across her, the weight slight and incredibly comforting, and heard her voice murmuring an expression of love into her sleep.

For a long while after, Mrs. Baines's mind raced over a turbulent sea in the crowded dark and came to rest at last, as the heaviness in her lids sank beneath the images of her mind, and she remembered that she would have to find some way to get food for her children tomorrow morning first thing.

TWELVE

MRS. BAINES was drunk, for Aggie Chance had been called again and her mother was giving a party. On the landing outside the Baineses' room, Mrs. Kinsella and Mrs. Slattery were singing and dancing the "Kerry Dancers." They had left the party and come up to coax Mrs. Baines back down, but she was drunk. Not gloriously, but quietly. On hops. The bottle stood empty at her elbow on the table across which Babby and her fella, Nick, sat with their mouths open in laughter, watching her. By the fire Danny stood with Neddo and Tucker Tommy, nursing tumblers in their hands from which they took leisurely sips so as to make their share last longer. Mrs. Baines was still sober enough to know that her children were making a mockery of her and that, to add to the fun, they were deliberately sending her off in the wrong direction in the songs she had begun to sing, by giving her the words to something entirely different every time she faltered. She knew, but laughed and smiled throughout her confusion at them and the women on the landing, and accused Danny of disrespect when he shouted down Neddo's attempts to set her right with a whispered word that she was forever on the point of grasping, only to lose it in the noise of their laughter. She chose those moments when their laughter was loudest and their attention distracted by the others on the landing, to shift her position and ease her body's weight and its fullness and the day-old pains that had taken her from the party going on in the hall below.

It was seven months since Pat Baines had gone away, this time to a job in Wexford. On the day she had received his scribbled note telling her to send his toolbox, came the discovery that she was pregnant. At first she had seriously considered an abortion, and only rejected that remedy because it went against the canons of a church that said you failed in your duty to God by not having as many children as He saw fit to bless you with. It was this that prevented her from taking the first step towards Mrs. Ennis's door over Connell's vegetable shop. But it was her intense aversion to destruction and her inordinate love of life, and children in particular, that turned her irrevocably from the back room, with its unaccountable sulfurous light and smell, to face instead the burden of bringing yet another child into the world of the Lane.

"Mother?"

She shook her head free of the balmy confused state brought on by port followed with hops, and rose unsteadily to her feet. She saw that Mrs. Kinsella and Mrs. Slattery had gone, and moved towards the window into the breath of a soft March that wafted into the room from the Lane.

"Are you all right?" Babby and Danny spoke together.

"It'd be lovely at home this time of year," she said. She looked at Nick. "It's awful, the way I go on. Like an exile." Her eyes traced his heavy beard mark, then clouded as the pains that had begun yesterday forced cries up into her mouth which she bit upon. Turning to Babby, she made quick desperate gestures for her to get the others out of the room.

Shocked into the realization of what was happening, Babby flew to do her bidding, and when they were gone, shouted out the window after Danny to fetch Mrs. Cogan.

The Lane said Mrs. Cogan was a witch. She knew herbs, and could cure ills. She had the Evil Eye, some said; and children peered at her between their fingers. She was a hunchback, and met the demands of births and the laying out of bodies for wakes with gruff nonchalance, and came wearing a hat of scarlet and black cock-feathers and a white apron reserved especially for births or a sack one for deaths. She had had a husband, who had died a year after their marriage, and seven children for nobody knew who, and she gave orders in a barrack-square fashion to Babby to get that fire goin' under that bucket a water, and when, arrested by a drowned moan from her mother, Babby turned back to the bed, she asked her what she thought she was doing.

Babby held out her hands. "Me mother."

The Witch drew tight the reins she was knotting together out of old stockings and tying to the head of the bed. "An' have you never seen her having a baby before?" Her question was directed at Babby, but she was watching Mrs. Baines.

Babby's reply was inaudible.

"Here. Take hold a that." The Witch held out the reins to Mrs. Baines and glanced across at Babby. "Then what is it ails ya?" Her gray eyes focused directly, not on any object seen but on something sensed. Babby twisted away to the fire, and the woman saw her being jerked upright by the beginning screams. She watched her, then turned back to Mrs. Baines. "Ah, now," she cried into the second outburst, "will ya quit? They'll say Martha Cogan's up to her devil's tricks."

Her briskness rasped nerves and sent Babby back to her mother's side, only to be pushed away by the woman's long-fingered hands and an appeal for help instead of hindrance that coaxed her back to reason. Reassured against her will, Babby calmed down, blinding her eyes and ears to the sights and sounds that wrenched her mother apart. "Oh, God," she said.

The dark gypsy face opposite laughed. "It's something," she

said, "the trouble we give getting borned and again on our way out. Though, mind you, there's some who go quietly enough. Like Nan Ockser, who got up from the table after devouring half a pig's cheek and went over to lie on the bed to ease her digestion, and when himself went to give her a cup of tea, there she was, stiff as a man's mitten, and death written all over her."

She began to hum now, in time to the sound of the melodeon coming up from the Chances' and out in the Lane where people were dancing round the door. She heard a girl's voice call, "Danny!", and recognized Queenie Mullen calling Danny Baines. She glanced at Babby, who was watching her mother and not listening. But Mrs. Cogan was, and not only to the sounds coming up from the Lane. As she tore an old pillow slip into strips, she could hear Mrs. Slattery and Mrs. Chance round the pipe that morning, and herself with them. It was Mrs. Chance who had brought up the subject of Mattie Baines and his English wife, and one word borrowing another led to where Alice Slattery was swearing that she'd seen Mrs. Baines letting Annie the Man get away with a loaf. —Funny, wasn't it? And she'd been on the verge of telling her she saw nothing funny about it, but she hadn't, there was something coarsely placid and implacable in the round fat face that towered over her, a childish bewilderment in the sensuous full-moon eyes looking out from the folds of smooth short-haired lids like pampered animals, that stopped her angry retort and made her instead agree. —But why did she? Mrs. Chance had asked. And Alice Slattery had made a pretense of shaking her head, stopping short of the actual effort, and hoping the others would accept the thought for the deed. —To stop Annie from informin' on them an' her. —And a lot better she'll be for it! Mrs. Chance said. Them two don't give her much except trouble. —Do any of them? Her own don't give it to her, Mrs. Slattery said. —Isn't it a terrible-thing to rear ungrateful childer! Mrs. Chance agreed. There's that Kitty in America, an' Teasey in England, an' not a penny piece has passed out of their hands since they left her. —Schenectady, Mrs. Slattery said very distinctly. But Mrs. Chance ignored her. —An' as for

Danny! She bent forward then, Mrs. Cogan remembered, before she said, He'll have to watch his step with Queenie Mullen. The hint, dropped, was savored to the last, and brought Mrs. Chance for once into the limelight as the bearer of actual tidings instead of in her usual role as recipient, and from pleasure she passed into delight. —Nooo! Mrs. Slattery's exclamation was a sough of startled breath. Her eyes devoured Mrs. Chance, who nodded. —He's been in the hall with her for the past few months, an' Aggie saw them on the Canal at Leeson Street Bridge twice in the past week. Mrs. Slattery showed her first doubt. —I've never seen him go from here to there with a girl. —Well, you can't have been looking very hard. The swift retort was, Mrs. Cogan thought, underlined with spite, and she could guess why. Danny's good looks and easy charm irritated many of the women in the Lane, but especially Mrs. Chance, who resented his lack of interest in her daughters, and especially his lack of interest in Aggie who, when she wasn't chapel-an'-convent-haunting, showed herself only too willing where he was concerned to give more than the friendly neighborliness with which he regarded her and which goaded her into spying on him and reporting his comings and goings whenever she could. —I wasn't looking at all. Mrs. Slattery's reply was equally swift. I don't have to, she added meaningfully. Mrs. Chance, aware that she had sounded more snappish than she had intended, said, Well, it's true. —Ah, well, sure there might not be more in it than meets the eye, Mrs. Cogan said, and Mrs. Chance sniffed. —Oh, there's more in this than meets your, or anybody else's, eye! She had closed her mouth tightly on the prophecy, irritated, Mrs. Cogan knew, by a prevailing attitude in the Lane that Danny was incapable of doing something he shouldn't. But was he?

"I wish they'd quit their roaring." Babby's remark brought Mrs. Cogan's mind from where it had strayed.

"What was I saying?"

"You were talking about Nan Ockser," Babby said.

The Witch nodded and laughed. "Yes, an' I was thinking of the caution that inspired Nan to leave an empty chocolate box with

King George's picture on the lid on the mantelpiece, and 'Let Erin Remember' lying open on the piano. Nan's husband," she said after a while, "is in the I.R.A. Like your Uncle Mattie."

Babby turned quickly, with the same tingle of astonishment and fear that she always felt when yet another neighbor revealed knowledge of Mattie and his doings, and as always suspected the hidden threat.

But the Witch was innocently testing the water's temperature and saying, "Speaking of which, I don't know when I saw him last."

Babby, forced to speak, was forced to think. "They were here last week," she said. But not together. They came less often to the Lane now, Mattie and Zena, and never together since that night when Annie the Man had watched them leave. Her mother was still paying for that night—shillings, sixpences borrowed by the way, a pinch of tea and a bit of sugar. And once she had lifted a head of cabbage off Neddo, and her mother had tried to stop her from going over to Annie the Man's room and demanding it back, and, what's more, getting it, for the woman was afraid of her, afraid of her temper.

"It'll soon be over." Mrs. Cogan tushed one thought and spoke another.

Babby looked at her. Some women wouldn't let the Witch inside their door, for fear of "influences," but her mother liked her and said the only influences she was afraid of were those that didn't interest Mrs. Cogan anyway—the Witch was a teetotaler.

"It's awful the way them poor creatures are chased from pillar to post," she said, and Babby knew she was talking about Mattie and Zena. "Ah, but sure they'll soon be able to call their own their own, now that the de Valera one is taking over."

Babby didn't know that he had, but before she could speak, her mother moaned and she had forgotten the I.R.A. and Mattie and Zena.

But the Witch ignored Mrs. Baines's sounds. "At least," she was saying, "whatever we get'll be Irish, and them murdering

Tans'll never be let back. . . . There now, me jewel," she said lightly, when she recognized the note in Mrs. Baines's scream. And in her hands, bearing down on Babby's mother, was all the strength of her body. "Push the hair outa me eyes, daughter," she said to Babby, and went on, "You'd think she was being hanged, drawn and quartered. An' now, wipe me forehead." Babby did so. "An' now, don't look."

And Babby spent shuddering the hours of labor that followed. She moved heavily over the shafts of agony drawn from her mother's side, handled the cloths and pans that Mrs. Cogan demanded in a numb attempt to cut herself off from the sight of her mother's pain, of the face twisted back in a bath of sweat on the pillow. She was staring with dull eyes when the Witch finally spoke.

"Well, whether you deserve it or not, you have a little sister."

Babby turned away from the thing held up to her and went to her mother, hiccuping pain on the sodden bed. She wrung out a cloth in a basin of cold water and wiped the pale forehead and face, bringing the wet rag onto the matted hair. Mrs. Baines, unable to voice her relief at the coolness, opened parched lips in a wordless groan before she sank back into an exhausted sleep.

Together then they changed the bedclothes under her, taking clean sheets from Babby's bed and wrapping the others in a bundle until Babby could wash them. Through the change her mother slept and when she woke again the bed was dry and clean and in it with her at the foot, the new baby, washed and dressed, was screaming loud and hungry. Mrs. Cogan picked it up and put it down beside her.

"That," she said, "wasn't in any hurry to see the light!" She was queerly pleased. "Sound in life an' limb."

Mrs. Baines glanced up at her. "You're very good."

The Witch stood straddled, her head not much higher than Mrs. Baines's on the pillow, her arms bare up to her elbows and crossed. "Musha!" She tossed her head at Babby, who was wetting a pot of tea at the fire. "Herself," she said, "was a great help!"

Mrs. Baines tried to see through the bars at the foot of the bed, but the effort was too much for her and she sank back. "She's great, God bless her!" she murmured. "I'd be lost altogether without her."

"You would, woman. Not a feather did it take out of her."

The Witch watched Babby pour the tea, then with a flurry of her skirts and apron wheeled about to her coat which was flung over a chair. From underneath it she took a freshly baked brown cake and held it up like a charm. "Here now, I was forgetting!"

Babby cut it, buttered the slices and passed them first to Mrs. Cogan, then her mother.

Mrs. Baines shook her head. "But I'd love a drop more tea." Her blanched face was tinged with yellow, and along her upper lip with its new white scar, beads of perspiration simmered on the tightly drawn flesh. Unable to raise her hand and wipe them away, she asked Babby to do so. She showed little curiosity about the new baby sucking with tenacious strength at her breast, losing its hold on the nipple in its haste to satisfy its hunger, causing the milk to splash over its red wrinkled face and burrowing angrily back towards the source with shrilled staccato cries. She made only the feeblest gestures to restrain the Witch when the latter swooped with a wiry strength to take the baby from her. She sipped slowly at the tea from the cup which Babby was holding to her mouth, seeing with dull-eyed unconcern its shiny whiteness cloud into the thick languorous smell of hot spilled blood that hovered in a vaporous swirl around her. Immune in her deadened tightly bound pain, she did not hear the baby's thumped cries nor see Babby's grave concern as she pushed the cup away. An arched anxiety shot away from her lids as they shut in the oblivion that sought her and snapped off the hope that all traces of birth would be gone from the room before Danny and the children came back.

"She's crying somebody out of the place."

Mrs. Baines spoke her superstition into the quiet that fell after

Dilsey's last whimper had died away. She straightened up from where the baby lay in blessed silence on the bed and spoke in hushed tones for fear of waking her again. Unlike any of the other children, Dilsey slept a fitful light sleep and for the past eight months had keened night noon and morning, and as far as Mrs. Baines and the dispensary doctor could make out, for no reason. She was a cranky child even from the first and unlike all the others, who had been placid sleepy children dropping off wherever she happened to put them, contenting themselves all day long with a crust of bread dipped in sugar or a short rounded marrow bone, nothing either contented or amused Dilsey.

Neddo and Tucker Tommy had to be kept from school to mind her the two days a week that Mrs. Baines went out to work at Miss Plum's, and on Saturday afternoons one or the other of them had to stay in while she was at Miss Fogarty's. Her low mournful keen disturbed their nights and drove Babby from her mother's bed back to Neddo's, and Tucker Tommy came out to take her place beside his mother. She was to be the last child of Mrs. Baines who, without knowing the truth in her jest, referred to her as "the shakings of the bag—the gatherings," puny, peevish and unhappy, forced to health and strength by what attention her mother could lavish on her.

Pat was hardly aware of his daughter's existence, having come home only once since she was born and staying only long enough to reap his usual harvest of destruction before he went off to another job. He denied either owning Dilsey or having any knowledge as to who did. He did not know that he was to have more to do with this last child than he had ever had to do with any of his other children, no more than Mrs. Baines knew the truth underlying the dread she voiced in her superstition.

"She's crying somebody out of the place."

Her belief in omens was as strong as her confidence that there was a god in heaven. And when Tucker Tommy came limping in at noon on one foot, it was not unexpected. The teacher had sent a note to the effect that his foot had had to be stitched in the

Meath Hospital and since he was barefoot, no blame could be attached to the school authorities. The postscript at the bottom asked if it wasn't possible to get him a pair of shoes.

It was then that Mrs. Baines decided she must search for more work and spent fruitless hours going from door to door around the big houses of Dartmouth Square and, having exhausted these, to the bigger houses in Fitzwilliam and Merrion Squares, all to no avail, except that at one house the servant she talked to gave her a bowl of dripping and a loaf of bread to take away with her.

"Times is hard for everybody, Missus."

The houses on the squares were being closed up, not one by one, but in sixes and sevens. Times *were* hard. Across the length and breadth of the city men were idle and Dublin, with the withdrawal of the English, was preparing itself for the inelegant ghost it was to become. But this was something Mrs. Baines knew nothing about. Politics was not the province of the poor. She would not have understood if she had been told. All she knew was that nobody could give her anything to do, not even washing, though she asked for it.

The last day of her search was the most discouraging of all, and rather than face the Street and the shops along it she went home by way of the Canal. At the bridge she saw Danny on the other side where he worked at the sandbank, shoveling sand onto the strainer that separated the pebbles. She didn't call out as was her custom, unwilling to draw his attention to what she felt must be her discernible oppression. After looking on his strong rising, bending body against the sweep of sky behind it, she walked away. The sight of him gave her pleasure, lasting over the hump of memory that caught her up by reminding her that his face was pockmarked now under its tan as a result of the skin disease he had picked up while sleeping anywhere he could the last time Pat was home. The dispensary doctor had pronounced it incurable, and in the skin hospital on New Street they had shaken their heads and plastered him with ineffectual ointments. Distressed at his discomfort and by half-heard taunts of "Scabby-Face," she reproached herself and determined to cure what they called incurable. She set about doing so with a tenacity that the Lane either marveled or scoffed at, until the scabs vanished under her ministrations of cold tea and the pets of bread soaked in grass and nettle juice, and all that was left to show the sores had ever existed were miniature craters scarring like pinpricks the lower halves of his lean cheeks. Her great fear had been that the plague of sores would attack his eyes, because for some reason inexplicable, sore eyes in the Lane remained sore, despite her concoctions and the Witch's and Sunday trips for the relic at Mt. Argus. Thank God, his eyes were left wide and black in their milky surrounds, behind the thick lashes that she could see now as she made her way home under the vast nakedness of the winter trees.

When she got home Dilsey was crying and Tucker Tommy was swinging her back and forth as he hobbled round the room on his one good foot. She stopped crying when her mother fed her, and for a while slept; but on the whole her petulant whinge continued through tea and the early evening, until it now seemed as though they would have to discover some relief for the maddening consistency of her secret misery.

"Put her into Babby's bed." Neddo, who showed only a mild tolerance towards what he and Tucker Tommy still called "the new baby," tried to be helpful.

"Jesus, Mary and Joseph! I'll down youse if you go near her." Their mother's whispered threat was fiercely uttered, angrily emphasized by the way in which she swept aside the clothes hanging on the line before the fire. "Get ready for bed," she said to Neddo, who sidled between the bed and the chair in the corner towards Tucker Tommy, who was cutting a notch in the top of a stick. "An' you too," she said to the latter, as she raised the wick in the lamp that had been lowered to darken the room while she got Dilsey to sleep.

Tucker Tommy grimaced at Neddo, and both pretended not to have heard as they watched her move quietly around the room tidying and straightening things before Babby and Danny came in.

They sat close together and occasionally raised their heads to look at her when they thought she wasn't watching. Then gradually growing bolder, they began to speak. Mrs. Baines listened to their quiet confidences, with a glance now and then over to the bed when one of them raised his voice too loud or when a muffled giggle found an answer in herself and she forgot her tiredness and her fear of waking the baby as she smiled with them. She finished the washing and left the clothes rolled up in the empty basin to be hung in front of the fire just before she went to bed. When she took up the sink bucket, Neddo jumped to his feet.

"I'll get it."

She gave in easily, but from habit warned him not to delay, and showed no surprise when he came back with the bucket full and without her having had to go to the window to call him.

"Who's in the hall?" she asked, as the door closed on the sound of a man's cough.

"Nan Chance and her fellow," Neddo whispered, as though they might hear him in the darkness below.

Mrs. Baines wondered how the girls could stand the cold damp of the hall hour after hour and night after night and still not get their deaths from colds and pneumonia. The room's warmth and the fire, glowing red enough to roast an ox, suddenly pleased her. Babby and Danny would soon be in wanting a bit to eat before they went to their beds.

"I wonder if she'd move?" Her eyes were on the clock, but Neddo and Tucker Tommy knew what she was referring to.

"She's fast." Neddo was eager to get rid of the necessity for silence and afraid that his mother might change her mind.

"Look. She's fast." Tucker Tommy joined in.

Convinced, Mrs. Baines swiftly picked up the child, her hands gentle and sure. Only her face showed her anxiety lest by a clumsy movement she should start Dilsey crying again, but apart from a brief whimper which died almost as it began the baby slept through the change of beds. The relief from her uneasy presence appeared on all their faces, Neddo and Tucker Tommy grinning broadly with expectations of staying up late and Mrs. Baines softening into wonder at the peace and contentment with which she could face the night, its surface ruffled by nothing more urgent than what she could make out of scraps and crumbs to surprise them for their supper.

When Pat was out of the house and Dilsey soundly asleep in the little room, the hour before bed was often these days filled with talk and laughter. Lately Babby had taken to bringing Nick in with her, his welcomed presence giving a festive air to the pot of tea and the fish and chips he and Babby might bring in or to whatever Mrs. Baines could manage to put on the table before them. Tonight she would make a brown bread, and as she took the flour from the press she sent Neddo out to the dairy with the jug for a penn'ort of milk. The cake was hardly off the fire and the cups on the table when Babby, out of breath and flushed as though she had been running against a breeze, came in the door with Nick behind her. He hesitated for a moment as though to give Mrs. Baines time to adjust herself and the room, before he bent his head and followed her.

"Nick's with me." Babby sought permission.

And her mother gave it smiling, "Haven't I eyes in me head?" And ears, she had almost added, because she had heard him on the stairs. She had been hoping Nick would come in tonight and at the back of her mind now was wondering if she could, before the night was out, bring Babby to some decision about their future; because being Babby's fella, year in and year out, was not the future Nick had dreamt about. Nick Ryan was ambitious. He was the youngest son in a family of seven and had apprenticed himself to a building contractor when he was twelve. The man had taught Nick all he could, and he had learnt the rest himself. He was an electrician and wanted only to put a ring on Babby's finger to get to England to do there what he couldn't here. There was a future for a man in England, Nick said. And there was a future for Babby with him, Mrs. Baines believed, and she wanted her to take her chance with Nick now, while she was young, while they were both young.

Nick came in smiling, holding out to her a white paper bag of fish and chips dripping vinegar, which she placed on the hob to keep warm until she had wet the tea. There was no shyness in the exchange or show of strangeness as Mrs. Baines and her daughter's fellow surveyed each other. Nick was taller than Babby and on a level with Mrs. Baines, but in the low-ceilinged room he appeared to dwarf her, and had developed a trick of inclining his head forward so that she had to raise her eyes to meet his. He was not handsome by the Lane's standards, which liked men dark and rough and to walk with a swagger. He was light-skinned, with soft brown eyes behind thick lashes that compared oddly with the sparsity of his hair, receding as it did far in on his temples. His face was thin and his nose definite but well-shaped over a mouth widely good-humored and curved into kindness. His manner was gentle except when he sometimes lost his temper at Babby's refusal to marry him. Then while the argument lasted, his words and temper blazed. He danced, not because he wanted to but because she did; and because he loved her, he could not understand her persistent refusals to say yes. The fact that Mrs. Baines was on his side encouraged him to believe that he would eventually wear down Babby's resistance.

"Sit over, Nick." Mrs. Baines drew the chairs to the table, and at that moment Danny came in. "You're just in time," she said, doling out the fish and chips while Babby poured the tea. "You can cut the bread," she said, handing him the knife.

"An' where was our wandering boy tonight?" Babby's smile was slightly mocking.

"He's far from home every night, if you ask me," Mrs. Baines intervened. She had not yet got used to Danny rushing out almost before he finished his tea these evenings, nor did she approve the secrecy with which he went, never telling her where he was going or with whom.

He grinned at Babby. "Wouldn't you like to know?"

"How do you know I don't?"

"Do you?"

"Oh, I know all right. But what class of a girl is she when you can't be seen around the Lane with her?"

"How do you know it's a girl?"

Babby laughed. "Because I do. Though what she sees in you beats me."

Danny passed Nick the plate of brown bread and bowed. "I can return the compliment," he said, then abruptly changed the subject. "Where were youse?"

"Willmore's," Nick said.

"Why don't you come with us next Saturday?" Babby suggested, sorry because she felt her joking had distressed him. "It's a carnival dance."

"Now you know I can't put a foot under me!" Danny dismissed the idea with a gesture that made Nick think the resemblance between Babby and her brother was strongest at night.

"You wouldn't be the only one," Babby answered. "Besides, between now and then, Nick and I could give you a few lessons."

Danny laughed. "Can't you just see me?"

"Why not?" Nick asked. "If I can, you can."

Neddo in all seriousness joined in. "You can take me mother."

"An' we could mind the new baby," Tucker Tommy added, anxious to overcome obstacles before they were put in his way.

"That's all I'm short of," Mrs. Baines laughed. "A night amongst the girls an' their fellas in Willmore's."

"Older women than you go." Babby's voice was doubtful.

Danny winked at Nick. "That's right," he nodded solemnly. "Take me mother."

Afraid that the suggestion was getting beyond control, Mrs. Baines threw up her hands. "Ah, now!" Her alarm was real: once a thing like this started there was no knowing where it would stop. She remembered the excursion to Skerries Nick and Babby had taken her on one Sunday in August, and the dance hall they had taken her into that evening, and how Babby and Esther

Fitz had forced her onto the floor for a waltz with Nick. She had to admit the waltz was lovely, and Nick a beautiful dancer, and while it lasted she had enjoyed herself, but when they coaxed her out again for the Lancers—she said afterwards she'd gone too far. At least, she pretended she had to Babby and Nick, who weren't convinced.

"You loved it at Skerries," Babby said, cutting into her thoughts, as she often did, with uncanny accuracy. "And you would again."

"No," Mrs. Baines said, but the idea had taken hold. "Why not?" Babby said excitedly. "You needn't dance this time if you don't want to. You could just sit and watch." She looked to Danny and Nick for confirmation, but Nick had his ear to another sound.

"I thought I heard somebody call you." He looked at Mrs. Baines.

She jumped up, as at a danger averted, and listened until the call was repeated, then went and flung open the door. Babby glanced at Danny, as their mother went out into the darkness of the landing.

"Oh, it's you, Queenie." They heard her exclamation and her mild complaint that the call had put the heart across her, not knowing who it was or what at this hour of the night.

"She'd like to go," Tucker Tommy said, thinking of his mother and the dancing. But the others had forgotten, and sat silent until Neddo shut the door after his mother.

Mrs. Baines had no time to wonder what Queenie Mullen wanted from her, but the sight of her standing hatless with her coat dragged loosely around her in the shadows of the hall door filled her with foreboding and made her sound cold, harsh without knowing that she did so.

"Yes, Queenie, what is it?" She stepped out into the light of the gas lamp at the corner, but Queenie drew back into the door as though afraid to be seen by anyone from the windows.

"I hope you don't mind me calling, Mrs. Baines. I didn't want to go up in front of Babby an' her fella." Her breath jerked from her in convulsive starts like the nervous rears of an animal under a fondling hand. Her face, slashed by shadows and the green glow of the gas lamp, was taut and her eyes, which had held her only appeal until Mrs. Baines spoke, leaped into a flash of arrogance.

"Musha, not at all, child!" Catapulted into a new dread, Mrs. Baines spoke kindly, her eyes devouring the darkness for a complete sight of the face before her. Instinctively she was aware of a change in the girl since she had last seen her, but she could not define it nor guess its cause. She reached to draw Queenie out into the light again, but Queenie shrank back into the folds of sounds coming from the Slatterys' room, cleaving her mind through the torment of the things she must say. But, O Jesus! if they'd only stop screaming and fighting just for one lousy minute: the thought pressed Queenie up against the end of the bannister. Its square stab sank familiarly into the small of her back. Against her face, the darkness was crowded and suffocating.

"I'm in trouble." She pushed herself away to stand at the edge of the open door. "I'm going to have a baby," she said out into the diffused light of the Lane.

Mrs. Baines stood behind her, watching her. "For Danny," she said, quietly, without moving.

As though she had not spoken, Queenie said, "For Danny. Me and Danny." Her head snapped round. "How'd ya know?"

How could she answer that one? Mrs. Baines thought.. "You're sure?"

"What do you think I am?" Queenie's voice rose hysterically. "What are ya tryin' to make a me? I've never been with anybody else."

"Christ! child, I never said you had." She took Queenie's hands. "All I meant was are you sure you're carrying?"

"Nothing surer." After the wry mockery, her next words could scarcely be heard. "What am I going to do? Me ma will kill me."

"Whisht!" Mrs. Baines pressed herself against the wall. Tom Flanagan passed them on his way to the pipe, but without turning his head.

"Where'll I go?" Queenie began to cry, the sounds muffled against the hand she raised to her mouth.

"Where indeed?" Mrs. Baines looked past the girl's head, across to the houses opposite. "Do they know?"

Queenie shook her head, and Mrs. Baines wondered how she had hidden her state from them and the three sisters she slept with.

"I'm not showing," Queenie answered her thoughts. "But it won't be long before they know. The oul' wan I work for sacked me today. She caught me being sick when I was doing out one of the rooms and said I was in the family way. I swore I wasn't and she wanted to send for Father Rex Aurealis and asked me if I'd be willing to swear the same thing to him. But I couldn't. She threw me out without a penny an' told me I needn't ask her for a reference because she won't give me one." The tide of words stopped suddenly, then: "She screamed out the door after me when I was going, an' said I was a whore, an' even when I was down the steps an' in the street she still screamed after me."

"I suppose Danny knows?"

Queenie's "Yes" was slow, almost an "Of course."

Tom Flanagan passed slowly back from the pipe, spilling water as he did so, but neither noticed.

"How near are you?" Mrs. Baines asked through the confusion of thoughts scurrying across her mind.

Queenie hesitated. "I'm not certain. About two, three months."

"In that case you must be married at once."

Queenie was startled. "Married!" She sounded incredulous. "How? On what?"

Mrs. Baines shook her head. "That's up to Danny." Her voice had lost its softness. "You don't mean to tell me he doesn't want to marry you?"

Queenie sighed into a sag against the door. "He asked me, but I don't want him just because he feels he has to. That way no fella's worth having."

Because Mrs. Baines agreed, she didn't contradict. But Danny would be different. He was quiet and gentle and had never given her a back-answer in his life, nor had she ever seen him raise a hand to a soul, only after a lot of provocation. He would be good to his wife: this she believed, and if she hadn't, she wouldn't have wished him on the worst woman going.

"But what'll you do if you don't marry him?" she asked. "An' what about the priest? Because don't you know that oul' wan will do as she threatened; they can't resist it." When Queenie didn't answer, she went on. "I couldn't let you lie up in my place, child. Not only would your mother have me life, but Father Tithe wouldn't let me give you a drink of water. He'd say I was encouraging you and leading you into sin, the way he did when Mrs. Slattery tried to help Nancy O'Byrne." She touched Queenie gently. "Besides, pet, if not for your own sake, then the child's, you have to get married."

Queenie looked up coldly. "I want to get rid of it! I don't want to be saddled with a baby."

Mrs. Baines stared at the calm despair in the face turned up to her. It was an old face, with lines wide and deep drawn from each side of the nose to the mouth, the eyes not visible, only the narrow brows which met like a brand on the twin rises of the forehead.

"I went to see Mrs. Ennis." Her matter-of-fact tone contrasted with the static darkened gap of her mouth, immobile even while she spoke. "But she won't do anything. I'm too far gone, she says." Then suddenly she gasped out in an uneven incoherent plea what she had come to Mrs. Baines for. "But she gave me the address of a nurse in Wexford Street who'll do it. For five quid down and another five when it's over." She clutched, desperate, and pulled the woman to her until her hot breath washed over Mrs. Baines's face. "Ten quid th' oul' bitch wants, an' I haven't a farthing, I haven't a penny."

Roughly Mrs. Baines disentangled herself. "Stop it! Stop that now an' talk sense! D'ya hear me?"

"I haven't the money." Queenie bent to half her size, a trick

Annie the Man had. "I haven't the money." Her voice dropped to a whinge, pinched out of her between a streel of incoherencies that stopped abruptly. "I've got to get rid of it," she cried. "I've got to." She clutched at Mrs. Baines.

"Dear Jesus, will you stop it!" Mrs. Baines tore herself free again, and sent Queenie staggering against the hall door which slammed against the door behind it. They heard Alexander Chance shout a complaint, accompanied by a bang as if he had flung something, and Mrs. Baines held her breath, lest somone come out in search of the disturbance. No one came.

Queenie dragged herself upright. "I'm sorry. I didn't mean to . . ." And with a young dignity, she asked, "D'you think you could get me a lend from one of the Jew men? I'd pay you back, Mrs. Baines."

And she would, Mrs. Baines knew; but she shook her head. "Child, I couldn't get you that kind of money if my life depended on it."

She looked away from Queenie, then out in the Lane, feeling sickened and cold and gray. She remembered that she herself had considered abortion; wasn't there every reason then why Queenie should?

"Could you try, Mrs. Baines, could you?" Queenie plucked at the sleeve of her blouse.

"No, Queenie, I couldn't, an' even if I could . . ."

Queenie dropped her hands into the fog which had had its beginning earlier in the night on the Canal, and now rolled down the Lane in clouds, while through it the lights in the windows were dimmed like the dull hearts of what had been roaring fires.

"You'll have to marry Danny." She drew Queenie down onto the bottom stair.

"I can't."

The whisper hardly reached her. "You can an' will. You'll go over to Father Rex Aurealis first thing in the morning an' tell him he's got to marry you." She felt the girl's withdrawal, but held on tightly to the hands between her own and gradually felt them relax.

"I don't want to force him an' that's what I'd be doing."

"Be sensible, child. It's right the man that fathered your child should marry you. If a marriage is anything, it's that," she said, puzzling Queenie. "Besides, what other decent man is going to look you straight in the eye if he knows you've had a child by somebody else? Do you think for one minute they're going to line up wanting to marry a girl like that? You'll be another Nancy O'Byrne, any man's fancy, an' the leavin's of all. If Father Rex Aurealis doesn't put you away in a home first." She went on tiredly, "I'm older than you, child, and know what I'm talking about. Let you be guided by me."

"But what would we do an' where would we go?" Queenie searched the darkness for Mrs. Baines's face. "An' how would you manage without Danny?"

Aye, it was put into words before she allowed herself to think it! "Don't fret yourself," Mrs. Baines shook her head. "Danny isn't keeping the teeth in my head. I'd manage, pet, as I've always managed. And as for where you'll go? Once you're married, you can come in with me till you get a place of your own."

Queenie leaned her weight against Mrs. Baines. "What'll I tell me ma?"

"The truth. What else?"

"Nothing." Queenie sat up. "I didn't think you'd take it like this. I thought . . . You're very good, Mrs. Baines."

Mrs. Baines sighed. "Whisht, child." She shivered suddenly. "Somebody's just gone over me grave," she said and reached forward up onto her feet again. "You'll go over to the chapel in the morning, like a good girl?"

Queenie pulled her coat close round her. "Yes, ma'am," she nodded, docile, ready now to be ordered and to do as she was told. "Will you tell Danny?" Her request was whispered as a breath in the dark of the hall.

"Aye." Mrs. Baines surveyed the girl now, standing where the light could touch her. "I'll tell him."

Queenie showed the trace of a smile, but there was no comfort in it, only a waiting watchfulness as though she were expecting to hear something she hadn't yet heard. But Mrs. Baines had nothing more to say, at least not to Queenie.

"I'll see him at the corner on his way to work." Queenie reached out a timid hand, roughened and hard, the calloused palm resting light and like sandpaper on Mrs. Baines's forearm. "I better go," she said.

And when she removed her hand, Mrs. Baines ran her own over the spot where Queenie's had rested.

"Good night," she said, and darted untidily across the yard to her own hall door.

Mrs. Baines stood where Queenie had left her. Her eyes roved the desolation of the squat crowded houses that at night sagged like breasts from which too many mouths have sucked. Her tongue sought the gaps where her teeth had once been and moseyed over the ones that remained like tombs standing on uneasy earth, loose and moving under the pressure of her tongue until it came to rest at last in the mouth left open to the night as she looked from the houses surrounding her to the high wall of the railway and above it to where she knew the sky must be. Denied the sight of the sky because of the fog that sealed the Lane, her eyes fell back on the gapes on the halls and windows, and on the man who was approaching her with silent footfalls. She watched him without any alarm, too wearied under the fresh burden laid on her by Queenie and Danny to care one way or the other who he was or what. She watched him touch the brim of his soft hat and drew back only when he thrust his face too close to hers, as though he wanted to make sure that her face was unknown to him.

"That's a bad night," he said.

"It is."

"The I.R.A. threw a bomb into a lorry-load of Free Staters in O'Connell Street tonight and killed every one of them. You live here?" His voice was low and thin as he nodded towards the darkness behind her.

She nodded but said nothing, thinking of Mattie and Zena, as he stepped past her into the darkness, finding his way up and down the stairs like a bat, then emerging beside her again with an apology for troubling her.

"It's no trouble," Mrs. Baines told him.

"I wonder if you could help me?" he asked.

With the Lane's mistrust and dislike of strangers, she looked him up and down before answering. And unconsciously, her eye flickered in the direction of Annie the Man's darkened window. "That depends on what it is you're wanting?"

Offhandedly, but without taking his eyes from her, he said, "I was looking for Nancy O'Byrne."

"What do you mean, you was?"

She hadn't meant to be funny, but the man grinned. "I am." His tone, more than the name, alerted her to a danger threatening, putting her on her guard against what as yet she could only surmise.

"You mean Cocky's daughter?" She was in control again, her voice matter-of-fact.

He nodded. "That's what they call her." It was hearty and false, his joviality.

"Well, you've come to the wrong house," Mrs. Baines pointed behind him. "She lives over there."

"Aye, I know," he said softly. "But she's not there now."

"Isn't she?" Mrs. Baines was all surprise.

"You know she isn't," he replied sharply.

She glared at him. "It isn't my business to know, or not to know!"

"Don't rise yourself, ma'am," he said placatingly. "I only asked a civil question."

"Well, you may not know it, but you got a civil answer."

"That I didn't, but we won't fall out." He grinned. "An' you can't help me at all at all?"

She delayed her answer, and then disguised it in a question. "What do you want with her?" she asked.

"We want to see her, ma'am, that's all."

"You an' the priest." She thought he might deny this, and

when he didn't she went on, "You're from one of them homes, aren't you?"

Her manner was now answer enough for him. "You're a great help, I must say," he said sarcastically and turned abruptly away.

"I never intended to be," she said after him, and remembering Mrs. Kinsella's usual parting shot, she called, "And tell that to your mother and your friends in America!"

She watched him disappear into the dark of Cocky's hall, and come out again and go into Queenie's. His soundless steps supported a bulk that glided noiseless, sinister, as he went from hall to hall in his search for the girl. She looked up at Cocky's window which was open and dark. Behind her Babby came out onto the landing and called her, claiming her from sadness and anger. "I'm coming, child." She turned back into the hall and began the slow ascent of the stairs. She met Nick at the door and, after bidding him goodnight, told Danny to see him down to the hall.

"Mother, what kept you?" Babby asked, as she closed the door behind them.

Mrs. Baines looked to see that Neddo and Tucker Tommy were in bed asleep, then walked over to her chair and drew it as close as she could to the fire. "I was getting a breath of air."

"There's a cup of tea, will I pour it for you?" Babby held the teapot in her hand, and her mother nodded. As she poured, "What did Queenie Mullen want?" she asked.

After a long sip, Mrs. Baines said, "She's going to have a baby for Danny," and raised the cup to her lips again.

"Queenie Mullen!"

Her mother looked past her to Danny, who had come in quietly behind her.

"You're codding." Babby looked from one to the other.

"I wish to God I was!" Mrs. Baines put her cup onto the hob, and Danny sat down where he could see her sideways.

"Is it true?" Babby swung round to confront him.

He spoke across to his mother. "I was going to tell you."

"Sweet Jesus!" Babby said. "As if we didn't have enough to put up with!"

"Shut up!" Danny jumped to his feet but spoke quietly, moving to place himself between his sister and his mother. "Why don't you mind your own business?" he said, as Babby pushed herself in front of him.

"That'll do." Mrs. Baines ended the threatened flair between them just as she had done all their lives when they seemed on the very brink of a row. "You sit down, the pair of you."

Neither of them moved.

"Do what you're told."

Babby, exasperated at the command, sat down, her face set in suppressed anger, bound to erupt before long.

"An' you, too."

Without a murmur, Danny did as he was bid. "I was going to tell you." He spoke before she could.

"Why didn't you?" She drew her hand across her face. "Did you think it wouldn't be necessary? Did you know Queenie was down to oul' Ennis an' out tonight looking for money for that nurse in Wexford Street?" She leaned forward. "Did you know?"

Danny sprang to his feet; the shock of his weight upon the floor shook the room to a trembling silence. He stared his unbelief. "No, I didn't. How would I?" His eyes snapped on his words.

"Don't you dare shout at my mother!" Babby, white-lipped, sprang up again.

"Well, she was." Mrs. Baines's glance met her son's over Babby's head. "And it was your business to know." She sat down suddenly, slumped in misery and disappointment, her eyes fixed in a sightless stare at a broad smut that clung to a bar on the grate, fluttering in the draft sweeping down the chimney.

"I wanted to tell you about myself and Queenie. But I didn't want to worry you about it."

"You might have had the girl's death on your hands." Mrs. Baines uttered the weight that had lain on her since Queenie's first mention of Mrs. Ennis. "You'll have to marry Queenie, as quick as you can."

"She doesn't want to get married." Danny shifted on his feet awkwardly.

"She does now." His mother proceeded to tell him what had passed between herself and Queenie, omitting nothing.

When she had finished, he asked, "Why didn't she tell me?"

"It doesn't matter. All that does is that you should know, and you do now." Mrs. Baines looked away and Danny sat down close to her.

"We'll go to England," he said.

"You won't have to," Mrs. Baines said quickly. "You can stay here till you get a place of your own."

Danny shook his head. "What happens when he comes home?" The question was final and decisive and gave shape to the dread they lived with. "We'll go to England the minute we're married."

"There's nothing here, Mother," Babby said softly. "Sure they'd be better off in England where there's work and the chance of a living."

Mrs. Baines tore her glance from Babby, made gentle by her brother's question. She didn't want Danny to go to England, to disappear into the vastness of a country that in her ignorance she imagined to be at the other end of the world, to go where she would never see him again, as Teasey had, and Kitty. Babby stretched out a hand to her, but she moved out of its reach.

"Stay here as I said, an' maybe he . . . maybe something will turn up." But it was the unspoken fear that would not be resolved.

Danny stared at his mother as she stooped forward from her chair and began to poke at the fire, as though in its dying glow she might yet find an answer to this new trouble just arisen. Something in the stoop of her shoulders and in the white face bent beneath the weight of white hair caught Danny's attention, forced his own problems not out of mind but to one side, and impulsively he rose and went to her. She rested the poker against the hob and stayed stooping for a moment.

"Mother."

She turned her face up to him. "Yes, son, I know," she said, forestalling any attempt he might make to explain why it was necessary for him to take Queenie not only from the Lane but

from the country. "If only there was something we could do."
And because she admitted the fact that there was not, she felt
old suddenly, older than she had ever felt, and utterly useless.

"It's the only way," Danny said.

Her mind spanned the years, to hear again Teasey and Kitty
as in a chorus saying the same words exactly when they went from
her. She shook the sound of their voices from her head, their
images from her sight, her mind lingering on what she knew to be
Danny's farewell to her, before she hurried to say all that she felt
should be said in her desire to detain and keep him near her a
little longer.

"You couldn't take that girl away in her present state. God only
knows what you might be landed into in a strange country with
not a soul to hand either of you a glass of water if youse were
dying. Couldn't you wait until the baby is born?"

"We have to go now, Mother," Danny said. "Queenie's mother
won't let her cross the door once she knows, and we can't come
in here."

"You can," Mrs. Baines answered desperately. She looked from
Danny to Babby, reading their thoughts. "We'd manage."

Danny shook his head. "No, Mother."

She recognized the determination in his face, as he got to his
feet. "I'll get the baby." Silence was a pressure and she went into
the little room where Neddo and Tucker Tommy were asleep. Her
heart was cold, and in the dark her voice was coarse: "Not yet,
Lord! Not yet!," as she took Dilsey off Babby's bed to bring her
out to her own.

As she was fixing the covers round her, their voices sucked at
her.

"He's right," Babby said. "It's better for them to go now."

Danny had stopped his pacing and stood tall and powerful before her, wanting her sanction for the decision he had made contrary to her wishes. She gazed at him across the table littered with
the remains of the supper.

"Go so." She sounded proud, dignified, even formal. "Go with the help of God and His Blessed Mother." But she looked gaunt, gray. "You better go to bed," she said.

Carefully she began to hang the clothes she had washed earlier in the evening over the line. Danny watched her, anxious for feelings he could only guess at, and when behind her mother's back Babby signed for him to go, he said, "Good night, Mother," and went through the curtain to the little room.

Babby waited with her mother until there was nothing left to tidy for the morning, and as she said good night, Dilsey began to cry.

"I'll take her," Mrs. Baines said, as Babby bent to pick the baby up. She took the child in her arms, rocking it gently, and the cries subsided to the familiar pettish whinge. "Get you to bed," Mrs. Baines said, but Babby stood for a moment looking solemnly from the baby's face to her mother's. Long after she had got into bed, she could hear slow steps pacing the other room and the mingled sounds of the mother and the child.

THIRTEEN

DANNY and Queenie were married after seven o'clock Mass on Thursday morning in Haddington Street Chapel: two days after Queenie's talk with Mrs. Baines and one day after the scene with her mother who, after the girl's first words, forbid her ever to set foot inside her door again. She refused to allow Mrs. Baines to take her in either, and so Queenie came to the chapel and her wedding from the Regina Coeli Hostel where she had lived for a day and a night cursed by her mother and admonished by the priest. The service was short and hurried and witnessed only by Babby and Nick and a handful of early workers who showed no interest or surprise at the sight of the couple standing not before the main altar but a smaller one to the side of it.

The marriage over, Danny and Queenie went off to sit and wait for the night and the boat to Liverpool up in Mrs. Cogan's room in Rock Street, while Babby and Nick, after taking leave of them outside the chapel, hurried off to their jobs. Mrs. Baines had wanted to prepare some sort of a wedding breakfast for them, but Queenie was afraid of the consequences her mother had threatened if she so much as showed her face around the Lane again, so the few shillings she had pawned for or borrowed, Mrs. Baines gave to Danny to put towards their fare. The rest he had borrowed himself. It was the way of a lot of marriages in the Lane and the Street, and caused only a mild ripple of excited gossip that died in the larger events that cropped up from day to day, and was remembered only by Mrs. Baines, whose last glimpse of her son was caught through Babby's description of him as he stood with Queenie in the chapel and outside saying good-by. And in time, Danny was remembered by her only in silence and at night when she looked up to the stars and the sky, and only out loud when one of the children going through the contents of the tin trunk came across a snap of him.

He wrote two letters, the first telling her his son had been born, the second with an address and a pound note and his apologies that it wasn't more. Then, like Kitty and Teasey before him, a silence followed, for a long time unbroken. Her letters to him, as to her daughters, were returned unclaimed and unopened. She went out of her way to establish relations with Mrs. Mullen in the hope that through her she might hear something of him, but Queenie's mother knew even less about Queenie's whereabouts than Mrs. Baines did, and refused to discuss her at all except abusively and, when drunk, to cry aloud Queenie's shame to the Lane.

The Lane's titter was worn thin by the following spring and the spectacle of Cocky O'Byrne's great body being dragged from out of the locks of the Canal on a Sunday morning. It was typical of Cocky that she should be discovered, floating with her face down in the water and only her hand above it at the hour of the day when half the Lane and the Street were on their way to the last Mass of the day, the Drunkards' Mass, at twelve. "Shameless of her!" some said—not to have chosen another day, even another way, but no mention was made of the hour. For a long time after-wards, Cocky's desecration of the Sabbath was the marrowbone of contention around the pipe and the corner of the Lane. They for-got the diversion her death had offered them, the wild specula-tions over the marks, visible and clear, on her face when they laid her out, and the rumors that followed her daughter from hall to hall as she fled from the reach of Father Rex Aurealis and his agents. They stood outside of it all to watch Fawan Barton and Mrs. Baines do what neither love nor charity could bring them to do: bury the woman.

It was Fawan, the Witch's niece, quiet gentle deaf Fawan, the mother of four sons fathered by her own father, who came running to Mrs. Baines to tell her about Cocky and ask her help in getting Cocky the Christian burial which the Church was denying her and, despite Mrs. Baines's quiet pleas to Father Rex Aurealis, did deny her, so that Cocky's end was as secretive as her daughter's, and no more honest.

Up at the Union, where they eventually secured a grave, neither Mrs. Baines nor Fawan was allowed beyond the gate to see the body, nor Mr. Pughe who, made more timid by grief, stood in the shadow of the two women as a novice might in a wide important assembly of Reverend Mothers. Turned away from the gates, they made their way to the chapel where just six months before, Danny and Queenie had been married, where what was Caesar's was rendered to Caesar and Father Tithe was Caesar, and where they lit three candles for the soul of the woman none of them could have known and only vaguely guessed at.

Cocky was dead and in her pauper's grave a month before her daughter Nancy showed up in the Lane. During that time Cocky's rooms had been stripped—down to the paper on the walls—by her neighbors, who showed no shame when they came across each other burrowing like mice among her pathetic possessions, not even good enough for the pawn but all that remained of what had once been the envy of the incautious, the lazy. They met each other now on the stairs or coming out of the room under cover of darkness or at an hour in the morning considered too early for anyone else to be about, taking with them whatever they could, proud and boastful like cats with rats clenched between their teeth and begrudging each other the size or the usefulness of some article that in their hurried greed they had overlooked and now marked out of the corners of sly eyes so as to fling it into some arrogant face at the next row. It was as though locusts had passed through the room the morning Nancy came back to it, exhausted and looking for a refuge for herself and, in her arms, the one baby she hadn't lost to Mrs. Ennis, for some place where she could hide. But there was no such place.

Mrs. Baines, who saw Nancy disappear into the hall, knew this, and sent Tucker Tommy in after her to tell her to come over to her room.

Nancy O'Byrne was barely sixteen when she had the abortion that drew Father Tithe's attention to her and only eighteen when the baby was born that she now carried in her arms. She had been singled out of the many, in that district where neither incest nor rape caused any but a passing commotion, and where hardly a family could in honesty say that all the daughters had been entitled to go to the altar in virgin white. Nancy was led to no altar, and so she was chosen. Chased from hallway to hallway by endless relays of little men set loose like ferrets to find her, and behind them at a discreet distance the Hierarchy in the formidable shape of Father Rex Aurealis, she was shadowed—by them and by a van that resembled the Black Maria. So far Nancy had escaped them. How, only God knows! Mrs. Baines did not, nor would she ask as she took the baby from the girl crossing the threshold and placed it in the bed beside Dilsey. Nancy looked starved and was filthy, although the signs of efforts to clean herself were visible. Her face, pale and thin, had been washed, and her light brown hair combed and drawn in under the hat that shadowed it. But the hat itself and the green coat were caked with dirt and creased from having been slept in, and the coat fell open on a worn red skirt that showed where the dirt had been but rubbed off. Her thin legs, mottled by fires someone had let her huddle over, bore silk stockings that were laddered to ribbons, and as Mrs. Baines saw, her shoes matched in their uselessness the blouse that was the remnants of some boy's gansey.

"God help you, child, but you look famished!" Mrs. Baines drew Nancy up to the fire. "Sit down there and I'll get you a bit to eat first."

Nancy sat down and watched Mrs. Baines place the heavy kettle on the fire. "Would you turn the key in the door?" she said and made as though to do it herself, but Mrs. Baines restrained her.

"Sit you still." She crossed the room and turned the key in the lock. "You'll be all right, pet," she said and busied herself with what little food there was in the press, out of which she hoped to make a meal. "You heard about your mother?" she asked gently.

Nancy drew her eyes away from the baby, still wrapped in its shawl on the bed. "I saw her," she said.

Mrs. Baines's knife stopped halfway down the piece of a loaf in her hands, jagging the pet that broke into big pieces over the blade. "You saw her? When?"

"When they stretched her onto the bank." Nancy drew her hat off and put it in her lap.

Mrs. Baines waited until the gesture was completed. "But how? Where were you?"

"In Kevin Hely's room."

The tenement where Kevin Hely had a room overlooked the lock and was next door to the pub at the bridge. Kevin was the man that had at first seduced Nancy, then paid for her abortion, then let her live with him as his wife. She had given herself to him willingly, believing then, as now, that he would eventually marry her.

"I heard the kids roarin' out," she began. She stopped and glanced from Mrs. Baines to the window, the mantelpiece. "I thought she was just drunk. An' I went to the window. I told Kevin to go an' tell them to stop, but he wouldn't. Then I saw.

She had buckled up, like she had a pain or something, an' Micky Connors put her on the grass. Soaking." She stopped and lifted her hat off her lap. "Kevin wouldn't let me out. He told me I'd get caught. He wouldn't let me, an' when he *put* me out she was gone. Nobody put the fork back." Her mouth began to distort itself over the small, hollow, hammering sounds that came from her. "They took her out with the fork."

Mrs. Baines reached for her with an embrace that was clumsy and tight and gentle, muffling the ends of words spoken against her face as, over and over, Nancy told her that the ground was wet.

Neither of them noticed Tucker Tommy, his face lost in the wide stare of his eyes as he went past them into the little room. His slight body in its solemnity was erect as the calf's lick of his fair hair rising stiff and straight, like a cock's comb, from the pale span of his forehead. He made faces against the window down at Mrs. Chance who stood, alone in the Lane, looking up at the Baineses' windows, and wondered if she could see him. When he realized that she could not, he stuck his tongue way out and, as if it was a signal for her, she began to scurry down the Lane towards the Street. Behind, he heard Nancy crying, and began to frost the glass with the heat of his breath. He had drawn his initials when the crying stopped and his mother called him. Emerging into the big room at the same time as a blowdown from the chimney, he noticed his mother's failure to say: We'll have rain, as she pushed a cup of tea across to him and a cut of bread and dripping.

He gazed at Nancy who stared unseeing, her face taut and streaked and pressed hard against the cup she was holding to her mouth. On the edge of the bed, Mrs. Baines was sitting with Nancy's baby in her arms feeding it from a medicine bottle with a yellow tit on it.

"What'll you do, child?" Mrs. Baines raised her face with the question.

Nancy put her cup down carefully, like one grown used to

caution. "I don't know," she said. "I can't stay here, they haven't left me a screed or a stick. Even if they had . . ." She paused. "The curse of God on them! That the hands may wither off them!"

"Don't, child. Leave them and your tormentors to God. 'Tis yourself and your child you must look to now."

But how? Where? The questions went unspoken. Into Nancy's mind leaped hope that the passing of days and hours might in some miraculous way have altered Kevin, and she knew she must go to him. She looked up at the clock on the mantelpiece. He had not been in his room when she had gone to him earlier that morning, but he was sure to be there now.

"I'll go," she said, getting to her feet.

"Go?" Mrs. Baines looked up from the baby in her arms.

"To Kevin."

Mrs. Baines set the baby down again and stood up. "Is that man going to marry you?"

Nancy looked away from her to the window, through which she could see the window of what had been her mother's room. "He says so."

"Does he say when?"

She shook her head. "He will now. He'll have to, now that me mother's gone."

"What's holding him back?"

Nancy shook her head. She didn't know. All she knew was what he said, and he said little except that they must wait. She never asked what for, afraid that if she persisted he might tell her the truth which, in her heart, she sensed, or, what was worse, leave her altogether. Because she loved him, she had believed him when he suddenly refused after her mother's death to let her stay in his room, telling her that it wasn't safe and that too many people knew. And she never thought to ask why he threw caution to the winds on the nights he wanted to sleep with her. But even this was happening less and less, and only when she forced herself upon him and ended nearly always with his abuse, when, thinking him bemused with love and sleep, she tried to force him to the ever receding brink of an immediate marriage. But things were different now, her places of refuge known and exhausted. Now he would have to marry her.

"He has to," she said, not aware that she did. She looked at Mrs. Baines. "I have to go." Her brown eyes softened as she saw in Mrs. Baines's face that same concern she had seen long ago in Cocky's, before her father had died in France.

"Wait, child, till evening," Mrs. Baines said. "Wait till night falls, then go an' see him."

Nancy reached down for her hat which had fallen to the floor as she stood up. "I'll be all right," she said and gave herself a quick look in the looking-glass.

"Wait, child." Mrs. Baines laid a restraining hand on the girl's arm, but Nancy only smiled. "You'd never know what trouble you'd walk yourself into now, or who saw you coming into the Lane."

"Nobody did. I was careful." Nancy gathered the baby in her arms, settling it with care into the crook of her elbow. "She's the spit of me mother."

Mrs. Baines smiled in agreement. "She is, God bless her!" She looked at Nancy. "What'll you do, if he isn't beyant? Will you come back?"

"I will." Nancy looked at the clock.

Against her will, Mrs. Baines turned the key in the lock and Nancy slipped past her onto the landing. There was nobody on the stairs or in the hall.

"Come back, now mind you." Across the bannisters, Mrs. Baines's whisper came to her as she set foot in the hall.

She waited, but Nancy did not come back. Less than an hour later she knew, with the rest of the Lane, why not. It was Mrs. Kinsella who came charging up the stairs to tell her.

"I was coming out a Miss Fogarty's with a few potatoes for the dinner," she began. "Musha! Let me sit down." In the room, over the table, she continued. "An' Miss Fogarty said, 'Will you have a look at Nancy O'Byrne?' 'Where?' I sez, but it was barely

out a me mouth when I saw her talking an' showing the baby to
the Witch at the corner of the Lane, an' her looking as if she
hadn't a care in the world on her. Now whatever it was going
on between them I don't know, because I'm not great with the
Witch this long time, but I wanted to see the baby, so I thought
I'd hold me ground till she left her, which she did, an' no sooner
had Nancy put one leg in front of the other an' before you could
bless yourself, they had her. Two of them. Though I on'y saw one
at first, a dyin'-lookin' puke with a raincoat an' a hat, an' he
stepped out a Corrigan's doorway, as I thought, to talk to her,
but not at all. The next thing I saw was Nancy trying to shove
him from her with her elbow an' she trying to duck your man,
but he caught her by the arm an' Miss Fogarty said, 'Ah, Jesus,
they have her!' With that I shouted, but before I could set foot
under me, the van drew up an' another bowsie jumped out of it
an' between them they pushed her into it an' away it went down
the street." Mrs. Kinsella stopped. "A motor van, it was. Or so
Miss Fogarty says, but I never thought to look because I was
roaring after the dirty hoor's ghosts till she told me an' the rest
of us to shut up because Father Rex Aurealis was coming. I don't
know where he came out of. One minute that slieveen bastard
wasn't there, an' the next he was." She stared at Mrs. Baines.
"How do they shaggin' well do it?"

"Did he say anything?"

Mrs. Kinsella threw her a quizzical mocking glance. "Does he
ever?" she sneered. "All he did was give us a look an' bless us
as he went by." She paused. "He's very free with blessings, but I
wonder if he'd be so offhand if they cost anything. I don't care,
but there's something about that man you couldn't trust. An'
don't tell me he wasn't watching them bowsies haul that poor
unfortunate off the street, because he was. An' don't tell me,
either, he had nothing to do with it, because he had."

"She should've stayed with me till evening," Mrs. Baines said,
distressed.

Mrs. Kinsella looked up at her. "Was she here?" Her voice rose in surprise, and when Mrs. Baines nodded: "An' was there anyone with you?"

Mrs. Baines shook her head. "Only Nancy. An' I asked her to wait till evening, but nothing would do her but she must rush out to see that corner-boy in case she'd miss him. There was something over me though, as she went out an' down them stairs. I should've known. I should've stopped her."

Mrs. Kinsella stirred herself into a protest. "How could you? How is anyone to know?" She looked thoughtfully, perplexed, away for a moment, then stood up. "It's a terrible shagging state of affairs altogether when a body can't walk the streets without wondering whether you're going to be kidnaped or murdered on them. England's going to be in the halfpenny place compared to the way the priests an' the chapels are going to be running us before long. Jasus! Talk about the Lords a Creation! Ya won't be able to blow ya nose without Rome's and the sanction of the priests, God blast them! There was that poor creature not meddling with anyone an' minding her own business, whipped off the streets without a by-your-leave into Christ alone knows what sort of a place by them ruffians, acting at the behests of the priest."

"If you could only be sure!" Mrs. Baines interrupted.

"Sure!" Mrs. Kinsella's exclamation rang to the rafters. "I'm as sure as I'm looking at you, an' so are a great many others if they had the decency to admit it. 'Sure' how are ya!" she said dryly. "Since when now did you need to be told it takes twelve pennies to make a shilling?"

She moved over to the door, her hands gathered round the bib and the potatoes in it. "But I'm sure of one thing. We won't hear any of today's dirty work from the altar on Sunday." She laughed. "We'll be given no penance for this. There won't be a word out of them."

And there wasn't.

Mrs. Baines didn't dare go near Father Rex Aurealis to ask him where Nancy was, but she did go out to the convent in Drumcondra where it was rumored she and her baby had been taken. But there the nuns could not or would not tell her anything, and at the Mary Magdalene Asylum in Gloucester Street which she tried on the off-chance that Nancy might have been taken there, she stood mute and dumb while a nun, a mere slip of a girl, chastised her for what seemed to her Mrs. Baines's unwarranted interference in something which didn't concern her. Had she nothing better to do, she was asked when she explained that she was in no way related to the girl she was searching the convents of the city for. She could only answer that she was a neighbor of the girl, who was without a soul in the world to care what happened to her and that she wanted to be sure that wherever the girl might be she should be all right. Mrs. Baines could not explain the promptings of her heart that made her care what might become of Nancy. She had never recognized her enormous capacity for compassion, and the nun before her was too absorbed in regulations to see it. In her learned ignorance she saw only an elderly busybody in need of rebuke, which she proceeded to administer both at length and with a thoroughness that would have pleased and heartened generations of hardened Reverend Mothers. When she had finished telling Mrs. Baines that she had never heard of the person she was looking for and at last closed the great door behind her, Mrs. Baines felt, as she afterwards said, fit for nothing.

Nancy was lost, irrevocably and forever; the fact, a speck before her eyes as she hurried home to get Babby and the children their tea, rose to grow lifesize beside her on the crowded streets, stepping out of place to confront her whenever she turned her head away from the sea of faces around and above her to catch a freer breath of air or to reach for an answer from the bewildered thoughts crowding her mind. But there was no answer to be had, except from the priest, and him she would never ask. He would no more have understood her than the nun did.

The December sky over the Lane was strident, impudent in its flaunting crimson and purple gashes. The vaunted heavens, tousled as though still trembling from the aftermath of a storm, had pushed the evening star higher into a darking blue like a paper sailboat flung onto the spread face of a stilled lake. Mrs. Baines looked up to see it before she set foot in her hall door, and at that moment in Kilkenny town, seventy-three miles from where she stood, a pub door was flung open and out into the gathered dusk Pat Baines stepped, black-booted and heavy-footed, onto the silvered fragility of sparkling frost that crinkled into dull sieved dust under his weight, turned towards Dublin.

FOURTEEN

Mrs. BAINES sipped her glass of invalid wine and admired the ceiling and walls, garlanded with paper chains and holly. And Mrs. Chance, sad and pale-faced, remarked, "I, for one, will be glad when it's all over."

It was Christmas Eve and, as was traditional, they were sitting in Mrs. Slattery's room, to which they had been invited to celebrate the great feast. Mrs. Baines sat beside Mrs. Kinsella, across from them Mrs. Slattery and Mrs. Chance, and around and beside them Mrs. Slattery's children playing and making serious efforts to kill each other, prevented from actually doing so only by the odd swipe of their mother's powerful arm, which swung out indiscriminately to down whichever of them happened to get in its way.

None of the other women quite agreed with Mrs. Chance, but refrained from saying so and waited politely as they did every Christmas Eve for her to say what they knew she would say, while

Mrs. Kinsella, who had made other visits around the Lane earlier in the day and was well past giving anyone her undivided attention, suppressed a giggle. The sweep of Mrs. Slattery's arm, like a lighthouse beam over the heads of her children, made her want to laugh as it flailed always the head or shoulders she guessed it would. When it skimmed and missed the head of Theresa, who was making silent sideways darts at Mrs. Baines's glass, Mrs. Kinsella laughed outright.

The laugh froze Mrs. Chance in mid-speech and Mrs. Slattery sank imperturbably past it lower into her chair. Her great face turned in what looked like silent meditation towards Mrs. Baines, who leaned slightly past Mrs. Kinsella and without looking at her said to Mrs. Chance, "What was it you were about to say?"

Mrs. Chance gazed sadly from Mrs. Kinsella, who sat up straight-backed with the laugh wiped clean off her face.

"It won't be the same without Aggie," Mrs. Chance continued, then paused. "Christmas or Easter, makes no difference when you haven't your childer around you."

Mrs. Baines nodded her agreement and Mrs. Chance sighed.

"Ah, now, isn't Aggie better off where she is?" Mrs. Kinsella said quickly, making amends not for her old enemy's sake but for the sake of the moment.

"She is," Mrs. Baines said.

Mrs. Slattery said nothing.

"Sure, she's praying for you," Mrs. Kinsella smiled over to Mrs. Chance who knew as well as they did that the amount of time Aggie had for praying was harmless.

The pretense was kept up, however, even by Mrs. Kinsella, that Aggie might one day be a nun. But, now as always, they awaited the girl's return to the Lane and after a stay of four or five weeks, Mrs. Chance washing and hanging out the navy blue serge dress and beside it the navy coat, beaten and brushed as if it was a carpet, because it meant that Aggie had been called again and that for another while the girls' fellows were safe. Then there would be another Good-by, to which everyone was invited and which highlighted the dreary routine for most of the people in the Lane: a farewell laden with bread and butter and tea and port and stout and whole plates of Jacob's fancy broken and whole biscuits spread out on a table the width of the room and covered with a cloth which was reserved for these occasions only and which Mrs. Chance had had blessed by Father Rex Aurealis. Everyone ate as much as they could off the cloth and even saved a biscuit —as some people save a bit of a wedding cake—to take home with them, hoarding it like a relic until the next time, and by then it was too stale to eat unless you dipped it into your tea. They gathered around Aggie, who stood fat-faced and dull-eyed at the head of the table in her washed navy dress that did nothing to enhance the mousey lashes and matching hair already drawn back into its former straight drabness where only the day before it had hung in Medusa twists from a more than generous use of the curling tongs. Her unsmiling face was thought pious as it drooped on the short fat neck around which she had replaced the silver Child of Mary medal and to which a hand fled, coarsened and red from constant contact with ruthless washing sodas, whenever anyone asked her to remember them in her prayers. They forgot for the moment that they did not believe in her prayers. Lulled by the plenty, they even went so far as to tell her she had God's ear and to beg His intercession for them, which she gravely promised to do.

But she had stayed in the convent in Ranelagh longer this last time than she had ever stayed before and her mother, for reasons of her own, felt that it was now safe to assume that she would stay away forever. Mrs. Chance prayed constantly for her daughter's ordination until it was no longer just a desire to be able to say that her daughter was a nun but her one and only consuming ambition, claiming all her thoughts, sleeping and waking. She changed from a stupid woman into a scheming one, and suffered Father Rex Aurealis's rebuffs ever since Mrs. Kinsella had put it into her head that his influence might help her achieve what money would have done. She lay in wait for him around the

chapel and his house, assuming he thought their meetings acci-
dental. She went to Confession once a week and to Mass every
day and sometimes twice. It was by accident that she should have
been on her way home from Mass the morning Nancy O'Byrne
came back to the Lane, but it was deliberate calculation that made
her turn back to the chapel and Father Rex Aurealis who, when
he had heard what she had to say, smiled indulgently and confused
her by asking why she had thought he should be concerned in
the girl's whereabouts. So uninterested did he appear that she
could only believe that she had made some terrible error and beg
his forgiveness, and she began to turn away to escape what she
felt would be his just but dreaded admonishment. But the serv-
ants of God were as good as Himself, as she afterwards said, and
instead of the priest eating the head off her he had called her back
up the steps to the hall door of his house and had talked to her,
asking kindly after Aggie while he hinted obliquely that on his
next visit to the convent he would remember her to her daughter.

But it was Christmas and Nancy was gone and if Mrs. Chance
felt that she had any part in her going, she had forgotten it by
now. And our sins are *not* always with us: not when nobody but
yourself knows about them and not when you're God-and-priest
fearing and when any day now a child of yours may become a nun.

"This time I have a feeling she'll take the veil." Mrs. Chance
smiled superiorly.

"Ah, God willing," said Mrs. Baines.

Mrs. Kinsella looked narrowly at Mrs. Chance's pronouncement.
And Mrs. Slattery raised the cup in her hand and said for the
first time, "Happy Christmas to youse!"

"Mind!"

Mrs. Baines reached out to halt the downward path of the cup,
but it was too late as cup and arm landed with a dull thud onto
Theresa's head. The child gave a yelp of pain and stopped dead in
her tracks. She looked wildly at her mother, who showed no alarm
but gazed stonily back before she moved her head slightly, then
reached for another cup.

"Heads of shaggin' concrete they have," she said slowly, puzzled and with an effort.

Mrs. Kinsella laughed, and so did Mrs. Baines who had pulled the child to her. Theresa's crying stopped as suddenly as it had begun, pacified by the new shining penny that Mrs. Baines slipped into her hand.

"No feelings," Mrs. Slattery said, off on some track of her own about which the others were not aware.

Mrs. Kinsella reached out and took the bottle of glorified red biddy off the table. She proceeded to fill Mrs. Slattery's cup from it.

Mrs. Chance sighed. "God! an' you don't feel the years going by, do you? On'y yesterday was last Christmas, an' here's another one on top of us before you know where you are."

"If that's all you ever have on top of you, Madge Chance, you'll be all right!" Mrs. Kinsella said, tossing her face into her raucous laugh.

Mrs. Slattery raised her indolent eyes and to no one in particular said, "I told her, 'Your husband *used* to work in Jacobs but your husband doesn't work in Jacobs any more.'"

"Who?" Mrs. Baines asked, and Mrs. Kinsella gave her a nudge. "You're a hard nut," she said over to Mrs. Slattery. "An' sure, more luck to ya!"

Mrs. Slattery jerked her arm up. "I'm the light of Tom's eye, I am." Her great face, suffused and moist, broke into shadowed folds of laughter.

"You're Cleopatria, Julia-darling, that's who you are." Mrs. Kinsella was shouting now, and didn't notice Mrs. Chance's sideways glances, strongly disapproving.

"You're demons," Mrs. Baines said. She wasn't drunk and was aware of Mrs. Chance's disapproval, but she was enjoying the banter of the women too much to care one way or the other. She was relaxed in a mild contentment, prepared to postpone for the moment the hours of delight before her when she would set about making Christmas for herself and her children. Against her, young

Theresa pressed, taking sly sips from the tumbler when she thought Mrs. Baines wasn't watching, and at her feet under the table Mrs. Slattery's second set of twins crawled and buffeted each other in play, naked except for shifts as black as soot covering only their shoulders.

"Go wan, give us a song!"

Mrs. Kinsella's suggestion was dismissed by Mrs. Slattery with a lazy half-gesture of her hand coming to rest on the swell of her breast.

"Ah, go wan, Mother. 'Kerry Dancers,'" Theresa cried out coaxingly. "With actions."

"That youngwan's indecent!" Mrs. Kinsella shook her head.

"Well, then, what about 'Robert Emmet'?" Theresa asked; but Mrs. Kinsella dismissed this also.

"That'd turn ya white."

"Still an' all," Mrs. Chance demurred sadly, "it's a good song an' about our martyr." There was a perceptible tinge of admonishment in her voice.

"Martyr?" Mrs. Kinsella cried. "He was a Black Protestant! Not that I hold that against him, mind."

"No, he wasn't," Mrs. Chance flatly contradicted. "He died for the Faith an' Ireland."

"He was a Black Prod." Mrs. Kinsella knew she was right. "All our best men were. An' I have Neddo Baines, number wan in his class, to back me up, because it was him who told me. Am I right?" She looked at Mrs. Baines.

"You are, ma'am. That's exactly what Neddo said," Mrs. Baines replied laughingly.

"Well, it's a barefaced lie," Mrs. Chance said.

"It's the truth, but does it matter?" Mrs. Baines intervened.

"He was one of our own," Mrs. Slattery interrupted lazily, and as far as she was concerned, this was all that mattered.

"He was a ram," Mrs. Kinsella said, "an' he ran that Sarah Curran bowlegged."

"Where's me youth?" Mrs. Slattery asked. "Where's me youth gone to?"

Mrs. Kinsella eyed her suspiciously. "What youth? What're you blathering about?"

"Me youth." Mrs. Slattery rocked herself back on her chair. " 'Gone, alas, like our youth, too soon,' " she sang.

"Them I.R.A. will have an awful lot to answer for!" Mrs. Chance cried; and Mrs. Baines knew that what Neddo had said had reminded her of Mattie.

"With actions, Ma!" Theresa Slattery clapped the sides of her head with the flat of her hands the way she did when she was in a temper. "With actions!"

"Lured us on . . . on . . . with wild delight," her mother sang.

"You mean, Tom did." Mrs. Kinsella nudged Mrs. Slattery, who stopped singing and laughed. "Bejasus! I'm going to make the welkins ring tonight!"

"Ah, go wan with a song with love. Sing something with love in it," Mrs. Kinsella insisted.

"An' then you'll cry," Theresa said seriously.

Mrs. Kinsella grinned. "Ah, that's only because me bladder's near me eyes!" She nudged Mrs. Slattery again. "Go wan, something with love."

Mrs. Baines laughed outright. "I'd never blame you," she said.

"What about a hymn? Seein' it's Christmas an' all." Mrs. Chance's suggestion, quietly put, found favor only with Theresa.

" 'Star a the Sea'," she said.

"That's not for Christmas," Mrs. Chance told her.

"What is, then?" Theresa asked.

"I told you that youngwan had a bad mind!"

Mrs. Baines shushed Mrs. Kinsella, saying, "Go wan then, sing us a song yourself."

And Mrs. Slattery opened her eyes. "She's a disturber of the peace."

Mrs. Kinsella, on the verge of opening her mouth, closed it again.

"Ah, but sure, God help her, she wants to sing," Mrs. Baines said.

"What about?" Mrs. Slattery held out her cup towards the bottle at Mrs. Kinsella's elbow.

"I think she's had enough." Mrs. Chance's voice, though hardly more than a whisper, was heard.

"Sure I haven't started yet, woman." Mrs. Slattery giggled. "Wait now," she said, "till I wet me thirst, an' then I'll sing youse all to hell an' back again."

"No need for you to get yourself riz," Mrs. Kinsella said. "Keep your drawers on. I'm pouring for you."

"Ah, gowa' a that!" Mrs. Slattery waved her hand with the cup in it, sending the wine splashing in all directions.

"Ah, God blast ya! Sure can't ya hold easy?" Mrs. Kinsella drew away, wiping a streak like blood from her face with the back of her hand.

Mrs. Slattery muttered incoherently and languidly sank, as onto a bed of feathers, deeper into her chair and the space between it and the table.

"Will you look at her?" Mrs. Kinsella laughed. "A lovely sight she'll be for poor Tom if he walks in!"

But Mrs. Slattery's collapse was temporary. She rose slowly upright and, drawing back off her face the strands of hair that had come loose from the untidy black and gray bun on the nape of her fat neck, she said, "Maybe youse'd like another sup?"

Mrs. Baines stirred herself and shook her head. In the room above she could hear Babby moving. "I'll have to go," she said.

"Ah, what's your hurry?" Mrs. Kinsella asked her. "Sure can't you enjoy yourself?"

"Oh, I have," Mrs. Baines laughed. "I don't know when I enjoyed meself more." She leaned across the table to Mrs. Slattery. "Don't forget to come up in the morning."

Mrs. Slattery nodded her head, then turned to look over her shoulder at the children behind her. "Shagging savages they are. I can't hear me ears with them," she said, before she shrieked suddenly and the children stopped in their play to stare at her dumfounded.

For one moment nobody spoke or moved, then Mrs. Chance said into the silence, "You shouldn't scream at them. It's bad for their nerves."

Mrs. Slattery turned slowly, her massive head lumbering around to where she could see Mrs. Chance. "What's them?" she asked, vaguely serious.

Mrs. Chance gestured towards her. "You know," she said lamely. "Ah, you know, things inside you . . ."

"In your head," Mrs. Kinsella jumped into the breach.

Mrs. Slattery stared up at her. "God forgive you," she said, "but you have a terrible dirty mind."

Mrs. Kinsella was exasperated. "Youse," she said, "are ignorant." And she broke into sudden hiccupped giggles. "Nerves is . . ." she went on. "Nerves is . . ."

She was still hiccupping, unable to go on, as, with a laugh, Mrs. Baines left the room, followed by Theresa.

A great mouth blew a breath through Moore Street and stirred scents into the air to cloud the damp warm darkness through which the Christmas crowds poured. Mouths opened on roared laughter and eyes squinted in the wind and opened again, impatient. Faces drew back from the sudden barbs of holly, and were pressed against shopfronts from which turkeys and geese hung by their feet and dripped still warm blood which children caught in their open mouths or the palms of their hands. Pink hams like jewels hung beside living white-feathered plump hens and scarlet-combed cocks that struggled against the cord around their chrome and yellowed claws, and fluttered their snowy cropped wings like plumed headdresses in a rowdy ballroom. Cold, stiff, furred rabbits were piled on boards flung across barrels in which pigs' cheeks were pickling in salt water, adding a piquancy to the cloy of yeast tossing in clouds from the opened doors of pubs and the exotic aroma of fruit piled high on trays flung across prams and orange boxes lining each side of the street. White-bibbed dealers with strange-shaped earrings and high button boots and without their shawls roared from behind mountains of fruit and vegetables and soft glittering tinsel, wound like frost around billows of multi-colored balloons netted by showers of streamers. The mysterious dark of Christmas trees was entered by hands and elbows and showered the ground with needles. And overhead, fairy lights and paper chains transformed the night.

It was cheaper to buy in Moore Street the last thing Christmas Eve. The shops and dealers let food and fruit and meat go at less than half the price, and, without bargaining, bargains could be bought. Mrs. Baines, with Tucker Tommy and Neddo each side of her, had bought what she had come for and was carrying it home in a pillow case held tightly in front of her. The only thing not in it was the pig's cheek, which Neddo was carrying wrapped in a bit of newspaper under his arm, the brine already robbing the dye from his gansey. From time to time he heaved it against his chest, breathless at some new wonder to which he drew his mother's attention. Tucker Tommy, lost on the other side of her, dragged behind, awed at first by the real live hens, frightened as the beady-eyed fowl made swift darts at his hand held up to them, becoming brave when his mother told him they couldn't eat him. Now as he dragged behind, he tapped the live birds on the head with his palm and set the dead ones swinging with a push of his fist, shrieking delight.

Mrs. Baines, caught up on their delight, laughed, surprised with them, mindful all the time of the things she had bought—necessities—and of the things they must go without. The pig's cheek for their Christmas dinner wouldn't be very Christmasy. She would have preferred to be able to get a fowl of some sort or a bit of beef, but even at half price they weren't to be thought of. Still, she had got the makings of a pudding and, for their breakfast tomorrow morning, a rasher apiece. Miss Fogarty had given her a few vegetables and a bunch of holly by way of a Christmas box that afternoon and a punnet of damaged fruit, which when washed and the bad parts pared away looked grand, and the kids would love it, also the box of sweets that Mrs. Cogan had given her for them. For Zena, she had crocheted a collar; but the children worried her—clothes were expensive, beyond the reach of what she and Babby between them earned, for even with the extra work at Miss Fogarty's the total amount coming in every week was twelve shillings and sixpence. With care and thrift, she managed, but there could be no luxuries, not even a gansey for one of them, nothing except the makings of the Christmas pudding and the rashers, and a sugared cake apiece from the shop towards which they were now headed.

She bought the cakes at three ha'pence each: one for Neddo, one for Tucker Tommy and one to take home to Babby. For herself she got a ha'p'orth of lemon drops in a small white paper bag, which she began to share with the children once they had finished the cakes and were gazing again in wonder at the shops and stalls in Henry Street which they turned into as they made their way home.

In O'Connell Street they stood to listen to the carol singers under the arch of the GPO, their nasal voices thickly sliding over the words of the songs half drowned by the vigorous rumble of the coins they were collecting in cardboard boxes; and further along, a Republican standing beside a woman with a pram talking about brother killing brother. . . .

While at home in the Lane, Babby was coughing blood onto a cloth which, when the coughing was finished, she flung into the fire and then began hiding in the little brown trunk the gifts for them that she had spent her share of the week's tips on. Later, when Neddo and Tucker Tommy were gone to bed, she and her mother would put them into the stockings they hung on the line at the fire. Tomorrow morning in the excitement of their discovery she, much to their consternation, would feign disappointment because she had been left nothing and would put her face close to the fire and call out to the man Tucker Tommy still believed to be somewhere up the chimney. . . .

In O'Connell Street the wind, with soft wet snow on it, bit into

Mrs. Baines and wet the heads of Neddo and Tucker Tommy, driving them from the carol singers and through the crowds swarming over the wide street through which they tried to hurry now in their eagerness to be home. Up Westmoreland Street they went, past the café where Babby worked, which they stopped to peer into, past Trinity College dark and outrageously Protestant in its gloomy withdrawal and behind its defense of black iron railings, and into Grafton Street lined on either side with glittering expensive shops before which they began to dawdle. For the length of it, they forgot they were cold, mesmerized by what they saw, and remembered again only when they left it behind and saw the bare branches of the trees in Stephen's Green, stark against the dark sky.

In Harcourt Street they met Annie the Man, walking close to the railings that surrounded the areas of the big houses, bent on some mysterious errand of her own. When she stopped dead in front of them, Mrs. Baines pushed past her and said, "Go long with you!" They heard her muttered curses following them, shadowing their excitement and anticipation for a moment until Mrs. Baines laughed down at her sons by her side and said: "Th' oul' reprobate!" They laughed then and repeated what she had said and were still repeating it, though her laugh had faded into a thoughtful expression, when they at last turned into the Street and into Mr. Pughe's shop for the oil and the candle.

Mr. Pughe gave them the tall red Christmas candle every year. It was his Christmas box to them for having bought the oil for the lamp all through the past year. He was sitting behind the counter when they came in, and rose neatly to greet them.

"The oil, Mr. Pughe," Mrs. Baines said, easing the weight of the pillow case between her knees and the counter.

"It's ready for you," he said, taking the can from under the counter and handing it over.

"And the candle, Mr. Pughe," Neddo suggested, anxious lest their Christmas box be forgotten.

"Whisht!" said Mrs. Baines.

"Yes, I have that also." Mr. Pughe took the red candle down from off the shelf behind him. "Here you are."

Before Neddo could move, Tucker Tommy, who had to stand on the tip of his toes and even then did not quite reach the top of the counter, stretched up his hands and said, "I'll carry it."

Mr. Pughe looked from him to Mrs. Baines.

She nodded and said, as Tucker Tommy took the candle gingerly, "If you let it fall, I'll take your life." As she thanked Mr. Pughe and counted out the money for the oil, she saw his eyes roving over her and the children with the new restlessness that had come into him since Cocky had died.

"It'll be a quiet Christmas."

"Faith, an' you wouldn't say that if you saw the sights and crowds across the city!"

"I suppose not." He brought his gaze back to her. "But I haven't been across the city."

She looked pityingly at him. "It would've done you good."

"I suppose so."

"You don't get out enough."

He smiled and shook his head. "It's little there is to go out for."

"Our Uncle Mattie an' Aunt Zena's coming for Christmas," Neddo said.

"Are they?" Mr. Pughe wasn't very interested.

"Do you hang chains up, Mr. Pughe?" Neddo asked.

Mr. Pughe shook his head.

"Neither do we," Neddo said. "Our mother an' Babby says chains are common."

"Are we common?" Tucker Tommy asked.

"I'm not!" Neddo's reply was definite. "Our Babby's going to get a wristlet watch from Nick because she doesn't want an engagement ring."

Mr. Pughe looked at Neddo blankly, but Tommy Tucker inquired, "Why?"

"Because . . ."

"That'll do," Mrs. Baines shushed him.

"She doesn't want to get married," Neddo whispered.

"Why?"

But Neddo had his eyes on his mother, who had hers on Mr. Pughe, thinking about the change that had come over him within the past months. His face was still fat and white, and his little mouth pursed, red as always, but his eyes wandered now in small orbs and had lost their surprised roundness. They were narrowed, lined, and, when he looked directly at you as he did now, puzzled, and made you think he was going to speak, even when he wasn't. His hands had lost their trick of coming together and lay slovenly in their collapse on top of the counter, matching in their grayness the stiff collar, no longer as stiff as it had been and nowheres as clean. His wig, though, as blackly preposterous as ever, still sat neatly on his head; but it no longer glistened, its purpose now sadly functional and dull as widow's weeds.

"These are a few sweets for the children." He pushed a paper bag across the counter to her.

"Ah, I don't like to, Mr. Pughe." Mrs. Baines shook her thoughts from her. "You're too good altogether."

"Take them," he said. He smiled vaguely. "They won't break me."

"Have you got your bit in for tomorrow?"

He nodded.

"I'll send you up a bit of pudding. Are you making one?"

He shook his head.

"Well, in that case I'll send you up a piece." Mrs. Baines gathered up her pillow case and the sweets he had given her. "A happy Christmas and many of them, Mr. Pughe."

He inclined his head slightly, and Neddo and Tucker Tommy echoed her. "An' the same to you," he said to them, "an' to you, ma'am." And after they had gone, he sat down neatly again on his stool near the window to peer again between the jars and boxes filling up his small square window out into the street.

The Lane was aglow with lamp and candle light, trembling narrow flames from the candles stuck in jam jars in the windows and

behind them the rich amber thickness from the lamps lighting up
the rooms and the gaudy paper chains strung across ceilings. Neddo
and Tucker Tommy watched from their own window, absorbed by
the decorations and the people they could see moving about in
the rooms of the houses opposite. Behind in their own room,
Babby cleaned up the mess that was left after bathing them, while
Mrs. Baines hurried the preparations for the mixing and making
of the Christmas pudding. They worked quickly, deftly and without stopping, even though Mrs. Baines laughed or exclaimed every
now and then at something Babby said or at the relay of news and
events passed back to her from Neddo and Tucker Tommy at the
window.

She was soon ready to begin the ritual that making the pudding
had become. In answer to her call, Neddo and Tucker Tommy
flew from their perch to post themselves on chairs at the table,
kneeling with their heads on a level with Babby's between them,
and all three waiting, as was the established custom, to be told
what it was she had decided they might do. Tucker Tommy hoped
he would be given the job of cutting up the candied peel and had
already said so. Mrs. Baines remembered that Danny had always
done it before, and before him Kitty. For a moment the memory
brought their faces, and Teasey's, to hover just outside the yellow
glow of the candle on the table, behind the heads of the children
that were left to her, and in the sudden rise of longing for the
ones gone, she passed, without seeing, the green and orange peel
across to Tucker Tommy.

"All right, son," she said, "you can do it now."

His triumphant laugh shook the candle's flame, dissolving the
images before her, and in the minute's sadness her eyes flew to
the altar and the freshly painted statue of the Virgin.

"You nearly put the candle out," Neddo told his brother
roughly.

"I didn't."

"You did," said Neddo, who had had his eye on the peels himself, and turned away from his brother, who was gazing at the steady flame to make sure he had done it no harm.

"You can do the nutmeg for me."

Mrs. Baines held out the small brown cones to Neddo, who immediately forgot his grievance; but Tucker Tommy had sensed that his brother was annoyed, and while his mother got out a loaf of bread to grate into crumbs, he nudged Neddo.

"You do the candy peel."

His whisper to Neddo was overheard by Babby and Mrs. Baines, who was picking and cleaning the black currants and American raisins. Babby's glance met her mother's.

"I don't want it," Neddo shrugged.

Tucker Tommy paused, then bent slightly to his brother who had turned his shoulder to him. "Ah, do," he said coaxingly. He held out the candied peel. "Here."

Neddo did not answer for a moment, then his smile was quick and white. "You keep it."

Tucker Tommy looked doubtful, but seeing that Neddo meant what he said and guessing that the altercation between them was at an end, he grinned.

Babby lowered her eyes from the ceiling.

Mrs. Baines laughed softly. "Thank God!"

"Alleluia!" Babby said, and for the Baineses the most important and exciting part of Christmas had begun.

They embraced the contentment with a joy that was all the more joyful because of the consciousness of the rarity of contentment in their lives, savoring to the full the time and the mood and the well of peace in which they lived for what afterwards would seem like one long blissful moment, its every sound and word and smell remembered and set down into its place like the pieces in a mosaic. They stored up the night's minutes as carefully as Mrs. Baines gathered the stray currant or the odd splashes of flour with a knife blade from the table, their hoard of pleasure growing as they laughed and listened to each other, and to Mrs. Baines singing "Holy Night" and telling the story of the Nativity through the squelch of pudding being mixed by her fingers, and sighed when she came to its end, for by then the pudding was ready to go into its bit of a flour bag which had been washed and got ready the day before and which she lowered into the fat black saucepan, all to be eased before their eyes onto the red fire. They sighed then, because for Neddo and Tucker Tommy the moment was more than half gone. What was left of it would be spent in their getting ready for bed and sleep. Babby and Mrs. Baines lingered for the sight of the happiness remembered and the sure knowledge that the moment going might be the last because into the next Pat Baines might walk. But he did not, and until he did Mrs. Baines would keep the pretense up of fearlessness, prolonging the hour for them by an exalted rise in her voice which she refused to lower even when Babby warned her through her own laughter that she might awaken Dilsey. Mrs. Baines knew that worse than waking the baby on the bed was Pat coming up the stairs and catching them unawares. Even so, until he did, she thought, the night must have its proper end.

"Musha," she laughed, "it won't do her a bit of harm if she does wake," and found an unlooked-for reward after her display of courage in the bright eyes of the faces raised up to her. "We'll have a cup of tea," she said, and bent down to the press for the small slab of cake covered with yellow marzipan, which she brought to the table high in her hands.

"Rich cake!" Neddo's and Tucker Tommy's exclamations burst from them and they did a small dance round the table.

"We have to save a bit of it for tomorrow though." Mrs. Baines cut the first slice and Babby poured the tea. "For your Uncle Mattie and Aunt Zena."

"Will Nick be coming?" Neddo asked.

Babby nodded.

Nobody minded saving some of the rich dark cake for tomorrow, since there seemed so much of it for tonight, and with eager anticipation they gathered around the table that somehow at once looked festive. They heard Ruth and Martha Fay in the Lane

singing, a prelude to ructions to come before the night was out.
Across the landing, Mr. Kinsella was reciting "Dark Rosaleen,"
despite his wife's screams to put a sock in it, and the Erne ran
with blood through the supper and Neddo's and Tucker Tommy's
pleas for another bit of cake, and Spanish ale gave Ireland hope
when Mrs. Baines had got them ready for bed. They hung clean
socks up on the line and put into the toes as payment for anything
Father Christmas might leave, the penny each that Babby gave
them, then gazed with momentary awe up the chimney, after the
trail of steam from the pudding in the black saucepan.

"Do you think he'll come?" Tucker Tommy asked Babby.

She laughed as she caught him up in her arms, and Neddo forgot the two pink-and-white sugar Santa Clauses and the two white-
net Christmas stockings alongside the game of Snakes and Ladders
which he had seen at the bottom of the tin trunk and about which
he said nothing.

"Of course he will," he said, as Babby tucked him and his
brother into bed in the darkness of the little room, ridding his
mind of the knowledge it held for the sake of the make-believe
that he could not have borne to go without.

Neddo slept quickly, but Tucker Tommy stayed awake strain-
ing his ears for the sound of someone coming down the chimney.
He heard his mother and Babby talking and the sound of water
being poured into the basin, and knew that his mother was washing out something belonging to one of them, and when the door
opened he knew Babby was on her way down to the pipe, for he
heard his mother tell her not to fill it—that a drop would do. . . .

"I wish it was morning." He spoke aloud.

His mother came in quietly and bent over him. "Whisht, son!
Go to sleep now."

"Are you going to bed?"

"In a minute," she answered, brushing his hair from his forehead with the palm of her hand.

But she would not for a long time yet, and when she did she
would still have to get up several times during the night to keep
the fire in and make sure the water didn't boil away from the

pudding. Tomorrow morning the pudding would be done, still steaming, she would cut a slice each and give it to them in bed with a hot cup of tea. Tucker Tommy sighed happily. The morning was something to look forward to, a prolongation of the wonder that Christmas was. He felt his mother's lips brush his face and knew she did the same to Neddo before he closed his eyes. He was asleep before she left the room.

Christmas was passed over on a wave of opulence, suspending for a few hours the specter of want and hardship in the Lane as puddings were shared and sips of wine carried in small glasses from room to room and people discussed or displayed the things they had been able to manage, marveling at the ingenuity of those who had contrived not only food but clothes as well.

"An' the style of some!" as Mrs. Kinsella remarked when she watched Mrs. Chance go off to eleven o'clock Mass wearing a new green coat and a navy-blue straw hat that would take the eyes out of your head.

After twelve o'clock Mass, Mrs. Slattery, along with Mrs. Chance, dragged herself up the stairs to Mrs. Baines's room, followed by Mrs. Kinsella, who stayed after the other two women had gone and who left only when Phillo and her children came looking for her. Neither Mattie nor Zena showed up for dinner, but Nick did, and in the evening accompanied the Baineses, including Dilsey in her mother's arms, to Fawan Barton's hooley. Fawan's hooley climaxed Christmas in the Lane, and women who from one year's end to the other didn't put water to their faces or a rack to their heads came washed and shining and smelling of carbolic ready for the spree, while behind them their husbands rubbed hands at the sight of the table dark with bottles of stout and tried to look as though they hadn't seen them. Upon a table beside the one laden with food and drink, Fawan's aunt, the Witch, sat, pink-bloused and black-skirted, her dyed black hair crimped and bobbed. She sat upon the table for fear of being walked on in the crowded room from which the bed had been removed for the occasion and left outside in the Lane. Mrs. Cogan had a reputation as a fortuneteller and was in great demand at hooleys. While Fawan played the accordion and the eldest of her children saw to the comforts of guests, her aunt read palms. She never asked for money as the tinkers did who came around the Lane, but it was clearly understood that silver, in the shape of a sixpenny bit, must cross her palm the minute she'd finished.

Babby and Esther Fitz were over to her first and, as always, came away pretending a belief in every word she had said. And though neither of them believed her when, after looking at both of Babby's hands, she said she saw a death "in the space of three," Babby was worried. She didn't tell her mother what Mrs. Cogan had said and asked her not to either, knowing that her mother's belief was stronger than her own where the Witch was concerned. She warned Esther about letting it slip during the course of the evening. Even so, while she was dancing, first with Nick and then with the fellows who came in as the gaiety progressed, the Witch's prophecy refused to leave her. When, at eleven o'clock, Mrs. Baines suggested that it was time they were going, Babby gave in with an alacrity that made her mother wonder and Nick raise both eyebrows.

"Are you all right, pet?" Mrs. Baines asked, her eyes traveling Babby's flushed face as she rose from her chair to go.

Babby laughed. "Of course, I am. It's just, it's getting a bit rowdy." She laughed again at her mother's concern, grabbed Neddo and Tucker Tommy, and followed Mrs. Baines from the room. "Well, it's all over for another year," she said.

"Please God!" Mrs. Baines said.

Babby and Nick lingered behind her in the hall.

"Good night, Nick." Mrs. Baines turned back to them. "Don't keep her in the cold too long, will you?"

Nick, as concerned as herself over Babby's air of fatigue, readily assured her. . . .

"A peaceful Christmas it was," Mrs. Baines said as Tucker Tommy opened the door to the room, and as Neddo closed it behind him she said, "Thanks be to God and His Blessed Mother!"

FIFTEEN

ANNIE the Man would leave her and hers alone now. It was Mrs. Baines's first thought, but she said, with compassion uppermost, "Why did you not come in before? You know there would've been a bit to eat and a place to rest your head." The question jumped others that she wanted to ask, to ask again, but the answers so far had been couched in terms intelligible only to the politically informed. She knew little of the forces behind the events shaping and changing Ireland, because they only remotely, and only through Mattie and his wife, concerned her. She wished Neddo was in from school, and that she'd paid a little more attention to him when he talked about executions and reprisals and about the people shooting to kill in Kerry, as if, she thought, they shot in other parts of the country just for laughs. She remembered him listening with her at the pipe to Mrs. Chance talking about the train that was set on fire over at the Broadstone with the passengers in it and her saying it was the work of the

Republicans, and Mrs. Kinsella denying it and saying it was the
Free Staters to blame, and both women looking to Neddo, who
had shrugged like an old man and said nobody knew who it was
for sure. He had surprised Mrs. Kinsella, who gathered most of
the opinions she aired from him at the pipe. Well, she would
get a few from him the minute he came in from school today,
Mrs. Baines thought.

And at the fire, Zena drew her hand across her eyes. "I couldn't.
It might well have caused trouble for you, if I'd come near the
Lane."

"Trouble!" Mrs. Baines said wryly. "But how did you manage
today?"

"Because it no longer matters," Zena said. "Now that they have
him."

Mrs. Baines reached deep for understanding. "How could they?"
she asked. "Seven long years. Jail a man like Mattie who's done all
he has, and indeed the pair of you, for this country?" She stared.
"It's beyond belief and reason that this country should turn around
and jail him."

"Oh, it isn't the country, Molly."

"Then who, if not the country? Tell me that."

But before Zena could answer, she had hurried into the little
room at Babby's call.

"We woke you, love," she said.

"No, I was only dozing."

Mrs. Baines bent over her. "Are you feeling any better?"

"Yes, I'm grand now." The smile was reassuring.

"It's your uncle Mattie. He was arrested by the Free Staters an'
they gave him seven years in Maryborough."

"When?" Babby tried, but failed to raise herself onto her elbow.

"A week ago."

"And we never knew."

Mrs. Baines shook her head.

"But why?" Babby asked. "I thought it was all over with Dev
deciding to join the parliament. Oh, God! Is it going to begin . . ."

"Hush! Hush, child! Don't excite yourself." She sat on the bed, and held her daughter's hands. "I'll find out all about it from Zena, though, to tell the truth, I can't take in all she's been saying, so we better wait for Neddo. He'll know."

Babby, sinking back, willing herself to calm, smiled at her mother's confidence in Neddo's powers. "Yes," she said, "he'd know. The Scholar."

"I'll bring you a cup of tea," Mrs. Baines said, and she hurried from Babby back to Zena.

"We were on our way in to you when it happened," Zena said. "We tried to get in on Christmas Day but couldn't, because eight of our fellows who went into Rathfarnham that morning were caught in an ambush. Actually," Zena said, as if the point must be made with cold detachment, "the Free Staters took them in the chapel."

Mrs. Baines stiffened by the fire. "At their prayers," she said.

Zena hardly heard her. "Then on New Year's Day, we were told it was safe, that there was a letup all round of surveillance. So we came down, and we might just as well have written them a letter beforehand. I had some things for the children, but Mattie had an idea we must also have sweets. Couldn't appear at Christmastime without them, he said. So we went into a small sweet and tobacco shop on Rathmines Road, and when we came out they were waiting. I remember them now in their hundreds, but in fact there can't have been more than twenty."

"Twenty? An' all soldiers."

Zena nodded. It had been a long time since she had talked so much. She took the tea Mrs. Baines put into her hand, but made no attempt to drink it. "They refused to let me see him."

Mrs. Baines thought of her futile attempts to do so, the trek she'd been driven to make through fifty miles of snow and slush of country roads over every inch of which she'd walked, down to the jail where they'd taken him, only to be turned away from the gates and made dirt of and called an English whore by the army guarding it, by the very sons of the country for which she and her husband had wrecked their lives.

"Maybe if you went to see your friends? Surely they'd be able to do something." She was thinking of the Countess Markievicz whom she had recognized a few weeks ago giving a speech to a handful of people on a dark corner of Rock Street. In Zena's sharp glance and the strong curve of her lips, there was a remembered wryness, a suggestion of a smile. She reached out and placed her cup onto the hob. Irrelevantly, Mrs. Baines noticed it. "Won't they do anything?"

"No." The flat final sound was delivered with a grandeur of gesture and tone that alienated her from the room in which she sat and from the people with whom, for good, bad or indifferent, she had chosen till now to live her life. "Any of our friends who *would* help are as powerless as I. Any of our friends who *could* help are too preoccupied with their new positions, standing in the Dail grabbing away like children in a glorified sweet shop."

"But they should help him. Isn't he one of themselves?" Mrs. Baines asked in anger.

"Mattie? He and a handful like him are the Hard Core. That's their tragedy," Zena said bitterly.

"Up to this I haven't agreed with the charges people round the place made against the Republicans," Mrs. Baines said. "An' many the time I stood up for them when Mrs. Chance and the others were saying what a bad lot they were, but it'll be a long time before I utter again in defense of them."

The protest Zena was about to make remained unsaid, as Mrs. Baines left her to bring a cup of tea in to Babby. Babby had been lying with her eyes closed; now she opened them and searched but found no answering smile on her mother's face.

"I'm all right," she said. But she wasn't. And hadn't been since before Christmas, her mother thought. Ever since then she had been sick on and off, lying in bed for a day, sometimes a day and a half, and returning to work when she shouldn't have been on her feet at all. Twice, the dispensary doctor had come to see her.

Each time he had been drunk. Each time he had said: Nourishment and cod liver oil, give her lashings of both, and, while he talked, he shook and fingered the bottle of whisky in the pocket of his soiled frayed overcoat before he went with exaggerated caution from the room out to the women standing round, waiting to draw him into another room to look at an ailing child or themselves. "Ah, now, stop worrying. I'm all right, I tell you." Babby reached out and her fingers brushed her mother's arm. "I'll be as right as rain tomorrow, you'll see." Her coaxing gentle smile was playfully mocking. "God," she said. "An' you love to worry."

"I'll ask Zena to take a look at you," Mrs. Baines said quickly.

"No." Babby reached forward again. "I don't want Zena to look at me. Promise."

"But, sure . . ."

"No, Mother. Promise."

"All right. All right." Mrs. Baines stooped and kissed her swiftly on the brow, stifling the sigh of love and impatience that was on her lips, and the longing to gather her into her arms. She straightened up. "You'll be better. With the help of God and His Blessed Mother." She withdrew, reluctantly, determined that however she did it she would somehow between now and tomorrow get the money she'd need to call in a paid doctor. As the curtain fell to behind her, she glanced over to the altar and the red Sacred Heart lamp she never allowed to go out, and for one moment her face was naked, her thoughts unguarded, in their familiar appeal, before she turned to Zena standing beside the fire.

"You let your tea go cold." Her hands flew to her hair to tidy back into the bun the white strands that had come undone. "I'll pour you another cup."

Zena, sucked back into other times in other places, stared. "No," she demurred eventually. "Don't bother, Molly."

Mrs. Baines forced herself to lightness. "And you must be wall-fallen," she said, spreading her lips in a smile meant to comfort.

"Molly!" For the first time Zena saw the soft scarred dinge of the lip and the gap, dark where teeth had been. "Your teeth!" she exclaimed, and was instantly flooded with embarrassment.

Mrs. Baines nodded, as though the remark were of no possible consequence. "Aye," she said lightly, "I've lost them."

Immediately aware of the cause, Zena hated Pat Baines with a virulence that choked her. She stared at Mrs. Baines as though she were seeing her for the first time, and found her older now than she had thought her, and thin, her gestures more angular, though still graceful, swift, without trace of awkwardness as she moved from the fire to the table, her bare arms in white flight as she prepared the small bits of beef meant for Babby. But she was old, old, and the thought astonished her when she remembered that Molly Baines was not more than forty-five, five years older than herself, and already a crone. All those years, Zena had not been aware of the gradual physical destruction which had taken place in this woman who had tried to mother and guide her ever since they had first met. Her flying periodic visits to the Lane had been too occupied by her own and Mattie's needs to give more than the occasional thought and thanks for the shelter, the change of patched but clean clothes and above all the love, sensed and shown in the understanding she had received from the hands of this suddenly old woman to whom she had come in all her trials, to whom she came now to take her leave possibly for the very last time. Zena felt contrite and suddenly violently guilty that she should have taken so much for granted. As she looked at the stooped shoulders and white head bent over another of her endless tasks, she felt a burst of compassion.

"I'm sorry, Molly," she said suddenly, holding herself rigidly stiff as she made her apology. "I'm an awful fool."

Mrs. Baines wanted to laugh at her sudden strange Englishness. "Musha, you meant no harm. An' you'd have to be blind not to see that I'm getting as gummy as a baby." She laughed her admission. "But you sounded very strange when you spoke just now, child."

"Did I?"

"Aye. English."

"But I am English."

Mrs. Baines nodded. "Aye, but I never remember you are. You must think us the queer lot."

But what Zena was thinking, she wouldn't tell. She was still seeing the ravages of change that had taken place since her last midnight visit to the Lane, and, bewildered by what she could see and what she could only guess at, she shied away, by her own burden made powerless to shoulder another's. Molly Baines, and Ireland, and me, she thought. Jesus! what do men think they're doing! The profanity, as strange to her thoughts as her lips, startled her and measured the depth of her hopelessness. She looked away over to the altar and the statue of the Virgin to whom the Romans prayed and who remained indifferent, impassive, pitiless to all appeals.

"Is it all right," she asked tonelessly, "if I go in to see Babby?"

"Of course." Mrs. Baines hurried to hold aside the curtain in the doorway. Anxious as she was to hear how she thought Babby was looking, she didn't go in with Zena, and when the latter came back her smile was reassuring.

"It wouldn't do her any harm to stay in bed for a couple of days."

"I know," Mrs. Baines answered, "but you might as well be talking to the wall as telling Babby what she should or should not do."

"She has seen a doctor?"

"Twice."

Zena nodded. "They took my thermometer. They took all my instruments. But I shouldn't think it was a dangerous fever. How about her job? It seems to worry her."

Mrs. Baines was relieved at Zena's diagnosis. "Once they have the doctor's certificate, it's all right to stay out."

"Well, I think she'll do as you tell her," Zena said, and went on to mystify Mrs. Baines by saying that Babby had appeared receptive to advice.

There was no time to ask Zena to explain, for she announced then that she would have to go if she wanted to get through some "lawyer business" in time to catch the night boat to England. Mrs. Baines had not thought what Zena might do now that Mattie was in jail, assuming without thinking about it that she would find herself a room somewhere, maybe get herself a job in a hospital and wait until Mattie came out again, but somehow the idea had not entered her head that she would go back to England.

"I can wait there better than I could here," she explained. "There are people there who might help me more than any I know in Ireland. That's what I shall see this solicitor chap about." She spoke without much hope. "Besides it's unlikely they would allow me to stay, even if I wanted to. Persona non grata, Molly." She smiled weakly.

Mrs. Baines wiped her hands on a cloth and put the saucepan with the beef in it onto the fire. "An' who'd stop you?"

Zena gestured a half circle with her hand. "The New Ascendancy," she said simply. "The New Tuatha de Danaan." Which didn't mean much to Mrs. Baines. "The New Cromwells." Which did.

"Does Mattie know you're going back to England?" she asked, trying to bring the woman's eyes to meet her own again.

"Yes," Zena said quietly, almost to herself. "We discussed this long before it happened."

"Child, you don't look well," Mrs. Baines said gently, her eyes moving up the slim straight body to the thin tanned face, somber under the brown soft eyes and the broad sweep of dark brows that seemed merely to touch the flesh from which they grew. "Couldn't you stay with us for a few days and rest yourself, before you face that journey?"

Zena shook her head. "Oh, Molly, as if you didn't have enough troubles of your own already." She bent forward and kissed her sister-in-law, committing to memory the worn gentle features and the touch of the dry cheek. When she drew away, she withdrew her hands as well.

"I hope to God you'll be all right."

"I shall be." Zena put on her hat and then her scarf and fastened the top and last button of her coat.

Mrs. Baines watched her. There were a lot of things to say and yet nothing. Zena was going out of her and her children's life as suddenly, as abruptly as she had entered it. She would miss Zena, Mattie's English wife who had devoted her life with him to a cause that seemed to her so worthy. She and Mattie said that what the Republicans wanted for Ireland was reasonable and fair, but events in Ireland were a great deal more complex than they would appear to the clear-thinking minds of a good man and woman, and Mattie and his wife were certainly that—for with her brother-in-law in prison she couldn't bring up against his character his consorting with willing hussies.

"And give my love to the boys," Zena was saying.

"I will indeed."

Zena looked back from the door. "Take care of yourself, Molly. I'll write to you. Will you let me hear from you sometimes?"

"I will." Mrs. Baines moved to embrace her, murmured a parting blessing, and without another word, Zena went out onto the stairs. . . .

"Leaving me as wise after the event," Mrs. Baines said afterwards, and only long afterwards, and after she had wiped away the tears of loneliness that came with Zena's going, "as before, because I still don't know why the Staters jailed Mattie."

"Well, I'll tell you," Neddo said, and he would, and make a song and dance about it if she wasn't careful, because he liked nothing better than to have herself and Babby on the other end of the receiving line.

"But softer, son," she said, "otherwise you'll waken Babby."

Neddo pushed his hand through his hair and said, "I forgot." He leaned his elbows on the table and supported his chin on his hands. "There are thirty-two counties in Ireland, aren't there?"

His mother nodded. "I'm not sure, son, but I'll take your word for it."

He looked at her wonderingly. "Did you never know that?"

"Never mind whether I did or not. Get on with the story."

"Well, there are," Neddo said.

"So they jailed Mattie for that?" his mother asked with a straight face.

"No," he waved his hand impatiently. "But Uncle Mattie wants Ireland to have all the thirty-two counties, and England wants six of them. And the Staters are willing."

"But they're Irish, aren't they?" Mrs. Baines asked with interest now.

"Yes," Neddo answered, "but they're willing."

"No," his mother interrupted. "The counties. They're all part of Ireland. Why can't Ireland have them? Why shouldn't your Uncle Mattie want them?"

"Because England wants them." Neddo began to grow impatient.

"England!" Tucker Tommy, listening solemn at the table, swung his head back and forth.

Neddo went on to his mother. "The Staters want to stop all the murder."

"Why?" asked Tucker Tommy.

Neddo gave him a black look. The lesson the master had given the class had been clear, but he could not make it so to his mother and was inclined to blame his brother's questioning presence. "The master said the mistake the Free State government made was in the executions last year. Because now they're afraid of reprisals, and are filling the jails with men like Uncle Mattie as hostages. They're afraid."

"An' well they might be!" Mrs. Baines declared.

Neddo grinned. He thought it was funny, the way people's minds tilted from one side to the other. People like his mother and Mrs. Kinsella especially, with no conception of a political struggle and who normally lived submerged in a world that had nothing to do with Dails and Constitutions and Ministers, women who eyed with absolute mistrust all speechmaking and street-corner eloquence, but who could yet be moved by the beaten, the losers, and never mind what motives impelled them to a ready energetic human feeling for what seemed to them the common faith of mankind and its shared passive acceptance. He suddenly wished he was grown up, like his schoolmaster, with a tweed suit and a waistcoat with a gold pocket watch and a red face with black hair sprouting out of his nostrils, who seemed to Neddo, when he talked about History, to be connected somehow somewhere to the far far past.

"I'm going to learn things like cause and effect," he said suddenly, and eying his mother he asked, "What's for dinner?"

"Tripe and onions," she told him, as he crept towards the little room to peep in at Babby.

The next day Babby went back to work to escape Pat Baines, who had come at the hour when his brother's wife walked onto the night boat on her way back to England. He came in wet and drunk, carrying a gramophone and an armful of stout, and, what was rare, jovial, until Mrs. Baines told him about Mattie. Then he began to cry. But proudly, he said, with tears of pride: for a brother he had not seen for two years and for whom he'd had nothing but abuse. But now he cared; his eyes compelling agreement, "I love him," he cried. "You know that, don't you? And those bastards, those peasants, go and incarcerate a man like that! Throw him into their filthy jails, a man who was one of the greatest jockeys in this or any other country, an educated man who could have gone to any country in the world and lived the life of kings! But it was her," he said, shaking a finger in Mrs. Baines's face. "It was that Englishwoman, that doctor's daughter with her middle-class yearnings, who's responsible. It was she who destroyed him, filling his head with . . ."

"Zena filled his head with nothing." Mrs. Baines braved a contradiction. "He was a Republican before they met."

"She told you that, but it's not true."

"No." She sighed at the futility of this. "It was Mattie who told me. The first time he brought her here."

"It was her, I tell you," Pat shouted.

Mrs. Baines gestured with her head. A reason had to be found for Mattie's imprisonment, and a reason was found.

"And now she's deserted him," Pat said, and she knew she could not contradict this either. "Packed up and gone running, leaving him to face alone what she began."

"Mattie himself settled beforehand, that if anything happened to him she was to get away to England immediately."

"The hell he did!"

"It's true." Mrs. Baines was stubbornly persistent, that he should not blacken Zena. "She told me."

"She told you," Pat sneered. "If she told you to put your hand in the fire, would you do it?"

"I might an' all," she replied lightly, edging towards an easier mood from the one her remarks seemed to be leading to.

"An' did she tell you what was to happen to him?"

"What could? Other than what has?"

"A lot," Pat grunted. "They could shoot him, or hang him."

"But he's had his sentence. That's another reason why Zena's gone to London, she had friends there and they maybe can help her get a year or two taken off the seven." It was out before she knew what she was saying. She hadn't told Pat what the exact sentence was.

"Seven years!" His face was dark trouble, for himself and past generations of Baineses. He began to cry again, and she let him, alert to his every changing mood and tone. When he stopped at last, he asked for a drink and, still half crying, slobbered a laugh that gave way to the opening lines of one of Mattie's poems that trailed off into a song before he stopped and, on a new mood, he said, "I'll see you all right," bragging, loud.

"A course," she sighed, as she had done before to his promise of the elusive fortune. She tried to smile confidently at him.

Laboriously he got to his feet and dragged off his rain-sodden overcoat and, brushing past her, threw it across the bed in which Dilsey was sleeping. "Give the man a drink," he said, gay, hearty, looking her in the face with a broad smile before he staggered past her into the little room. She watched him go with dread.

The sight of Babby lying in the bed stopped him short in his groping for the slop bucket. Beside her, Neddo and Tucker Tommy had been sitting close together, but now they sprang to their feet, each trying to get behind the other as they edged away towards the far end of the room.

"What's going on here?" he muttered thickly, suspiciously, blinded by whiskey fumes and the flickering light of the candle on the chair drawn up beside the bed. Stooping, his massive body lurched forward and in an effort to steady himself he grabbed hold of the back of the chair which swayed precariously until he leaned himself across it.

"It's Babby." Mrs. Baines appeared beside him and spoke quickly. "She's not well, an' I put her to bed."

"Isn't she?" he asked.

Slowly he straightened up and whipped the bedclothes off her.

"Leave me alone," she screamed. The cry was jerked from her as, with a desperate effort, she flung herself up in the bed and close to the wall out of his reach.

"Get up!"

"No!" Mrs. Baines pushed towards the bed, and her husband's arm flung against her, knocking her against the wall. The candle rolled off the chair, still lighting.

"All right, mother. All right," Babby cried quickly, slipping over the edge of the bed and struggling to her feet.

Cautiously Neddo picked up the candle; the gesture, unseen by Pat, whose eyes were following Babby, was seen by Mrs. Baines, who was drawing Babby from him in towards the warmth of the other room, helping her into her coat and drawing on a pair of stockings, just dried over the line by the fire, to slip over her feet.

Behind them, muttering obscenities, Pat found the bucket, used it and let it drop onto the floor with a clattering thud. His glance measured his virility and without stopping to do up the fly on his trousers, he staggered out after them. Neddo and Tucker Tommy, too terrified to stay, parted from their mother, blew out the candle and followed her out to where the screech of the new gramophone had begun to mingle with the slobbered phrases of Pat's songs. Turning bleary eyes to where Babby and Mrs. Baines sat, with his sons crouched behind them in the corner of the fireplace, he defied them, then went to the window and defied the Lane, to contradict a word he said about himself and his martyred brother. As he waltzed from topic to topic, he abused Zena and praised Mattie, and switched to a multitude of varying moods, none of which lasted for more than a minute. He sang, recited his brother's poems and, made maudlin by them, he cried. He clove the air before their faces with sweeps of his arms and made promises of how much better off they were going to be from now on, emptying his pockets of the few coppers in them onto Mrs. Baines's lap, with the grandiose gesture of a gambler playing a trump card, all the time shouting aloud his own genius, not newly discovered, but simply unrecognized until someone—he had forgotten who; and anyway it didn't matter—had pointed it out to him, but from now on the world was his oyster and the pearls he was going to bestow on them would be nobody's business. It was just a matter of waiting.

Diversion followed diversion, interrupted only by Pat going to the bucket every twenty minutes, and stories were begun, left unfinished and forgotten as he began something new. With the vicious clarity of mind and sight possessed by all habitual drunks, he saw, and when he didn't see, he fancied, that Babby and her mother were not as taken up by his talk and promises as they should be. Outraged at any attempt to diminish his importance, he flew at them, demolishing momentarily their utter exhaustion in sudden slaps of fright and pain. Dilsey woke when once he fell against the bed and he forbid Mrs. Baines to lift her up, then, forgetting, he screamed at her for not doing so and flung a bottle clean out the window at the sight of what he said in a new burst of rage was another bastard. He wept for them, and for his brother, but mostly for himself, and the night wore away long after the oil in the lamp had done so, and ended only when the last bottle had been emptied and the gray light coming in through the curtains of the window found the brown-stained remains of it, a havoc of splashed and spilled and vomited sud over which Mrs. Baines's eyes streeled, old and dull in her gray drawn face.

At last unable to stand any longer, Pat crazily crossed over to the bed and fell across it. Mrs. Baines and Babby between them got him into it.

"Please God, he'll sleep," Mrs. Baines whispered.

Babby didn't answer, but turned away. Neddo, with Dilsey in his arms and Tucker Tommy just behind him, followed. They heard Pat curse and call.

In the little room, Mrs. Baines spoke to Babby. "Go to bed, child."

Her daughter gazed at her despairingly. "Mother," she whispered, as Mrs. Baines took Dilsey from Neddo's arms.

"Whisht! Go to bed." She spoke gently and reached out to touch and kiss Babby and the children beside her, solacing, comforting them, and by so doing, easing a little the desolation that had so completely taken possession of her.

Pat called again, muttering curses.

Her own misery and revulsion must be prolonged for what would be another eternity, but for the moment her children's had come to an end. She looked back at their faces, told them to say their prayers before they went to sleep and took the first slow dragging step away from them out to Pat, whose passion and lust had yet to strangle her in a flood of loathing, degraded by his touch, by her passive cursed hatred for him, by its terrible futility, its low shameful helplessness. . . .

SIXTEEN

"THERE'S no mistake about it but God does very funny things," Mrs. Chance said wisely.

"Oh, He's a comic!" Mrs. Kinsella said mockingly. "A bloody riot!"

Mrs. Chance tried not to look scandalized. "Ah, no, joking apart," she said.

"Who's joking?" Mrs. Kinsella plunged her hands into the bucket of cold water at her feet to grab what was left of a blanket she was washing.

"Well, if you're not, an' if I was you, I'd waste no time in asking Him to forgive you," Mrs. Chance said.

Mrs. Kinsella's laugh was dry. "If there's any forgivin' to be done between Him an' me, I know who should do it." She was irritated beyond endurance by the sanctimonious manner of Mrs. Chance, especially since Aggie had been accepted as a novitiate. The infallibility of that wan'd turn your stomach, saying earlier on that she saw the hand a God in Mr. Pughe's disappearance whereas everyone else saw suicide or murder or, as Mrs. Baines said, maybe he had just gone off to escape the burden of loneliness that Cocky's death had plunged him into. After all, God didn't just stretch down out of heaven and pluck a man up by the scruff of the neck, leaving his shop behind him with a strange little fat woman behind the counter. But Mrs. Chance, dissatisfied with the conclusions drawn, was voicing her own which amounted to the fact that anything could happen to a non-Catholic and that nothing could be too extraordinary to befall out an' out sinners which in effect was what Mr. Pughe was, not going to Mass, not being christened or baptized in the Holy Roman Catholic Church. She knew this and said so, and only Mrs. Kinsella bothered to contradict her. Mrs. Slattery felt the effort to do so beyond her. Furthermore, she didn't much care one way or another where Mr. Pughe had gone to. And Mrs. Baines, because she had liked him and understood something of his grief over the death of Cocky, was silent and hoped that what she surmised was true. But the only known truth was that Mr. Pughe had gone and in his place was a woman who wouldn't give you a candle nor a bundle of sticks on tick if it was to save your life, and refused to give any information about Mr. Pughe's whereabouts, when questioned, thereby proving as far as Mrs. Kinsella was concerned her own suspicion that he lay murdered and buried under the floorboards of his own shop. How else could one account for the new green lino that had appeared on the floor the day after his absence was discovered? If that wasn't put down to cover up some dirty work, what, she wanted to know, was? It was easier to clean, suggested Mrs. Slattery, easier than boards, all lino needed was a rub of a damp rag tied on the head of a brush. Mrs. Kinsella, knowing her neighbor's aversion to work of any kind, dismissed this.

She rose up from the bucket at her feet, wiry and damp. "Would you ever let me throw this across your line?' she asked Mrs. Baines. "Mine's broke."

"Aye, indeed." Mrs. Baines's gaze swept the line that Pat's presence and his whims made practically unnecessary.

It was nearly a year now since the night he had brought home the red-horned gramophone, an acquisition that had long since gone, as had everything else that could be sold, pawned, or in a fit of drunken generosity given away. Only Pat stayed, no longer looking for jobs, neither in Dublin nor in the country, so there had been no relief to free them like birds from the caged peevish passionate dark into which he threw them.

Babby, in the middle stages of consumption, crawled from her bed in the mornings to her job that she dared not lose, because he refused to let her lie up, because she feared the consequences of his anger on her mother if she went against him. And Neddo found that his black eyes were no longer a novelty but the source of shame, to escape which he began to mitch from school. Mrs. Baines discovered this and, though understanding his reasons, pointed out what would happen if his father got to know. Neddo promised he would go to school, for always at the back of his mind was the vague idea that someday Pat would go off again and there would be no more beatings.

But as time went by and Pat remained, the promise he made receded in the growth of a humiliation that he was unable to laugh off. And so he mitched again, unbeknownst to his mother whom he kept in ignorance by intercepting the pencil-scrawled notes that the master sent to her, until, angered by what he assumed was Mrs. Baines's high hand, he turned the matter over to the school committee from whom it went to the police.

Unaware of this new threat against which she was to prove absolutely powerless, Mrs. Baines, free for the first day this week of Pat's presence in the bed and the room, had stood at the pipe listening to the singing going on at Mary Thraill's wedding, but mostly to the controversy raging around Mr. Pughe's disappearance, and only occasionally interrupting, when it seemed to her that Mrs. Kinsella was going too far in her direct accusations of murder against the woman in the shop. She lingered, too, because she was enjoying the bright sharp air of a fine autumn day blowing under the pale sun the new chrysanthemums in her window box and the lines of clothes that gave off staccato sounds as they were slapped together in the breeze and reminded her of Babby's low labored coughs, before the sounds were drowned under the great-bellied noise of the Lane and the thunderous screech of trains passing overhead. But in the meantime it was good to feel the rare urge to laugh, to dwell, to be lost for even so short a time outside her own immediate now.

"Well," Mrs. Slattery began. She raised a massive hand up to the rag tied round her head. "As I was saying . . ." She stopped.

"What?" Mrs. Kinsella asked at last.

"Gone out a me shaggin' head," Mrs. Slattery said tiredly, her eyes meandering over the great spread of her breasts. The thought she had lost remained lost, perhaps somewhere at her feet.

"You'll never find it there, Alice," Mrs. Kinsella laughed. Still irritated by Mrs. Chance and wanting to annoy her, she continued, "You'll have to let it alone till Tom gets home."

The suggestion of a grin touched the folds of Mrs. Slattery's face. "You're the low oul' thing," she said.

"Oh, I'm as low as a duck's belly." Mrs. Kinsella's retort set them all laughing, except Mrs. Chance.

"You've shocked her," Mrs. Slattery said.

"Well, be Jasus! If I shock *her*, I'd turn thousands white!" Mrs. Kinsella shot her answer, but without quite losing her temper. She turned to Mrs. Baines. "It never dawned on me before, but do you think that depraved oul' bastard went off with some fancy woman or other?"

"Oh, holy be to God!" Mrs. Slattery cried and looked pityingly from her to Mrs. Baines.

Mrs. Baines laughed. "Poor Mr. Pughe! Where do you get such notions from?"

Mrs. Chance's snigger implied that she could tell if she had a mind to.

But Mrs. Kinsella ignored her. "What makes you so sure?" she asked Mrs. Baines.

"I'm not, but he wasn't that sort of a man."

"It's as I said," Mrs. Chance remarked. "You have a low mind."

Mrs. Kinsella eyed her. "You'll be tellin' us next ya don't know what this is!" She swung herself round and slapped her pregnant belly.

"God, but you're disgustin'!"

Mrs. Chance bent down to pick up her bucket of water, assuming that she had brought a halt to her neighbor's lewdness. But the enmity between them was too old and suddenly too raw for Mrs. Kinsella to let the remark pass. Her normally pale face flushed a mottled red and, with a sudden shriek, she raised her foot and kicked the bucket of water crashing out of Mrs. Chance's hands.

"Disgusting am I? You piss-pot!" She bared her arms, easing into a ready tenseness onto her hips before she screamed a streel of black oaths that drew the Lane to a halt and stunned her opponent more effectively than any physical violence could.

Mrs. Chance stared aghast, her mouth trembling in a palsied effort to regain the breath that shot from her on a roar as Mrs. Kinsella made to fling herself on her.

"Ah, Jesus God!" Mrs. Baines screamed as she rushed to separate them.

Mrs. Slattery edged herself aside with a shout that drew the Lane out. In an instant the air was filled with shrieks of abuse and laughter and advice as women dropped whatever it was they were doing and came running.

Mary Thraill, a bride of two hours, tried in vain to bring her guests back into the room when they rushed out to see the rucky-up. She turned mortified eyes to her new husband who, because he lived in a Corporation house over in Drumcondra, couldn't be imagined ever to have seen the likes. But from the look in his eyes and the sound of his voice when he bent down and told her she was gorgeous, which she was, and from his apparent lack of interest in anyone but her, she fondly and foolishly but happily imagined that he hadn't noticed any of it.

The row that was not a row ended on a stream of name-calling and with threats of summonses both from Mrs. Chance, who was being brought back to her room across the yard, and from Mrs. Kinsella, who with unrealized vengeance was following behind uttering dire threats of what she would and wouldn't do the next time.

"She's a shocking temper!" Mrs. Slattery had still not recovered from her fear of being pushed over.

The crowd were diminishing now, although the more interested of them hung about the pipe, rooting at the cause, which was not quite clear to anybody, and hoping for a recurrence, because both women could still be heard screaming abuse to each other from the safety of their rooms and because there was a feeling that this wasn't the end. . . .

"She's an overbearing oul' bitch, that Mrs. Chance." The opinion was voiced behind Mrs. Baines and Mrs. Slattery.

"An' very thick with Father Tithe." The remark was accusing.

"She'll be over to him about this, so she will," another said.

"What'd she do that for?" someone asked.

Mrs. Slattery herself was wondering that, for although Kinsella had never had much time for Mrs. Chance she had less and less this past twelvemonth. She looked at Mrs. Baines, as if for an answer.

But the latter had had enough. The lovely crisp morning had been destroyed, torn asunder by a violence that sickened and filled her with a desperate urge to run from the Lane and the dirt and the smells, the sight of tears and the stench of blood. Out anywhere, she thought, as her mind leaped free over the maze of walls that confined her. Away, Christ! away anywhere, only let me go, she thought, before reason and remembrance reasserted themselves and, with a shudder, she shook her head in answer to Mrs. Slattery's unspoken question. Filling her bucket with water, she turned from the pipe and went back up to the room.

Shortly after, Pat Baines came home, driven back by his unsuccessful attempts to borrow money from the dealers in Camden Street. He was hardly back in his bed when Neddo crept in, throwing wary glances at his father, not daring to speak in case he drew Pat's attention to him. He carried his schoolbooks in a canvas bag his mother had made, and after a quick searching look at Mrs.

Baines he grinned swiftly and hurried into the little room where Pat's eye couldn't fall on him and where he would wait for his mother to follow. He was wondering if she would have the money for the broken bread which was sold cheap in the new bakery in Kevin Street, or whether he would be sent up to the pawn with a gansey or the pressing iron for the money, as he so often was, or over to Miss Warr's, when a knock came on the door and through the slit of the curtains he saw his mother go and answer it.

"Mrs. Baines?"

Neddo heard the question and his mother's reply and saw her glance at his father, as a woman gently but firmly pushed past her.

It was Miss Cahill, the policewoman, who stepped into the room, all gray and neat and big and carrying a large black handbag. At the sight of her, Neddo drew back from the curtain. He heard her introduce herself and then his mother offering her a chair and then no more. Wildly he looked round the room, as if he were searching for some way to escape, but there was none. Sick with fright, he flung himself under the only bed that was left now in the room, where he slept with Babby and Tucker Tommy.

Miss Cahill smiled easily and gave the impression that she had just dropped in to continue a conversation left off, rather than to begin one never started. If she felt any surprise at seeing a man lying up in bed in a room that was spotless and bare with poverty, she showed none and seemed unaware either of Pat or her surroundings, although her shrewd eyes, shadowed by the sensible gray brim of a felt hat, had been instantly conscious of both. She was too old and good at her job not to be, too much depended on her accurate assessment of a scene and the people in it, for her not to know that her visit was ill timed and that she would have trouble from the man on the bed before it was over. Her smile, meant to disarm, was ordinary, as was the way with which she settled her stoutness onto her chair, while the facts of the case ran through her mind, and she took from the black bag on her lap the leather-bound notebook in which were recorded the dates of Neddo's attendance at school for the past year. They were few, but perhaps there was a reason. The boy mitched, but he might have a job, in which case a warning from her and the threat of the courts should have the desired effect. It was normally all that was needed. If not, then the boy was sent to an industrial school, but only as a last resort, since neither the law nor the politicians welcomed additions to these already overcrowded institutions. It was, however, her business to find out, but first she would like to know if Neddo was home, and if so, could she see him?

Mrs. Baines, distressed at the effect of the policewoman's visit upon Pat and consequently upon Neddo, hardly heard, and moved only when Pat shouted at her. She threw Miss Cahill a harried glance and went into the little room.

Neddo, hearing her come in, peeped from under the bed. "I'm here," he whispered, and drew himself out and up beside her.

Angered by her fear for him, Mrs. Baines clutched him. "You mitched again, didn't you?" Her hoarse whisper was a statement.

He made no answer, except to stare dumbly up at her and wait, isolated by her hands on his shoulders, keeping him at a distance from her. But she said no more, only gently brushed back the lock of hair off his forehead, before she drew him out face to face with Miss Cahill.

Recognition was instant.

"We haven't met before," Miss Cahill said, "but we've seen each other in the Art Gallery in Merrion Square and in the museum, haven't we, Neddo?"

He gazed quickly at his father then back to her before he replied. "Yes, ma'am."

"I must say you choose the most congenial places to mitch, don't you, Neddo?" He did not answer and Miss Cahill went on. "I gather you're not overfond of the parks or the swings up in Palmerston, are you?"

"No, ma'am. I like pictures."

"And history." She smiled. "According to your master."

He nodded.

"Why do you mitch, Neddo?" Miss Cahill asked suddenly, hoping to get an unguarded reply. When she got none, she said, "Don't you like school? The master says you were doing very well."

"It's all right," Neddo said.

"Then why don't you go when you're sent?"

"I haven't sent him every day," Mrs. Baines broke in suddenly. "Some days he had to stay home to mind the baby."

Miss Cahill raised her glance from Neddo to his mother. "You work then, Mrs. Baines?"

"Yes, ma'am."

"How often?"

"Four days a week."

"But you leave the baby up in the Crèche?"

"Not always."

Miss Cahill smiled carefully. "More often than Neddo goes to school." Mrs. Baines did not answer and Miss Cahill looked again at Neddo. "Why don't you go to school, when you're sent, Neddo?"

He threw a glance to his mother, then to his father, before he looked up at Miss Cahill, who sat close to him, waiting.

"The kids jeer me," Neddo said quickly.

"Why?"

Neddo would not answer. Nothing would have induced him to tell her why in front of his father. She turned from his stubborn tight-shut look to Mrs. Baines. "Do you know?" she asked, anxiously.

Mrs. Baines knew, but she also knew she dare not say so. "Does it matter why?" she asked.

Intuition, as well as the deep penetration of Mrs. Baines's gaze warned the elderly policewoman. She guessed the reason was in some way connected with Pat Baines, and knew it, when she saw Neddo and his mother start back as Pat sat up in bed and spoke suddenly.

"I'll tell you why," he said.

She turned her eyes full upon him, a faint hostility in the raised contours of her smooth jaw line and in the rounded slightly prominent chin. "You will, Mr. Baines?"

"Aye, I will," Pat replied arrogantly before he reduced his voice to the whinge Irishmen adopt, with its keening informer quality strangely unmasculine and only a shade more pronounced in the women beggars in the streets of Dublin. It was into this he lapsed in his indictment of his son.

"Our hearts are broke," he began. "He's a liar and a cheat and a thief, an' not a day or a night passes without him doing some harm." He went on, recalling every misdemeanor Neddo had ever been guilty of and some he was not, shocking Miss Cahill not by the magnitude of the sins but by the venomous way in which he uttered them. She gazed appalled as his first insinuations that his wife had encouraged his son became open accusations which only once did Mrs. Baines attempt to deny. She was standing with Neddo, her hand on his shoulder, her fingers moving his gansey in agitated rotating circles and roughing the skin off his flesh under it. Once she drew him protectively to her as Pat poured forth his vicious spleen, and when at last he stopped, she drew over to the table.

"It isn't true," she said, uncertain, as though she expected to be halted either by a shout or a blow. "He's no worse than any of the boys around the Lane," she cried, "and better than most!"

Pat interrupted her loudly. "What are you blathering about?"

She turned to Miss Cahill. "He's a bit headstrong, an' that's all. But there's no harm in him. He's a good boy. Except for the school."

"Shut up!" Pat's shout stopped her, but only for a moment. She swung round on him, and the cup that had been on the chair at the bed beside him flew past and crashed on the mantelpiece behind her.

Miss Cahill jumped to her feet and with an unaccustomed alertness that dispelled all trace of her former easygoing manner was between Mrs. Baines and the bed in an instant. "That wasn't necessary," she snapped. "And I would advise you to control yourself."

Pat glared past her, as if she had not spoken, as if she were not there. "I told you—he's no good!"

Mrs. Baines stared at him. "Whose fault is it," she asked, "if he won't go to school? Who gives him the black eyes?" In a deadly calm, she said, "It's your fault. You shame the child . . . treat him like a beast." She stopped, gasping. "You're not fit to have children. You should be locked up. You're a madman, that's what you are." She leaned against the table, overcome with tired misery. "You're not natural," she concluded with her one enormous consciousness; and only Pat's low laugh broke through the sudden wrath-filled silence.

Miss Cahill drew forward a chair and forced Mrs. Baines down into it. "Get your mother a glass of water," she said to Neddo. She made Mrs. Baines take a drink and waited before she said, "Perhaps, Mr. Baines, we can discuss this calmly and without losing our tempers, because that's not going to get you or me anywhere."

Pat's broad back under the collarless striped shirt arched away from the squashed pillow, pulsing forward in what for the moment was impotent rage. "By Christ!" he hissed. "I'll swing for you! And your bastards!"

"That'll do!" Miss Cahill barked her command. "Let's have no more of this."

Pat jerked his head back with a swiftly violent gesture of monstrous proportion in the small room, which shrunk Lilliputian before the expanse of his strength. "I've put up with enough of your interference," he said calmly. "An' I don't want any more of it."

Miss Cahill made a visible effort to control her temper. "If you don't behave yourself, you'll get a lot more interference than you bargained for. You'll cool that temper off in the Bridewell."

Pat, cautious but not cowed, stared. Miss Cahill sat down again and turned to Mrs. Baines and Neddo standing beside her. His hands in his mother's lay on her lap, and his face, like hers now that all her fight had left her, was drawn, knowing what the inevitable outcome of her outburst would be once the door closed behind the policewoman.

"What are we going to do about Neddo, Mrs. Baines?" Miss Cahill spoke her question kindly, lightly.

"He'll go to school in the morning," Mrs. Baines said quietly.

"He won't," Pat said suddenly, pointing at Neddo. "We can't manage him, and I won't be responsible for him."

"Mr. Baines." There was a world of patience in the voice.

But Pat had had time to think and, with sullen persistence, held his ground. "Who's going to look after him if I don't?" he asked. "An' I won't. I can't get any good outa him." His eyes narrowed. "I want him put away where he can't rob and plunder. I want him put where he can be controlled."

Miss Cahill laid a restraining hand on Mrs. Baines's arm. "You can't put a child away simply because you want to," she said quietly.

"Can't I?" Pat grimaced a short laugh. "If I can't control him, I can," he said smugly. He heaved himself forward. "He's mitched from school for nearly a year, hasn't he?" Without waiting for a denial or an acquiescence, he went on, "You have to bring him into the courts, don't you?"

"No, I do not," Miss Cahill answered coldly. "Not if he returns to school tomorrow and not if you undertake to see that he does."

Pat brought his hand down upon his thigh. "Well, I won't." After allowing the full significance of his refusal to sink in, he nodded spitefully. "So put that in your pipe and smoke it! I'll do nothing a the kind!"

He lay back and Mrs. Baines got to her feet. "I will, Miss," she said. "I promise you I'll have him in school tomorrow."

Miss Cahill drew herself up beside Mrs. Baines. "I'm sorry," she said, "but if the child's father is alive, he is the person responsible." She paused and regarded Pat—and with his father, she thought, wouldn't a boy be better off in a school. "If the father refuses to accept that responsibility, the court must then decide what is to be done." Pat remained still, mute, his lips fixed in sullen temper. Miss Cahill looked down at Neddo. "If this is your husband's decision, it leaves me with no alternative but to bring the boy into court." She spoke slowly and whatever she was feeling for Mrs.

Baines was hidden by her head bent to the bag on the table before her, from which she extracted a sheaf of neatly bound documents. She found the summons for Neddo's appearance two days later in the Children's Court, but instead of handing it to Pat or Mrs. Baines, she left it on the table where it lay formal and white against the scrubbed bare board. "You will not change your mind, Mr. Baines?" she asked.

"I will not." He shook his head flatly.

In silence they watched her prepare to go, not noticing her hesitation as she was about to close up the black bag, not noticing the little white and pink wax angels with fat legs and dimpled arms outstretched, until she held them out towards Mrs. Baines.

"These might amuse the younger children."

Mrs. Baines stared at her before she was aware the woman had said anything, and only saw the wax figures when they were actually in her hand, their heads covered with tight golden curls, their fat smiling faces delicately tinted, and from the voluptuous curves of their backs, white wings arching made of real feathers. She closed her hand on them before she put them down on the table beside the summons.

"Thank you," she said quietly, and moved to open the door.

"Good-by, Neddo," said Miss Cahill, turning back on the landing.

Neddo's reply was inaudible, and to her "good afternoon" Pat made no reply. She smiled at Mrs. Baines, who was looking far beyond her, and as the door closed she saw from the corner of her eye a sweep of white and knew that Pat Baines was springing up from his bed. Without actually hearing it, she sensed the cry that followed her as she went out the hall and into the now darking lane.

Pat's vengeance was full but guarded, and Neddo on Thursday morning emerged unblemished by the brunt of his anger, which Mrs. Baines and Babby had borne alone. For them the intervening days throbbed as they dragged themselves from under his hands, out of his reach, and Thursday arose, phoenixlike in its resurrection as a day in which Mrs. Baines was to mourn in its swift flight the passing from her of another of her children, and Babby was to grieve for the loss Neddo would mean to her mother as well as to herself. She had loved him, the Scholar, loved his gaiety underneath his owlishness, his capacity for laughter which even now he could not suppress though behind it fear lurked while he tried with his strange adult awareness of his mother's grief and her own to lighten the weight of the terrible passing minutes.

Neddo's father was taking him to the courts, was actually for the first time in his life about to walk into the Lane and through the streets under the high narrow stripes of Heaven with one of his own children. It might have been a momentous occasion if his wife and his children had not had the unquestionable undoubting knowledge that at the end of the journey Pat would swear his son's life away for six years. As yet, Neddo and his mother were ignorant of the length of time and mercifully oblivious that this leave-taking was to be the last they were ever to take of each other. His mother had washed him, not with cold water as was the custom on weekdays, but with hot, a luxury and unusual when Pat was at home because he said it was pampering them. But this morning while Pat slept, she smuggled the kettle into the little room and with Babby and Tucker Tommy watching, had stripped and washed him thoroughly. She had also washed out his gansey the night before, thinking that the sight of him cleaned and neat might give lie to the accusations Pat was bound to heap upon his head and warning him while she made him ready to say Sir and Ma'am if anyone should address him and to remember to say Please. And all the time her hands moved over his body and her fingers, like those of one blind, ran lovingly over his face. She shook her head when he asked if he should go down and search for cinders as he had done every morning for the past few years, and when he was dressed and ready, she left him and went out to prepare the breakfast.

Vividly conscious of the ordeal of the past few days and not wanting to add to it by any display of the fear he felt for the one ahead of him, Neddo touched across it lightly. "It won't be so bad, will it?" he whispered.

Babby, her head supported on her hand, gazed earnestly back, and behind her in the bed Tucker Tommy kneeled across her in his shift.

"No, not too bad," she answered gently.

"Will there be a judge?"

"Oh, twenty at least," she smiled.

"Ah, no, no joking," he begged.

"All right then, joking apart," she said. "Yes."

"With a wig?" Tucker Tommy asked.

Babby shook her head. "No. No wig."

"No wig? Gonny!" Tucker Tommy, for Neddo's sake, was clearly disappointed.

But Neddo didn't mind, and said so.

"I'd be afraid, wouldn't you?" Tucker Tommy asked Babby.

Neddo waited; and Babby knew it.

"Not a bit," she said. "I think it'd be great gas. It'll be a new experience. You'll be able to fill a dozen copybooks with it."

Neddo laughed, a little uncertainly at first before he grew solemn again. His wide blue eyes fastened on Babby's. "Will they send me into a school?"

Babby, questioned directly, felt bound to give as direct an answer, but was so long in doing so that Neddo asked a second time. "They might," she said, "but if they do, it'll probably be Artane. And that won't be too bad. You'll be able to come home for a day every now and then, like Tom Dunne. And mother and me will be able to go out an' see you."

"An' me!" Tucker Tommy interrupted quickly.

Babby smiled. "Yes, an' maybe Florry Connors."

Neddo grinned.

"Florry'll be mad jealous of you."

"An' his new clothes." Tucker Tommy remembered Tom Dunne.

"Yes, an' new boots."

Mrs. Baines came back in with a cup of tea in her hand and two slices of fried bread, which she handed Neddo as she told Babby it was time for her to be getting up. Babby did so, pushing her legs before her, filigreed with black and yellow bruises, over the side of the bed. She stood before them in her flour-bag shift and took a mouthful of the tea that Neddo held up to her. Her shoulders, hunched against the morning's chill, were also bruised into spattered colors that distorted the creamy white of her skin.

"Does it hurt?" Neddo asked.

Babby, knowing what he meant, shook her head.

"Theresa Slattery got murdered yesterday," he said, taking back the cup.

"What for?" Babby began to wash in the basin of fresh water that Mrs. Baines had left on the brown tin trunk.

He giggled. "For calling Granny Quinn 'False Alarm.' Her new teeth fell out while she was hanging clothes on the line." He held his hand with the bread in it up to his mouth to stifle his laughter.

"Oh, that's terrible!" Babby tried not to laugh.

"She went right up to her and said it," Tucker Tommy broke in.

"Yes, an' Granny Quinn chased her, an' then she told Mrs. Slattery," Neddo finished.

The first sounds reached them from Pat, who was now up and going about the room, and Babby held her hand up to signal quiet, then drew on the black dress that she wore to work. In silence Neddo and Tucker Tommy regarded her as she combed her black straight hair and the even short bang fell smooth and shining onto her broad brow. They started when the curtain was pushed aside, but it was only Mrs. Baines.

"Come on to your breakfast," she said before the curtain fell into place again.

For a second none of them moved.

"You'll be a good boy, won't you?" Babby's whisper broke the sudden hush and her hands went out to touch her brother as he got to his feet beside her.

Neddo nodded as he felt her arms go around him, manfully forcing back the tears that rose in his mouth and the longing to throw himself against her. He felt the warmth of her body, protective, wonderfully familiar. His cheek felt the sudden wet of a tear as she pressed her mouth to his. Before he could reach her again, she had raised her hand to his eyes and was gone. He listened to the familiar clatter of a cup lowered into a saucer, and when the door opened and closed he knew that Babby was gone.

"Eat your bread." Tucker Tommy brought Neddo back to the room to stare at what was momentarily the angular unfeeling world of walls and the trunk and the bed, relieved only by the human presence of his brother.

Tucker Tommy was lucky, Neddo thought, his eyes lost in the fumbled crumbled world of the bedclothes. Tucker Tommy would have his cup of tea with his mother when he and his father had gone. Tucker Tommy would go to school and this day would be for him like all the other days. Engulfed and wizened by loneliness and a terrible longing to escape what lay before him, Neddo began to tremble like the pinkeens in the Canal that he had fished for and caught in his bare hands.

"Don't cry," Tucker Tommy said, and stared solemnly at him before he wriggled from under the bedclothes to come and stand beside him.

They gazed at each other, lost in a world they could not control. Defenseless, they waited for Pat to get ready.

"If I don't come home, you can have my lesson books and bag," Neddo said. "But maybe I will." He looked at his brother hopefully.

"Aye," Tucker Tommy said, and at that moment Pat called in to him to come on. He gave the fried bread that he had not been able to eat to Tucker Tommy before he went out to his father.

Pat was ready and standing with his hand on the knob of the door. Mrs. Baines stood at the table which was littered with the remains of the mean breakfast, aware of what was taking place but hardly seeing it until Neddo, small suddenly and thin in his bright blue gansey, stopped in front of her, shy before the mute appeal in her eyes and uncomfortable, because he knew himself to be the center point of her distress.

Pat swung the door open and went out onto the landing.

"You're going so," Mrs. Baines said down to Neddo. Her question did not demand an answer and he made none. "You wouldn't do as I bid you!" she said suddenly, passionately.

He stepped back quickly from the anger that blazed down at him from her eyes, and gave a whimper between a cry and a half-uttered word.

"You'll do as the strangers tell you," she said. "You'll . . ."

Neddo made a childish gesture towards her.

Emotion rippled across her face, distorting the high cheeks and the planed bareness of the flesh, and with a swipe of her bare arm she flung his hand from her. He cried a rough short animal cry, and with a twist of her tall body she grabbed him to her.

"Oh, Jesus!" she said, and between her arms Neddo saw her face bent down to him until his sight was blacked out in the hollow of her throat. "My son, my son." The words came out of her without effort and without moving a muscle of her face as it stretched in a great yawn of grief up to the sloping ceiling. She rocked him with a sway of her body, mumbling incoherent words of love and advice that he couldn't hear, accompanied by Tucker Tommy's low crying.

Pat's shout from the hall drew her away from him, and kissing they withdrew. She didn't hear Pat ask Neddo what kept him, but moved to the window to look out after him. She saw them cross the Lane, Neddo small, blue, his legs bare in the short trousers and white as the face which he turned back to her for a second; and beside him, Pat tall and black, striding arrogantly forward, implacable as he went to rid himself of a son he had always, with no sense to it, hated, invulnerable to the bitter curses that were falling on him and had yet to fall from her lips.

Behind them, Florry Connors came slowly out of a hallway opposite, her dawny face intent, as though with purpose. "Neddo." Her cry wasn't meant to carry, but the second one was. She moseyed after them until she neared her own hall door, into which she ran muttering his name through dry-eyed sobs, and was gone when

Neddo looked back down the Lane for a last sight of his mother.

She watched them out of sight, and when she turned in from the window, the change that Zena had seen in her was stronger and more pronounced than ever, as though all life and, at last, hope had been drained from her, leaving her beaten and spent, like a body from which the soul has fled.

Neddo did not come back, and neither did Pat, only Miss Cahill, with the dusk of evening, her approach down the Lane heralded by the screams of a straggling gull hovering in aimless flight over the Lane's rooftops and by children's warning shouts as they fled into hallways out of her way. Mrs. Baines heard her footsteps on the stairs and recognized that they were strange and yet expected. She made no move to open the door, even after it had been knocked upon, not until she heard Mrs. Kinsella say in answer to a query:

"Without making you an impudent answer, ma'am, why don't you find out for yourself?"

Then and only then did she move from where she was sitting at the fire to open the door.

Miss Cahill glanced back to Mrs. Kinsella, who closed her door firmly in the policewoman's face.

"I'm glad I found you at home, Mrs. Baines," she said as she stepped past her. Mrs. Baines had not yet lighted the lamp and the room's dark seemed only a shade less tense after the darkness of the stairs, yet both women could see each other sharply and strangely clear. The thought crossed Miss Cahill's mind just before Mrs. Baines spoke.

"Neddo! What happened to my Neddo?"

Miss Cahill looked startled, but only for a moment. "Didn't your husband tell you?"

Mrs. Baines shook her head. "He never came back."

"Oh, Lord!" The ejaculation was out with the resting of the handbag on the table. "I'm sorry it has to be me."

The pause that had been long and labored came to its end. "Yes?" Mrs. Baines's mouth stayed open.

"The court sent him to St. Michan's in Tipperary until he is sixteen. . . . It's a good school, they'll teach him a trade. . . . Sixteen." The policewoman repeated.

"He's eleven!" Mrs. Baines's mouth shut on the last word; and her sight, on Miss Cahill's grayness.

"I don't know what I expected," Miss Cahill went on. "But your husband's attitude couldn't have been more unhelpful." She spoke to herself: "Why would he do such a thing? He stood there and swore that little fellow's life away. Mrs. Baines, why would your husband do such a thing?"

Mrs. Baines stared blankly. "Why?" she said. "Why . . ."

"Perhaps you could persuade him to accept responsibility. . . . I'm sure if he would, I could . . ."

"Why!" It was Father Tithe that Mrs. Baines could see, and she was not aware that she had spoken at all. The question was skeined between the priest and herself, poured through them like silver in the veins, until the priest snapped it in a gesture that was a blessing, and it was left with her then and became a drum beat. . . . —It is not your place to question you know that. —I know that. —There is a reason. God does nothing without a reason. You know that. —If I was a sinner . . . if I was a wicked begrudging woman . . . if my children were liars and thieves . . . if I brought them up in the dark of ignorance . . . —Haven't you discovered that Christ never closes one door but He opens another. . . . He has his reasons but it's neither your place nor mine to question but to accept . . . obedience, humility, acceptance, these are the laws that distinguish us from the beasts of the field. The consequences of sin are hard to bear, and they must accompany men as long as life lasts. —But, Father, how have I sinned? —To suffer and endure, that is the lot of humanity. The priest's smile was wafer-thin, framed by the bleached arch of his hands. You must pray for him, you must stay with him, it's your duty to God. —You must pray for him, the nun said. . . .

Mrs. Baines looked around. Tucker Tommy was plucking at her sleeve and on the stairs Mrs. Kinsella was saying to Miss Cahill's back:

"Youse are a shaggin' unlucky lot, an' I hope to Christ I never live to see one of youse darken the door again."

Miss Cahill never looked back, and Mrs. Kinsella wondered if maybe she hadn't shouted loud enough, and that maybe the wan hadn't heard a word she'd said.

That night Tucker Tommy slept with Babby alone, and the bed seemed lonely and big and terribly empty. In the other room in the other bed, Mrs. Baines lay down with Dilsey, and only Babby heard her get up and go to the window; and only Dilsey, with no understanding yet of what they meant, heard the soft moans that clung round her mother's mouth before, with a pettish whinge, she flung herself against the mouth and slept.

SEVENTEEN

"COME into the parlor and say before the Sacred Heart what you said to me at the pipe!"

Mrs. Kinsella laughed. "Is it in the parlor you want me?" she asked mockingly.

And from the open doorway, Mrs. Chance watched her, then rushed and with a cry flung the bucket of water she was carrying right over Mrs. Kinsella. In the ominous silence the empty bucket clattered to the ground, zigzagging the damp dusk as the two women faced each other. Mrs. Chance's hands shot up and out. "You rotten sow, I'll swing for you!" she said, but her hands slid off the wet head; and with a twist Mrs. Kinsella doubled up and charged as a bull would, for the pit of Mrs. Chance's belly. Her scream tore itself around the whitewashed walls of the Lane and bounced in an echo as doors and windows were flung wide, showing patches of lamplight behind pale faces crowding to watch the rucky-up.

Mrs. Chance dragged herself up off the ground. Her mouth, knocked open, gushed blood over her bottom lip and poured itself out in a wide waste onto the high front of her white bib. She cursed and staggered towards Mrs. Kinsella who waited, fists on spread hard hips, glaring through a plastered black mane of hair that half hid her face and fell below her thighs.

"Stop them!" Mrs. Slattery screamed from the pipe, but nobody moved. "You lousy dirty informer!" Mrs. Kinsella shouted when Mrs. Chance's hands reached her and before they both fell in a tight grip down into the muck.

But the fight had gone out of Mrs. Chance, and she could do no more than grab fitfully at the hair blinding her and give little moans as Mrs. Kinsella kneaded and pounded and tore whole handfuls of hair out of the head beneath her, muttering: "Judas, Judas, Judas . . ."

Suddenly from the dark of a door Fawan Barton tore and flung herself down beside them, to be joined by other women who came screaming blasphemies as they struggled to separate the contorted mass on the ground. Somebody shouted, "Get a scissors!" And when the screams and struggling stopped, they were carrying Mrs. Chance into her room, and on the ground Mrs. Kinsella lay filthy and bloody, with suds on her mouth, and twisted through her fingers and wrapped in wide bands around her hands was Mrs. Chance's hair that had to be cut away.

Tucker Tommy came out slowly from the corner of Mrs. Chance's windows and stared at Mrs. Kinsella's naked buttocks.

"Shag off!" Fawan Barton, who was trying to lift Mrs. Kinsella up, shouted at him.

Tucker Tommy tore his gaze away and darted towards the hall and stairs. He flung the door of the room open and rushed in. It was in darkness except for a fitful flicker at the bottom of the fire-grate and the glow of the altar lamp at the feet of the Virgin. The light didn't touch the table standing in the middle of the room, nor the big bed. But he knew the table and the bed were there, just as he knew that his mother had not yet returned, although he did push aside the curtain on the door of the little room and call out, not to his mother but to the darkness. He dropped the curtain back into place and rushed out into the dark quiet emptiness of the Lane again.

At the top of the Lane he passed Theresa Slattery on a swing on the lamppost outside the pub. "It's a new one," she called out to him from halfway up the shop window.

He glanced at the new yellow rope without answering, and darted across the streets between the Park tram and a yellow bakery cart, and hurried past Miss Fogarty's, Miss Keogh, the bootmaker, who was standing at the door of her shop with her saffron-colored hair frizzed up and her painted face raised to a bottle of red biddy that would start her singing as soon as the last drop was drunk, round the pub at the corner and along the Canal and its tall tenements, and here he began to run until he reached the gaping door of the pawn office.

Inside, gas jets blazed over the high counter behind which the assistants, with only their heads showing, scurried backwards and forwards; and before which the crowd waited. Late evening was the best time to make a pledge, since the gaslight wasn't as searching as the daylight, and a shine from wear or a neat patch in a suit didn't show, with the result that the place was always crowded from the minute darkness fell. There was no pushing or shoving, despite the crowd, only a patient waiting, and Tucker Tommy was able to edge his way through the women and children until he reached the counter.

He saw Mick, the foreman assistant, open a bundle wrapped in a sheet, and heard a woman say: "Four shillings, Mick, an' I'm only leaving them with you till morning."

Mick raised his head. "An' could you not find the time to give them the belt of an iron?" He held up a shirt that had just come away from the front of a fire.

"Well, it's a pity about ya! You'll be wantin' them starched next!"

After looking over and through the crowd, Tucker Tommy saw that his mother wasn't there. He edged in beside the woman and hooshed himself up so that he could see over the counter. His eyes swept the mountain of clothing and articles of every description lying in piles on the floor and came to rest at last on his sister Babby's blue cloth coat. He knew then that his mother had come and gone.

"You should hang that," he shouted to Mick, and pointed to the coat. Then he dropped back onto the floor, suddenly nervous in the gradual mounting of a familiar terror. After one more wild sweep of his eyes around the shop, he ran back out onto the Canal again. He ran with his head down and didn't stop until he burst open the door of the room, saw his mother bent over the dying fire raking it to life again, and the panic ebbed.

"Lift your feet, can't you? You come up them stairs like a herd of cattle," she said in complaint.

He didn't answer. His look took her in. "I was looking everywhere for you," he said. Then quickly: "There was a rucky-up. You missed it."

"Well, *you* didn't," she said. "Who was it?" And she raised a hand to brush a wisp of hair from her face.

"Mrs. Chance an' Mrs. Kinsella."

His mother sighed. "Ah, well, I suppose that was inevitable."

Tucker Tommy listened for a moment to the sound of a new word. "Aye," he nodded.

"Go now," Mrs. Baines said, "and fill the kettle. Babby will be back before I know where I am."

"What's for tea?" Tucker Tommy asked with his hand on the knob of the door.

"Potato cakes."

He caught her near smile and was grinning as he took the stairs in one jump on his way to the pipe. The Lane was quiet now after the row, but at the pipe Annie the Man stood getting water into the can she used for beer, and the soup she begged of the convents in Dartmouth Square and Ranelagh.

"Is that yourself?" she said hoarsely, her lashless eyes hidden under the brim of the hat she always wore, as black as the hole in her face where her nose should have been. The sight of it never failed to paralyze him.

He stood at a safe distance and said, "Yes, ma'am."

"Wasn't Chance the bad pill to give poor Nancy away?" she tittered. "An' her down on her bended wans twenty-four hours of the day."

Not sure of what she meant, Tucker Tommy didn't answer.

"Is Babby up on her feet again?" she asked directly and sympathetically low, as though she cared.

"Yes, ma'am." He dangled the empty bucket against his knees.

"Isn't that grand!" Her lips made a sucking noise as though she had a sweet in her mouth, and having filled her can, she said, "Come on, put that grand bucket under."

Tucker Tommy held back.

"What are you waiting for?" she asked roughly.

"It's all right, I can do it myself."

"Ah, to hell with you then!" She let the handle of the pipe go and twisted into a crouch. "A pox on ya, ya imperdent bastard!" she snarled, and as he stepped back, her spit landed on the ground between them like a full stop. Muttering, she dragged herself away into her own hallway.

Tucker Tommy stared after her, remembering the "lends" his mother had called the endless sixpences and shillings and sometimes the odd half-crown that at one time, and with great frequency, had passed from her hands into Annie the Man's. "Lends" pawned and borrowed for. "Lends" demanded until Miss Fogarty had raised a green white and yellow flag over the door of her shop one day, and the next he had heard his mother scream at Annie the Man, who had called again to borrow, that she had nothing for her and from now on wouldn't. "If you can find anyone to listen to the things you can tell, go right ahead," his mother had said airily, and made a run at Annie the Man, who went back down the stairs quicker than she had come up them. And out the window Mrs. Baines had put her head to sing "The Wearing of the Green." And in the Lane, people said there'd be no more rents to pay, but there were;

and his mother had said they'd be pinning medals on his Uncle Mattie now, but they didn't. He was still in jail, even though there was no more fighting in the country. And Annie the Man was still in the Lane—the only difference was that she no longer came to borrow, and his mother was no longer afraid of her.

Slowly and cautiously and with his eyes still on Annie the Man's door, Tucker Tommy approached the pipe. He was glad there had been nobody about to see the incident. If so, he would have been forced either into a show of bravery, such as answering her back, or calling up to his mother, which he might have done if he wasn't so conscious of the grown-up responsibility that had fallen almost unbeknownst to himself onto his shoulders ever since Neddo had gone away. Neddo had been gone for two years now, and not once in that time had his mother or Babby been able to scrape enough together to pay the train fare down to see him; and except for two short visits, his father had been gone the same length of time.

During those two years, Tucker Tommy had grown up. It was he who went out in the morning to gather the cinders that his mother was raking to life in the room above. It was he who went to beg old clothes from Miss Warr in the orphanage in Northbrook Road. He had, without knowing at first that he was doing so, taken over all that had been Neddo's contribution to the house and gradually more. For, now that Babby had lost her job in the café, he had to scrounge and hunt for work outside the house as well, mean jobs and temporary, depending on the whims and day-to-day busyness of the shops around the Street, those who sold fuel and thought he was overcharging when he asked for a half a crown for a whole week's work of delivering sacks of coal up to the houses on Ranelagh Road and undercut him when they could, or didn't employ him at all if they could get another kid to do it cheaper. He worked for less when he had to, which was frequent, now that Babby was almost constantly sick.

Even with the extra burden, however, there was peace in the house; and his mother, who still had her jobs, and Tucker Tommy, between them, kept the rent and the insurance paid regularly.

And it could at least be said that not once in the last two years had Nick Ryan, coming in with Babby from dances or lately coming to visit her, had to go without a cup of tea and at least a bit of gur cake. Life was quiet except for Dilsey's crying and Babby's lonely night coughing. But the crying was the worst, and it was Dilsey's persistent keen which today had so unnerved Mrs. Baines, who believed the child's laments to be unlucky and to forbode only evil, that to escape it she had turned in anger upon her and threatened to dash her brains out if she didn't stop. But Dilsey had persisted, and Babby, who was going down to meet Nick and sit on the Canal, had taken the child with her.

Tucker Tommy, letting the handle of the pipe go and bending down to lift the bucket of water, saw her coming home again round the curve of the Lane with her sister in her arms.

"You shouldn't be carrying her," he said at once, aware of the weight of the child, now going on three.

Babby, with a coat draped around her shoulders shawl-fashion, waited for him to cross the yard. Her face lost its tautness and only her eyes shadowed a memory before she became amused and touched by his resemblance to her mother in his concern for her.

"You're growing into a terrible bully," she said, and her voice, she thought, didn't sound strange.

He noticed that she didn't laugh and that the breath seemed gone out of her as though she had been running. "I'll take the bucket up," he said, "and then come down for her." Dilsey had fallen asleep, and it was better to make two trips and carry her up, than wake her and risk the keening again.

At the door, Mrs. Baines stood with the amber smoky glow of the lamplight behind her, waiting. Her face, chalk-white, showed her alarm. "What's the matter?" she asked, her hands reaching out to take Babby's coat from her shoulders.

Babby made a desperate effort to smile, but her short labored gasps betrayed her. Unsteadily she stumbled towards the table and the chair beside it. She leaned heavily against the table, resting her breasts against it, trying hard to raise herself up when she heard her mother murmur: "Oh, God!" but her strength had been exhausted. Closing her eyes, she stayed still. . . .

. . . —Look! It's no good your shutting your eyes like that. All I asked was a simple question, an' all I want is a simple straightforward answer, do you hear me?

She shook her head and opened her eyes.

—Well? Nick asked and waited.

—Ah, Nick, I don't want to get married, I told you. I've told you a hundred times.

—Yes, but never why. You've never said. You don't now.

She shifted the weight of the child on her lap. —Do I have to? she asked, and saw that she did. It's only . . . her voice trailed away, and her eyes fled past Dilsey's head to the green swell of the Canal.

Nick leaned towards her. —We could get a nice house, either here or in England. I've got a good few quid together now, and my job here is safe. Though I could get a better one. In England.

—Ah, Nick, she said suddenly, still looking away into a dream-distance, give us a bit a peace.

—Why won't you marry me? He spoke quietly, forcing anger back. You love me, don't you? Or you were supposed to.

She watched him get to his feet and begin to pace back and forth. —I do, she said quietly. I do, but I can't marry you, and I've told you over and over again, only you wouldn't believe me.

—I thought you were codding. He stopped his pacing and stood over her. There's no reason why you won't. Why have you gone with me then, all this time, if you never intended it to amount to anything?

—Because I wanted to! she said, feeling defiant.

—What have you got against me then?

—Nothing. Nothing in the world, she said softly.

Anger burst out with his voice. —Who are you waiting for, Babby?

—Ah, Nick! she cried.

The darkness was opening wide again, and clear, and she could see into its loneliness, its unbearable emptiness, and in anguish she turned towards him and saw the darkness crowd again with the wonder and glory of everything that she knew and loved and was familiar with, at bay now and held in check until the next time the empty dark, wide with room and space, that she sensed would come rushing back.

—It wouldn't be any use, she said into the gray eyes that had come back down to her.

—It would be, darling. It would. I love you.

His urgency made her grave, sobered her after the ecstasy of her return from the nearly constant companion the darkness was becoming.

—I know you do, sweetheart. I know you do. An' that's why.

—I'll go away so. I'll clear off over to England.

Babby made no answer. —Would you take her till I get up?

Nick reached out and took Dilsey from her, and when she stood up beside him he handed her back, waiting silently to see what effect his threat would have on her.

But all she said was, —Will you?

—Aye, I will. His tone was sharp.

She drew the coat flung round her shoulders closer. —I won't be seeing you so.

Nick shook his head. His face was closed now, and showed no emotion. Neither was there any in his voice. —If you want to, an' if you change your mind, you know where to find me. He was half turned away, as though he expected her to refuse even this.

She nodded, not wanting to trust her voice. There was a chill in the air, in the trees overhead a wind stirred cold, and when Babby released a hand to touch him, Dilsey drew them apart with her beginning keen, as though she mourned the two beginning delicate deaths. . . .

Terror, fierce and wild, swept through Mrs. Baines. "Darling heart, what is it?" Her hands flew and touched Babby, but lightly, afraid to add the extra pressure of their weight onto the bowed shoulders.

Under their hovering restraint Babby moved, a movement frail and slight as though borne up by a will outside her own. Like a leaf on a still autumn day responding to the pull of earth, her head pressed back into her mother's outstretched hands which cupped its raven glossiness.

"I'm tired, Mother."

"You are, my heart. You are indeed. You're dead tired."

"Ah, no, Mother. You're just humoring me." She looked straight ahead of her to the altar and, hanging near it, the glassless life-size picture of her father's brother, Mattie, sitting black-suited and black-hatted on a square cane chair. "I'm just tired. Honest."

Mrs. Baines did not answer, nor did her fingers, which continued to massage her daughter's head, halt; and only faltered when Tucker Tommy spoke.

"Will I go down to the dispensary doctor and tell him to come up?"

"What for?" Babby drew her head away. She looked up at her mother. "I'll be all right, I tell you. It was only a weakness, that's all."

But it was no ordinary weakness, such as was common in the girls around the Lane, or like any she had had before. This had lasted longer, for—it seemed—eternity.

"Will I, Mother? Will I get the doctor?"

The dispensary doctor was useless. He would be drunk when he came or as close as made no difference. Yet, without money to call in another one, there was no alternative. Torn between common sense, which admitted that the dispensary doctor was better than none at all, and her longing to please her daughter, Mrs. Baines sought to pacify her. "Just let him look at you."

"Ah, Mother, no." Babby's plea was plaintive.

Mrs. Baines turned away, afraid of the brilliance of the eyes raised to hers. "You'll have to." She tried to sound as though her mind was made up, which it was not.

"Well, all right then, if it'll set your mind easy."

With the battle won, Mrs. Baines smiled. "You're a good child."

"Oh, I'm the limit," Babby replied, with a touch of her old capacity for the quick retort. "But I warn you, Mother," she went on, as she remembered the stock phrase of Dr. O'Carroll, with which he concluded all his diagnoses, "if he tells me it's 'nourishment' I need, I'll brain him."

"Esther Fitz says you ought to eat fry bread an' run against the wind," Tucker Tommy suggested.

His mother's indignation and Babby's laugh relaxed the tension of the room, and after supper Tucker Tommy was sent down to the doctor's house to tell him that he was to call the first thing in the morning. When he came back, Babby was asleep in his mother's bed while Dilsey had been put into his in the little room.

"It's warmer," Mrs. Baines said when she saw him look from Babby to her. "Did you tell him?"

"He wasn't in," Tucker Tommy whispered back, "but I told the woman at the door."

"She won't forget it, will she?" Mrs. Baines anxiously wiped her hands on a towel. And he knew that she had been rubbing Babby's chest and back with the warmed camphorated oil. The room still reeked with the smell of it. "I'll keep the fire in tonight," she said, as he went to sit beside it.

Until it was time for him to go to his bed, she talked, mostly about Babby and what they would do for her, as if by hearing the sound of her own voice and by seeing his unspoken awareness of it, she was drawing some reassurance against the thing which was overwhelming her. The light and the air grew heavy in the room. Between them his mother's voice fell and went unanswered, and Tucker Tommy, close to the fire, began to nod. He struggled to wakefulness a few times until at last Mrs. Baines stood up and said it was time they went to bed. He watched her pile cinders on the fire and draw back the clothes on the line and saw her go over once to look down at Babby.

"Will she be all right?" he asked, and crept to the bed beside her.

"With the help of God and His Holy Mother."

But during the night Babby's fever rose, and in the morning, after a cursory glance at her, Dr. O'Carroll offered Mrs. Baines the inevitable ticket that would admit Babby into the Union.

"She'll be looked after up there," he said, trying to keep his hands steady as he filled out the card. "The sisters, you know."

Mrs. Baines knew. She made no move to take the ticket he held out to her. Her eyes were on Babby, who was staring up at her with a vacant look. "I thought she was a little better," she said, thrusting away the dread and the dust of death that had settled on the room overnight.

You always do, the doctor thought, but he remained silent.

"She's been like this before, an' got better."

"Her pulse is weak. Very weak," he said rapidly, as though afraid speech and thought might elude him. He took his black soft hat from the table. "I'll send the ambulance."

"No!"

"The girl is dying," he said abruptly. "She's in the last stages of consumption. What can you do for her here?" He set his hat on his head.

"I'll nurse her," she said piteously. "She'll get well."

"She won't," he said, harassed and made wretched by Mrs. Baines's overbearance and this delay that was forcing him into terrible sobriety.

Mrs. Baines did not answer, and finally he went to the door where he reached clumsily for the knob hidden under clothes hanging over it. She found it for him.

"I'll come back tomorrow morning," he said. Without another word he left the room and the house.

"I'm glad, Mother, you wouldn't let him send for the ambulance." Babby's lips stretched.

"No, my darling, never," Mrs. Baines answered, her voice a mixture of fierceness and childish tenderness.

"I'll get well," Babby said earnestly, and as Mrs. Baines stayed silent she added, "Won't I, Mother?"

"You will, my heart." She reached out and brushed the black hair back from the face, creamy white against the pillow.

Babby's eyes closed in a graceful quietness that matched the silence of the house, a silence maintained with effort as children were hushed and footsteps went softly up and down the stairs and in the Lane under the windows people spoke only in whispers, while Mrs. Baines sat listening to breath gasped, at times easily, and was sped upwards clutching false hope in wild adoration and thanks as the minutes and the hours went by.

Into days time went, and outside, people forgot and resumed the strident rhythm that for a while had slowed to a whisper, and in the room Mrs. Baines alone fought to save the life of her child. But her adversary stood on firmer legs, on more concrete ground, and playfully toyed against the barb and luxury of beef tea and dazed vigilance, biding his time willfully, like a child dissecting a fly: until Mrs. Baines was forced to tear her sight from the frail hands clawing timidly at the blanket, and face him.

It was evening on Saturday when she sent Tucker Tommy for the priest and in the fading light prepared the room for his coming.

"I got the candlesticks from Miss Fogarty," Mrs. Kinsella said softly, placing the shiny brass holders on the white cloth which Mrs. Baines had put over the table. "Will I put in the candles for you?"

Mrs. Baines, pouring a cup of holy water into a saucer, nodded. She set the saucer on the table before a crucifix, on either side of which Mrs. Kinsella placed the candles, lighting them with a paper from the fire.

"He's coming." Mrs. Kinsella said, and moved over to open the door for Father Tithe, who removed his hat as he bent himself in past her.

"*Pax huic homui.*"

The light in the room sank under the breadth of him, and

with a nod as greeting to Mrs. Baines, who stood ashen gray at the side of the bed, he began to remove his overcoat. Handing it to Mrs. Baines and looking round at Mrs. Kinsella whom he disliked and who had come forward to take it, he dipped his white massive head abruptly and put on his yellow and purple stole as Mrs. Kinsella bent her knee in the way of a curtsy. Onto the table with the white cloth, she watched him put the little silver-and-gold pyx case containing the Sacrament and beside it the silver oil-stock that reminded her of the shell Mr. Thraill had brought back from France.

He bent over the bed and murmured to Babby, who stared up at him with her eyes large, brilliantly black and strangely composed in the still beauty of her face, before they closed on remembered pain as she kissed the crucifix he held down to her. Her lips were flushed, parted, still, humorously away from her teeth which showed like a row of pearls between folds of ruby-ed silk.

"Adjutorium nostrum in nomine Domini."

He dipped his fingers into the saucer of holy water and sprinkled it around the room, making the sign of the cross as he did so; and all the time he watched Babby.

"Et cum spiritu tuo. I'll hear your confession, child." Father Tithe drew his gaze away and edged up closer the chair that Mrs. Baines pushed forward. He looked up at Mrs. Baines. And together she and Mrs. Kinsella went into the darkness of the little room, the latter going begrudgingly, reluctant to leave the priest alone with Babby. He might work some spell over the girl lying defenseless on the bed. You never knew with priests, a person was never the same after them. You couldn't trust them. And Father Rex Aurealis! She never had trusted him, thank God, but after the brazen way he carried on over poor Nancy O'Byrne, she trusted him less. "I'd put nothing past them," she whispered her doubts.

Mrs. Baines did not hear, for she was listening to the priest begin the confession, the words echoing through her brain like sounds heard in a dreary misery of a haunted close dream. She groaned softly, and her head in the darkness rolled between her hands which had reached up to hold its heavy swaying burden.

Father Rex Aurealis called her quietly, and Mrs. Kinsella touched her to life and helped her to her feet.

"I'll anoint her now." He waited until the two women were on their knees before he began the words of the Viaticum. *"Ecce Agnus Dei."*

Babby strove to repeat the words after him, then stopped to look down at her mother whose lips were moving silently over the responses.

"Domine non sum dignus."

On the landing Tucker Tommy, with Dilsey asleep in his arms, crept closer to the door and listened.

". . . from the malignant enemy, and bring thee to life . . ." The priest's words trailed into Mrs. Baines's long sobbing breath, her eyes tracing despairingly the beloved extenuated face that was staring down the length of the bed to where she knelt.

Father Rex Aurealis made the sign of the cross and Mrs. Kinsella's hand tightened on Mrs. Baines's elbow, helping her to her feet. The priest prepared himself for departure, taking in as he did so Mrs. Kinsella, then the stripped bare orderliness of the room. Mrs. Kinsella looked from the priest to the prison to which he had condemned the woman beside him and the girl on the bed. Her eyes met his, and from the clash both looked away and rested on Mrs. Baines, who had come to stand between them with her hands twisted together in front of her as though still in prayer.

"She was a good girl," he said.

"The *best* of a girl," Mrs. Kinsella said. The priest looked at her. "Them that God loves . . ." Mrs. Kinsella broke off under the stern rebuke of his eyes, gleaming in the room's dimness under the forbidding brush of his white eyebrows.

"She's dying," Mrs. Baines said, her glance piercing his through the haze before her. "My child is dying." Father Rex Aurealis nodded his head. She let her hands fall to her sides. "My child." The words were heavy with power, spoken above a whisper but no more, yet seemed to have been shrieked in the white anointed silence.

"God and His most merciful mother help you," Mrs. Kinsella said.

"Amen." Father Rex Aurealis's lips moved. "You must pray." He looked at the door. Mrs. Baines did not see him. She had moved back to the bed.

"How long, Father?" Mrs. Kinsella questioned directly.

The priest sighed. "An hour." He shrugged. "Maybe two." He turned to the door, bent his height, and did not see Tucker Tommy sitting on the landing outside. His exclamation was lost as he tried to steady himself from falling, while Tucker Tommy dragged himself and Dilsey up before him.

"Oh, Jesus!" Mrs. Kinsella cried as he lurched forward. Steady now, he straightened his long heavy frame in front of her. "Thank God," she said.

"I'm all right," said Father Rex Aurealis, then, "You took the Lord's name in vain." The rebuke was mild, but enraged her. "You go to Mass, don't you?"

Calmly, Mrs. Kinsella lied. "Oh, yes." Deliberately, she omitted the "Father."

He nodded. "See that you do," he said sharply, before he turned away and went down the stairs.

An' that's not all, Mrs. Kinsella thought. I'll see that you never condemn me to a lunatic of a husband, nor any daughter of mine to any Mary Magdillon Asylum! "I'll take her in with me." She reached out and took Dilsey from Tucker Tommy. The child whimpered during the exchange and Mrs. Baines turned away from the bed at the sound. "I'll keep her in with me tonight," Mrs. Kinsella explained.

"I'm troubling you."

"Troubling me! You should talk about trouble!" Mrs. Kinsella's gray alert eyes swept over the tall woman kneeling. "I'll have to go in now an' get them their bit to eat," she said, "but I'll come back. An' if you need me before that, call, will ya?"

"I will," Mrs. Baines said quietly, strangely calm now as she stood and came to the door, drawing Tucker Tommy into the room as Mrs. Kinsella went out.

She used him like a staff, her hand spread taut and flat upon the crown of his head, while he stared at the black crucifix with the black Christ whose limbs appeared to writhe between the greedy flames of the candles.

"Is Babby going to die?" he asked, squirming under the weight of his mother's hand.

She dragged on a breath and took her hand away before she answered him. Then all she said was, "Aye."

"When?"

"Soon."

Babby, dreamy white and flat under the white quilt, stirred out of the peace into which she had sunk. She murmured and her head moved on the shadowy black of her hair. Swiftly Mrs. Baines moved to her side.

"What is it, darling?"

Babby opened her eyes into her mother's face. "I'm cold," she murmured.

"I'll make you warm again, love." Quickly she grabbed the couple of coats hanging on the door. Gently and tenderly she spread them over the quilt.

Babby sighed pleasurably. "I'm getting spoilt." Her lips curved to a smile under a faint glistening of perspiration, like down.

"Would you like a drink, darling?"

"I'd love a bit of an orange," she said.

"Will I get her one?" Tucker Tommy came towards her.

Mrs. Baines shook her head yes and looked round to him. "Get a twopenny one, a good one. And hurry."

He held out his hand. "Where's the money?" he asked.

"On the mantelpiece. An' hurry."

There was fourpence on the mantelpiece. He grabbed half and hurried out. When he came back his mother was putting more clothes across the foot of Babby's bed.

"I can't get her warm," she said. "There's no heat in these." There was a desperate complaint in her voice.

He crept softly over to the bed. "Are you asleep?" he murmured.

Slowly Babby's eyes shifted themselves up, dragging after them the black silky lashes that streeled like lace over the polished gleam of the pupils. "Will I peel it?" He held up the orange so that she could see it.

Babby looked at him out of pure love. "Into six parts," she said and smiled while he did so. He held the peeled orange out to his mother, counting into her hand the cold juicy half-moons.

"Will I squeeze them into a tumbler, pet?"

Babby opened her parched lips, and her mother sensed her refusal. She took a segment with her mouth and swallowed the sucked juice in a few gulps.

"Will you have another, pet?" And, when Babby turned her gaze up to her, "Are you still cold, love?" Mrs. Baines reached up to feel the smooth brow which stretched towards the palm of her hand like a cat wanting to be fondled. Her forehead felt smooth as marble and as cold. "I'll put Tucker Tommy in to warm you, will I?"

Babby smiled yes, and Mrs. Baines turned to Tucker Tommy. But he had already begun to strip himself. Then, cautiously so as not to shake the bed, he got into it over the black iron trellis at the foot.

"That's grand," Babby murmured, as he got under the covers and stretched naked alongside her.

She closed her eyes then and so another hour wore on. The smell of oranges lingered around her head, mingling with the odor of the oil on paper that crinkled dustily, like dried old flower petals in a jar. Softly Mrs. Baines got up from the chair beside the bed and went over to the fire just as Tucker Tommy began to doze.

When Babby stirred against him, he opened his eyes again. Through the black iron scrolls he saw his mother hunched on her stool at the fire. Through a heart he could see her face, pale and thin and worn, her humorously curving mouth tightly and almost grimly closed, the strong nose, the resolute chin, the almost snow-white hair tossed and untidy now with despair. Stabbed into uneasiness with an as yet incoherent understanding of her anguish, but made aware somewhere along the short span of his years of her need for Babby, a thought came into his head: Babby was his mother's only comfort, almost the only reason for her existence; of all her children Babby was the one she cared for most, the one who had stayed with her all the time, the one child she would not be able to live without. She missed all the others and still nourished a hope that she would see them again and kept their memory fresh and before his mind by talking about them, recalling their most trivial habits and ways with such a vividness that it might have been only yesterday she was remembering and not five years, ten years, eleven years ago. *Their* loss had in some way been made bearable. Driven from her, taken from her as they were, always she had had Babby, the great loving prop to her spiritual hardihood, and now she was about to lose her.

A chill breath swept across his face as Babby stirred against him. Through the bars of the bed he saw his mother jump to her feet, dwarfing the mighty iron as she rushed past it and lowered herself over Babby. He sat up frightened at the swiftness with which she moved and at the gurgled drowning sounds that almost took shape before his eyes under the faded letters of Babby's shift as she struggled up into her mother's arms.

"Mother," she whispered, burying her face against Mrs. Baines's breast.

"My lamb. My baby child." Mrs. Baines cried a stream of endearments as she clutched her daughter to her. "I'm here, my darling. I'm here," she said, as Babby again called her, muffling the feeble plaintive cry that echoed as if it had come from some lonely and soft hollow place.

Tucker Tommy drew back against the wall. It was cold against his naked body, but not so cold as Babby's arms reaching with a weak branchy strength up towards her mother's shoulders, nor so cold as her legs which against him even through the coarseness of her shift had given off a piercing chill, like a bar of iron or an empty stout bottle pressed against the throb of bruised flesh.

"She's terrible cold," he said over to his mother.

Mrs. Baines was not aware that he did, nor aware of him at all. Fiercely, possessively, she held Babby, her arms tightly locked around the wasted body, her fingers spread and stretched to their limits as she gathered the girl to her, and all the time she murmured roughly, pitifully, begging the child's attention with an urgent tyranny.

"Babby," she cried, lowering her cheek to the bloodless face pressed to her heart.

Babby's eyelids stirred, and easing back her head onto her mother's arm she sighed. "Mother. Mother." Vainly she tried to see, but her lids fluttered like dark birds finding their wings and folding altogether under the weight. She gave a small sigh like the sometimes gentle sough of the wind in the chimney.

Mrs. Baines bent over her. "Ah, no," she muttered softly. "Ah, dear sweet Christ . . ." Her voice trailed into a wild moan as the life was drawn from the room and faltered before she whipped aside the terrible silence. She reared up as if she were ducking a fist and still clasping the body of her most beloved child, she screamed savagely, violently, like a beast suffering a mortal wound, and the Lane, listening, listening, crossed themselves, knowing Babby Baines was dead.

"I'm sorry for your trouble," they said when they came to look their last on the girl in her coffin on the bed.

But Mrs. Baines hardly heard, and her stare was disconcerting when she did, as though she would have had them explain what they were talking about. She sipped the tea Mrs. Kinsella or Tucker Tommy pushed into her hand, and when he grew afraid of her silence and cried she held him to her, hugging his face to her breast while all the time her eyes were on the long brown coffin from which she would not be drawn, not even to lie down on the bed in the little room to which they tried to coax her.

She left the business of the funeral to Mr. Kinsella, and made no requests except that the grave be bought outright. This proved to be impossible with what was left out of the insurance after paying for the shroud and the coffin. But Mr. Kinsella did not tell her that what was left was inadequate to do more than open an old grave, that Babby would be the last to go into it and that Mrs. Baines never would. They could tell her after, Mrs. Kinsella decided as she watched her—on the morning of the funeral before the undertaker's men were due to arrive—tear off a bit of a blanket, raise the shroud at Babby's feet and wrap it around them.

"She was cold," she said, drawing the shroud gently back over the blanket. "I couldn't get her feet warm, no matter what I did."

"No, God help you!" Mrs. Kinsella said. "You were telling me." She paused. "An' you got her the shift."

"Aye." Her nod was touched with irony. She held her hand up slantwise across her mouth. The finest shift Babby had ever worn lay flimsy and white under the blue shroud. A pound had been paid for it. "But I left it too late."

The hearse, shiny and black, drew up in the Lane under the window. Mrs. Kinsella hurried over and looked out. "They're here," she said, as the heavy footsteps came up the stairs.

Mrs. Baines moved slowly up to the head of the coffin and looked long and silently down at the face, set now in all its pure white beauty, stilled into marble as in a light sleep. Around the long hands rosary beads had been woven, and into the right hand a few primroses tied together with a bit of new twine of the parcel the shift had made. These were Mrs. Baines's flowers, of the spring that Babby had been waiting for to get well. There was a knock on the door and the hearse men, ruddy in black overcoats, entered, followed by neighbors who had come to help carry the coffin down and to follow it to the cemetery.

Mr. Kinsella emerged from the group and looked over to his wife who nodded and said, "The men are ready now," touching Mrs. Baines on the elbow.

She bent down and kissed the cold lips, and onto them, big

awkward tears the size of damsons fell. "Me little child," she murmured. "Me little Babby."

"We're ready, ma'am." The taller of the hearse men was harsh, impatient.

"God an' there's a great hurry on youse!" Mrs. Slattery said smartly.

"We haven't all day, ma'am," he countered.

"It's a bloody pity about youse," Mrs. Kinsella snapped, her eyes flashing under the shadow of her big best hat.

But Mrs. Baines was ready. With Tucker Tommy beside her, she stepped into the folds of people gathered in the doorway. Esther Fitz was crying now, openly and shamelessly. At a gesture from Mr. Kinsella, the hearse men went forward to screw down the lid. In the hall, Mrs. Chance, just risen from her bed, stood and shifted the bunch of flowers in her hand in order to bless herself as the coffin was carried past her. Outside, the hearse waited, and two prancing horses decked out with white plumes for the young footed the cobbles arrogantly.

As Mrs. Baines was helped into the cab behind the hearse, Mrs. Chance moved out and placed the flowers in her hands. "She's better off, God help her!" she said. "It's to heaven she's gone."

Mrs. Baines looked down at the flowers and when she raised her eyes again, the world had a bare ruined look. Yet all around her, things moved and made noise in the silence she had now begun to listen for. There was the swish of a whip, and beside her Tucker Tommy said: "We're going, Mother," but she heard none of it, nor felt the horse surge forward; for ahead of the cab she had already gone, way past even the hearse and its horses with their plumes and its burden away, eons away in her search for Babby.

EIGHTEEN

THROUGH a golden October haze, Mrs. Baines, with Tucker Tommy and Dilsey on either side of her, went through the enormous wrought-iron gates of Mount Jerome. Through them she had come every Sunday afternoon, hail, rain or shine, for the past eight months. She and the children were a familiar sight to the drowsy clerk who watched them Sunday after Sunday from his office inside the gate, and often on a weekday he had seen Tucker Tommy hurry by carrying up the green marble stones as they were collected, having been intended originally to mark the grave where Babby was buried but being used now as a kind of guard around the square patch of earth.

Tucker Tommy knew every twisted path in the cemetery, and often after tending the grave he would wander off on his own in search of hedgehogs or to stare with squinted awe through the trellis door of a vault, while his mother remained where she was, resting after her short loving labor, her hands grimy with clay folded peacefully in her lap as she sat with her back to the trunk of a dark yew tree that stood just a little to the side of the head of Babby's grave.

Tucker Tommy carried another green stone today and as usual walked ahead of his mother; for lately, and almost imperceptibly, her alert proud carriage and stride had bent and slowed and seemed no longer capable of the energy needed to catch up with him as she had so often done in the past. Now as had become usual, he turned and darted back to her, linking her arm with his free hand, pausing in his breathlessness to ask her if she felt all right, for with the constant habit of grave-visiting had come her sickness, no less constant in its attack. Often now the mornings would find her tired, her limbs paralyzed with an exhaustion that chained her to the bed from which she could not drag herself, where she lay preparing Tucker Tommy's and Dilsey's meals from a chair beside her while she herself broke fast on nothing but tea and a pink cream biscuit which she could buy only in penn'orts. But nothing could prevent her from taking the long walk along the Canal to Babby's grave on a Sunday, though frequently of late Tucker Tommy would beg her to stay in bed and let him bring up the wallflower plant that she had bought out of her few shillings' wages from Miss Fogarty on a Saturday, no more than she could be coaxed into giving up one or the other of her jobs now that he had a permanent one as a messenger in a chemist's shop at the end of Rock Street.

She smiled at him now reassuringly and lifted her face into the hurried breeze coming toward them down the center path bordered by dark yews with between them the elaborate graves of the rich and mighty, cast for perpetuity into black bronze and gray and white marble, ornate, baroque, sculptured stone, squat and frozen elegant banners over the graves of the dead.

"God help them all," Mrs. Baines said as they moved on towards Babby's grave, expectant, eager to reach the few square feet of clay under which all that had made her life bearable and worth while lay marked and remembered by a few dawny wallflowers and by the circle of green stones which Tucker Tommy found around the Canal and in the dumped refuse from the gardens and houses of Dartmouth Square.

Mrs. Baines approached as if she were expected. Her glance went before her and came to rest at the head of the grave, and her hands left their resting place over the center button of her coat and almost reached out as though they grasped and were grasped by someone who rose to greet her. The impression that somebody actually did was made more vivid by the way Tucker Tommy held back, feigning an interest elsewhere in case his awareness of something he did not understand should expose his consciousness of it and perhaps make her uneasy. To have gone ahead with her would have been an intrusion, so he waited until she turned to look back at him and Dilsey. Then he moved to kneel beside her and pray, as they always did. Afterwards they began to freshen the earth, stirring with their fingers the top layer of soil and clearing it of grass and weeds, before Tucker Tommy added the new stone that today completed the circle. At last, satisfied that there was nothing more they could do, he and Dilsey wandered off while his mother sat at the trunk of the tree. He knew she was thinking about Babby. And often, as now, after his wanderings over the cemetery, he would come back and find her sitting exactly as he had left her with her head turned towards his sister's grave, her faded blue eyes dried after tears shed, in vacant desperate loneliness, until he touched her back to remembrance.

As though she were withdrawing from a journey, she looked up at him for a moment before she smiled and said, "Yes, son, we'll go so." She rose to her feet slowly, reluctant to leave, prolonging the farewell by tidying her already austere tidiness while Tucker Tommy and Dilsey fidgeted, anxious to be away because they were afraid they might be locked in the cemetery; for the closing bell had rung long ago.

"We're the last," Tucker Tommy told her gently, as she gazed back down at the square of black earth she knew so well. He knew by her face that she was saying good-by, and moved ahead of her through the narrow strips of paths between the sea of graves and headstones rising straight or lopsided beside them. She followed after a moment. "We'll be back next Sunday," he said.

"Aye," she said quietly. He linked his hand onto her arm. "You're the great man." Her glance appraised his tousled calf's lick, rising in upright defiance from his wide brow. "You've been a good boy," she said, considering him seriously before she turned to look after Dilsey who was jumping onto the afternoon light that fell through the cypresses lining the walk. "But you were all good children."

His hand on her arm tightened, made uneasy by the finality of her statement. He looked up at her and was immediately calmed by the serene set of her face. And at the gate he forgot his pang of fear by the lightness with which she answered the gatekeeper when he nodded and said, "Well, ma'am, over for another week."

She nodded her agreement. "Yes. Till Sunday."

And for the last time she heard the gate clang to behind her, its sound reverberating through what was to be the latter end of the long wait. The long dreary interval began now to gallop to its end.

"You should have woke me," she said two mornings later when she opened her eyes and saw Tucker Tommy come into the room with a sack of cinders flung across his back. "I never even heard you go out," she said, as he dropped the sack into the corner beside the fire.

"D'you feel better now?" he asked.

"Great," she said. "I feel great." Her voice was jauntily confident. "Sure, there's not a feather out a me."

"You coughed all night."

"Aye. But it's only a bit of a cold. It'll be gone before the day's aired."

"Wait there till I light the fire and put the kettle on." He arrested her attempt to get up.

"All right," her voice was easy and soft as though humoring him and in the same tone she had used yesterday evening when she had come home from Miss Plum's house and he, seeing her exhaustion, had persuaded her to get into bed. "But I'll have to get up this morning." She watched him rake out the dead ashes from the grate.

"You shouldn't," he said over his shoulder.

"There's a few things to be washed. An' there must be good drying out, for the keen a the wind in the chimbly all night would've skinned the horns off a goat."

"I could wash them when I come home from work," he said as he handed her the cup of tea.

"God help you, son, but your washing is harmless." She smiled up at him.

"I'll leave them steeping now, then when I come back I could do them," he said, and thought she was going to give in to his persuasion.

She sank deeper against the hard straw mattress and pulled the scraps of bedclothes and old coats tighter across her. "You'll ruin me and leave me fit for nothing, if you go on pamperin' me like this." She closed her eyes against the worry on his face and readied herself for the effort to pull herself upright.

He turned away to slice her a cut of the half-loaf on the table.

"I couldn't," she said, when she opened her eyes and saw him standing beside her with the bread in his hand.

"I'll toast it for you."

She shook her head, but only barely. "Do a bit for yourself and Dilsey."

"She's asleep."

Dilsey raised herself up behind Mrs. Baines's back. "I amn't," she said.

"Keep yourself covered, pet." Mrs. Baines turned her head on the pillow.

"Will you not have any?" Tucker Tommy asked her as he gave Dilsey a piece of toast and a cup of tea.

"No, son." She sipped the tea slowly while he had his.

"I'll get you the messages before I go," he said, and a silence fell until he jumped to his feet.

"That would be a grand help," she admitted. "If you'd bring back a couple of potatoes and a few potherbs I could make a drop of soup."

He went to the mantelpiece and took sixpence from what was left of her wages of the day before, and hovered earnestly about her while he pleaded with her to stay in the bed. "Only till eleven. I'll bring the things in then and make you a cup of tea."

"All right," she called as he reached the door, "but aren't you the desp'rit youngfella!"

He grinned back at her, and in his relief took the stairs in two jumps.

The room was quiet after he left, peaceful except for the sound of crying in the Slatterys' room below. Mrs. Baines tried to think which one of the children it was, but the capacity for distinguishing one voice from another had left her. Her eyes closed tightly in her pallid face and against the sound of the crying she murmured a faint complaint before she sank into a deep heavy silence. Beside her, Dilsey played with the sleeve of a coat until, tiring of the game, she crawled along the bed and onto the floor, where she was still when Tucker Tommy came back.

"Will you dress us?" Dilsey got to her feet, her voice shrill in the quiet.

"I will in a minute, pet," Mrs. Baines said, opening her eyes.

"I thought you were asleep." Tucker Tommy placed the vegetables wrapped in newspaper on the table.

"I must've dozed. An' I had the grandest rest."

She dragged herself up and Tucker Tommy started, as he saw her shriveled lips tremble in a twisted grimace before they parted in a gasp. He ran to her. "Are you sick?"

She fell back against the cold sworls of black iron and forced a smile that was apologetic. "I think I will stay in bed for another while. Give me over the vegetables, an' I'll get them ready. Then you better hurry back to the shop or you'll be sacked."

"Will I put something round you?" he asked.

"Aye, do." She snuggled her shoulders into the white christening shawl he drew about them.

He pulled a chair up to her, put the vegetables on it and was turning away to get her a knife, when Dilsey, who had got up to the window, shrieked with delight.

"It's me daddy!" she cried, leaping back down off the window sill, her shrieks drowning the footsteps mounting the stairs, while Tucker Tommy hurried to get the chair and the vegetables out of the way. But there was no time, and for the second occasion in eight months. Pat Baines walked into the room, sober and dark, to stand in frowning contemplation of the scene before him.

"What's this?"

The explosion of his words was no less dramatic than his appearance, and his dark eyes fell like a lash on each in turn. They recoiled before his outflung arm, though all he did was throw his hat down before he said, "Didn't youse hear me?"

"Me mother . . ." Tucker Tommy was silenced by the battering blow of the eyes turned on him.

"I wasn't feeling too well." Mrs. Baines's voice was an uneven rasp.

Pat muttered a curse. "Ah, for God's sake, get up!"

"I am," she said quickly, dragging uselessly at the clothes covering her, which hung in her hands, a ton weight.

Tucker Tommy went to her and drew the covers back, and with staggered efforts she drew herself out over the edge of the bed. Her husband watched her draw on her skirt and her blouse while Tucker Tommy bent and found her shoes.

"Go back to your work, son," she whispered, when Pat turned to the mantelpiece. Tucker Tommy stood uncertain, ignoring her command, fearful of leaving her alone. "Gowan," she said. She drew herself painfully to her feet, and Pat went into the little room.

"I'm afraid," Tucker Tommy's whisper just reached her.

"You needn't be." She touched his face lightly, and with desperate effort she raised her hands to gather her hair into some sort of tidiness.

He began to go then, slowly, catching his breath in fright as she hit against the table and heaved herself into bent uprightness.

"Go," she said feverishly, impatiently. "Gowan!"

"I'll hurry back," he said from the door, but she didn't answer him nor make any attempt to. In a useless rage at his impotence against his father, he fled down the stairs.

Pat was gone when he came back, not finally but for the day; and gone, too, were the few coppers from the mantelpiece, gone unnoticed and unmourned in the face of the irreparable havoc he had wrought. After driving Mrs. Baines to provide a meal, robbing her of what little strength had been left to her, he didn't eat it. When the food was ready and set down before him, he sent it flying to the floor, screaming abuse at what he called the "pig swill" put before him, before his first blow, maliciously sudden, sent her sprawling senseless to the floor.

She lay where she had fallen, and when she was able to move again, Pat had gone. Unable to stand, she crawled across the floor to the side of the bed, dragging her body with tortured slowness over the bare boards strewn with the meal that had cost her the last spark of life to prepare. Her breath gasped itself in shuddering moans that sent Dilsey out of the room onto the landing.

Mrs. Kinsella found her easy to lift onto the bed when she came running, drawn by Dilsey's screams. She shouted wildly for her husband to come and help her, frightened by the pallor of Mrs. Baines's face. He went running for the doctor, leaving his wife alone with her until Tucker Tommy came in, followed almost at once by Mr. Kinsella and the depressingly familiar Dr. O'Carroll, clumsily fumbling through the fumes of drink.

"What happened?" he asked of no one in particular as he stooped over Mrs. Baines.

"How would I know?" Mrs. Kinsella answered him.

"Keep a civil tongue in your head, woman," he said testily, while he fumbled for Mrs. Baines's hand.

"Me father murdered her," Dilsey said through her whinging to Tucker Tommy. "He knocked her down," she said, beginning to cry all over again.

Dr. O'Carroll straightened up. "Are you the husband?" he asked Mr. Kinsella.

"I'm not then."

"Well, where is he?"

Mrs. Kinsella looked to Tucker Tommy.

"I don't know," he said.

"This woman will have to be moved," the doctor said slowly. "And I want no obstacles put in my way by you people." He looked at Mr. Kinsella, wrote a number on a card and handed it to him. "Go out, man, and telephone the ambulance," he said, and immediately began filling out the admission card for the Union.

"Will I?" Mr. Kinsella looked at his wife, who hesitated, unwilling to commit herself.

"Do as you're told!" the doctor snapped.

Mrs. Kinsella nodded. When her husband had gone, Dr. O'Carroll bent again over Mrs. Baines.

"Can you hear me?" he asked.

Slowly, very slowly, she opened her eyes.

"She'll have to be moved," he muttered thickly.

Mrs. Kinsella touched his arm. "She doesn't hear you. Let me tell her."

The doctor leaned against the table. "Not . . . makes any difference," he said, "with or without consent, I'm shifting her."

"Can you hear me, Mrs. Baines?" Mrs. Kinsella said softly. Mrs. Baines opened her eyes. "They want to take you to the hospital. Do you want to go?"

The cracked lips gave a quiver, but no sound was uttered. The eyes stared, uncomprehending, up into the familiar face above them.

The door opened softly. "They're coming," Mr. Kinsella said breathlessly, and the doctor, standing at the window, nodded his head.

Mrs. Kinsella took Mrs. Baines's hand, feeling for the weakened pulse. "She might be all right," Mrs. Kinsella said, "an' I'd hate to have it on me conscience that I'd let her go out of the place when she didn't want to go." She turned, distracted, to Tucker Tommy. "What'll I do?"

"Nothing. Except control yourself!" Dr. O'Carroll came across and stood beside her, looking down on the closed eyes, watching the soft rise of the flattened breast under the blouse Mrs. Kinsella had opened down to the middle, hoping to ease the labored breathing. "She doesn't care one way or the other where she goes."

"She does. She hates the Union." Tucker Tommy stifled a sob, and Mrs. Kinsella stepped up beside him.

"They'll look after her better than you could, son." A knock sounded on the door and she moved to open it.

Two men in uniform, carrying a stretcher between them, shuffled in, their faces firmly set in seriousness. Tucker Tommy stared at them, and a great dread swept over the beat of his quickening heart.

"No!" he shouted. "No, you're not to take my mother." He surged forward, but Mrs. Kinsella caught and held him, bundling his face into the folds of her sack apron.

"Hurry!" she cried. "For God's sake!"

When she released him, his mother had been carried out the door of her room. He rushed after her, peering desperately through the rungs of the bannisters for a glimpse of her face, but the red blanket hid her from him, and all he could see was a stray rib of white hair peeping through as though it sought a final look on a life not only known but known well.

"Mister!" he shouted out the full of his voice as he flung himself down the stairs after them. "Bring my mother back!"

"Jasus! what's going on?" Mrs. Slattery's voice joined the mounting commotion as women ran to the hall door and gathered round the ambulance pulled up outside it.

"What's up?" they asked, and the more belligerent, touched by Tucker Tommy's distress, cried, "What do youse think youse are doin', youse gurriers?"

Unmoved, unafraid, the men ignored them. Swiftly, efficiently, their gestures and movements gathered momentum until, with a final twist of the black doors, the stretcher was hidden from sight, closed tight against the tight face of Tucker Tommy. The ambulance moved suddenly in glossy impudence. Beetle-black, it shot across the cobbles, followed by a crowd of children who screamed abuse and laughter after it. At the hall, the crowd fell back to let Dr. O'Carroll pass through. Fortified by a quick swig out of the bottle in his overcoat pocket, he faced them, his red-veined eyes sweeping over them contemptuously.

"Have another look Rasputin," Fawan Barton cried shrilly, brazenly.

There was a nervous titter. The doctor's reply was lost to Tucker Tommy, but he heard a woman new to the Lane ask Queenie Mullen's mother what was up.

"It's Mrs. Baines, She's going to the Union."

"Who was she?" asked the woman, who had moved a few days ago into Mrs. Chance's rooms.

Mrs. Mullen raised her sharp pointed nose. "Don't tell me you don't know, an' you in this place a week now?"

The newcomer shook her head.

"God!" said Mrs. Mullen. "The countrywoman—did you not know her?"

"The Countrywoman": the phrase caught at Mrs. Kinsella and reminded her of the summer's evening years ago when she had first seen the tall blond woman with the baby in her arms coming into the Lane, and the look of surprise on her face and her trick of averting her proudly held head as she gazed at the houses around her, and her explanations afterwards that she felt they might all fall down on top of her. Well, they had! Mrs. Kinsella thought bitterly. Them and her husband and the priest between them had done the job proper and no mistake about it. Between them, they'd massacreed her. She shook herself and leaned across to the newcomer.

"Anything you don't know, ask Sadie. She'll enlighten you."

Her sarcasm was not wasted. Mrs. Mullen leaned forward. "Is that so?"

With superb unconcern, Mrs. Kinsella drew herself erect. "Ah, go an' have a Mass said for yourself," she said. She drew Tucker

Tommy apart. "Go on to your work, son. I'll look after Dilsey till you come in."

"I want to see me mother," he whispered hoarsely.

"This evening you can. They'll let you see her then."

He stared, and without another word walked away, tears of self-pity rolling down his cheeks. His hand, fumbling for the bit of rag in his pocket, found the paper bag with the little pink cream biscuits he had bought for his mother and not given her. Roughly, he wiped his face on the cuff of his coat, a black parson's coat with rounded ends that Miss Warr had given him. She knew, she said, that his mother was good with her hands and clever with the needle and would be able to make something useful out of it. "But not that clever," his mother had said, and even after all her labor it was still a man's coat.

It was still a man's coat, but a good coat, with pockets large enough to hold a dozen oranges, although that evening they held —besides the pink biscuits—only two that he had swiped from under Miss Fogarty's nose, and he hurried now with them, up the Lane and into the Street, his hands closing on what Mrs. Kinsella had called "the little luxuries," when he had told her what he was bringing up to his mother. Cheerfully, she had agreed to mind Dilsey again and apologized for not being able to add anything to the things he was taking with him.

"But I will a Sunda'," she said. "Maybe a little cake or something. You can ask her what she'd have a longing for. An' don't worry about Dilsey, I'll mind her," she shouted as he rushed out into the night on his way to his mother.

Through the streets he went at a trot, his runner shoes making no sound in the night through which he ran: silently anxious, feeling forward in a lonely way, thinking the things he would say to her, unmindful of the drizzle falling like baptismal drops through the patchy darkness. He moved nimbly, side-stepping the corner-boys who shot out a foot in an effort to trip him and twisting away from the stretching arms of derelict cadgers who mooched for a breathless moment after him like a disease reaching from a sore.

Around the Protestant black of Christ Church, he fled out into James's Street, lined with hucksters and pubs around whose lighted doors kids played, drawn to the green gaslight in a forest of stone whose foundations palsied under the steel and iron clank of panting trams. Briefly, they passed him, swaying with bulging transparent bellies exposing for a moment the tortured faces of the already devoured, before tearing ahead to guzzle the darkness; and always he was left streeling behind.

But ahead of him was the Union, and holding its high wall and great gate in his sight, he slowed down, taking his eyes off it only when he drew level with the pub beside it in order to take a look of himself in the looking-glass in the window. He angled round the giant whisky bottle and saw that his hair had lost what smoothness he had forced upon it and stood up in a damp profusion. He drew the flat of his hands across it, and without another glance hurried over the last few yards to the big shut gate. There was no knocker, but on the wall beside it was a bell. Tucker Tommy pulled it out towards him and stepped back expectantly. On the other side, he could hear people moving and talking, a quiet bedlam of voices mumbled and shrilled, through the louder commands to shut their lousy gobs!

"Whadd'ya want?" a man shouted to Tucker Tommy.

Startled, he turned from the gates he had expected to see open and noticed a little door beside them, through which a man poked his head and shoulders.

Tucker Tommy ran towards him. "To see me mother."

Tall, thin, with cropped gray hair, the clerk eyed him doubtfully. "Come back tomorrow."

"I can't." Tucker Tommy darted as he saw the door closing.

The man drew back and brought the door with him. "Why not?"

"I'm working."

The other shook his head as though a new burden had been added to those he already carried. "All right," he said and jerked his head. He beckoned him in. "What's her name? When did she come in?" he asked, and when he was told: "Follow me."

He led him through a low arch of utter blackness out into a bleak square lit by a single gas lamp and flanked by four-story buildings of grim gray stone. At the building nearest the gate, a crowd of men and women hung around an open door and a single lighted window which had "Office" written in black capital letters across it. Inside the door, a high counter separated most of the room from a narrow square space where the most forward of the crowd were standing. Two gas jets burned over a high desk on which a vast black-bound ledger lay open. A man sat on a high stool bent over it, the noise of his furiously scratching pen drowned by the loud complaints and abuse hurtled at him from the crowd lining the counter.

The man Tucker Tommy was following pushed his way roughly past them, causing one old man to stagger uncertainly before he fell cursing to the stone floor, but nobody paid any attention except Tucker Tommy, who stared as the old man rose shouting to his feet again, his quavering voice womanish in its stridency.

"The Tans was gentlemen compared to youse!" he cried. Ousted now from his place against the counter, he turned on the crowd, who were standing body to body in the scanty space. "Youse lot a mealy-mouthed paupers!" he cried, his wiry body under a multitude of old mackintoshes, cavorting unsteadily in a pecking movement like some grotesque ancient bird risen from some old long sleep. He appeared to trail as if suspended, as he rose and fell in his futile attempts to reach the faces of the people in front of him. "Youse are doin' me in," he shouted. "The way youse did in old Ireland!"

"That's the spirit, Micky!" A woman turned a blotched and bloated face towards him. "Tell the buggers what you think of them. The country's with you." She screamed a laugh that was echoed here and there in the crowd.

"Give me me ticket for me bed!" the old man screamed.

"Ah, gowan! Give the man his bed!" someone else cried.

"There'll be no bed for any of youse if youse don't watch out."
The man Tucker Tommy had followed beckoned him towards
the far end of the counter. "When did you say she came in?" he
asked, holding his head sideways.

"Today."

"Ah . . . I thought you did." He was pleased with himself.
"Well, she's gone." He brought his face, which he had turned
up to the semi-darkness of the ceiling, round again. "Removed."

"Eh, son, got a fag?" A cadger unnoticed had moseyed up and
was reaching a dirty hand out.

Tucker Tommy drew closer to the counter and shook his head.

"What about the price of one?" the man asked. "I'm gasping."

"Nip that!" The man behind the counter snapped. "Or out
you'll go, whether you like it or not."

The beggar replied with a muttered obscenity and turned away.

Stretched to the utmost on his toes, Tucker Tommy asked,
"Where's me mother? I want to see her."

"She's gone. Amn't I just after telling you?" The man was
irritated. "Are you hard a hearin' or what?"

"She can't be!" Tucker Tommy fell back and shouted. "She
isn't! Where'd she go then?"

This time the man stared hard. "Listen," he said, "I'm not here
to deal with chiselers. I told you oncet an' I won't repeat meself."

He turned away and Tucker Tommy jumped forward. "I want
to see the nun." He was trying hard not to scream.

"What nun? The man halted in his tracks.

"The nun in charge!" Driven by what was now becoming in-
supportable fear, Tucker Tommy spoke at the top of his voice.

"T'row him out!" The voice of the crowd rose sullen and surly.

The man ignored them. "Out a me way," he said, vaulting over
the counter. "Come on," he spoke to Tucker Tommy. "Come on
then." And he brought him back outside the door. His glance took
in the minister's coat and the runner shoes and the mud-splashed
bare legs. "Your mother," he whispered, bending, "was taken to
Greenfield. If you want to know."

The name staggered Tucky Tommy. "Ohhh!" he cried softly. His face shot up as if a steel point had been pushed into the base of his spine, snapping him into action. "Why?" he shouted. "Why?"

In a flash he turned and ran. The clerk called out, "Ey, son!"

Tucker Tommy did not wait. He found the cobbled yard under his feet, and was running, running across to the gate that stayed tightly shut despite his frantic hands until, mercifully, the great lock was turned by someone who pushed him roughly aside. Another push sent him blindly out on the path and the wet lighted street that stretched before him. He stopped to ask the way and was running again without waiting for an answer, through side streets that he had never gone through before, possessed like a bird by some uncanny knowledge that the direction he was going in was the right one. Faster and faster he ran, with the sweat trickling down into his eyes, murmuring, murmuring as he sped into a distance colored like the inside of an empty porter bottle. Faces, blank and white, shot past, while he plunged on ahead of the ever reaching might of terror following, catching up with him on a drunken halt at corners. Over the bridge and the gray swell of the Liffey under it, he tore, panting to a stop in the shadow of the Four Courts where he asked the way, then plunged again into a maze of back streets, stumbling on numb legs the last dizzy steps that brought him finally to the high redstone wall surmounted by the high railings of the madhouse. Behind them somewhere was his mother.

Sweat seeped out through his gansey and down his back and thighs in cold beads, as he panted under the great gate and the handle of the bell placed high upon it. He leaned heavily against the gate, drawing his breath on painful gulps before he could spring up to pull it. Away in a distance he heard its peal, reproachful in an imagined stillness. He shivered. Hours passed before he heard the slow approach of heavy feet and the creaked whinge of the iron gate as it moaned its consent.

"What do you want?" It was querulous, impatient, and uttered by a garrulous wisp of a man no bigger than Tucker Tommy himself, but broad, as though he had grown out instead of up.

"Me mother." Quickly he added the particulars, now a litany to his ears.

"Have you a Dying Pass?"

Tucker Tommy shook his head. Ferret eyes probed the darkness and a sparse brush of black hair on an overlarge head jerked backwards, beckoning. He went quickly onto a gravel drive up to a redstone house which shone a light here and there onto the scraggly withering bushes growing in front of it up to a pillared hall door which the gatekeeper, going before him, opened with a key. The hall was square, stone, bare except for a wire-framed electric-light bulb fixed against the high ceiling. Its fierce brightness lighted up the four dark oak doors that led into the building proper.

"Here." The gatekeeper pointed to a spot on the floor, unlocked one of the doors and locked it again behind him.

Tucker Tommy drew the two paper bags from his pocket. He was smoothing them out when the man came back, accompanied by a nurse who, with a leisurely inquisitiveness, surveyed him coldly.

"Well!" and it was a comment. "You won't want for lack of cheek, will you?" Her voice was coarse, level and without a trace of feeling. "Don't you know this isn't the visiting hour?"

He stared at her mutely.

"Who do you think you are? The Lord Mayor?" She waited. "What do you want?"

"To see my mother." He was heedless of rebukes.

"At this hour?" The nurse shifted her weight. "You haven't a pass."

"I can't come in the day." He moved forward. "I'm working."

The gatekeeper raised his head.

"All right," she said. The man shuffled away. "You have a nerve haven't you?"

Tucker Tommy pressed his lips together.

The doughy, heavy-featured face broke into a slovenly grin.

"Come on. But only for a few minutes, mind." She held up her hand in sudden warning. "And if you make a sound . . ." Her voice threatened.

"Yes, ma'am."

"Nurse." She corrected him.

Doubt clouded his face until she twirled skittishly at the door with a billow of her starched white apron and of the loose blue fullness of the dress underneath.

"Nurse," he said, reassured. The gesture was ordinary, the kind of a twirl a girl in the Lane might have made.

"That's better." She drew him into another hall, and he saw her sort out a key from the bundle in her hand and slip it into the lock of the door nearest them. It swung open with heavy slow caution, and beyond it he could see the widening ward, coming reluctantly into his sight until she pushed him into it. "Go on."

While she locked the door behind them, he stood and stared stupidly around the long narrow room, lined on both sides with white iron beds from which rose a babble of sounds, like the beating of wings against his face, baffling him in their singsong crescendos of lament and exulting, regulated and modified in their rise and fall as by some crazily swung baton. This was one of the so-called sick wards of Greenfield. In its forty narrow beds were women, more than half of them dying reluctantly while the rest lay sinisterly quiet or strapped, and moaned unheeded their minds' griefs.

The nurse pointed to the far end of the ward.

He narrowed his vision to keep out the sights on either side and moved over the bare wood floor to where his mother lay, dying but with all her senses, in silent white isolation upon a bed in the corner. Stonelike, he approached, his every sense averted, every step placed as though he went on thread that unwound from a spool held before him. A woman in a striped calico shift left her bed, her white feet silent on the bare floor, her legs below the shift a continuation of the long arms held to her sides, her gaunt face sunken under the high ridge of her cheekbones, expressionless yet purposeful, as though she were about to perform a great deed, a moving stone in some old ceremonial. Her eyes flashed a feverish urgency and need, mighty and proud in their black glittering determination—until she fell meekly into step beside him, mumbling incoherently her mind's gnaw.

"There is monkeys on the wall," she said suddenly and stopped herself dead in front of him. "There is monkeys on the wall."

Tucker Tommy stepped back, frightened.

"Sh! The whole place is filled with monkeys. Look!" She flung her arms in a wild gesture. "Look. Along the wall."

He forced the spit into his mouth just as the nurse bore down upon them. The woman shrank back but the nurse caught her arm in a man's grip.

"Have you no shame in you?" she asked her. "Are you not enough trouble all day, without starting your tricks at night as well?" In answer to the woman's low moan, she went on, "I'll settle you, Lady Ann!"

Tucker Tommy hurried on, his fear lessening as he came up to the bed where his mother lay, and where both of them, each in a different way, were coming to the end of a search.

Mrs. Baines lay flat under the bedclothes, her eyes shut as though she were sleeping and only flickering to life when Tucker Tommy whispered: "Mother." Softly the eyelids curled back and the majestic blue eyes rose from their tenuous rest to consider him. The calm dreamy glance welcomed him, thrusting back the cry which rose to his lips at the sight of her and which he could scarcely repress. She had changed. In the past hours a startling difference had come over her. It was as if his mother, whom he had handed a cup of tea that morning in bed, had already gone and someone who only resembled her had come to take her place. Thin and shallow and hollow, she looked. Her forehead, high-domed and smooth, stretched away to a fine silky cloud of white hair spread sideways on the pillow which seemed hardly to dent under the weight of her head. And her hands, those loving capable hands, were now long thin shadows folded over each other lightly on her chest, but open as though they had let go.

"Tommy," she said, gently following his name with her slow smile. "God bless you."

"Your voice isn't changed," he said and grinned.

"No, pet."

"I brought you two oranges and the pink biscuits." He held them up so she might see them better.

"You keep them."

"No, they're for you. Do you feel better?"

"Yes, I'm grand now." She gazed at him.

"Does the noise worry you?"

She moved her lips together. "Ah, no. I don't mind it. I sleep now. I'm getting lazy," her voice sank to nothingness.

"Mother!" his cry roused her from the grateful quiet.

She saw the tears on his cheek. "Ah, son."

"Will you get better?" He put his hand out to touch and hold hers.

"Aye."

Hardly had she spoken or her gaze begun to trace his features when the nurse came and said, "It's time, sonny."

Afraid, he looked up at her. "Couldn't I stay for another bit?" His eyes begged her indulgence.

She shook her head, and he looked from her to his mother. But she didn't intercede for him. For the first time in his life he had called on her in vain. He felt small and lonely and unwanted, and his eyes grew brilliant behind unshed tears.

"Please," he begged.

The nurse rustled impatience.

He bent down and kissed his mother on lips that were cool and dry, and the blue eyes, agleam now with a new pity, watched him. "I'll be up and about again, son," she said; and the nurse said, "Come on."

He held up the two paper bags to her. "These are for my mother," he said, handing them to her before he turned swiftly back. "I'll be up tomorrow, Mother."

She gazed. "Yes, pet," she murmured, but the nurse laid a hand on his shoulder.

He had forgotten the noise. It had receded while he was looking on his mother and sounded only in their pauses, like the faraway murmur of the water pouring into the locks on the Canal in the dead of night. But now he met it head-on again: the soft tormented howls of the mad and the near-mad and the sighs of the sick, gaining in violence as the darkness deepened its black mystery and haunted with its probing ghost fingers, rooting hands in search of cinders in a bin, the jellied tracery of the brain. He kept close to the shape of the nurse, trying not to see the hands held out to them as they passed, or to hear the sometimes clearly audible sane voices craving some attention, some small attention, before a guttural lewd or holy word was screeched after them.

In the milky darkness at his side, a low but defiant voice sang:

"The sun shines down on Charley Chaplin.
His boots are crackling
For the want of blackening.
An' his poor torn coat
It needs a mendin'
Before they send him
To the Dardanelles."

"They're a right pack, aren't they?" the nurse said as she hurried him up the ward to the door. "I'll deal with you later, Mary Jane!" she threatened a woman kneeling up in her bed in busy confusion, with her hands held up before her while she argued with them or cajoled them, each in turn, to some secret bidding.

He shivered as the night air met him, and high up the sky was black, and in the wind there was snow. His mother would get well, he thought, then remembered that she hadn't asked for Dilsey, or whether or not Pat had been at home when he left. She hadn't asked him how he had found her. He would have liked her to know, and about the chase. It would've pleased her, and maybe made her know how important she was to him, if he could've told her. He skirted the thought that followed: maybe she didn't know that she'd been moved from the Union to that place. Maybe she didn't know where she was . . . or care. She would get well, he thought, and turned up the collar of his minister's coat, and headed with a pang of loneliness for home.

Pat Baines was in when Tucker Tommy reached the hall. Mrs. Kinsella, who had been on the watch-out for him, heard him on the stairs and quietly opened her door to intercept him.

"He's home," she said. "An' moldy!"

"Where's Dilsey?" he asked.

She nodded over to her bed, where Dilsey lay at the foot alongside the youngest Kinsella child, blissfully sleeping. "I'll keep her here tonight. She can go back in to you tomorrow."

"What about me father?" he asked, anxious lest Dilsey's absence cause another commotion.

She laughed bitterly. "Judging by the racket he kicked up on his way in tonight, he won't miss her." She flung her head up. "The man's stocious!" Then: "How was your mother?"

"She's grand. She was asleep, but she woke up when I came in."

"Ah, sure, with the help of God, she'll be outa that kip and home again before we know where we are."

He wondered for a minute whether to tell her where his mother had been taken, and decided against it. The name of the madhouse, rare in the Lane, meant shame. "I better go," he said.

"If you have trouble with him, get out. Don't stay to be murdered, will you?"

Tucker Tommy shook his head. I'm not afraid, he thought.

"I'll keep the door on the jar," she continued, "till I hear how you get on."

From long habit, as he entered the room his eyes flew to the corner of the fire, where his mother had liked to sit, desolate now in its gray vacancy. A flood of despair came over him as he felt the room's emptiness, which despite Pat's presence hung like a pall over it, chilling him to the bone with longing.

Pat staggered from where he sat at the table, knocking over a tumbler half-full of whiskey at his elbow. "Where's you mother?" His voice blurred as he teetered to a halt.

Tucker Tommy drew back against the door. "She's in the hospital."

Pat thrust out a hand and grabbed him. "Th' hospita'!" His sodden breath slid in disgust over the word before he flung Tucker Tommy from him. "Who she think she is?" He slobbered a reel of curses that took him from one end of the room to the other.

Tucker Tommy's blood waxed into angry heat. He longed to smash and beat the black malice-wreathed face into sensibility, into regretting all the suddenly now vividly remembered vicious pains and anxieties that it had rained into the minute-by-minute hours of his mother's life, the malicious inflictions that had driven everything she had ever cared about from her and withered her into crippled ill health and old age when she was still young. He had thought that his mother's going to hospital might bring some change in Pat, but it had not. But maybe, if he knew into what class of a place they'd taken her, if he knew, mightn't that make the difference. Surely he would remember, and remembering regret.

"They put my mother into Greenfield."

Pat stared.

"The nuns did," Tucker Tommy said.

Into the silence, Pat roared, shattering it with a blasphemy before he retched out, "She's mad!", and a weird delight shook him. "She's mad!" Thrusting his face close to Tucker Tommy's, he said, "Your mother's mad." The words twisted from his panting mouth between the strong square teeth. "D'ya hear?" His face touched his son's. "D'ya hear what I'm telling you? She's mad."

His breath blasted Tucker Tommy's terrified eyes, and he ducked and ran crouching to the other side of the table. "You're a liar," he screamed. "You're a filt'y rotten liar! An' I'm not afraid. Do you hear? I'm not afraid. I'M NOT AFRAID OF YOU!"

Pat swiped out, but misjudged the distance and lost his balance with the flight of his fist. Crashing heavily to the floor, he lay and cursed his wife and his children, and the drunkard-tears of self-pity coursed down his face. Tucker Tommy watched him, not moving, lest Pat should try some sly trick. Tense, he watched every move of the wild thick arms as they beat with savage vigor on the floor. Finally their tattoo trailed away, and with a slow heave Pat staggered to his feet, glared stupidly, searched for the drink he had knocked over, and sent the empty glass smashing to the floor.

"Where's my drink?" He turned clumsily in crazy circles.

"You spilt it."

Pat raised his hand, then drew it flatly along his face as he lurched towards the bed. It was over, Tucker Tommy saw, seeing the long moment pass. He went forward to take off Pat's boots and help him into bed, taking a vague relief from the continuance of a ritual he had seen his mother perform, hoping by doing so to retain some sense of her in the dreary emptiness of the room. He let the boots quietly onto the floor and began to take off Pat's jacket, but his father pushed him away and staggered upright to remove it himself, grinning soft curses as he did so, and stopping only when he had stripped himself down to his startlingly white skin, tinged with a faint flush of blue across his massive shoulders, fading into the black maze of hair on his chest.

"Get into bed," he said, and his glance down at his nakedness was sly and slanted.

Without answering, Tucker Tommy began to pick up the clothes that had been flung onto the floor.

"Didn't you hear me!" He swore.

Tucker Tommy, alert again, said, "Yes, I'm going."

"Here," Pat said. "Sleep here." He flung himself down into the bed, and for fear of discommoding him, Tucker Tommy did as he had been told. He lowered the wick in the lamp until it went out altogether, then quietly, hardly breathing, he crawled into bed behind his father. The room was quiet now. He had never sensed the house so still before, a breathless stillness as if, now that his mother was no longer in it, all life had left. Not a sound came up from the Slatterys' room below. Not a move was being made through the whole house. Quiet as a nun: the remembered thought was his mother's before he saw that the little altar lamp had gone out, leaving the room darker than he had ever known it. Lonely and dark it was, without the familiar crimson glow that she had never allowed to go out. Tomorrow, he thought sleepily, he would light it again. Tomorrow. Before the thought trailed away into a near dream, he jerked suddenly into wakefulness as Pat's weight bore down upon him and he felt the hands glide in a rough long caress over his body. A breath burst into his mouth, stifling his own, and against his face the sandpaper brush of coarse mustache hairs rasped, as the straw mattress groaned in protest at the sudden shifted weight. A burst of wild fear gave him strength, whipping him like an eel escaping the spread of a net, and in a moment he was free of the clutching arms and the powerful pillarlike legs.

He sprang up against the wall and out of bed in a single flash of fright. Standing still in the darkness he listened, waiting, but there was no shout. From the bed, Pat called twice before he began to snore heavily in a drunken and concussive stupor. Cautiously, Tucker Tommy crept away into the new cold and darkness of the little empty room.

In her bed, in the corner, in the sick ward of the madhouse, Mrs. Baines, in death as she had so often done in life, made room for another: Tucker Tommy, perhaps, or one of the many children she had brought into the world, now scattered across a good part of it, leaving her to make her way from it alone, unhelped, unwatched. She lay slantwise across the bed as if to make a place in it beside her for one of them. Her arm crooked to hold a head. Her glance slid down over the hump of her wrist to where she could just see the bright gleam of the silver ring that Danny had made for her, its worn polished glitter rising loosely from the skeleton mesh of fine veins and brittle bones of her hand. For a long time now she had lain so, her face set in gentle patience, ready to creep silently away as soon as the last of the fading light had been squeezed from her eyes; the white light, flecked with green, through which the faces had come, merging into each other, into an indistinguishable whole before she set the task of telling one from the other, elusive wisps of features so well remembered, yet no longer definable, as though made up of the vaporish stuff of dreams, closing into nothingness just when they seemed most clearly sharp. But the last of the loved remembered faces had faded with the last of her unshakable energy, of the fine intelligence that had helped her to bear, while fighting them fiercely, pain and dirt and want, conquered only at last by her own physical destruction in sanctified duress at the hands of a drunk. But remembrance, like care, had gone now. She was dying when all usefulness had left her, and her body reached with calm peace towards the earned rest, enveloped in a sweet peace born of her courage and of her indomitable, honest and gay heart.

She was very close to Babby now, and into the approaching shadows she gazed, fearless until death placed its diadem upon her brow. Towards it she reached as though she were rising into the sunnied hilarity of a summer's day. She sighed. Her hands opened into stretched ease. Her eyes closed finally on the deep shadows. All care had indeed stopped.

NINETEEN

"HE'LL die roarin', an' that he may!" Mrs. Slattery scratched her bare arms with relaxed chubby fingers.

"He won't, you know." Mrs. Kinsella angrily jabbed a large safety pin into the opening of her flower-patterned bib which she reserved for Sundays. "That's a lot of balls, us havin' to make up for the sins we commit. We don't have to do no such thing. That hoor's ghost will live to be ninety, an' even then they'll have to shoot the bastard, you mark my words!"

Mrs. Slattery heaved a great sigh. "Course," she said, "he has the constitution of a lion. Looka the height an' brea'th a him."

"You could sing that if you had an air to it," Mrs. Kinsella retorted briskly. She was raging.

And with good cause, Mrs. Slattery thought. "I can't get over the badness of him. When you think he let that poor creature end her days in a kip like that!"

"Whisht, for Christ's sake!" Mrs. Kinsella interrupted. And

what she had to say was meant to be heard by anyone who cared to listen. She raised her voice. "Wouldn't you expect him to have brought her home like any decent Christian, an' at least wake her properly an' send her off from here to the chapel before he put her under the grass? But no! That would've cost a little more, an' left him less to piss down the drain." Her eyes darted up to the window of the Baineses' room, to the window box without the small splash of color for the first time for as long as she could remember. The geraniums, wiry and delicate at the best of times, had withered and died without Mrs. Baines's ministrations, the once proud scarlet heads soot-caked on parched blackened stems.

"I can't believe he won't have to answer for it," Mrs. Slattery said. "Jasus! there'd be neither rhyme nor reason to livin' if he was allowed to get away with the things he's done."

Mrs. Kinsella eyed her. Slattery could be as thick as stone sometimes, an' about certain things as dense as a shaggin' monument. "Did Chance have to answer for informin' on Nancy O'Bryne?"

"Well . . ." Mrs. Slattery began with a wry glance at her neighbor, but she was interrupted.

"Did Father Rex Aurealis have to answer for putting that creature behind bars in one of his lousy convents? Is he havin' to answer for the way he taught that poor soul above in Mount Jerome to stay an' put up with that hoormaster all these years? Preachin' patience at her! Forbearing, understanding an' forgiveness. I know what he told her. I heard him with me own ears telling her where her duty lay. Who is he havin' to account to?"

"God," Mrs. Slattery said. "He'll have to."

"Ah, God, me bollix!" Mrs. Kinsella roared. Mrs. Slattery shied back. And Granny Quinn over at the pipe nodded her bugled bonnet and dipped her chin onto her cameo.

"Well, Chance had to answer for her badness in a way," Mrs. Slattery began again. "Thank God! Because you ran her out a the place."

"An' by Jesus, I'll run a few more out before I'm finished," Mrs. Kinsella replied.

"Ah, God be with the times!" Granny Quinn called, at the end of her prayer; but both Mrs. Kinsella and Mrs. Slattery ignored her.

"Well, I suppose we can be thankful he gave her a Mass," Mrs. Slattery said.

"It was the least he could do. An' he wouldn't a done that, if I hadn't told him to."

Mrs. Slattery shook her head. "True for you, woman, dear, you did your best."

"I did shag-all!" Then quietly: "She would've done a hell of a lot more for me. An' I couldn't leave the youngfella to manage alone with that blackguard. Heartbroken he is," she said softly. "An' he tryin' to act as if he were a grown man, move a stone he would the morning the word came. About six it was, when I heard that man in the hall shouting. An' Phillo said—when he heard—'That's Mrs. Baines. What's the bet?' I didn't contradict him. I got up and threw a coat round me and there on the stairs in his shirt was Tucker Tommy with the paper in his hands. 'What is it?' I said. Quiet, because I didn't want to draw the other ram's attention. 'It's me mother,' said he, 'she's after dyin'. It's written on this,' he said. Quiet, and with no commotion. 'Come in, an' I'll wet a sup a tea,' said I. 'No,' said he, 'I must tell my father.' And in he goes, and the other feller's up and out and down them stairs for the insurance before I'd time to bless meself."

"If *that* was one a your habits!" Mrs. Slattery's insertion was sly, and wryly put.

For the first time that day, Mrs. Kinsella grinned. "You know me too well, ya brasser!"

"Gowan," Mrs. Slattery urged.

"Broke his neck out, he did," Mrs. Kinsella said. "An' didn't come back till the half of it was gone."

"It was nice," Mrs. Slattery said, "of Miss Fogarty and that Miss Plum to turn up for the funeral, wasn't it?"

Mrs. Kinsella threw her head back. "It was the least they could do," she said contemptuously. "An' bejasus! between them you'd think they'd've risen to more than one glass wreath the size a me hand."

"Miss Fogarty brung flowers."

"So she did," Mrs. Kinsella said. "I was forgetting. She would've liked that, if she could've known."

"How do you know she didn't?" Mrs. Slattery asked.

"I don't. But, if it'll comfort you any, I'll pretend she did. I'll let on she hasn't forgotten she was ever born. . . ."

A silence fell.

"It seems years since she went," Mrs. Slattery said, "an' it only the other day."

"Ah!" Mrs. Kinsella cried on a burst of rage. "That's what I was saying this morning. Wouldn't ya think he'd've the decency to wait until she was cold in her grave before he starts turning the place into a brothel, dragging in his fancy woman!" Her eyes squinted gray fury.

"Whisht, for Jesus' sake!" Mrs. Slattery nudged her.

Above them a door opened and someone stepped out onto the landing. They turned as footsteps started down the stairs, and when Tucker Tommy came round the bend of them and into view, Mrs. Kinsella nodded thoughtfully to him.

"Are you going up to the grave?" she asked, shifting closer to the jam of the hall door as she made room for him to pass.

He nodded.

"How did your bit a dinner turn out?" she asked, her eyes leaving his pale thin face to meander over his black minister's jacket and his first long black trousers that the woman in the chemist shop where he worked had given him.

"It was grand." He edged himself past them. "I did what you told me."

Mrs. Kinsella nodded approval, and Mrs. Slattery searched for a comment that would bring the question of Pat Baines's fancy woman under discussion; but she was too long, and unused to finding the sharp opening. Sensing something, he hurried away.

With a halfhearted resentment at his closeness, she stared after him. "That youngfella's only thirteen," she said, "but the kids going nowadays are born with sense."

"Wouldn't they need to be?" Mrs. Kinsella replied. "That child'll have to fend for hisself."

He turned the Lane, out of their sight.

"I did the washing yesterday, in case I wouldn't a been able to do it tomorrow." Mrs. Kinsella stirred herself, shifting her weight from one hip to the other. "God!" she spoke the thought. "It's a terrible thing to rear ungrateful childer! A houseful of childer that benighted creature brung into this world, an' not one of them 'cept Babby an' that youngfella ever asked if she'd a mouth on her."

"Ah, a shaggin' lot a use they were!" Mrs. Slattery interrupted.

And Mrs. Kinsella continued as though she hadn't. "Not one of them to wet her lips when she was dying, an' a lonely oul' death it was, with only the uncaring hands of strangers to ease her into eternity an' put the coppers on her poor blue eyes."

"That Teasey'll have a lot to answer for," Mrs. Slattery said, "her more than the others, 'cause she had full an' plenty an' if she didn't, wasn't she in the way of getting it?"

Mrs. Kinsella sighed. "They'll all have a lot to answer for, her as well as the others."

"Sky, they were."

"What?"

"Her eyes. I remember. They matched the heavens on a fine day. An' they cared. You could tell. Soft an' caring no matter what." Mrs. Slattery sighed. "She always cared."

"She did," Mrs. Kinsella nodded. "For everyone and every thing. Th'oul' house is desperately empty without her," she continued on a sigh that ended the conversation, as she turned back into the hall and up the stairs on her way up to her own room.

Along the Canal, Tucker Tommy went at a trot.

He had caught the indignation in Mrs. Kinsella's voice the moment he opened the door of the room, had heard what she was saying before he closed it behind him. She was talking about the woman his father had brought home with him the night before. Snug size, she was, and in the lamplight her face and clothes were the color of onions fried in water, and when she spoke there was the sound of spite and mean mockery in her voice.

She had come into the room ahead of Pat, ferrety furtive, trespassing on the room's new hollowed-out silence with sniffing pinched nostrils and tight lipless mouth that opened for the first time on a snarled oath as she settled onto a chair at the fire. She didn't remove her hat or coat, nor did she seem aware of him, although he stood at the table before her, nor of Dilsey, who sat in the bed staring out at her. She seemed aware only of the fire's heat and of Pat's interruptions into the songs he began to sing and of the tumbler in her hand, from which she took long parched drinks that comma-ed her snarled jeers at Pat's spasmodic impatience as he tried to coax her into the little room and the bed.

It was late, Dilsey had long since fallen asleep, when at last she rose up from the chair and with garrulous lewdness allowed Pat to drag her from one room to the other, where her breath continued to soil with her ground-out moans the long night's blackness.

He was waiting his turn to fill his bucket this morning when to his surprise the woman came slowly out of the hall and forninst the women gathered round the pipe, made her way up the Lane. He saw the looks they threw each other, and into the sudden silence Granny Quinn bent and spit before the rest of them: "The dirty oul' vomit!"

There was murmured approval. "The priest should be sent on him," Mrs. Mullen said.

"The'oul' bastard should be bate decent," said Fawan Barton.

Now, Tucker Tommy ducked his head, remembering his shame as he ran from the pipe and the things the women were saying. But the talk was behind him now, along with the empty room, the terribly empty room, stunted like the growth of a child by a hump on its back, its eyes mirroring the withdrawal of all that had been good and gentle in its world. The cold was there, too, that had come with the transit of the coffin from chapel to hearse to grave, the damp cold, icy cold, when remembrance brought on his first terrible fear and he had raised his eyes in frantic search of her, and into his sight had wandered, slow and pitifully alone, the small glass wreath of white wax flowers lying on the brass-topped board that covered her now quiet heart. He had cried then, hysterically and noisily, like a baby still in his pram, Mrs. Chance had said. She had turned up for his mother's funeral and in a fierce whisper told him to be a man and stop making a show of himself and that his mother was with God. But he didn't stop until she had bent down to him again and accidentally jabbed him into physical pain as the bridge of his nose was lacerated by the rough edge of her black shiny hard straw funeral hat.

"Now look what you've done!" she whispered, as the blood spouted down the right side of his face.

It was Mrs. Kinsella who edged herself past Mrs. Chance and his father, to wipe his face. He let her do it, dry-eyed, in a sudden cuteness sprung on him like a flower from the well of his grief. They would go, if nothing occurred to prolong their stay, he thought, and leave him behind with his mother, because here was the end of the journey for them and only he, her son, could go one step further with her.

"You're all right again, love?" Mrs. Kinsella's words never reached through the thunderous noise of his impatience as he watched and waited for them to go from the now covered grave. With longing he watched their lips move, as they took their farewells, their platitudes soundless, yet stretching forward into an eternity of shapes that made the waiting unbearable. Why didn't they go? He almost said it aloud, and when at last Mrs. Kinsella turned away, he went with her, made dumb and obedient and foolishly childlike by utter exhaustion.

"You can go up a Sunda' to the grave," Mrs. Kinsella had told him as she put a cup of tea into his hand back in her own room, where she had taken him to lie down on her bed. And all through his sleep, her voice had repeated this promise. "You can go up a Sunda' to the grave."

The thought stayed with him, even when he woke, and along with it had come a new sense of aloneness. It was queer, this sense, and had lasted all week, separating him from the things round him, so that he walked in the room and along the streets without touching them, and at times withdrew his mind's eye from the faraway point it had settled on, to marvel at his detachment from all that before had seemed ordinary and real, but now in the aloneness moithered the life out of him, chained and confined him in a prison the making of which had been none of his doing, and from which there was no escape until, like the Resurrection, a Sunday had arisen to free him.

Sunday had come, its dawn stained and cold, the day's birth pangs muffled by the complaining nark in the women's voices round the pipe, shame-making and penetrating through Pat's muttered curses and the smell of boiling cabbages. But all morning and ahead, the promise stayed, glorious, shriveling in its strength all it did not touch, all that was with every step, now, receding shadow.

Through the big gates of the cemetery he went, his gangling black-suited thinness animated by wild bursts of energy, to which he gave rein the moment he left the wide somber main avenue, beginning to jump when he entered one of the smaller paths that was somehow gayer and lighter by its absence of trees. Swiftly he went, short-cutting familiar plots divided by paths lined with graves, every one of which he had come to know over the months of Sundays when he had come here with his mother to tend Babby's. He would tend it again today, but on his way out, after he had been with his mother, after . . . after . . .

He stopped running, and here the earth was churned, wet brown and so fresh that he could see the fat maggots, white and chestnut-colored, burrowing and emerging over its surface like an entrenching army. Beneath the maggots the new graves seemed squeezed, their surfaces sunk in apology. New wreaths of flowers, withered and knocked sideways, were flung wide, their momentary prettiness outrageously bedraggled on the earth's brown sprawl. Here among them was her resting place.

He moved forward, his body snapped into crouched attention, memory and sight riveted on a point ahead, towards which he went with poised caution, as if he wanted to come upon her unawares, almost conscious of his wish that she would be looking the other way. Expectancy made him smile, till he grew shy suddenly of the sight of the laugh that was in his eyes and on his mouth, and he lowered his face to hide it, to hide the fool he felt, and saw the earth cracked into squashed clumps, clinging to the ends of his trousers and covering altogether the sight of his shoes, approaching her. He stopped at the edge of an ill-defined border, a crude spade mark forming a boundary line, and before him on the opposite plot, in about ten yards from the lane, should have been her grave, marked by its small glass-covered wreath of white flowers.

He stiffened, and with his hands out before him sprang to scan the sea of graves.

"It was here," he said aloud, before, as in a game of Tig, he began to rush from grave to grave, desperation giving way to despair that sent him running in circles only to lead him back each time to where he felt her grave should be. But it wasn't there, nor was the wreath from Miss Plum, the wreath that was to distinguish her grave from all the others. In its place, he saw a cross of red, wired carnations surrounded by bunches of flowers piled against each other in plenty. The cards attached bore a strange name, one which meant nothing to him, but which he read over and over as though he must brand his eyes with the sight, or as if a miracle must change it.

"What are you looking for?"

He jumped, recovering breath punched out of him. "Me mother," he said quickly. "Me mother. I can't find her grave."

His eyes lit on the blue-veined face under a bowler hat and hardy gray eyes that surveyed him with a hazy concern.

The man's jaws closed on something that flooded his mouth with saliva. "Aye, an' where was it?" he asked, after he had swallowed.

"Here. Just here." The gesture was frantic. He looked away and back. "She was buried Wednesday," His eyes, large in his thin face, implored remembrance.

"Wednesday." A squelched spit hit the ground. "A Wednesday's a busy day. Always very busy on a Wednesday.'

"But on'y last Wednesday. After ten Mass." Tucker Tommy's hands touched the navy blue serge suit in front of him.

The man gave a glance to either side of him, and hope, wild and ready, swept through Tucker Tommy. "What was her name?"

He told him, hardly conscious of the words, as he watched the impassive face for some sign of enlightenment. But all the man did was chew, and the hardy eyes in their shifting wide scan remained untouched, thoughtless.

"She was buried here." Tucker Tommy fought back the thing that was withering his throat, and the man said, "Somewhere here, yes, a Wednesday after . . ." A new alertness made him hunch his shoulders as he dug his hands into his trousers pockets. "I mind now," he said, and stopped to stare at Tucker Tommy, who gazed back with his mind and mouth overflowing with prayer until the man went on: "I mind it well now, but that wasn't a bought grave."

He said nothing, then plaintively, "Me mother."

"Your mother," echoed the man.

"Her grave was here." His voice rasped fear.

The man threw back his head. "Somewheres," was all he said, but the gesture said, God alone knows, could be anywheres! "If it wasn't a bought grave, you haven't a hope of finding it." He stared curiously. "If it was bought outright and paid for, you'd have the receipt, and the number of the grave on it, and then it'd be as easy as tying a shoelace to find it." Tucker Tommy never took his gaze from the man's face. "When you don't buy the plot, anyone who likes can be buried in it. And youse didn't. Did you?"

"No."

His father had not bought it. There was no receipt. No number. Only a knowledge of where they had laid her, and the knowing was no use when you couldn't find the exact spot. He moved, to look round him. He had to find her. There were things to say. Questions and answers to be asked and told. A leavetaking. He hadn't taken his leave of her, because she had gone before he knew rightly she was going. She had gone without a word to him, quietly, and without as much as a by-your-leave.

"You're wearing out good leather." The man's voice halted him finally, and he came to rest before him.

"I can't find her," he said, and the man bit down on the thing in his mouth.

"No, son," he said. "An' what'd be the use if you could?" He braced himself heartily. "I'm afraid she's given you the slip this time, all right," he said. And even after he had walked away, Tucker Tommy could still hear his voice.

She had gone and was gone and there had been so much he had wanted to say, none of which he would say now because she wouldn't be there to hear. She had given him the slip, given them all the slip. He fought back the tears that sprang into his throat and flooded up to his eyes until a great sob tore through him, shattering his taut body in a burst of young despair. And when he finally cried, his eyes were dry, but his thin shoulders twitched as though he were being held in the grip of a black fit.

He came through grief to loneliness and the chiming of the cemetery's bell, which he was hearing now for the last time, the solemn, slow, lonesome peal matching the slow turnings of his body as he moved to go. His eyes swept the graves in this new plot without fixing their attention upon any one, for there was nothing to remember now, no need to know how it looked because she wasn't here any more and he wouldn't be coming back. She was gone. He wouldn't be able to come and worry her, and neither would anyone else. She was gone. She had escaped. The thought stopped him. He looked back. But all seemed as it had a moment ago. Yet somehow it was different. But only the thought was. The sea of graves looked exactly the same, and yet not quite, because in no way did it contain her. She had escaped from the earth, from his father, and from him. Mrs. Baines was gone. And the earth was cold, all brown clay and empty, its face scarred with headstones stunted in dejection, and their weight held nothing beneath them, and so—they were meaningless. He walked away.

This time he did not look back, but turned his face the way he had seen her do up to the sound the breeze made in the tops of the trees, and beyond the sound, to the sky streaked with the first dark of evening. The beginnings of the night she had loved. In the church at the top of the main avenue the service was coming to its end. Involuntarily he thought: the Protestants; and on the thought he heard her whispered: "Whisht!", lest his remark be overheard and give offense. For the space of a pulse beat he stopped walking to listen, but all he could hear now was the hymn straggling towards its end, and the words were louder than the thudded moan of the organ, and louder than the sound the wind made in the trees:

"Now the day is over . . ."

He moved. He measured his steps with an air of tidiness.

"Now the darkness gathers . . ."

At his right he saw the church and ahead he saw the great black wrought-iron gates, and beyond them the city. Now the darkness was gathering. . . . The sight filled his eyes, as the room at home had done when he was lying at Babby's back to keep her warm. The room then had held more for him than the city did now, but now the room was empty too, its vacancy cupped by hands that had destroyed everyone they touched. Now an empty city and an empty room lay ahead of him, both ingrained with the sights and sounds of her destruction superimposing themselves over everything else by way of a sigh, held in a draft coming down the chimney or under the door, or by way of the empty echo of a cinder falling onto the hearth, echoing again her trials, tribulations and the emptiness of her going.

"Through the long night watches . . ."

"Come on, youngfella. Time's up."

Tucker Tommy withdrew his gaze, the gatekeeper beckoned. "I'm going," he said. But not home: he was not going home. The thought and decision were sudden, but they did not seem new nor strange.

He took another quick look at the city at his feet, then quickly he went out the gates. He turned left. Before him the road led away from the room and the Lane. And when he thought again, his hand touched his chest and the patch on his shirt near the collar that she had put there. Fingering the patch, he walked into the coming night.

FOR THE BEST IN PAPERBACKS, LOOK FOR THE

In every corner of the world, on every subject under the sun, Penguin represents quality and variety—the very best in publishing today.

For complete information about books available from Penguin—including Pelicans, Puffins, Peregrines, and Penguin Classics—and how to order them, write to us at the appropriate address below. Please note that for copyright reasons the selection of books varies from country to country.

In the United Kingdom: For a complete list of books available from Penguin in the U.K., please write to *Dept E.P., Penguin Books Ltd, Harmondsworth, Middlesex, UB7 0DA.*

In the United States: For a complete list of books available from Penguin in the U.S., please write to *Dept BA, Penguin*, Box 120, Bergenfield, New Jersey 07621-0120.

In Canada: For a complete list of books available from Penguin in Canada, please write to *Penguin Books Ltd, 2801 John Street, Markham, Ontario L3R 1B4.*

In Australia: For a complete list of books available from Penguin in Australia, please write to the *Marketing Department, Penguin Books Ltd, P.O. Box 257, Ringwood, Victoria 3134.*

In New Zealand: For a complete list of books available from Penguin in New Zealand, please write to the *Marketing Department, Penguin Books (NZ) Ltd, Private Bag, Takapuna, Auckland 9.*

In India: For a complete list of books available from Penguin, please write to *Penguin Overseas Ltd, 706 Eros Apartments, 56 Nehru Place, New Delhi, 110019.*

In Holland: For a complete list of books available from Penguin in Holland, please write to *Penguin Books Nederland B.V., Postbus 195, NL-1380AD Weesp, Netherlands.*

In Germany: For a complete list of books available from Penguin, please write to *Penguin Books Ltd, Friedrichstrasse 10-12, D-6000 Frankfurt Main I, Federal Republic of Germany.*

In Spain: For a complete list of books available from Penguin in Spain, please write to *Longman, Penguin España, Calle San Nicolas 15, E-28013 Madrid, Spain.*

In Japan: For a complete list of books available from Penguin in Japan, please write to *Longman Penguin Japan Co Ltd, Yamaguchi Building, 2-12-9 Kanda Jimbocho, Chiyoda-Ku, Tokyo 101, Japan.*